DARK PACIFIC

DAVID E. MEADOWS

BERKLEY BOOKS, NEW YORK

THE BERKLEY PUBLISHING GROUP
Published by the Penguin Group
Penguin Group (USA) Inc.
375 Hudson Street, New York, New York 10014, USA
Penguin Group (Canada), 90 Eglinton Avenue East, Suite 700, Toronto, Ontario M4P 2Y3, Canada
(a division of Pearson Penguin Canada Inc.)
Penguin Books Ltd., 80 Strand, London WC2R 0RL, England
Penguin Group Ireland, 25 St. Stephen's Green, Dublin 2, Ireland (a division of Penguin Books Ltd.)
Penguin Group (Australia), 250 Camberwell Road, Camberwell, Victoria 3124, Australia
(a division of Pearson Australia Group Pty. Ltd.)
Penguin Books India Pvt. Ltd., 11 Community Centre, Panchsheel Park, New Delhi—110 017, India
Penguin Group (NZ), Cnr. Airborne and Rosedale Roads, Albany, Auckland 1310, New Zealand
(a division of Pearson New Zealand Ltd.)
Penguin Books (South Africa) (Pty.) Ltd., 24 Sturdee Avenue, Rosebank, Johannesburg 2196,
South Africa

Penguin Books Ltd., Registered Offices: 80 Strand, London WC2R 0RL, England

DARK PACIFIC

A Berkley Book / published by arrangement with the author

PRINTING HISTORY
Berkley mass-market edition / September 2006

Copyright © 2005 by David Meadows.
Interior text design by Kristin del Rosario.

ISBN: 0-425-21219-X

BERKLEY®
Berkley Books are published by The Berkley Publishing Group,
a division of Penguin Group (USA) Inc.,
375 Hudson Street, New York, New York 10014.
BERKLEY is a registered trademark of Penguin Group (USA) Inc.
The "B" design is a trademark belonging to Penguin Group (USA) Inc.

PRINTED IN THE UNITED STATES OF AMERICA

10 9 8 7 6 5 4 3 2 1

To the Maritime Sealift Command

Acknowledgments

It is impossible to thank everyone who provided technical advice and support for this and other novels. I deeply appreciate those who visited www.sixthfleet.com and who read my column on www.military.com. Your comments are welcomed and I do try to personally reply to everyone.

To the Master of the USNS *Denebola*, Captain Joe Gargiulo, and Mr. Matthew Cull (PM5 Sealift Surge Detachment), who took time from their busy in-port schedule in Norfolk, Virginia, to guide me around this massive ship. There is no way anyone unfamiliar with these large aircraft carrier–size ships can appreciate the impact they bring to the deployed warfighting forces until they have been aboard them. It was hard to believe the *Denebola* is 946 feet 1-1/2 inches, while the newest aircraft carrier, the USS *George Bush* is 1092 feet in length—a difference of less than 150 feet. The Nimitz-class aircraft carriers, of which USS *George Bush* is one, have a crew of over 5,500 people with ship's company and air wing embarked. The USNS *Denebola* has fourteen merchant marines assigned when in port, growing to the overwhelming crew of forty when the *Denebola* sets sail. The staterooms on the Fast Sealift Ships convinced me there are better ways of going to sea than in open bay berthing areas belowdecks on a warship. I recommend that the Navy ban sailors who are up for reenlistment from seeing the berthing accommodations on these Fast Sealift Ships. Twin beds, a recliner, a private bath, a desk, and a huge stateroom made me want to up anchor and head out to sea again.

My thanks to the support of my cousin Joan Cox, who continues to encourage me to write the Great American Novel.

I would like to express my thanks to Terry Smith, Vincent Widmaier, and William Cross for their security insights. To a wonderful Middletown, Maryland, readers group who call themselves "Not Your Ordinary Books Club"—Tara Cocchia-Little, Kathie Reed McKain, Nikki Dierman, Linda L. Corsiatto, Dianne Shelton, Anne Paxton, Julie M. Littrell, Cathy Davidson, Leesa LaCroix, and Lori Benedetto (maker of fine purses). I spent a wonderful time with this group who honored me by reading and critiquing my *Joint Task Force Liberia*. And, of course, the indomitable Tim Bovill and Greg Klitgard, who showed up to provide their own objective insights from the Navy perspective. My best wishes to Mary-Michael Lyons whose parents, Clinton and Christine, encourage her to write. All young high school–age writers should have her zeal.

As always, my continued thanks to Mr. Tom Colgan for his editorial support, and to his able right-hand person, Ms. Sandra Harding.

Rest assured any and all technical errors or mistakes in this novel are strictly those of the author, who many times wanders in his own world.

David E. Meadows

DARK PACIFIC

ONE

Kiang Zheng searched Pearsall Park as he walked. His eyes shifted from side to side to front, as he tried not to turn his head. Today may be the day. Occasionally, he glanced over his shoulder.

This was too public of a place. He could be caught. Once caught, his parents would die. Why such conspicuousness? Maybe there was some irony in meeting in a park that brushed up against Lackland Air Force Base.

The April sun of San Antonio was a shadow of its summer relentlessness. He envied the fun surrounding him by a lunchtime crowd of secretaries, airmen, and office workers spread across the lush green, laughing, eating their sandwiches. As if no worries pulled them down.

They had better enjoy it, thought Kiang, for by summer the green would be gone; dust and brown leaves would cover the park. Die-hard runners convinced of their invincibility would be the only things pounding through the dry heat of Pearsall Park.

Kiang wiped the back of his hand against his forehead. The motion shifted the baseball cap, allowing a slight breeze to send a momentary coolness across his brow. The hot summer sun of Texas was only two months away, but for Kiang the heat was already building. Nothing like West Texas summer heat. Then, the heat would be like an oven, baking everything beneath it, sending the crowds scurrying for air-conditioned diners and bars.

Several women lay on top of towels, tanning: their eyes shut, blouses pulled up to their bras and dresses tucked high—glimpses of the whites of panties drawing the attention of the young men and bringing forth smiles and memories from the older men. Some of the tanners slept, their chests moving rhythmically, mouths open, heads tilted to the side. Probably recovering from the nightlife along the Riverwalk, thought Kiang. A nightlife missed since China. The joy of the Riverwalk was lost in the stress of being pulled between two masters and the worry for his parents. So his days melded into one—go to work, come home, and wait for the telephone call or slip of paper between the pages of morning paper telling him where to go.

The barks of playing dogs came from behind him, causing Kiang to glance back and watch for a moment as two Labradors chased a spinning disk being thrown between two men.

When he faced forward again, he saw her. She was in the same place he saw her yesterday, as she was the day before that, and the day before that, and so on. It was Thursday and she'd been here every day at this time. Every day she had been there as he had walked the same path heading to a different spot, waiting for a meeting that never happened.

Today may be no different. The meeting may never occur. This could be another one of their inane tests of his . . . what? His loyalty? Was it loyalty when you did it out of fear? Was it loyalty when you did it so your parents would live? He took a deep breath and sighed.

The young lady's camouflage shirt lay folded to one side as she sunbathed. Her camouflage trousers were rolled up high on her thighs. Air Force sunglasses hid her eyes. A tattoo of a bird was on her right ankle. Four days he had seen her and for a brief moment he wanted to know the color of her eyes. He knew her body. It reminded him of his neighbor in Culebra—shapely, the spiral legs of a dancer. The nipples on the small breasts poked the airman's light undershirt upward like tiny hills on a smooth plain. Small breasts, like the Chinese.

His neighbor was forever working in her yard. And she was forever smiling at him, engaging him in conversation. Though never overt, Kiang was sure that if pushed, she would be willing. But he could ill afford any relationship that would endanger his parents. Especially one with a married woman and all the emotional danger it presented.

He crested the small rise, surprised to find today's meeting place, the bench, empty. Every bench from the car park to here had been filled. When he reached the green bench, a WET PAINT sign taped on the back of the bench explained why no one sat there.

Kiang touched the bench with his finger. Nothing. He lifted the sign and ran his hand lightly along the seats, satisfying himself that the paint was dry.

Kiang glanced around, wondering if the trip today would be another useless sojourn to Pearsall Park. He shivered at the thought that the colonel would come. It had been three years since he had seen the colonel. Three years since he had seen his parents. The colonel had never come to see him, leaving these meetings to others—less important handlers. Why would the colonel come? Kiang ran his finger along his faint mustache, brushing away the sweat.

Kiang took off his suit coat, folded it in half, and draped it across the wooden rails of the bench. He sat down. After several minutes, Kiang shut his eyes. The hot sun, fatigue, and a sense that no meeting would occur combined, and within a few minutes he slept. His body shivered as memories washed through his noonday dreams.

CONSCIOUSNESS *rides a fickle sea, submerging beneath harsh realities, drifting along uncharted depths of the mind. The quiet current above Kiang rippled, disturbed his floating solace.*

His mind reached out to hug the smooth bottom, moaning as the upward drift pulled him away from the quiet nothingness. His grip loosened and his mind turned from the bottom, the faint light at the surface drawing him. Kiang drifted upward. The moaning increased. Terror flooded across tumbling thoughts at the rippling edge of consciousness. Then, pain exploded like a mirror shattering into a thousand shards. As if fired from a cannon, he shot upward, breaking the surface, gasping for breath.

Pain greeted him with its familiar tendrils, wrapping around his body. He suddenly opened his good eye. The iron bars of the cell filled his vision. Gasping, he fought to remember where he was. He shut his good eye, his vision clouded by the film of sleep, tears, and blood.

A second explosion of pain ricocheted across his body, knocking the air out of his lungs, loosening the clogged mass in his nasal passage and shooting it out of his mouth and nostrils.

His mouth wide open, Kiang fought to breathe. A couple of gasps and his throat opened, bringing in air. And when it happened, more of the loose mass dislodged, slipping down the back of his throat, getting stuck for a moment, cutting off the air in mid-breath.

Choking, he jerked his head an inch off the concrete floor, bringing a fresh wave of pain washing across his senses. He swallowed, clearing most of the airway; a cracked rib rubbed against a bruised lung. Kiang kept his head raised, afraid to lower it. He reopened his right eye slightly, but the unexpected assault of a halogen lamp inches from his face caused him to shut it again. His head fell back onto the floor, splattering the liquid beneath him. He started choking and was forced to raise his head again. He twisted onto his side, drawing his knees up as protection from the boots surrounding him.

"Move the light away. I want him to see me."

It was the familiar voice Kiang had heard for days, weeks—or maybe he'd been here for more than a month, he didn't know. He'd lost track of time. The light in the cell was on constantly. There was no window to mark the transition from day to night and back to day.

Kiang shivered involuntarily. The whimper he heard was his own. It mattered little how much he knew or how much he told. He had told them everything he knew, would know, and had known. He'd told them things he had forgotten, things heard from others. And he made up his own pieces of information sometimes—pieces he doubted were true, but they filled a void that helped keep the torture at bay.

As bad as the pain was, he knew was going to live. To live, he had to give them something, and when he did, the beatings stopped for a while and he was allowed to escape reality until the next time.

He knew the routine. The Chinese checked everything, trusting no one, not even their own sources of information. So everything he said was run through the same process as information from their own trusted sources. Their spies were scattered across the globe, masquerading behind the guise of professors, business-men, diplomats, and even students. Each independently collect-ing tidbits of information that was sent back to the Ministry of State Security. There, equally untrusted puzzle-makers sorted pieces, developing analyses and best-guesses. By comparing the same information from multiple sources, the Ministry of State Se-curity determined who was to be trusted and who was to continue work abroad. It was within those gray walls that senior leaders bounced his stories against the ever-changing puzzle to see if they fit. Seldom did any piece of the intelligence puzzle fit per-fectly, so they continued to return. And he continued to die a lit-tle with each return.

A shoe scuffed on the cement behind him, drawing a fresh wave of shivers. He pulled his knees tighter against his stomach, causing a long audible release of gas. Laughter bounced off the cement walls of the cell. Ribald comments kept the laughter going. Kiang pulled his knees up, trying to get them tight against his stomach, trying to ignore the pain accompanying the act. The sound of gas passing rose in intensity as Kiang's knees moved closer to his stomach.

Adrenaline rushes through the body of even a tortured pris-oner. But as days pass and "interviews" become routine, the adrenaline burst fades quickly as fatigue and depression take their toll. He couldn't hold his legs against his stomach for long and slowly they uncoiled, exposing his stomach. He tried to squeeze his eyes shut tighter, recognizing that only his right eye responded. The left remained swollen shut.

He waited for the boot to explode into his body again. When it didn't come, he still waited. Anticipation can be far worse than the event itself.

"Good work," the voice said, and he knew the man wasn't re-ferring to him, but to the "nice work" of the others for nearly beating him to death . . . not quite dead. Kiang wanted to kill the man. To kill the man he had to live, but unless some miracle hap-pened, he would die. That death would come when they ceased to have use for him. If they would only leave him alone for a few days and let him recover . . . If it reached the point where death was preferable to the chance to live, he would take his own life. But to either live or die, he needed time to recover.

Kiang would have laughed at the irony of the wish for the beat-ings to stop long enough for him to regain enough strength to *take his own life.* Ah, to have the strength to commit suicide, *he thought. There was definitely irony in that wish, but he didn't have the energy to think about it. He just knew it.*

He opened the eye again, only a small slit this time. The light was to the side and not directly in his face. He tried opening the left eye, but there was no light. He wanted to touch it, but fear stopped him from moving his arm. His left eye was swollen shut from yesterday's beatings . . . or was it two days . . . three days ago—he couldn't remember.

The shiny toes of three combat boots filled his vision. The fourth boot was dull, covered in red. Laughter echoed off the walls over something one of them said. The comment was in Cantonese and he didn't speak good colloquial Cantonese. His Mandarin was good—his parents spoke it. . . . And then thoughts of his parents and where they were and whether they were alive or not flooded his mind for a moment before another kick to the stomach sent their faces whirling away as he fought for breath. When you least expect it . . .

"Uggg," a voice said. "Look what he did to my shoe."

He opened his eye for a moment, the boot directly in front of him. A bloody mass of snot slid off the toe of the boot.

The boot rose out of sight for a moment before he felt the pressure of it on his head. His head rocked slightly from side to side as the soldier rubbed his boot against the top and sides of his head.

"There, you arrogant bastard! Your hair shined my boot."

The pressure of the boot moved away. The laughter of the others at the soldier meant more pain for him.

He rolled onto his back, raising his head and turning it slightly. The dull boot moved suddenly, drawing back before rushing forward, kicking him in the stomach. His eye rolled back and liquid trickled from the side of his opened mouth. His breath came in short, rapid gulps, and his right arm fell to the side and lay limp next to him. He couldn't hold his head up any longer, so it fell backward, the impact softened somewhat by the thin film of rancid liquid in which he lay.

"Do you think he is dead?"

"Not our worry. If he's dead, then we'll find another one. If he's alive, his parents live."

He feigned unconsciousness, hoping they would believe him incapable of feeling pain and would leave him alone for a while.

The odor of stale onions filled his nostrils and he knew the man was squatting beside him.

Kiang squinted. The man's crooked teeth filled his vision.

"I know you see me, Kiang. I know you think this will end, but it will end when I say it will end."

A muffled scream echoed from somewhere down the concrete hallway, rising in intensity for several seconds before collapsing into a long, oscillating series of moans.

The man laughed. "That gentleman has been here for over two years. You know something, Kiang? He doesn't even remember his name . . . or, so he says."

Kiang shivered.

The man laughed. The others in the cell joined in the laughter. "No, you haven't quite been here that long. Only a month, but even a month can be an eternity."

I've been here a month. A month. Now, I know. . . .

The rustle of the starched uniform fabric as the man stood told Kiang the visit was about done. He couldn't recall telling them anything, but his thoughts were jumbled. He had quit lying to them the first week. Only the truth can set you free, they kept telling him, laughing at the joke of using the Central Intelligence Agency's mantra. Kiang believed only the truth could stop the pain. So he told them the truth . . . whatever truth they wanted.

They would return, but every moment alone was a moment without pain—without thoughts.

He listened intently as the boots splashed across the floor, and when they neared the door leading from the cell, he breathed in deeply and held it. When the metallic echo of the cell door clanged shut and the noise vibrated through the small room, he released the breath—a breath of relief. He should be home now, watching the San Antonio Spurs play. Why had he listened to his parents when they asked him to take them back home to visit long-missed relatives? This wasn't his home. But he was a dutiful son and, in China, where his parents were born and raised, sons were dutiful. So, the dutiful son took his parents back to the small village they left decades ago. Why else would they have a son? he thought.

No, he was American. As American as apple pie. As American as football. As American as that short-skirted neighbor of his with the nice thighs. . . . He wondered for a second whether she even knew he was gone. He must remember. He mustn't forget who he was. That was what they wanted. They wanted him to forget . . . and, at times, he did. A Chinese was a Chinese was a Chinese. This idea of passports determining a Chinaman's nationality was so much bullshit, if he believed his tormenters.

He was . . . yes, he was, and he agreed, realizing for a fraction of a second he couldn't recall his name. Kiang slowly drew in a deep breath, stopping when a cracked rib touched his lung, bringing pain to the effort. He rolled to the side again, bringing on another sharp blast of pain. Pain was a series of radiant spokes emerging from the hub—his body—shooting through every muscle, bone, and organ. He felt warm wetness on his thigh as what little was in his bladder trickled over his leg to join other puddles from other visits. At least he wasn't wearing the suit he bought for the trip. But, then, he wasn't wearing anything.

Who am I? he asked himself. He forced himself to answer the question—thankful he knew the answer. The man had used his name. He had a past, and at first when he was thrown into this cell where the floor titled slightly toward the open hole in the corner, he promised himself he would have a future.

He had started . . . when? He couldn't recall, but it was after the first week here. He had started a mental checklist to keep his identity whole—to ensure he remembered who and what he was.

His home was a small, white Cape Cod house in San Antonio. He was single. The nice looking next-door neighbor was married. She was his number one fantasy. He was an engineer. He had a good paying job with a large American contractor. Weeks ago he was that someone. He had a car. He had a dog. He didn't have a cat and would never own one. A lawn service cut his grass and who . . . Who was taking care of his mail?

He concentrated for several seconds before the vision of his short-skirted neighbor filled his thoughts. She was picking it up for him. Even his fantasies failed to bring relief into his thoughts. She was as far away as a fairy tale.

Now, he was nothing. He wanted to live, but if he couldn't live, then he would decide his death. It was the only thing he could take away from the satisfaction of his torturers. His ancestors would understand. They would accept him. His parents would follow him shortly and they would forgive him. The colonel, as his torturer was called, would send them on to him before his body was destroyed. He would explain to his parents when he met them on the other side. They would understand.

*Survival was an instinct, a desire to live, and while he still sur-
vived he knew it was only because his captors wanted him to live.
His life rested in their hands. They did not threaten him with
death any longer because they knew he would welcome it.* "And,
this too shall pass," *he mumbled through cracked lips.*

"He spoke."

*He didn't mean to speak! His breathing picked up in tempo as
his fear grew greater. He whimpered, knowing . . .* They hadn't
left the cell. They are still here!

*Three swift kicks struck the sensitive area right below the
kneecap even as Kiang tried to draw his legs up to protect his
body.*

"Enough!"

*A few tears fought their way through the swollen eyelids. If
only they would ask a question. What did he know now that he
didn't know before? Whatever he knew, they could have—whatever he knew, he had given. He thought of his job. He had not had
to come into the company from the military like most others. He
had been recruited near the end of his first master's degree. He
was proud of his job. They had paid for his doctorate. He owed
them and he had paid them with his loyalty for five years. He ran
his tongue lightly over his teeth, surprised to discover they were
still all there; or, at least, they were as far as his tongue could
tell. A tongue painted with something that had burned and blis-
tered the tender skin, making him think of a time that seemed so
long ago when he inadvertently picked up and bit into a raw
jalapeno pepper. It had been nearly two days before he could eat
again. He had spent a lot of money to straighten his teeth. He
would have smiled at the hypocrisy of them cracking his ribs, rearranging his insides with their boots, and breaking his nose with
the miracle of still having all his teeth. He wondered how long he
would have them? His thoughts ran together in random ways,
bouncing against each other before tumbling backward through
the mind.*

*He took a deep breath; the rib jammed against the lung again,
but no new gratings when he breathed. He realized the hopeless-
ness of his situation. They had told him it was hopeless. He believed them. He had also believed in the first week that, given
time, he could escape what was happening. Now, he wished for
an escape through the doorway of death. He whimpered.* Kiang
tried to raise his hand again. It didn't move.

"Just kill me and be done with it."

"Why would we want to kill you?" the colonel asked. *"You are one of us. You are Chinese. We are just here to reeducate you to where your loyalties lie."*

He whimpered aloud. Let them do what they want. He heard the laughter of the others in the cell.

"We will continue our talks until you understand."

They wanted him to do something. If he did what they wanted, he could live and his parents would live. If he didn't, then his parents would meet him in death. If he agreed to do whatever it was, then he may have the opportunity to kill himself.

"No!" the man said.

Kiang didn't know what the *"no"* meant, but when the expected kick failed to come, he knew what the *"no"* meant.

"Thank you," Kiang mumbled. It was the first time he had directly addressed the man the others called Colonel.

"You are welcome," came the reply from the man with crooked teeth. *"Come."*

Kiang tried to stand, but only managed to raise his head and slide one leg through the muck before exhaustion overcame him.

When he recognized from the sounds of boots splashing through the liquids of the cell that the men were leaving his cell, he knew the command had been toward them, not him. He wailed aloud. He wanted to go. He deserved to go. The colonel could free him—free him long enough for Kiang to go meet his ancestors.

"Take me," he gasped aloud.

The cell doors clanged shut. He wondered if they had truly left this time.

"Not this time, Kiang. You need your rest. I'll be back. Do you want me to come back?"

Kiang turned his head toward the cell door. The colonel stood there, his hands by his sides, gazing back at Kiang.

"Yes," Kiang said. *"I want to come with you,"* he said, his voice low, barely audible.

The colonel laughed. *"And, you shall, my friend. You shall."*

Kiang watched as the colonel smiled at the other soldiers, turned, and walked out of sight down the hallway.

He shut his eye. Fear faded within his thoughts as consciousness dove toward the depths of his mind. The waters of oblivion pulled him down, away from reality, and the smile *that eased across his face as he passed out broke open the scabs on his bruised lips.* But, I still have my teeth. *Fresh blood joined the liquid trickling from his open mouth, seeping down his chin onto the wet cement beneath him. He coughed, turning his head to the side so he didn't choke on his own body's rebellion.*

COLD water hit his face, bringing him around, but not suddenly as if he were emerging from a well-rested sleep. It was a slow swim upward as water flowed across his naked body, drawing uncontrolled shivers long before he worked the energy to open his right eye. It didn't seem he had been out long.

"He's clean; turn off the hose. Lift him." It was the colonel. "I told you I'd be back, Kiang."

Two sets of hands grabbed him under each arm and lifted him roughly. How long ago had that been? Hours? Days? He didn't know. He didn't care.

He moaned—a long, drawn-out moan like the deep bass of distant thunder. Laughter and ridicule erupted from the uniformed audience inside the small cell. Kiang felt no emotion. Their laughter and comments had become part of his day. He made out enough of the Cantonese to know they were making derisive comments about feminization of the Chinese male by American life. All he cared about was that he would do whatever the colonel wanted. The colonel is my friend.

They sat him on a straight-back chair and tied his hands and legs to it, using those little plastic things he had used eons ago to tie cables together.

"Please," Kiang pleaded. "Whatever you want."

"What did he say?"

"I don't know, Colonel. It is hard to hear him."

He heard the sound of the hard slap before he felt it on his cheek. He moaned again. Lightly he ran his tongue along the bottom row of teeth, wondering briefly why he was worried about his teeth. The colonel would protect his teeth. He'd need good teeth. Why would he? he asked himself. He ran his tongue along them again.

"Your teeth are fine. They will be fine as long as you are useful."

Whatever they wanted, they could have. Just stop the torment;

the pain. "I will do whatever you want," he pleaded, articulating each word carefully. The colonel agreed.

"Of course, you will, Kiang. I know that. You know that, but there are others who aren't sure you are telling me the truth. They are afraid that you will trick me with your American ways."

Kiang opened his eye and watched the thin, bad-teethed colonel walk from the right side of the chair to the left.

"As you know, Kiang, you lied to us when you first came here. You are lucky we didn't cut something more valuable off."

One of the soldiers reached forward with a baton and lightly tapped his balls. Kiang hardly moved. It was just one more pain in an opus of pain.

"I'm not lying. Whatever you want, Colonel."

"Hey, Colonel," one of the soldiers said, "He knows who you are."

"He is the master," Kiang whimpered.

They agreed. As one, the soldiers started agreeing with Kiang, telling him he was making the right decision. In the background of the voices, he did not hear the colonel. They thought he was making the right decision. They were proud of him—but they didn't untie him. What if he was lying to them? they discussed among themselves. Then, did the beatings began anew. Each hit, each kick brought waves of pain. Several times he rode a roller-coaster of awareness and unconsciousness, twisting between peaks and valleys of pain. His toes suddenly hurt, and through the salty film covering his right eye he saw the fingers on his left hand now curved to the left at an almost ninety-degree angle. It seemed the beating continued for hours. Back in the depths of his confused mind was a slight pride in staying conscious, though another part called him to hide beneath the sea of reality. Seek the bottom.

Kiang became aware during the "discussion"—as they called it—of being detached like a hovering spirit, observing from above what was happening to his own body. The pain was there, but it had been shoved into another part of his essence. He found himself noting the beating like the scientist he was—without passion. He would have smiled if he could have controlled his body, for the pain had vanished. He watched them slap, hit, and kick him. He even saw the colonel warn them to stay away from the face. He realized at that moment that he was dying. Elation filled his soul.

He reconciled himself to death, wondering how many more minutes until death arrived. Would there be a white tunnel with his ancestors waiting to greet him? As if hearing his thoughts, a bright, white spot on the edge of his dreams drew his attention. It grew in intensity, and the white tunnel grew in size; welcoming tugs pulled him toward it. He let the pull take him, just as his tormentors stopped. The white tunnel vanished and with horror he was jerked backward.

Kiang was back in his body. Pain rippled through him. He wanted to go back. He wanted to find the white tunnel. He wanted the peace he felt emanating from it.

His head flopped onto his chest. There were no fists working to keep his head up. The sound of the cell door opening brought a fresh reprieve to his senses, as he believed the Chinese to be leaving. But, they had tricked him before with the cell door. His consciousness swam furiously away from the waves of pain washing over him. Fear returned as he realized he was going to live and he shut his eyes, trying to recall how he had found the white tunnel. Within the turmoil of his mind, Kiang searched futilely for the white tunnel that had disappeared. The warmth and safety of the other side had vanished. So he dove, and within seconds was safe in the depths of his mind.

WHEN *he regained consciousness next, he was strapped to a moving gurney. The wheels made clanking sounds across the ridges of the rough concrete floor of the hallway in which he moved. The thin bed vibrated as the gurney rolled over uneven tiles. As they wheeled him, his thoughts were of death, and how they were going to administer the final coup d'état and bring a stop to his pain. He smiled as darkness freed him.*

"THAT should do it," the doctor said, lifting the swab away from the healing cut on his right cheek. "Give that another few days and it will be healed."

Kiang nodded, but said nothing, eyes down and looking away from the young doctor, afraid to look her in the face. Afraid the past two weeks of attention and condolences was some sort of deadly Pavlov experiment. His eyes registered the long white smock reaching nearly to her ankles above white tennis shoes.

The door opened to the room, causing him to jump involuntarily. He was seated on the edge of the examining table, his feet about six inches off the floor. Paper shoes covered his feet. A green paper gown covered his body, ending a few inches below the knees. When had they given him the green gown? His fingers touched the fabric-paper. Everything was paper in China. The plates, the cups, the shoes . . . He thought it was Japan where everything was paper, but China had lots of paper things also. No wonder the shoes were paper here; the real shoes were being worn in America. Would he ever see America again? He stifled a sob, but not so quick it didn't escape his lips.

Her hand briefly touched him on the shoulder. She leaned forward and in soft Mandarin said, "It's my assistant. You don't have to worry. Everything is forgiven. You are destined to be a hero of the people. Are you worried about being released soon? Don't. We are very proud of you. Many of our citizens journey abroad—"

She stopped suddenly and he wondered why. Without raising his head, he tried to lift his eyes enough to see who the newcomer was. A pair of black combat boots filled the edge of his vision. She had lied. It was no assistant.

"I'm sorry," she said. He detected a slight tremble in her voice and saw her feet turn to the side.

"Thank you, Doctor. You may leave us now."

"Yes, Colonel."

A moment later, she was out the door, leaving him with his colonel.

"I see you are better."

Kiang started to cry. Both of his eyes were open, but he stared intently at the boots that filled his vision, recognizing the dull shine on one of them. He pushed his legs together quickly, trying to stop his bladder from letting go. Was all of this some sort of experiment? Was he to be beaten and jailed again? His bladder let go and urine trickled down his leg to puddle on the floor.

"You can stop that now. You are a member of my team and we are going to be good friends." Hands gripped Kiang's shoulders. "You understand?"

He dug his chin deeper into his chest.

"I asked if you understand," the colonel repeated, his voice terse with a trace of anger.

The hands shook him for a second and then released him.

"Yes, Colonel," he mumbled.

A rough hand grabbed his chin and forced his head up. He caught a glimpse of the man's head and quickly shut his eyes, squeezing them shut.

"Open your eyes and look at me," the man said, the hand shaking his head back and forth, "Or, I shall cut them out so I can see what you are thinking behind them."

Kiang trembled. The man would do what he said. And enjoy it while he carved the eyes out. He knew there was a thin line of the colonel's need of him that kept the man from doing it. This colonel cut eyes, tongues, and ears from his victims as casually as others bragged about a marathon. Kiang hadn't been told that, but he knew it to be true. No one was as terrible as the colonel. No one had told him that, but he knew it to be true also. And the colonel was his friend; his master. Whatever the colonel wanted, he could have.

Kiang became aware the colonel was talking and he hadn't been listening. The fear of consequences made him focus on the man's words. If he failed to do what they wanted, not only would he die, but his parents would die.

They would die a horrible death. He didn't want to think about how they would die, because the many ways this man could do it left so many horrid possibilities that they swamped his thoughts. The colonel was someone who enjoyed experimenting with the ways of dying.

Kiang forced his eyes opened. The colonel released his chin.

"There! That's better, Kiang. When I tell you I want you to do something, I don't want any more of this shaking and crying and pissing on yourself like a little girl who has lost her dolly. Do you understand?"

"Yes, Colonel."

"Good."

The man had rough, dark skin that was only slightly lighter than the dark eyes that seemed to penetrate his thoughts. Heavy, bushy eyebrows hung over the colonel's eyes like misshapen awnings, accenting a leathery face weathered by years of wind and sun. The black hair was speckled with gray along the edges and in the center of the forehead a bright scar ran from the top of the right eyebrow to the edge of the hair over the left eye. Kiang fixed his eyes on the center of the forehead, avoiding eye contact with the colonel and trying not to trace the scar with his eyes.

"Did you enjoy that?" The man laughed, his eyebrows bunching upward. *"Most never forget my face once they've had the pleasure of my company. Your parents will meet me soon, but how long they enjoy my company depends on you, my friend and comrade."*

The door opened. His eyes remained fixed on the center of the man's forehead.

"Lay his clothes on the chair," the colonel ordered.

There were two of them, and they both acknowledged the man as "Colonel."

Kiang tried to swallow, but his mouth was so dry. He coughed.

"Bring our comrade a drink of water, Corporal."

Kiang heard water flowing from a tap behind him, but he kept his eyes on the colonel's forehead. Nothing must detract him from his concentration.

The colonel took the glass from the corporal and held it out to him. *"Here, drink."*

Kiang's hands shook slightly as he took the glass. How did the man know his mouth was dry? There was nothing about him this man didn't know. The colonel knew him. He knew everything. He knew where he had gone to school and even his first girlfriend, who had been a friend of a friend. A girlfriend in college, a relationship that lasted only a month, and this man knew her name. A fellow Chinese who had immigrated to America. A Chinese that this man promised he would meet again, if he accomplished his mission.

"Remember who gave you the water."

"Yes, Colonel."

"And, remember who freed you from the cell."

"Yes, Colonel."

"And, Kiang . . . remember who can put you back into the cell."

He shook involuntarily, but his eyes never left the colonel's forehead. A smile broke across the colonel's lips.

"Good, Kiang."

"What mission?" he asked aloud, and then shivered uncontrollably.

"I said stop that."

He stopped shivering.

"Relax."

His muscles relaxed. Relaxed so much the two soldiers stand-

ing nearby grabbed him to stop him from falling off the examination table.

The colonel laughed. "You're ready."

Kiang watched as the colonel turned and left the room. The soldiers pointed to the clothes, told him to dress. Minutes later he walked between them as he started down the long hallway, leading to what he knew was a new life. Whatever the colonel wanted . . .

KIANG jumped when a hand touched his shoulder, his eyes opening wide. When he saw the colonel sitting beside him, his mouth went dry and he was unable to swallow.

"Was it a nice nap, Kiang?" The colonel laughed.

Dressed in a dark black suit, a gold tie against a starched white shirt, was his nightmare. The man's black hair was neatly combed as if nailed in place. He was sunburned. The sunburn highlighted the red scar running from the beneath the heavy bushy eyebrow on the right across the forehead to the left edge of the perfect hair.

"Colonel," Kiang replied, his voice shaky.

The colonel smiled. "You are surprised to see me, no?" he asked in Mandarin.

Kiang nodded.

"Sometimes it is nice for me to travel across America and see those who serve the People's Republic. To remind them of their native soil." He laughed, facing forward and putting both hands on his knees. "It is also important for those of us who defend our country to know our enemy. What better way to know our enemy than to visit it; to send others to live here; and, to invest in its economy."

Kiang nodded. This was not the giant in his dreams. This man who sat beside him, bending forward, with both hands on his knees, was short. Shorter than him. His stomach hung slightly over the belt of the trousers. The colonel's arms tightened, sending ripples along the muscles of the forearms, up to the lower upperarms, to disappear beneath the short sleeves of the white shirt.

"You don't speak much, do you?" the colonel asked.

"No, sir. I am only here to serve," he said, dropping his gaze. He looked for a water bottle, knowing he didn't bring one. His throat was dry and Kiang found it hard to swallow.

The colonel laughed. "You are very important to us, Kiang. We have a task for you and, should you do it well, we think you should come home and visit your parents."

He looked up at the mention of his parents. "Are they well?" he asked.

"They are enjoying life in their hometown. I don't think they want to return to America. They are happy, surrounded by their relatives. They talk with their ancestors at the native ceremonies of the area." The colonel touched his chest. "Personally, I have always found it hard to talk with my ancestors. But, there are many in our country who believe deeply in seeking and receiving advice from the dear departed."

Kiang forced a swallow.

The colonel stopped talking as a young couple walked by, holding hands and laughing.

When they disappeared around a nearby bend, the colonel said, "Young love is so nice, don't you think? Here are this country's finest, laughing and playing, little realizing the downward slide of greatness that they ride."

Kiang nodded.

The colonel sighed. "Kiang, you are familiar with this American project called Sea Base?"

Kiang nodded.

"Answer me when I speak," the colonel snapped, his arm jerking upward quickly.

Kiang jumped. "Yes, my colonel."

"And quit acting as if I'm a mugger about to beat the shit out of you." He waved his arm across the scene in front of them. "The park is full of lunchtime loafers. Why, Kiang," he said, his voice softening, "you could get up and walk away any time you want. I wouldn't try to stop you."

Kiang's breath came in deep, rapid gasps.

"Now, stop that."

His breathing returned to normal.

The colonel laughed. "I always amaze myself when I command something and it immediately happens."

"Yes, my colonel."

"Yes, what, Kiang?"

"Yes, I know about Sea Base."

"Tell me what you know."

"It is a concept developed long ago by a chief of naval operations to build a large floating island capable of going anywhere on the oceans. It will—" Kiang coughed, ran his tongue around his dry mouth a couple of times, and continued "—be capable of carrying aircraft; docking ships and submarines; it will be a hospital, a supply depot, a repair facility. It will be everything."

"How big is it?"

"I am told it will be over eighty acres of American territory."

"Do you know how and where they are going to build it?"

"There is a prototype test—a beta test, as some of the contractors call it—that will be conducted starting in June."

"I am told, Kiang, that you turned down an opportunity to take part in this test."

Kiang stretched his neck, turning his head both ways, trying to stimulate some moisture. He shook his head. "I didn't turn down the opportunity. Jack Sward was selected to go. He knows the antenna systems better than I."

"What if Mr. Sward was unable to go?"

Kiang shrugged. "Then I would have gone, but Jack really wanted to go. He went to the director and got his name on the list. There was never any discussion about me going." He looked at the colonel. "I wasn't sure if I was supposed to go."

"We would have liked for you to go."

Kiang let out a deep breath, unaware he had been holding it. "It is too late now. Everyone is to be in Hawaii by June third."

"Oh, you have a sail date?"

He shook his head. "No, my colonel. We only have a date for everyone to be in Hawaii."

The colonel nodded, his head going up and down several times. "Kiang, I think this Jack Sward will meet with an accident. I think when this happens, you will volunteer to replace him. I suggest you appear reluctant to volunteer, but you are doing it for the company."

"There are others who they may choose to go other than me. This is a magnificent scientific endeavor, my colonel, and there is no shortage of volunteers."

"Then I suggest you don't be too reluctant in your volunteering, Kiang." The colonel stood. "You are only useful when you do what I ask. You go to your bosses—you go to this Jack Sward today—you let them know you would like to accompany Mr. Sward on Sea Base. For the next two weeks, you become a shadow of Mr. Sward; so much a shadow that when something happens to him, they will immediately think of you."

Kiang shut his eyes, nodded, and said, "Yes, my Colonel." He knew Jack Sward. Jack had been with the Layer Institute of Research for over twenty-five years. He had three boys, all in high school. Kiang had visited the Swards. He had sat at their table and partook of their meals. He couldn't do this. He opened his eyes, gaining the courage to protest, but the colonel was gone.

Kiang stood up and looked both ways, but could not see the colonel. He turned and started back to his car. By the time Kiang reached his small blue compact, any thoughts of giving up his parents for Sward was gone. On the trip back to the Institute, Kiang formulated his plan for becoming indispensable to Sward. If he could convince Sward to remain behind—let Kiang, a bachelor, take the six-month deployment . . . But he knew Sward would laugh at him and continue plans for being in Hawaii.

A month later, when Sward died in a car accident, Kiang was so involved in Sea Base that he was immediately selected to head the team going out on this great adventure. For Kiang, it was one more sin that he added to the others. He had been surprised to discover he felt no remorse over the death of Sward. The police said he had spun out of control and hit the revetment of an overpass, being killed instantly. His death was ruled accidental and by the time Kiang flew out to Pearl Harbor, Sward's wife and children were starting to learn how to live without their father. While Kiang had no remorse over what had been done to assure him a place on Sea Base, he was satisfied to hear that Jack Sward had left enough insurance and a large annuity to his wife. The Institute had also been benevolent. The remaining Swards would be all right.

TWO

Senior Chief Alistair Agazzi slowed the car to a crawl, turning the ignition off. The vintage 1957 Chevrolet rolled to a stop, the right tire bumping against the curb in front of the white stucco house on Malapai Lane. He leaned over to the passenger window and smiled. The faint muffled shout of *"You son-of-a-bitch"* reached his ears. He straightened, placing both hands on the steering wheel, his fingers drumming on it for a moment. He shook his head and chuckled. Just like old times.

Agazzi opened the door and stepped out. On the lawn across from the car, a growing pile of shirts and pants covered the grass near where the sidewalk and walkway met. A row of disheveled shirts, jumbled together, decorated the hedgerow that ran along the left front of the house.

Agazzi glanced up. A batch of white underwear emerged from the second story window. He caught a glimpse of Helen's bare arms. The whites tumbled down, some landing across his shipmate Master Chief Boatswain Mate Jerry Jacobs's back. His friend, the venerable master chief, was working methodically along the hedgerow, casually picking up the clothes, snapping them as if pulling them from a dryer. Then the career sailor nonchalantly draped them over his shoulder.

Agazzi opened his mouth to say something.

"You are dancing on my last nerve, you know?" Helen screamed from somewhere inside the upstairs room, her words echoing through the open window.

Helen, Jerry Jacobs's wife, was packing her man for sea.

Jacobs picked a few clothes from the lawn as another load shot from the second floor window. Agazzi thought he heard the man humming. Wouldn't surprise him. This was vintage Jacobs. A master chief's master chief. If the sea wanted him, then kiss the wife good-bye, slap her on the butt, and tell her to have the post-man out of the house by the time he returned. There was only one slight problem with that: Jacobs didn't believe in telling his wife when he was going to sea, heading out for a few months' deployment.

During the many years Agazzi had known Jacobs, to the best of Senior Chief Sonarman Alistair Agazzi's knowledge, the master chief had only once achieved his goal of deploying without his wife finding out. To escape what was waiting for him on the pier when he returned, he had sneaked off the ship in a laundry hamper.

"You said, *No more! I've had it!* you said. *We're going to settle down!* you promised. *I'm on a shore tour and when that's up—I'm getting out!* you lied. That's what you said! And look what the hell you're doing! You're going back to sea again, you lying, thieving bastard!"

A mix of T-shirts and skivvies flew out of the window, wadded in a ball, traveling a couple of feet before inertia took over and separated them like little parachutes as they fell.

Agazzi reached inside the open driver's window and pulled the emergency brake up. It wasn't as if this vintage car was going anywhere with the wheel turned against the curb, but . . .

Even at this early hour, the rising Hawaiian sun was settling its blue sky heat across the island. Another beautiful day in God's country, as Jacobs would say . . . if they had been on the golf course improving their par, chugging their beer, and griping about whoever was playing in front of them.

Agazzi walked around the front of the car, pulling his hand-kerchief out and rubbing the chrome hood ornament as he passed. Near the right door, he leaned back against the car. Wasn't anything to do but stay out of the way until Helen and Jerry finished their "good-byes." Helen stuck her upper torso out of the window, her hands holding each side of the frame, her rich black hair bouncing past her shoulders. After six kids she was still a fine figure of a woman, Agazzi thought.

"No, you can't even tell me you're going to sea! I've got to find out from Frieda, Julie, and Roxanne. They know!" She pounded her chest, her housecoat opening to expose her right breast. "I'm the wife of the master chief in charge of a bunch of misfits and their wives know and I don't." Her head disappeared back inside the house.

"Um, always the right one; never the left," Agazzi mumbled. *You would think,* he thought to himself, *a six-kid woman would have lost a little of the firmness around the breasts.*

Jacobs crossed the walkway leading from the house, holding a bundle of clothes cradled in his left arm while bending to pick up others as he moved toward the sidewalk.

"Hi, Alistair," Jacobs said, tossing the clothes on top of the growing pile. "She's nearly through." He reached up and pushed his ball cap up and off the front of his head. "At least, I think she is. There shouldn't be many . . ." he said, scratching his head.

Movement to the right caught Agazzi's attention. The neighbor was standing on her walkway, hair in curlers, holding the morning paper in her hand. The other hand gripped the top of her housecoat closed as if this somehow protected her from the ongoing action with her new neighbors.

"Damn civilians," Jerry said, following Agazzi's gaze. Jacobs cupped his hands. "Hey, Mrs. Davis, would you come over and give me a hand with these clothes? My wife's not very good at packing."

The woman shook her head, her lips curling in disgust, and quickly disappeared back inside her house.

"What would we do without the neighborhood watch?"

"Nice neighbor?"

"Like the Maryland Vehicle Administration, only less helpful."

Agazzi wondered how long the Jacobses would last here before they wore their neighbors' welcome out. Civilians just didn't understand the stress of military families or the difference the occupation of the sea made in lifestyles. *Come to think of it, not many of* us *understand this farewell dance of the Jacobs.*

From the window above, a fresh stream of obscenities and castigations spewed forth.

"Yeah, I am too going to get out!" Jacobs shouted up at the window as he turned back to the house, heading toward the hedgerow. "Just as soon as the Navy will let me!" he added. Then in a whisper he mumbled, "Eventually, of course, when I'm old and gray."

Agazzi grinned. Sure, his shipmate had promised Helen he was leaving the Navy. Retiring. Settling down. A good nine-to-five job, pumping gas, sacking groceries, or being one of those roving security guards at a shopping mall. Take the boys to scouts and Little League, even drop off and pick up Deep Freeze from ballet. Every lifer promised the missus they were going to get out. Some wives actually believed it. Frieda, Alistair's wife, believed it. The difference was that Alistair intended to retire. Either he was going to make master chief this time up, or when this deployment was over, Alistair Agazzi was going to take his twenty-two years of service, put in his papers, and kiss the Navy bye-bye.

Frieda warned him this morning when she kissed him goodbye that Helen had been furious last night when her suspicions had been confirmed.

Agazzi tuned out the tirade as he watched Jacobs meander around the yard, picking up clothes. Maybe he should retire now—the hell with waiting to see if he was going to be one of the one percent of senior chiefs to be elevated to the two-star rank of master chief. Maybe he should march right down there to the personnel office, call his detailer, and tell them, "Yo! I'm hanging up the single star of senior chief and going home. Mail my papers." But, where would he tell them to mail his papers? Another challenge for lifers was determining where they were going to settle down after retirement. So many of them failed to plan, and they ended up spending the rest of their lives near their last duty station. The good thing would be he'd be home all the time. He grunted. The bad thing would be he'd be home all the time, growing old, and being bored over finding things that were as exciting as being at sea.

He pushed away from the car and uncrossed his arms. Agazzi made a mental note to think about retiring while they were out to sea. Everyone *thought* about retiring. Once a lifer, always a lifer, the short-timers joked.

Agazzi frowned, surveying the clothes piled up and those still scattered on the lawn. "Jerry, uniforms?"

Jacobs turned. "Uh?"

Agazzi pointed, "Uniforms? Where are they?"

"Naw," Jacobs said, shaking his head. "I took them out a few at a time starting a couple of week ago. They're on the ship."

"Here, ya bastard! You're going to need these at sea!" Several pairs of Navy dress shoes—white and black—sailed through the window, en mass, before inertia tumbled them apart and scattered shoes across the lawn and walkway.

"Except the shoes," Jacobs added.

"Except the shoes," Agazzi nodded in agreement.

"*Never again,* you said! Settle down; keep a mortgage long enough to make some money; sow roots for the kids! Get a little something for their college education. Let Enduring Freedom and Clean Sweep play Little League!" Helen's head poked through the window. "You're a son-of-a-bitch, Jerry Malone Jacobs! You're a low-life—"

Helen glanced up, saw him, and stopped. Agazzi smiled and waved.

"Alistair, don't you pull that friendly shit on me. I might have known you'd be part of this. Frieda told me you were going to sea, too. I should have known!" she shouted, pointing at her husband who was bent over, picking up shoes. Helen's housecoat parted again for a fraction of a second before she pulled it back together.

"Ah, Helen. I'm as surprised as you are," Agazzi said, placing his palm against his chest. "Just as surprised as you are."

"Alistair Agazzi, you lie; your feet stink; and, you don't love Jesus. So don't you stand there and tell me you're not part of this." She dropped her hands onto the windowsill, her housecoat coming partly open. "And quit trying to look at my—"

"Helen," Agazzi interrupted. "How can you say that? Frieda washed my feet this morning."

"Alistair, if Frieda even got out of bed in the morning to say good-bye, you'd think she was having an affair." She looked down at Jacobs and leaned out the window. "Which I may do while you're out to sea this time!"

Jacobs looked up. "Honey, there any black socks up there?"

"Shit!" She pulled halfway inside the window, then leaned back out, jabbing her finger at Agazzi. "I should have known if Jerry's going to sea, you'd be behind it, or part of it, or agreeing to some other scheme of his to get out of the house for six months. Why don't the two of you go off and marry each other?"

Agazzi opened his mouth to explain that neither he nor Jerry had asked for this assignment, but stopped. He wasn't going to be sucked into the middle of this Jacobses' "going to sea" ritual. He was as close as he was going to get. He pulled a comb from his back pocket and ran it through the receding light-red, quickly-going-gray hair.

Jacobs straightened and stared at the empty outline of the second-story window before glancing back at Agazzi for a moment and smiling. Then, the master chief returned to scooping up the clothes.

Helen reappeared to toss a bunch of black uniform socks onto the grass.

"Well?" she asked, looking at Agazzi, her thick eyebrows rising. "Are you going to stand there like some jackass, or are you going to answer me?"

"Answer what?" Agazzi asked. *What was the question?*

"Don't pull that dumber-than-shit stuff on me, Alistair Agazzi. You know you're part of this conspiracy of Jerry's to get his sea-struck ass away from me and the kids for six months."

Agazzi spread his fingers across his chest. "Helen, how can you think that? I'm only going because Frieda doesn't want her fine figure of a man ditty-bopping off to sea without me along to watch over him."

"Jerry, any time today, shipmate," Agazzi whispered.

The sooner Jacobs finished, the sooner they'd be aboard ship, having breakfast. He glanced at his watch. How long do Fast Sealift Ships serve breakfast? On a Navy warship, the chow hall would be closing in thirty minutes.

He looked at Jacobs, who was bending over to pick up the socks, and noticed the bulging midriff of his friend. It wasn't as if he had the bulging midriff Jerry had to sustain him, plus he'd only had one cup of coffee this morning. His body would go into withdrawal soon if he didn't have that second cup. Thoughts of last night with Frieda caused him to smile. Last nights ashore were usually packed with a sailor's fantasy—except maybe for the Jacobses. He would put theirs in the nightmare category.

"Then you and Frieda can raise him when he returns," she said, her voice slightly lower. "I'm getting tired of waiting for him to grow up."

"Give her a few days and she'll calm down," Jacobs said softly, his head nodding slightly. It was true. Helen always got over it . . . a few days after he returned.

The Jacobses had been married twenty turbulent years. They had six kids—*six kids!* He shook his head, his lips tightened. He wondered if he and Frieda had had six kids, if he'd want to stay at sea as much as possible, too. Jacobs crudely claimed every time he returned from a cruise that he put six months of sperm savings from his own natural bank to a good retirement cause by impregnating his beautiful Helen. They even called their kids by nicknames commemorating the deployment from which he returned. Jacobs called them Daddy's retirement investment.

Agazzi would be hard-pressed to tell anyone their real names. There was the oldest, Deep Freeze—the only girl in the family— a tribute to Jacobs first deployment in the Navy where he wintered in Antarctica for nine months.

Then the boys came in back-to-back pairs with Deny Flight and Joint Endeavor in the 1990s after Jacobs returned from the Balkans operations in the Mediterranean.

Then, in the early 2000s, after 9/11, came his sons Enduring Freedom and Clean Sweep.

The youngest had just turned one. He was Maritime Claim, a show of force two years ago to repudiate the international claim by the People's Republic of China of two hundred-nautical mile territorial waters. Twelve nautical miles was the accepted international claim.

Economic claims were a different matter, but that was beyond Agazzi's concern and it hurt his head whenever he tried to figure it out. He was just a poor senior chief trying to make the best of a Navy that seemed to realign and reorganize every time some chief of naval operations read a new business or management book.

Agazzi was the acting division officer for this deployment. The usual junior officer assigned to the job wasn't coming. Agazzi was looking forward to running the sonar division on this deployment without having some young just-commissioned college kid to train.

Agazzi didn't read business books; he didn't try to reorganize his division—well, not as often. Nor did he try to calculate the "return on investment" from how his Anti-Submarine Warfare control center operated. Which was probably why he and the other khaki-clad enlisted in the Navy figured they were truly the last warriors in the Navy—all the officers were too busy trying to learn to be businessmen. As he and Jacobs had discussed, the sailors were still sailors to those in the Goat Locker—not human capital, as the Pentagon called them.

The fact that he was going to be the division officer was a good side of the new philosophy, even if it meant he had two jobs rolled into one. He would be the division officer, but he would still be the division chief for the Anti-Submarine division—the ASW division. The ensign probably could have been of some use, if the young man had been allowed to come.

The ensign—Agazzi couldn't even recall the young man's name—had gotten himself thrown in hack a couple of weeks ago for an undisclosed liberty incident. *Probably screwed up a balance sheet.*

Enlisted sailors went to the brig, but not officers. Oh, no. For minor infractions they were sent to their BOQ room to remain there until their hack-days were over. They couldn't drink, but they could watch television and were allowed to eat three times a day.

So, the skipper thought it would be good for the newbie officer to spend time confined to his bachelor quarters room for the entire time of the deployment. The junior officer was being punished by not being allowed to go to sea! *Wow! If word gets out that's all it takes to avoid a six-month deployment, a long line will be forming at the skipper's door.*

Agazzi didn't have the whole story. If the new ensign was doing stuff on liberty to get thrown in hack, then maybe that ensign had some cojones. Maybe some day, way down the line, he'd become a fine Navy officer who not only had his Surface Warfare qualifications, but his CPA credentials, too.

He'd get the story eventually. Good news travels fast; bad news faster. Why would anyone need a soap opera series when you had situation reports—sitreps—telling everyone from your command to the chief of naval operations how you screwed up.

Jacobs scooped up several pairs of skivvy boxer shorts, snapping them out, and in two quick moves the master chief folded them into the long, creased style taught in Navy boot camp.

"I cut the grass yesterday," Jacobs offered, not looking up as he tossed them unceremoniously onto the pile, the shorts falling apart as if never folded.

"You both ought to be shot." Helen disappeared back inside the house.

"Between these grass shavings from yesterday, the morning

dew, and high humidity, these whites are going to have a nice permanent shade of stained green." Jacobs laughed. "That should give the laundrymen something to think about—green hashmarks instead of brown in the crotch of your skivvies.

"Looks as if she's blaming me for your lack of bravery."

Jacobs pushed the pile of clothes with his shoe. "Bravery! She loves me. Just last night, there I was tied to the bed when she walked in with jumper cables and a saddle. I knew then, the night had just begun."

"Master Chief, anyone ever tell you you're a sick puppy?" Agazzi asked, bending down and pulling a light-colored fabric purse from the pile of clothes. "Yours?"

Jacobs took the purse. "I'm a boatswain mate, Alistair. We have certain standards we are expected to live down to," he said, holding the purse down along the side of his khakis.

"And, it is my humble opinion that you have not only achieved, but have established lower standards in which to excel."

A faded sea bag sailed out the window, landing directly at Jacobs's feet, causing him to jump and look up at Helen.

"Thanks, honey!" He grabbed the sea bag and began cramming clothes into it.

"Don't 'honey' me, you bastard! You don't think I'm going to keep anything Navy in this house, Jerry Malone Jacobs!" she shouted, her arms emerging through the open window, holding several pairs of slacks and a sweater. She stuck her head through, her lower lip pushing against the upper, and majestically opened her arms as if welcoming the Lord. The clothes fell across the hedgerow. "Ah!" she gasped. "I'm feeling better already and he isn't even at sea."

"Ah, honey. At least throw them farther out." He held his hands up in a begging posture. "Those bushes are rip—"

"Then get one of those young hussies in those ports you and Alistair are going to terrorize to sew them up. As far as I am concerned, you have everything you're ever going to get out of this house!"

"Helen, it is really nice how you pack Jerry for sea. Most wives would—"

"Alistair Agazzi, don't make me come down and shove your head up your butt so far you'll look like a Greek water fountain. Your wife is just as upset."

Agazzi frowned. "I just left her, Helen. She isn't upset."

"She will be when I finish talking to her!"

Jacobs handed the purse to Agazzi. "Here, hold this. If she thought I took one of her Lori Benedetto purses with me, she'd think I was fooling around." The master chief returned to shoving clothes into the sea bag, throwing the shoes in willy-nilly.

Agazzi held up the purse. "It'd go nicely with your khakis. Or, you could tell her you decided to come out of the closet."

Jacobs held up three fingers. "You read cipher?"

Agazzi glanced at his watch. It was nearly seven o'clock. Jerry could worry about straightening his clothes out when he got to his ship.

Agazzi opened the trunk of the car. "You think she'll call my wife?"

Jacobs tossed his sea bag into the trunk. "Alistair, how long have you known Helen?"

"You're right. She'll call Frieda."

Jacobs closed the trunk. "Of course she's going to call Frieda. Here, hand me that purse before you become too attached to it."

The front door opened and Helen Jacobs stepped onto the small cement porch.

"Well!" she shouted. "You gonna leave without kissing me 'bye?"

"Go kiss the missus 'bye, Jerry, so we can get out of here. And, tell her Frieda is out of town."

Jacobs turned and sighed.

Agazzi whispered, "I'd keep my head down just in case she—"

"Crank the car, just in case," Jacobs said over his shoulder as he walked toward the house, stopping at the front steps directly in front of his wife.

"Here, honey," he said, handing her the purse.

"How long are you going to be gone this time?" Helen asked, taking the purse from him.

He shrugged. "It's just a proof of concept trial. Not supposed to be more than four months."

"Why don't you tell me when you're going to sea? Why do I always have to find out from others?" Her voice trembled.

Agazzi shook his head slightly, hearing them talk. He could never keep a thing like this from Frieda. Other men rose to the occasion and told their wives. Why the hell Jerry didn't, no one knew.

"Every time you're about to go to sea, you know how I know?"

I'll tell you. Your uniforms disappear a little at a time. A shirt here; a pair of khaki trousers there; and, your skivvy shorts start disappearing. And each time I tell myself I'm imagining things even when I know you're moving them to the ship. Or—" She pointed at Agazzi who was sitting in the car. He waved at her. "Maybe they're being kept over at Alistair's or someone else's house. You could tell me, you know?"

"You're right."

Jerry's excuse for not telling Helen he was deploying until the day of deployment was what just happened. Instead of a couple of hours of yelling on the morning of departure, it would be two to three weeks of holy hell, according to Jacobs. But Agazzi learned a long time ago that the master chief's spin was much like a fisherman's tale: Not everything was as clear as he said.

"Next time—"

Agazzi saw Helen's eyes widen, a fire blazing behind them.

Jacobs must have also, for he paused. "Sorry, honey. I mean this is the last time. It truly is. I have put in my papers."

"You've put in your papers?" she asked, a hint of disbelief and a tone of hope in the question. "Your retirement papers?"

"Well," he said, his head nodding in both directions. "I have written them. They're in my locker. All I have to do is take them to personnel. They'll mail them to Millington, Tennessee, to the Bureau of Naval Personnel, and in a couple of weeks I'll have my retirement date."

She shook her head and put her arms on Jacobs's shoulders. "Jerry, you're a liar, you know. I know it; Alistair knows it; and even your children know it. BUPERS probably has it stamped in big red letters across your service record. We both know you won't retire until they kick you out," she said softly.

"Of course I will—"

She held her hand palm-up toward him. "Stop. Don't tell me more lies. The day you sleep in, get up, and don't put on a set of khakis, then I'll know you're retired." She wrapped her arms around him, and hugged him tightly. "I love you even if you are the worst damn thing that ever happened to me. You're screwed up and you don't listen to what's best for you."

"I like it when you talk like that," Jacobs said.

Agazzi poked his finger at his lips, making a vomiting motion. Helen saw him and raised the middle finger of the hand behind Jacobs's back.

Jacobs returned the hug for a few seconds, then pulled back to kiss her. "I love you, too, honey. Kiss the kids for me and tell them I'll be back soon."

"Does this cruise you're going on have a name?"

"Operation Sea Base."

"Christ! Don't you even think it when you come back. Sea Base? Hell, no. No more. Maritime Claim was the last one. By the time you return, I will have gone to the doctor and had him close the shipyard."

Two minutes later, Agazzi and Jacobs were on the road, dodging the morning traffic and heading toward the port at Pearl Harbor.

"You okay?" Agazzi asked.

"Of course I'm okay. Why wouldn't I be?"

Agazzi shrugged his right shoulder. His left hand steered the car. "Just thought maybe this time she bothered you."

"She's no bother. What would life be like without a Helen? It'd be boring as hell. Every sailor worth his salt should have a Helen. Haven't you ever heard of the face that launched a thousand ships?"

"How's Maritime Claim doing?"

Jacobs smiled. "Just like his old man," he said. "Got a set of lungs on him that keeps Helen awake at night and a set of his daddy's baby-blue eyes to accent the fabulous Jacobs family black hair." Jacobs paused and shook his head.

Several minutes of quiet passed between the two shipmates as Agazzi shifted lanes, fighting the urge to look at his watch. He reached down and switched on the radio.

". . . explosion destroyed the front of the building. Authorities do not have a clear picture yet if anyone died in the explosion. The Chinese attaché to Hawaii has expressed his outrage to the Secretary of State over the incident. . . ."

"Another one," Jacobs said.

Agazzi nodded. "Three in the past month. Looks as if these self-styled anarchists have shifted to Hawaii."

"You gotta ask yourself what in the hell do they hope to accomplish going around the country bombing everything Chinese."

"Not just Chinese. One of those explosions hit the Russian embassy in New York."

". . . fire is out. Roads are shut down surrounding the area of the explosion as authorities collect evidence, and also to give the city workers an opportunity to help clear the debris. Earlier this morning, ABC was on the scene when several ambulances left the site carrying the injured to area hospitals. Many of those injured were some of Hawaii's homeless who spend their evenings along. . . ."

Agazzi reached over and turned off the radio. "We're nearly there."

"You think she'll be out?" Jacobs asked as he leaned forward.

Agazzi nodded. "She hasn't missed a day in a month. If she isn't, then we won't see her again for six months."

"She must the healthiest woman we know. You ever notice when she bends over those little butt cheeks peek out beneath her shorts. Almost as if they're winking at ya, don't you think."

"No, I don't think."

"That's because you're a senior chief and I'm a master chief. Master chiefs are prone to deeper thought."

The "she" was a young blonde whose early-morning calisthenics at the nearby park had brought more than one car to an unexpected stop. Short pants, sweatbands, short cheerleader socks, and tight high-riding shirts that revealed the lack of a sports bra—or any bra for that matter. She was the highlight of the day ahead.

"You think she knows—"

"Of course she knows, Jerry. Why do you think she does it right there at edge of the park directly across from the stop sign."

"I bet she keeps score on the number of fender benders caused by her deep knee bends. I'd like to see those deep knee bends up closer."

"You're a sick puppy, Master Chief."

"How many times do I have to tell you master chiefs aren't 'sick puppies'? We may be rabid Dobermans; ill-tempered wolves; or, even, mad mastiffs—but never sick puppies." After a couple of seconds, he added, "The top one-percent of the Navy are never puppies."

"Yeah? Then, what are we senior chiefs?"

"Toy poodles."

The car rounded the curve, braking for the stop sign. Across from the stop sign, her back to them, was the blonde in a tight red outfit, her slender, exposed arms stretched above her head, her hands spread wide. As they watched, she stretched from right to

left before bending over to touch her feet. Then, she started deep
knee bends.

"Maybe more of a lapdog than a Doberman right now," Jacobs
conceded.

"Red is a little too vibrant for me."

"If you ask me, red ain't vibrant enough for her."

"Panty ridge," Agazzi said, the car idling at the stop sign. He
put on the left turn signal.

"I should hope to shout," Jacobs added. "A fine butt like that
without a panty ridge is like a fine oil painting without a frame."

The car eased away from the stop sign and several seconds
later picked up speed.

THREE

The door to the conference room clicked shut behind Agazzi and Jacobs.

"Let's get out of here," Jacobs said. "I could use a good cigar and something to clear my mind from all that mental masturbation we just heard."

"You mean psyche satisfaction." Agazzi chuckled in agreement.

"Is that with or without foreplay?"

"Nothing like having a Ph.D. with a degree in engineering, or something, explaining how Sea Base is going to work to a bunch of us high school graduates. I was lost by the second slide. Was that math or physics on those slides?"

"I think it was Egyptian hieroglyphics, and don't pull that high school graduate on me. I know you've got a Master's degree somewhere in that brain."

"Feels more like a GED after that session," Agazzi said.

"If I hear another person say 'intricacies of the model' one more time."

"I think Ph.D.'ers perfect saying that over the years."

The two men weaved through the crowd in the narrow hallways of the Maritime Sealift Command headquarters building, squeezing past sailors and merchant marines shuffling among the various offices. Most appeared unfamiliar with the layout, their eyes scanning the signs hanging above the doors, bumping into others doing the same. The building was one of those many 1980s building that had been remodeled so much that the original purpose was known to only the most ardent of researchers.

The narrow hallways forced everyone to turn sideways to pass. A tall, lanky sailor they had fallen behind, using him to blaze a way through the crowd, knocked a sign with his head. The way he continued walking, the experience must be a common one. Agazzi and Jacobs exchanged a smile at the incident, Jacobs shrugging his shoulders to Agazzi's unspoken comment.

Ahead of them, near the water fountain, an older man stood— must be in his sixties, thought Agazzi—dressed in blue jeans with a large gold earring in his left ear, having a quiet argument with a young Navy officer. The index finger of the man was jerking toward, but never quite touching, the khaki-clad officer's chest. The young officer looked down pleadingly at the old merchant marine.

As Agazzi neared, he heard the officer call the man "Dad." Must be hell to work in the same organization as your father.

"Excuse me, Senior Chief," a young sailor said, turning sideways as he hurried by the two.

"What about me?" Jacobs asked. "Don't he know a master chief when he sees one?"

"He was just working up the chain of command."

" 'Eat shit and die' is what I have to say about that."

TWO minutes later, the two blinked their eyes in the bright noon sun. The tall sailor was sauntering off down the sidewalk, his hands swinging freely.

Jacobs sighed. "I hate being inside. I've been on Spruance-class destroyers that had more room than that building."

"Let's find some shade," Agazzi offered.

"You believe that crap in there?"

Agazzi stepped off the curb, looking both ways as he crossed the road leading from the quarterdeck. "I'm not what you'd call a marine engineer or whatever those people called themselves. They say this has been fully tested. Operations Test and Evaluation Forces—OPTEVFOR, or whatever those folks from Norfolk call themselves—have put it through its paces."

Jacobs rubbed his stomach. "That is great to know. Now I have this great warm fuzzy rumbling around inside. Kind of like when we were *recapitulizing* the Navy or *transforming* it or whatever the shit the officers called it. If I recall back then, that *recapitulizing* cost 30,000 sailors their careers; cost the Navy every good overseas liberty port we had; and, managed to let the French, Russians, Indians, and Chinese move into them."

"You need to come out of your shell, Jerry. Be more forceful about your opinions. I think this bottling them up inside . . ."

"Okay, okay, okay," Jacobs said, waving him away. "Bottom line is, if they're going to brief us on this manmade island bullshit, then they should use layman's terms so people like you and I can understand it. Most of those in the auditorium are just sailors like us. We could give a shit less about tensile strength and drooping drawers."

"They didn't have to brief us, you know?"

Jacobs nodded. "I know. The Navy gives them a set of orders and tells them they're going to be analysis and test-checkers. Next thing you know, they have a clipboard with graph paper on it."

"Drooping drawers?"

Jacobs shrugged and shook his head. "It was all I could think to add."

Agazzi stopped at the curb and waited for Jacobs to step up beside him. They walked across the grass toward a picnic table some bright, enterprising sailor had built under the palm trees. Another small thing in the life of a Navy, thought Agazzi, where a lone sailor did something for everyone and no one could recall his name.

This picnic table was here when he was chief years ago, and the only change when he came back this time was that someone had sanded it down, replaced some rotting wood, and repainted it. He'd driven by here during the workday and seen people using it. He wondered briefly what ever happened to the person who did this. What ever happens to a lot of people who cross your life for a moment, enriching it in ways they never knew, and then disappear forever?

Jacobs was talking about painting something, but boatswain mates were always painting or sanding something, even when it might not need it.

Agazzi had been in the Navy for twenty-two years. Rich years. Years of doing the Navy's work and enjoying not having to de-

cide what color tie went well with white socks. He thought back
to his first tour of duty in Rota, Spain, as a young man in his late
teens, barhopping with the young coed backpackers who mean-
dered into the Navy village to earn a few coins before continuing
their treks through Europe. Whatever happened to the young
ladies he knew and the sailors he matured with during that tour?
He shook his head. He'd been doing this a lot lately—reminisc-
ing about his early career and the people he knew. People he
wished he now knew where they lived; what they had done with
their lives after Rota; and what they were doing now. Who was
alive and who was dead? Frieda said it was because he was thinking of retiring. And retire he would, if he didn't make Master
Chief off this list.

"Hey, I'm talking to you," Jacobs said, slapping him on the
shoulder. "Don't go doing any of that deep thinking shit on me.
I've had all I can handle this morning."

A red cigarette can, filled with brown stained sand, sat beside
the table. Crushed cigarette butts protruded from the sand. It had
been a while since someone had done a working party and
dumped the butts.

"OPTEVFOR has civilians who have been doing this type of
stuff for years," Agazzi answered.

"Considering most of the Navy folk assigned to OPTEVFOR
are as bright as you and I, whatever anxiety I may have about riding around in the middle of the Pacific on an eighty-one acre . . ."

". . . eighty-one-point-five acre . . ."

". . . platform mounted on top of eight aging MSC ships powered by 1970–era steam plants, is somewhat relieved. If we
needed a repair part for those ships, we'd have to go to the Maritime Museum in Norfolk."

"Or the one at the Navy Yard in Washington."

Jacobs stepped around one of the small palm plants encircling
the picnic table. "Well, answer me this: What's to keep those
MSC ships' movements synchronized? A bunch of scientists? It
took three of them to get the projector to work this morning." Jacobs tapped a finger against his head a couple of times. "They
may be maritime engineers, as that bunch in the auditorium
called themselves, but they sure as hell ain't boatswain mates and
they sure as hell haven't spent a lot of time out at sea. The ocean
doesn't like people who don't respect her."

"I don't think they're going to keep something like this secret, do you?"

"Sometimes, she doesn't like those who do." Jacobs snipped off the end of his cigar. "I hope to hell they don't think they're going to keep it a secret," he said as he flicked what he called his blowtorch lighter and fire-blasted the end of the cigar. "I'd hate to be floating around in the middle of the Pacific with no one knowing where I'm at when this thing goes tits-up and those eight ships head belly-down. You ever seen a ship sink?" he asked curiously.

"If it sinks, Jerry, at least you will have the benefit of being topside and, to answer your question: No, I haven't seen a ship sink—except in movies." Agazzi pulled out a bunch of rolled papers from his back pocket. "And, that's the only place I want to see it."

"You know it doesn't look militarily sharp to have things wadded up and stuffed into your pockets. Sets a bad example," Jacobs joked, blowing a huge smoke ring into the near-still air. "Next thing you know, all these sailors who want to grow up and be like you will be seeing who can have the most things wadded up and stuffed in their pockets."

"Oh, yeah!"

"Wow, Alistair. You really have the gift for comebacks."

Agazzi grinned. "You're standing there blowing smoke all over the place, giving everyone second-hand cancer, and you tell me wadded up papers set a bad example? Go figure."

"Not my job to figure. My job is to keep the ship afloat and looking nice for congressional junkets. Wadded papers in the back of senior chief trousers distract from the purity of shipboard life."

Agazzi laid the papers on the table. "Here, I've got something you can wad up."

"Probably not wide enough for my liking."

"What were you going to say about ships sinking?"

"What I was going to say is that when ships sink they're like giant Hoover vacuum cleaners, sucking everything down with them when they go. It won't matter whether I'm topside or with you or with your sailors *way down* below the waterline. It's going to be one moment of sheer skivvy-filling terror. But, it won't last long, because the suction is going to pull your frail little human body to where it is chasing those tons of steel heading down to the bottom of the ocean. I think your eyes pop just before the water pressure crushes the bones into your body. Then those eyes will deflate as the water pressure caves the skull. . . ."

Agazzi looked at Jacobs for a couple of seconds before shaking his head. "You know, Jerry, I always sleep better after one of these conversations." He turned and tapped his finger on the papers he had rolled out on the tabletop. "This is where my sonar technicians and I are going to be," Agazzi said, pointing to the pamphlet at the United States Naval Ship *Algol*. "Our unmanned underwater vehicles are going to be located two ships away on the USNS *Bellatrix*. If we have a problem with the machinery that loads and delivers them, I'm going to have to come up six decks to the main deck, cross another ship to reach the *Bellatrix*, then walk down six decks to where the UUVs are located."

Jacobs stuck his arm out and flicked the ash away. "Well, that breaks my heart, Shipmate. At least you'll be beneath the six-foot-thick canopy of Sea Base out of the wind, sun, and most other weather that may come along." He lowered his voice, put his hand on Agazzi's shoulder. "You know, since you're going to be inside the ship, your eyeballs will pop later than those of us topside. I'll wave at the porthole as I pass you heading downward."

He shrugged off the hand. "Jerry, this may work on young seamen and junior officers, but this is Alistair you're talking to. How many times have we gone to sea together?" He put his hand on Jacobs's shoulder. "You should save this for them. I mean, it's really good. Really, really good, but I know you," he added, dropping his hand. "Save it for new meat."

Jacobs dropped his hand and shrugged.

"Where was I? Oh, yes, they expect eight of us to run sonar and handle the UUVs twenty-four/seven." Agazzi unzipped his carry bag and pulled out a bottle of water. "I have discovered during my career, my fine Master Chief Petty Officer—whom everyone loves and admires; whose every word is weighed with caution and concern—that every time some admiral in Washington decides we can do more with less, he's right. We do more with less, but the more of before is less than today."

Agazzi held the water bottle out to Jacobs, who took a deep swig. "Even warm it's good," Jacobs said, using the back of his hand to wipe the moisture from his lips.

"It's good because you didn't have to pay for it."

"How can you ask a man with six kids to pay for it, Alistair? Some of us aren't as lucky as you and Frieda."

If you only knew, my friend, how many years we tried to have children before coming to terms with the fact that we were going to be a two-person family. "Yes, but all you have to do is wander around the top of Sea Base, stay off the runway when those Air Force jocks start playing 'Testosterone Charlie,' and shove your deck apes to where the rust is."

Jacobs blew out a series of smoke rings. "Deck apes are so non-PC. You're going to get yourself in trouble one of these days."

"Me?" Agazzi exclaimed, placing his hand against his chest, fingers spread. "Who's had more EEO complaints against him for inappropriate comments than—"

"They weren't EEO complaints. I am an equal opportunity—type of guy. They were 'sexually inappropriate' comments. Besides, Alistair, you aren't doing your job in today's Navy if someone hasn't made a hotline phone call, filed an equal-employment opportunity complaint, or written the inspector general. Oh! And, don't forget congressmen . . ."

"Congress-people."

". . . Everyone writes their congressman at least once a year. Personally, I list every complaint in the bullets I give the division officer when he writes my yearly evaluation. What's a good master chief if he doesn't take credit for the hard work he gets out of his sailors."

The sound of gravel shifting as cars left the meeting was accompanied with dust drifting over the table.

"You think this thing will support two squadrons of Air Force fighters?" Jacobs asked.

Agazzi shrugged. "How would I know? I don't even know how many aircraft are in an Air Force squadron. Come to think of it, I don't know how many are in a Navy squadron."

"It's an airdale thing. They don't have many secrets, so the number of aircraft in a squadron is well protected."

"Besides, how do we know the Air Force will let them fly aboard Sea Base?"

Jacobs laughed. "That's a good question. Sea Base doesn't have a golf course or officers club."

"Wait until they discover there's no alcohol, either."

Jacobs's eyes widened. "But, I thought . . ."

"Well, you thought wrong."

Jacobs shrugged. "Either way, this is an opportunity the Air Force can't afford to miss, even without those necessary amenities." He took another drink of water from Agazzi's bottle. "The Air Force has been trying for years to prove we don't need aircraft carriers. All they need is a bunch of tankers and they can fly from mainland America to anywhere in the word using their air-to-air refueling capabilities. Go anywhere, be anywhere, do anything within hours of being ordered."

Agazzi reached over and took the water from Jacobs. "Reminds me of the old United States Navy before business books became our tactical mantra."

"It is still the United States Navy. We can deploy anywhere, be anywhere, and do anything."

"Yeah, but we use aircraft carriers. The Air Force uses the air," Jacobs added, his voice intentionally high and whiny. "Piddle packs are their key to mastery of the globe."

"Piddle packs?"

"Well," Jacobs said, his voice derisive, "fighter aircraft don't have heads, do they? They gotta pee somewhere."

Highlighting anything negative about the Navy irritated Jacobs. Jacobs had this perverse enjoyment of making others uncomfortable. Highlighting the Air Force against the Navy was one way the master chief irritated a myriad of Navy audiences. In today's military force the military services were so entwined that seldom did only one service operate alone. They operated together, drawing on the skills and expertise of each other. The U.S. military was smaller today because of the economic burst of 2015, but it was still the most powerful in the world. Hard to believe six years had passed since then.

Agazzi tapped the center of some architect's drawing on the pamphlet.

"Jerry, I suspect you're going to be involved in putting up this tower," Agazzi said, changing the subject.

"If they're smart, I will be," Jacobs said, jamming the cigar between his lips and leaning over. "What tower?"

"According to the briefer, this is where the main operations control center for Sea Base is going to be located. It'll be a combined aircraft control tower and combat information center. The commanding officer of Sea Base will have his office and staff there. They will fight Sea Base, launch aircraft, and maneuver this eighty-one-point-five acres of American territory all from this tower."

"So this is where they're going to fight this floating bucket of industrial bolts guided by information age computers?"

Agazzi sighed. "I believe so, but the main computer server farm for Sea Base is on this ship: the USNS *Denebola*."

"Main computer server farm! What the hell is that? Makes me think of tractors, dirt, and cow shit."

Agazzi tapped the image of the *Denebola*. "Once Sea Base is fully deployed, the ships holding it up must operate as if they are one. This is done with computers and the *Denebola* is the home for those computers."

"And what happens when this so-called farm decides to have a bad crop?"

Agazzi shrugged. "I guess they'll switch over to the back-up servers on board the USNS *Pollux*."

"And all of this is going to be done from this tower in the center of Sea Base?"

"Jerry, are you and your people going to put this tower up, or aren't you?"

Jacobs nodded. "No. They have a Seabee company tasked with putting up the topside buildings, including the tower, once Sea Base has been fully expanded. My job will be overseeing a lot of the basic work such as connecting the walkways between the ships. And we can't forget our lovely friends in the Air Force. They tend to get pissed-off when a little nail or screw is sucked up into an engine causing it to explode." Jacobs jerked his arms apart. "Boom! Ergo," he continued, pulling his cigar from between his lips and dropping his arms by his sides. "We'll be helping with foreign object disposal—FOD walkdown, for those of you who have flown in a previous life. *FOD this, FOD that, and FOD you*, is what I always say. Plus, we'll be doing the normal shipboard preservation stuff such as removing rust and painting, rolling up lines—little things that need strong backs and weak minds until some admiral at the Pentagon gets this brilliant idea that modern technology can replace us. Then, like the early 2000s, another rating will bite the dust."

Agazzi smiled. "It should be quite a sight."

"*Another one bites the dust,*" Jacobs sang mockingly. He shoved the cigar back in his mouth, took a puff, then, holding it between his fingers, pointed at Agazzi. "As for the tower, it's more a raising than a set-up. One of the Fast Sealift Ships nearer the center has the tower on it. Once Sea Base is connected, they'll raise the tower from a horizontal position on the ship into a vertical configuration. It'll come through a precut hole. It'll tower about four decks above the main deck of Sea Base. Those working in it will be able to walk belowdecks directly into the ship and their berthing quarters without ever leaving the confines of the spaces. Wow! Makes me want to be something other than a boatswain mate. Why don't I shoot myself now?" Jacobs waved away dust raised by a couple of passing cars.

"Sounds dangerous?"

"Everything about this adventure not only sounds dangerous; it is."

"I can see having a little apprehension over whether this thing is going to work, or drown 3,000 sailors, civilians, and Marines. Just thinking how they're going to mitigate the waves and currents—"

"Giant sea anchors."

"Sea anchors?"

Jacobs nodded. He dropped his still-lit cigar into the bucket of sand. "Every one of the Fast Sealift Ships—FSS, we the initiated call them—has two expandable sea anchors about seven hundrd feet in length. Considering the ships are only slightly more than nine hundred feet in length, once the sea anchors are filled with sea water, it'll be like having sixteen more things to keep Sea Base steady." He shook his head. "Or, sixteen more things to pull us faster to the bottom."

"You know more about this than you let on."

"I'm a boatswain mate. No one ever tells us anything so we have this *proclivity*—"

"Proclivity?"

"—to find out about things like this. Also—*another proclivity*—to discover every little tidbit of nautical lore to ensure the real truth of our Navy is passed from one generation of real sailors to the next."

"I hear they're doing away with the Boatswain Mate rating. Changing the rating to Mariner."

"Don't make me gag, Alistair. Mariner—what a wuss of a name!"

"You know more than you're letting on. High and tight, right?"

Jacobs grinned. "Okay, I have been involved in some of the stuff concerning the setting up and taking down of Sea Base." He slid into the bench across from where Agazzi stood.

Agazzi lifted his right foot onto the picnic bench, resting his right arm on his raised knee.

"So, what things have you learned?" Agazzi asked.

"A few things," Jacobs said, frowning.

Agazzi put his foot down and slid onto the bench directly across from Jacobs. "How many days should I wear a life vest?"

"My intentions are to never be without a life vest. I have discovered in my ancient wisdom from twenty-seven years of Naval service that anything complex going to sea eventually *stays* at sea—most times at the bottom."

Agazzi lifted his hand and twisted it in the air a couple of times. "Someday, is this enlightened master chief going to write his words down?"

"Of course," Jacobs agreed, nodding sharply. "But first I have to finish my other two books: *New Lights on Masturbation* and *Know Your Body Nude*. Those two I expect to be bestsellers among those who go to sea. Young men when they first have sex need someone more experienced than—"

"While I find your ideas for great books fascinating, tell me about the sea anchors," Agazzi interrupted.

"Well, since you don't want to talk about my books . . . As the sea anchors take on water and sink, the stability of Sea Base increases. Kind of like giant keels over a thousand feet down when you add the sea anchors to the normal depth below the waterline of these ships."

"Wow."

"Along the tethers running between the sea anchors and the parent ship are air hoses and electronic cables so those server farms can change their depth. Sensors on the sides of the sea anchors will constantly monitor current, bearing, and drift so the computers can rapidly change the depth of individual sea anchors to keep Sea Base stable."

"You're going to be manning some console somewhere that monitors this?" Agazzi asked.

"Not me. I ain't no computer geek. You know more about that than I do. Until you told me about the *Denebola* and *Pollux*, I didn't even know we had two ships completely dedicated to keeping Sea Base stable."

"I don't think the ships are completely dedicated to the server farms. I just said that was where they're located."

"Probably explains why we have a bunch of information professionals and technicians running around back there," Jacobs said, jerking his thumb toward the Maritime Sealift Command building. We have finally reached the real world where we are going to pit computer geek against the sea. I think I know where I'm going to place my money."

"How do you know they're IPs and ITs?"

"You can spot them by their pasty complexion. Those computers won't only have the data from the sea anchors to help determine depth, but also sensor data coming from the ships, the meteorologists, Naval Postgraduate School, and when—notice I didn't say if—when an emergency arises they will also have a one-nine-hundred number to an astrological service."

"I thought we did away with the meteorologists."

"The Navy did. Shows what happens when you put a bunch of warfighters in charge. There's nothing they don't think they can do and do better. If they can't see it, touch it, feel it, experience the thrill of a concussion as it blows up, then it don't exist."

"Tell me what you really think, Jerry. Don't hold back," Agazzi said with a smile.

"If they can't see it, then they can't paint it on the side of their ships. Ergo, it doesn't exist."

"What happens if both sets of computers go? I'm sure they have an emergency breakaway plan to bring Sea Base down?"

Jacobs guffawed. "It is hard to break away when you have two squadrons of aircraft parked overhead." He sighed. "Kind of wish I'd listened to Helen and retired."

"Unlike you, I'm enthused over being part of something that once again projects America's power back into the Pacific. Since leaving Japan—"

"Whoa, shipmate! I never said I was unenthused about going to sea. I love the sea. It's ideas like Sea Base I'm unenthused about. Ships are meant to bore holes through the ocean." He stuck his arm straight out. "A bow that slices through the water." He dropped his arm. "Huge bow waves sweeping along the side of the ship cascading into the prop wash past the stern. Dolphins riding the bow waves. Phosphorescent simmers at night as the moon races across the sky. That's going to sea for me. Not stumbling across the top of the Pacific on a metal island waiting for it to go tits-up."

Agazzi grinned.

"We don't need Sea Base. We just needed to stay in Japan. Remember when we had to send a couple of carrier battle groups steaming . . ."

"Another quaint Navy term: steaming. We don't steam anymore. We turbine or nuclear wherever we want to go."

". . . to show our support for Taiwan. But without forward bases in Japan and Okinawa, the only thing we had forward was a lone carrier based in Guam."

"And it's our oldest aircraft carrier and rust is the only thing holding it together."

Agazzi looked at Jacobs for a moment before continuing. "Do you have anything good to say about this venture?"

"Yes, I do. It is an opportunity to excel, which every God-fearing, seagoing manjack of a sailor looks forward to."

"Well, from the way—"

"Of course, that doesn't mean we aren't all gonna die when this thing goes tits-up, belly-down. Sea Base is going to give new meaning to FUBAR, FOAD, and Holy Shit."

Agazzi grinned. "Well, I can't express how much better I feel after discussing this with you."

"What do you think of those fancy weapons they're putting on Sea Base? I mean, whatever happened to good old five-inch/62s, blazing away with their lone barrel, shooting a myriad of different rounds at whatever enemy confronted us?"

"I think the same thing that happened to the battleship sixteen-inch guns. We haven't had an enemy confront us on the high seas since the Soviet Union up and imploded."

"Back before my time."

"Bullshit. You used to tell me—"

"Well, there are a lot of things I tell you. You don't expect me to blow a good sea tale by sticking to the truth, do you?" Jacobs smiled. "I guess I'm old Navy after all these years and whenever something new comes along out of these laboratories, I wonder if they work because maybe I don't understand them. Take that railgun, or whatever the shit he was talking about."

"It does sound like science fiction, doesn't it?"

"That it do. It's also about the only one I can recall because the others the professor from the Office of Naval Research Navy Research Laboratory mentioned had too many words to remember."

"You mean like the kinetic energy weapon, high-energy laser, and coil gun?"

Jacobs nodded. "Yeah, those are the ones. The railgun I paid attention to because it was the first one he talked about and I actually believe I understood how it operates."

"Well, you're doing better than me."

Jacobs turned, shifting his feet out from under the table. "I wouldn't say that. You're one of these technology ratings sonar technicians; you understand things that aren't real things, just things in the mind like electricity, magnetism, radio frequencies, sexual urges. Me, I understand rust, paint, line, anchors. If you can touch it and it's ship-related, I know it. But if you have to think about and visualize something that isn't real, then it ain't me. That's why I like surface warfare officers—I get to paint what they kill on the side of the bridge," Jacobs said, and then in a low voice added, "Of course, my last captain didn't like me painting the pier on the side of the bridge and putting a red X through it."

"I understood the high energy laser weapon. We've been experimenting with them for over three decades—since the twentieth century. The Air Force has some sort of laser weapon mounted in the nose of its heavy bombers."

"Kind of like a white stick for a blind man."

"And they've had great success in knocking out multiple targets with near-instantaneous firings."

"Well, lasers are supposed to be at the speed of light. Now, railguns use the movement of electromagnetic force. I think I understand the concept for both," Jacobs started explaining, his words coming slowly. "The electromagnetic forces shoot along the barrel, propelling the projectile in front of it until the shell is going so fast that when it reaches the end of the barrel the last thing you see is a blur heading over the horizon, heading toward its target."

"That's what I understood."

Jacobs shook his head. "Won't ever make it as a Navy weapon." He spread his hands apart suddenly. "No boom. No smell of cordite." He dropped his arms. "No stinging of the eyes as the smoke whiffs back across your face. What kind of Navy gun kills without some sort of explosive music to the shooter's ear?"

Agazzi ran his hands over the pamphlet, smoothing the paper once again. His finger jabbed the four corners of the Sea Base diagram. "Supposed to have two of those railguns. The high-energy laser weapons are supposed to be belowdecks somewhere, available for raising, if needed. I guess their components are so complex they want to keep them away from the salt air, spray, and weather."

Jacobs reached down and pulled his cigar from the butt can. He brushed the sand from the end, sucked on it a couple of times, saw no smoke, and unceremoniously tossed it back into the can. "Hell, what good is a Navy weapon if it won't work in any weather. What we gonna do? Ask the Chinese to wait until the sun comes out before we fight them?"

'We'll never fight the Chinese," Agazzi said as he stood up.

Jacobs looked up at him. "You're full of shit, if you believe that. It might not be us who fights them, but our children or our children's children will fight them."

Agazzi shook his head. "They have even less a chance of fighting them than we do."

Jacobs stood. "Okay, smart-ass, why won't we fight them? We have a treaty with Taiwan."

Agazzi pointed at his military shoes. "Shoes. That's why we won't fight them."

Jacobs looked down. "Shoes?" He looked up at Agazzi. "What do shoes have to do with fighting the Chinese?"

Agazzi sighed. "If we decide to fight the Chinese, they won't let us have the shoes our troops will need."

Agazzi looked past Jacobs. "Company coming." Ambling toward them was Petty Officer First Class Elvis Keyland, the leading petty officer for Agazzi's sonar team.

"Before Keyland gets here, Jerry, tell me anything else you know about these computers that are supposed to keep Sea Base level, functioning, and operating. I'll be taking my people over to the servers while we're heading to the operating area to test out our programs."

"The computers monitor every compartment, every walkway, every connecting device between the Fast Sealift Ships. The ships are going to shift individual control of their bridges to the computers. These computers will coordinate rudders and speed to keep Sea Base as motionless and level as possible. Of course, the engine rooms on those Sealift ships will have to be up and running the whole time we're out there." Jacobs jabbed his finger at Agazzi. "A question I have is, how do we refuel those ships located in the center of Sea Base? Do we run a hose from one ship to the next to the next until all of them are refueled? And how big a logistic supply line will be needed between Sea Base and shore?"

"I'm sure the officers have thought of that."

"Just as they thought of shutting down our overseas bases, moving our ships to American ports, and wondering why we have little to no influence on old allies and even less on adversaries." Jacobs shook his head. "I really enjoy watching how decisions are made based on the latest book someone in charge has read. Why don't they improve morale by reading something along the lines of *Debbie Does Dallas*?"

Petty Officer Keyland lifted his hand and waved as he crossed the street and moved toward them.

Jacobs turned, saw Keyland, and shook his head. "Elvis has left the building."

"Stop kidding him about his name. He's going to make chief before we return. If the chief's board misses him this time, it will be a travesty."

"You and your travesties. He never should have had that DUI when he was a seaman. DUIs and bad body fat get the same degree of attention before a promotion board, and Lord help you if you're a fat drunk!"

"Heh! He's had fourteen years of sterling performance. He'll make chief."

Jacobs nodded. "You can make First Class Petty Officer with a less-than-perfect record. There's no promotion board reviewing your record. But, mark my word, my friend—when they see the DUI, his promotion opportunities will fall faster—"

"Trust *your* predictions? I'm not the one telling everyone we're going to drown out there. All I'm saying is, Keyland is going to make chief."

Jacobs pushed himself up. "I know you're right, Alistair. He should make chief. He's a good leading petty officer. It's just I've seen a lot of good sailors wonder why they never got promoted when every one around them knows why. Guess I will leave you to your leading petty officer and wander down to the ship." Jacobs stood.

"You're on *Capella*?" *Maybe he's trying to tell me I'll never make master chief and he knows why,* Agazzi thought.

"I was." He pulled a folded piece of paper from his pocket. "But they shifted me to the *Antares.* Don't know why, but usually when they start moving us enlisted, it means to less comfortable quarters. Probably want me near the computers in the event they rust." Jacobs's eyebrows bent into a V shape. "Do computers rust?"

"They're called servers."

"They the moving bits and digits through this virtual world of information I keep hearing about?"

"Yeah . . ."

"Then they're computers," he said in a voice letting Agazzi know that, as far as Jacobs was concerned, the argument was over.

"Okay, you win. So, they've moved you to *Antares.*"

"Yeah. She's not the newest, but at least on board these MSC ships we get private staterooms. Staterooms with twin beds, a La-Z-Boy chair, television, telephone, and the list goes on and on—don't forget the private bathroom and shower. Next life, I'm going to come back as a merchant marine. They know how to live. You still on *Algol*?"

"The *Algol*, along with the rest of my men."

"Your sailors with you?" Jacobs shook his head. "I need to double-check and see if they've shifted their berthing arrangements, but assuming they haven't, then most of my junior first division personnel will be riding the amphibious warship USS *Boxer* until we reach the Sea Base operating area. Then, they'll helo them over to help with the setup. I'm going to try to get them berthed in several of the ships so I've got them spread around Sea Base. That way, if something happens and I need a quick reaction team, I'll have some sailors near wherever I need them. Otherwise, I'll have to put them in one of the prefabricated buildings the Seabees will put up."

Agazzi stuck his hand out. "Guess I won't see you until we reach the West Pacific."

Jacobs shook hands and shrugged. "I doubt that. We'll be doing a lot of cross-decking during the two weeks it'll take for us to convoy out. Got to check everything and make sure we're ready when we arrive. Of course, nothing ever goes right, but it helps to do what you can before you start. Reduce those ankle biters so major catastrophes are averted. I'm going to grab my gear from your car and hitch a ride with the other boatswains down to the ships."

"See you north of Taiwan."

"Let's hope it's not south of sea level."

AGAZZI watched as Jacobs spoke to Keyland as the two passed each other. Jacobs was seldom wrong when it came to anything having to do with ships and the ocean. On the other hand, the venerable master chief had never seen a ship, a deployment, or an officer he didn't believe was heading toward disaster.

He promised himself he wasn't going to lose sleep over worrying about it. The two friends balanced the ying and yang of the sea when together. Their two jobs were as far apart as their personalities. Jacobs brought disruption into Agazzi's life that otherwise might be a bland career of daily routine and nights in front of the television. Helen did the same for Friéda and, for Frieda, the six kids of the Jacobs household helped make up for never having children of their own.

"Senior Chief," Keyland said when he was a few feet away. "I inspected the weapons bay on board USNS *Bellatrix*. The unmanned underwater vehicles are secure. The loading device works. I had Petty Officer Taylor and Seaman Gentron do a maintenance check on the loader. Everything is working well."

Agazzi nodded. "Good job, Petty Officer Keyland. Have they turned the keys over yet?"

Keyland shook his head. "No, Senior Chief, not yet. I think they want you to sign for them, but when I talked with the lead scientist of the Office of Naval Research, she said we should have them by the time we reach the operations area."

"Doctor Malone give any reason?"

"She said they wanted to run some more diagnostics. Told her we had just done a maintenance check, which involved the diagnostics, but she was insistent that she do it, too. If I had known that, I could have saved some wear and tear on our troops and sent them off to do something else."

Agazzi acknowledged Keyland's comment and went on to explain how Sea Base was a grand concept designed and funded by the Office of Naval Research. Lots of prestige, future programs, and jobs probably rested on the success of this enterprise. There was one weak spot and that was underwater. The future weapons of the twenty-first century were designed for warfare above the surface and on the ground. Very little had been done since the end of the Cold War to keep anti-submarine warfare on par with the zooming advances in weapons and technology in anti-air and anti-surface warfare. Even the Marines had better technology and weapons than the anti-submarine forces of America.

China was fast becoming an ocean-going Navy with a submarine force that presented a formidable threat to America's hegemony under the waves. The keel of a second aircraft carrier had already been laid in the Shanghai shipyard. The first aircraft carrier had been a disaster, but the Chinese learned a lot from it. Expectations were that this one would be capable of making its own water and steaming in the open ocean.

On the positive side, recently some far-reaching thinkers at the Pentagon and at the Office of Naval Intelligence had realized Chinese submarines were venturing farther and farther out from their own shores. The Office of Naval Research had an ASW project using unmanned underwater vehicles that were going to be tested during this deployment. If they worked, then Big Navy at the Pentagon was going to fund them to replace torpedoes. Agazzi and his team were the "testees," as Jacobs called them. Agazzi was excited over the prospect of using the UUVs in the coming six months. He and his division had spent the last five months training on operating them.

The UUV project was on a shoestring budget in comparison to Sea Base. The UUV concept had lain dormant so long on the shelves of ONR that many of the components in the program were already out of date. The officer corps had focused on surface and air warfare over the past twenty years, with only the less gifted finding themselves involuntarily assigned to the ASW forces. Even destroyers, the ship class designed to fight submarines, were discovered to be better equipped to fight inbound enemy aircraft and missiles than to defend against enemy submarines.

Only the Japanese had recognized the growing threat of the Chinese submarine force and focused its energies on fighting and winning the underwater battle. A lot of the modern technology in the UUV system installed in *Bellatrix* came from Japanese defense forces.

Japan had also recently laid the keel for its second aircraft carrier. Agazzi bit his lower lip. Here was America rushing to the Sea Base concept as the weapon system to replace aircraft carriers, while both China and Japan were beginning to build the very ship class America was replacing. *Let's hope we're right*, he thought.

"I'll see you back at the ship," Agazzi said as Keyland headed off toward his car. Keyland still needed to load his sea bag on board the *Algol* and drop his car off for long-term storage.

They both admitted they were looking forward to experimenting and playing with the UUVs. While UUVs may replace the legacy torpedoes, the fact was that the UUV was nothing more than a souped-up torpedo.

Agazzi couldn't see the Navy getting rid of the cheaper torpedoes in favor of UUVs. As long as you didn't break the wire that guided them to the targets, torpedoes worked fine. If the wire broke—and that happened a lot as the torpedo got farther away—then the torpedo would go into an automatic search and destroy circle, each turn growing the circle wider, until it locked onto a target and shot toward it, exploding when it reached proximity. The problem was that the torpedo didn't care what the target was; it could even be the ship or submarine that launched it.

Agazzi stepped across the street toward where he had parked the 1957 Chevrolet. Minutes later he was driving slowly along the Pearl Harbor Naval Base streets, weaving his way toward what had been the battleship piers during World War II, enjoying the beauty of Hawaii in late morning.

The sight of the eight huge Fast Sealift Ships lining the four piers blocked the view of the other side of the harbor as Agazzi came around the bend. They towered over the tractor-trailers and piles of supplies being craned aboard. Only aircraft carriers were larger than the Fast Sealift Ships, and that size difference was measurable in feet, not yards.

He pulled into the temporary parking across from the piers. Helen would bring Frieda down later this afternoon to pick up the car. No reason for them to see their husbands off. Agazzi stood beside the car. His sea bag was braced against the front bumper as he watched the activity on the piers.

The huge cranes mounted on the Fast Sealift Ships reached down like giant hands, clasping ready pallets—some weighed as much as 50,000 pounds—and swinging them easily aboard the ships. The ships stretched upward nearly a hundred feet from the pier. Each was over 900 feet long. What amazed him was the discovery that when in port each ship had a merchant marine complement of fourteen, growing to forty when underway—except for this mission. Another attraction to Sea Base was that it was going to show Congress the Navy could meet an increased mission at sea on a larger, bolder platform with less manning to do it. Less manning meant more work for him and his sailors.

Every couple of minutes, a group of merchant seaman, walkie-talkies welded to their ears, guided the tentacles of the cranes to a waiting boxcar mounted on the lead tractor-trailer. Each truck waited in line, idling fumes that joined the dark smoke curling upward from the stacks of the ships. The ship force scurried over the boxcars like ants, attaching cables and securing tempered clasps to the heavy weight. Then, moving quickly, they watched as the crane lifted the boxcar from the back of the tractor-trailer. Everyone stood out of the way in the event something happened and the boxcar came loose. It had happened before and would happen again. The trick was to be elsewhere when it happened.

Agazzi glanced at his watch, wondering how in the hell they were going to make the new sailing time of one o'clock when so much still had to be loaded, but then it wasn't his problem. The signs at the end of the pier next to where he had parked showed the USNS *Algol* tied aft starboard side. The ship on the pier in front being loaded was the USNS *Denebola*. He hefted his sea bag onto his left shoulder, glancing back once to ensure the car was locked. Then he stepped off, walking to the right toward the next pier where his ship was docked. Another forty-five minutes before they sailed, but setting sail and actually leaving the pier could be distinctly different. When all the lines were off the pier, a ship was technically underway.

A container rode lightly alongside the ship in front of him as the crane strained slightly lifting the heavy weight. The name *Antares* in large capital letters, painted black, was embossed on the side of the gangplank leading from the pier to the quarter-deck of the Maritime Sealift Command ship. Up there somewhere, Master Chief Boatswain Mate Jacobs was probably watching, counting every rust spot, every dent, and every material condition gripe he could find, bemoaning to whoever was listening how much this ship needed his attention. But then every ship needed the attention of its crew, and the less crew available, the more attention a ship eventually needed. In the American Navy of the twenty-first century, ninety percent of the Navy was at sea, going to sea, or just returning from sea. Unfortunately, when you had fewer than a hundred and fifty ships, there wasn't much of a Navy in comparison to the Navy of the twentieth century. *But by God, we know how to train our officers to be* good *business people.*

Agazzi said "Good morning" as he passed a civilian on the bench at the head of the pier where the *Denebola* was loading. The man raised his hand in acknowledgment, flipping open a cell phone as Agazzi passed. The man needed to lose some weight. Agazzi shook his head. Man was probably a reporter. Definitely wasn't used to the heat. No one wore a suit and tie outdoors. Especially in the middle of summer. *Go figure*, he thought as he continued toward his pier.

AGAZZI tripped, caught himself, and continued along the pier, walking to the port side to avoid the workforce loading the *Antares*. He came suddenly upon the *Algol* as he emerged from behind a large pallet of food supplies. He set his sea bag down, leaning it against the full pallet. Several sailors and merchant marines stood across the pier having cigarettes and talking.

The *Algol*, like the USNS *Antares*, was one of eight Fast Sealift Ships of the United States Navy. And, like the other seven, it was built either in Germany or the Netherlands. He wasn't sure which, but knew they were originally commissioned as merchant vessels. But when the cost of operating them outweighed the commercial profit margin, the United States government purchased them to support its sealift requirements. During Desert Storm and Operation Iraqi Freedom, some of these ships made as many as three round-trips between the Persian Gulf area of operations and the mainland United States. They had a top speed in excess of thirty knots and could load enough fuel to do a complete round-trip without refueling. They were one of the open secrets of American might, and now, for this unique experiment to return America to the West Pacific, all eight had been removed from their primary mission. Sea Base may be a secret now, but he knew eventually the news would be released. This was America at its finest, surprising the world with its might.

If Agazzi knew how much of this secret was already known,

he'd only shake his head and blame the press. Nothing is a secret if more than one person knows it. Agazzi believed in the American Navy. What was right for the Navy was right for America. He took a deep breath. He truly loved every minute when he was with, near, or on board a Navy vessel. No one could understand the intrinsic sweep of emotion from riding on a warship until they've stood on the bridge of such a powerful ship and controlled its destination through their own commands.

Agazzi stood silently on the pier, his head tilted back as far as possible, staring up at this gigantic ship. One that would be his home for the next six months. He took a deep breath, smelling the salt breeze coming off the port, noticing the absence of odor that usually rode port winds, and felt a moment of elation. He was going to sea. Something about going to sea excited him now, after twenty-two years of service, as much as it had excited sailors throughout history.

Once he was aboard and had stored his sea bag, he would find a place topside to watch the ship single-up all lines, and wait for the three blasts from the ship's horn as it backed away from the pier and eased into the harbor channel. The thought of the sea-and-anchor detail brought back the memories of a year ago when he was the khaki for the number-one line on the destroyer *Stripling*. When the line parted . . . He shook his head, forcing himself not to recall what had happened.

Once he heard the boatswain pipe *"Underway! Shift colors!"* he would walk around the edges of the open deck and watch the land and buildings slide away as the ship picked up speed in its creep toward the open ocean. It was something no sailor could explain to a landlubber. He couldn't even explain it to himself. Over the next few days, for the first time in his at-sea career, Agazzi would have little to do but to watch the merchant Navy move them across the surface of the clear Pacific.

A clear Pacific for those who fought above the surface, but for him and the few hundred anti-submarine warriors in the Navy, it was the dark Pacific beneath that was his battlefield. There were things down there that could swallow a man whole. But it was the manmade things that could destroy everything and everyone going to sea with him, and that was a concern he took seriously.

Others may not believe the Chinese were a threat, but Agazzi knew differently. He might kid Jacobs about the shoes, but he truly believed America was going to have to fight them eventu-

ally. Until that eventuality came, China would probe, push, and
pull back as it developed a profile of America's anti-submarine
capability. He lifted his sea bag. He might be testing these UUVs
on this trip, but he also intended to do everything he could to
keep their technology secret. Professionally, he believed the Chinese would send at least one submarine out when they discovered
the presence of Sea Base.

Agazzi looked at the amount of supplies sitting on the pier. Behind the ships, one of the Fast Sealift Ships was being eased out
into the channel. Like all sailors on movement day, he hoped they
hadn't changed the underway time. Missing movement was a
court-martial offense, though few were ever court-martialed for
it. You just never got promoted again, for second chances were
seldom in the modern Navy.

FOUR

When a ship the size of the USNS *Denebola* gets under way, it isn't like a smaller ship such as a sailing craft, or even a destroyer or a cruiser. Aircraft carrier–size ships don't just throw off a few lines, back astern, and come about smartly, twisting into the channel. They're cumbersome and dangerous. As Sea Base prepared for a debut onto the world scene as a new way to control the seas and project power, only eight aircraft carriers remained on active duty. All were Nimitz nuclear-class carriers, and with the American economy in tatters because of 2015, full battle-group deployments were few.

There were no replacements approved for them, and unless Congress could find the funds to build new ones, the U.S. Navy would be a four-carrier force in nine years. Even with their age and decreased operational deployments, the U.S. Navy aircraft carriers were still the most dangerous warships on the seas. As the admirals sought ways to maintain the American presence at sea, it becomes more an economic issue than a capabilities issue. The cost and manpower to use aircraft carriers were becoming prohibitive.

A Nimitz-class aircraft carrier displaced 97,000 tons when fully loaded for a deployment. Some of those tons flew aboard once the warship is underway. Those tons are called aircraft.

When you combined the permanent members of the Nimitz-class ship's company of 3,350 sailors with the embarked air wing number of 2,480, you neared 6,000 sailors for a fully armed, power projecting weapon of war capable of taking out most anything by itself.

The USNS *Denebola* was fully loaded as she started her underway preps away from the Pearl Harbor pier. Even before the first of several tugs tied up alongside her, she displaced 62,000 tons. Once at the operations area northwest of Taiwan, she would still have those tons, along with the challenge of holding the Sea Base tons aloft and towering above her. The Office of Naval Research scientists estimated the displacement tonnage for the eight Fast Sealift Ships would exceed the design specifications for the ships. But their calculations showed the Fast Sealift Ships could handle this increase because the tonnage would be dispersed across eight huge ships that would, for the most part, be motionless.

Tied to the piers, eight lines ran from the eyes of each of the Fast Sealift Ships, stretching downward at a sharp angle to gigantic bollards equally spaced along the piers. Unbeknownst to most who were working that day, some of those bollards had battleships tied to them on December 7, 1941. Beaten by use, exposed for decades to weather, and remounted for use each time the docks were upgraded or repaired, the cast-iron bollards were as strong today as they had been during World War II.

Each of the eight lines of the USNS *Denebola* were doubled-up to hold the ship steady while the opened tractor-trailer-sized hatch on the starboard side of the *Denebola* allowed trucks, forklifts, and even the occasional car to drive into its main loading area. These Fast Sealift Ships had been earmarked for the scrap heap two years ago when the head of the Office of Naval Research, Admiral "Tablet" Bushnell, circumvented the Secretary of Defense's decision and convinced close friends in the Senate to use them for Sea Base. Bushnell was an astute politician, pointing out how many states would benefit from Sea Base. With unemployment slowly inching upward after the collapse of 2015, any work a senator or congressman brought to their states meant future votes in the next election. After 2015, many of their predecessors discovered themselves among the unemployed.

Ideas trickle up the chain of command. That's the way it's been and that's the way everyone expects it to continue. This trickle of ideas is like a salmon swimming upstream. Few make it to the spawning ground, and ideas swim slowly up the chain of command until they reach someone senior enough to have an epiphany so it becomes his or her idea all along. Then it becomes something to pursue with vigor. On the other hand, when an idea is given the imperial thumbs down, it is expected to die—die much faster than the vigor it would have received if it had been approved. Bushnell's idea had been given a thumbs-down years before he resurrected it through the backdoor: He went directly to his good buddies in the Senate.

In the strict, no-nonsense world of defense, no good idea goes unpunished. The chief of naval operations took credit for Sea Base and within twelve months, Bushnell found himself retired. Within eighteen months, the senior staffer on the Senate Armed Forces Committee was retired Admiral "Tablet" Bushnell. Newspapers had much fun at his expense when "old Annapolis shipmates" divulged the origin of "Tablet" as referring to Bushnell's propensity for seasickness. The Navy and Tablet always appeared friendly and close in front of the press and cameras; behind the scenes, it was pretty much a dogfight over Sea Base.

RICHARD Zeichner stood across the pier watching the activity. He had already loosened this tie and unbuttoned the top of his short-sleeve shirt. Sweat ran down his neck in little rivulets. His suit coat lay on top of a nearby pallet where he had tossed it. He took his handkerchief and wiped sweat from his brow. He hated Hawaii. Heat, heat, heat—everywhere. What he wouldn't give to be back in Chicago. What ever possessed him to agree to do this? In his mind, he heard his mother—*God rest her soul*—shaking her finger at him and shouting *"Pride goeth before a fall,"* which didn't make much sense. It wasn't as if he was a member of the Senior Executive Service or something. He was a GS-15, which was as high as you could go before being selected for the SES. But at fifty-five, he didn't see much chance of that happening.

The clang of metal on metal drew his attention as a huge truck drove up the ramp into the *Denebola*, the wheels drumming on the metal ridges of the ramp. The supplies loaded on the back of the open truck looked for a moment as if they were going to tumble off when the truck hit the bump where the ramp connected to the ship.

Richard draped the handkerchief across the top of his head. *Not much hair to protect that scalp of mine from the sun.* Despite appearances, he should have brought his NCIS ball cap from his stateroom when he disembarked from the *Denebola*. And he should have left his tie and coat there.

He picked up his coat and walked along the pier, looking at the two huge ships lining both sides. He shook his head, feeling a moment of coolness as he shook sweat from his face.

It was amazing that he was part of such a huge armada. He wondered for a moment if *armada* was the right word. Sure he worked for the Department of the Navy. He should be excited over being the lead Naval Criminal Investigative Service representative for this trip. Probably if he were ten years younger this would be a stepping-stone to promotion. Every job had stepping-stones, so why did NCIS send him here? It was as if he or his deputy, Gainer, spoke Navy. Didn't mean Gainer spoke law enforcement either, but their job was to keep order, ensure the myriad of investigations—there were always investigations—were efficiently documented and submitted, and keep out of the way.

The sharp sound of screeching hydraulics drew his attention. He shielded his eyes to look up at the main deck of the *Denebola*. The huge crane on the aft portion of the ship was lowering a container. From his vantage point, he couldn't tell if the container was being lowered onto the main deck or into the large hangar below it. He knew the top hangar amidships between the two forecastles of the *Denebola* was filled with computers, servers, and enough air-conditioning to knock his Hawaiian heat away. He didn't have any idea what was being loaded in the aft portion.

Zeichner enjoyed the idea of being part of such a huge undertaking, but he hated being here. This was something historic. No other nation in history had ever done what these eight ships were setting out to do and he was part of it.

He hadn't thought of it as historic until he spent two weeks with these energized bunnies called ONR scientists. "I guess you're an engineer when you don't have a Ph.D. and you're a scientist when you do," he said softly aloud.

Each of the eight ships were 946 feet and one and a half inches in length. *Who in the hell measured that one and a half inches?* he asked himself. *It's like adding a penny to the figure of the national debt. Doesn't mean shit.*

Zeichner had been on the USS *Nimitz* nearly ten years ago.

The *Nimitz* was 1,092 feet. Probably measured by the same anal-retentive scientist. He wondered whether they used a tape measure, a ruler, or just SWAGed it. SWAG stood for Scientific Wild Ass Guess.

These eight ships, only 155 feet and 1½ inches smaller than an aircraft carrier, were going to hoist up above them over eighty-one and a half acres of metal designed to fabricate a man-made island in the middle of the Pacific Ocean.

The sound of the crane twisting toward the pier drew his attention again. These aging merchant ships were designed for the rapid transport of heavy Army and Marine Corps warfighting vehicles ranging from tanks and helicopters to armored and unarmored wheeled vehicles. If it was bulky and weighed a lot, it found its way onto one of the Maritime Sealift Command ships. These ships were going to sail into the Pacific near Taiwan and somehow connect themselves together to form a floating island under the flag of the United States. And he was part of this. If this worked, and if you believed everything Office of Naval Research told you, then it would bring control of seas and power projection to a new level. The classified documents he saw argued that Sea Base could do more than several aircraft carriers at a cost significantly below that of a single carrier. Congress liked that idea. The aviation Navy didn't. It would be the death knell for large aircraft carriers.

He had little idea what all of this really meant. There were a lot of things to keep his days interesting until the six months were up. For one, he was looking forward to seeing how those computers on the *Denebola* were going to keep these eight giants steaming a perfect course and speed. He chuckled. Damn good thing it didn't depend on his nautical skills, which were significantly less than his bosses thought. His more practical father—God rest his soul—would say, "Never volunteer for anything. Just answer the questions and let them try to figure out what the hell happened."

Of course, they never did figure out what his father did. He hadn't. The investigators hadn't. And, if his mother knew she took it to her grave. He kept the farm. One day, after he retired, he would try to decipher what his father meant. Family rumor was that he buried the money somewhere on the property.

Zeichner stepped into a narrow space between two large pallets so several forklifts speeding in single file could pass without running him down. NCIS was right. Based on the background he had built over the years, on paper he was the best choice for this six-month deployment. Unmarried. He patted his ample stomach. *And not much chance of ever getting married for a man my age and girth.* The last forklift sped by. Zeichner stepped out and looked both ways; the fumes trailing the forklifts stung his eyes and caused him to cough. He blinked rapidly, clearing the fumes from his eyes before turning and continuing up the pier to where it met the main road. His cell phone should work once he was out of this metal valley created by the gigantic ships rising on each side of him.

The grinding sound of gears meshing accompanied by shouts of the merchant marines along the pier caused him to stop. The ship docked behind his, the USS *Pollux*, was lifting its ramp. He glanced at the gangways leading to the main deck.

It took two gangways to reach the main deck from the pier. The first one went halfway up the side of the ship to a small platform where the second one took you to the main deck. Huge steps on each of them reminded him of small porches. Maybe the huge steps were to take your thoughts away from the fact that the gangway was at a sixty-degree angle, you had to use metal rods held together by rope as banisters, and the gangway swung as you moved up it. If he had to climb them several times a day, the fat would fall off him like a waterfall.

Thoughts such as this made him think of doing something about what he preferred to call *girth* while others had less kind words for his size. Faded black letters printed on discolored tarps hanging from the gangway metal railings read USNS *POLLUX*.

It wouldn't be long now. The master of the *Denebola* had warned everyone to be on board by twelve-thirty. Richard glanced at his watch. It was past eleven o'clock. The new sailing time was one, so he had plenty of time. Forty-five minutes. From the amount of supplies still on the piers, he doubted the ships would sail by one. Original sailing time had been eleven and he still didn't see an appreciable reduction in the supplies on the piers.

Several toots of a ship horn came from behind the USNS *Pollux*. His brow furrowed. Was one of the other Fast Sealift Ships already under way? He glanced at the *Denebola*, saw the ramp still down. Supplies were still being loaded. He watched the huge stern crane of the *Denebola* spin out again over the pier to load another waiting pallet. No, his ship would be here a while longer. It wasn't as if Sea Base could become Sea Base without the *Denebola*.

He glanced behind him and saw the dockhand he had seen earlier near the bow of the Denebola walking in the same direction. The man stopped, examining a pallet. Looking around the pier, Zeichner saw other supervisors doing the same thing. Trying to hurry the loading, he thought as he turned back around.

Zeichner's inexperience on the waterfront clouded his natural inclination to analyze everything. How can you know when something is out of the ordinary when you have no f'ing idea what the ordinary is?

He reached the end of the dock. Across the main dock, a vintage 1957 Chevrolet parked and a man wearing the single star of a senior chief on his collars stepped out, the bright sunlight twinkling off the silver. Tall, lean. One look and Zeichner silently determined the man was one of those focused joggers who ran everywhere.

The sea bag told Zeichner the man was probably embarking for this journey also. He smiled. It didn't take a rocket scientist to figure out that most everyone here not working on the docks was embarking for the deployment.

He's cutting it close, Zeichner thought. But even if the man appeared to be a member of the Navy's fitness mafia, he was a real sailor. This senior chief would have a better idea how far along everything was than he did. He was just an aging NCIS agent with a couple of weeks at sea.

Zeichner tossed his coat onto a nearby bench, noticing as the coat headed toward the seat that some previous occupant had spilled coffee on the metal slates.

"Damn," he said, jerking the coat back up. The coffee was gone and he knew where. Sighing, he laid the coat on the back of the bench, the wet spot exposed to the sun. "Maybe it'll dry in this heat." He sat on the far side of the bench, leaning back so his chest muscles were pulled apart, letting the moisture beneath his shirt evaporate. The dockhand was examining the pallets at the end of the pier. *Good*, Zeichner thought. *The sooner we get underway, the sooner I can sneak away to my stateroom and take a nap.* The vision of the air-conditioning filling the stateroom with cold air caused him to smile.

The senior chief said "Good morning" as he passed. Zeichner

raised the hand with the cell phone in acknowledgment. He watched the senior chief for a few moments, wondering briefly what the man's job was on this deployment.

Dialing the number given him by the quarterdeck, he waited several rings before someone answered.

KIANG stopped as the NCIS agent tossed his coat onto the bench. He pulled his ball cap lower and stood at the corner of a waiting pallet, looking at the supplies and shuffling from one side to the other. If someone were watching Kiang examining the pallet, their eyes would linger little before continuing along and noticing other dockhands and supervisors doing similar things.

He thought Zeichner had spotted him earlier when the man turned unexpectedly. The colonel had been right about everything, including the man sent to lead the NCIS team. Kiang's eyes darted between studying the pallet and watching the agent. Clipboard. He should have brought a clipboard with him. No one questions a person with a clipboard. For a moment, Kiang doubted his guise, giving thought to head back to his ship, the USNS *Regulus*, and wait until the ship set sail. Several dockhands came around the corner, nodded at him, and continued on their way. Their passage convinced him he was all right and unnoticed. Kiang disappeared into the flowing crowd of workers focused on loading the ships.

The NCIS agent was using his telephone. Kiang wished he had not stopped but rather had continued past the man. If he had cigarettes, he could have stood in the parking lot behind the bench. The wind from the sea brushed his face. The wind would have carried the man's words to his ears. Kiang watched, noticing the man's face change as the conversation continued. One moment a smile, the next furrowed eyebrows, and at one point he could hear a raised voice that accompanied the NCIS agent's jabbing finger. The actions belied a man speaking to his family, but then the colonel had said the man was a bachelor—no family. *Maybe he is gay*, thought Kiang.

After ten minutes and no sign the conversation was going to end, Kiang shifted his attention to the pallet in the center of the three waiting rows.

*   *   *

THIRTY minutes later, battery nearly drained, Richard snapped the cell phone shut. This wasn't going to be the boring trip he had figured. He stood silently, letting his eyes travel the length of the Pearl Harbor piers, looking at each of the visible Fast Sealift Ships docked near the heads of the piers, knowing several were out of visual sight. The dockhand examining the pallets was on the third one. As Zeichner watched, the man nodded as if he was satisfied, then disappeared along the right side of the line, heading back down the pier.

Somewhere within this convoy was someone or some group who might not want Sea Base to succeed. While the Navy put out a lot of positive comments behind closed doors about Sea Base, everyone knew the senior flag officers and civilians in both the Department of the Navy and the Department of Defense were seething over how Bushnell had pulled this off.

Some of his NCIS comrades would have greeted the news from his cell phone conversation with headquarters with angst. He smiled. A couple of NCIS agents were probably kicking themselves in the butt for turning down this trip. Zeichner was no fool. He hadn't been the first choice, but he had been a safe one from the perspective of the director of NCIS. He laughed. It was too late for one of those budding sycophants to replace him. *Never knew*, he thought and laughed. It would be something if this late in his career this turned into a field goal for promotion.

He stood. His eyes scanned the waterfront. Two whistles came from the direction of the channel where one of the Fast Sealift Ships moved.

Where to start and how to figure out whom or what or why or even *if* the intelligence was true? Everyone agreed al Qaieda sleeper cells existed in the United States; no one had ever found any. It wouldn't be one of them on board Sea Base. From what he knew, the only sleeper ever found in America was at the beginning of the Cold War: Soviet Colonel Rudolf Abel. Arrested in 1957; eventually traded for the U.S. U-2 pilot Gary Powers.

It would be hard to base the premise of sleepers on this lone incident, but if he did, then whomever NCIS suspected of being on board Operation Sea Base had to be nation-state supported. Ergo, the only nation-states curious to the point of self-defense would be Russia, China, and the mercurial North Korea.

North Korea had all the tact and guile of a sledgehammer. Every attempt to send spies to the United States—at least the ones known— had been easily discovered. Six so far in federal prisons. Another five would have been, but in trying to slip them into the United States, North Korea had sealed them into a container—much like those now being loaded. The container had traveled a circuitous course to the United States and three months later, when it arrived in Long Beach, the smell of decaying bodies led authorities to them.

China. China had been waging economic warfare against the United States for years to the point where the United States had lost so much of its manufacturing capability it could ill afford to antagonize the Chinese too much. The United States still publicly swore to uphold the defense treaty with Taiwan, but this treaty threatened the U.S.'s self-interests. How do you go to war with a country that holds a third of your debt? It's like taking on your bank, only without the niceties of the law. If China flooded the market with U.S. treasury bonds, the economic collapse of 2015 would look minuscule.

"No," Richard said softly. He always suspected Russia of rising from the ashes like a great phoenix to resume a powerful role in a world where economic might was shifting to Asia. *Yes*, he thought, *let's start with Russia as the most likely candidate. They fancy themselves to be a world power, and what better way to prove it.*

All this analysis occurred in a couple of seconds. It wasn't as if Zeichner's analytical skills were legendary within NCIS. Most detective skills are nothing less than piecing together chronological events against a pattern of motives. It would take good ol' shoe leather drudgery, gathering facts, and putting them together like a jigsaw puzzle until a picture started to form.

Like every detective, Zeichner started with his own professional depth and biases. Unlike some of the younger detectives, Richard's ego was hardly tied to his preliminary ideas. He had given up long ago tying his ego to any position. He had seen several innocent people pinned to the legal cushion by detectives who twisted facts to fit their preconceived conclusions. In large organizations, those who did, didn't last long. In smaller ones, they sometimes lasted longer; no one wanted to snitch on those being admired.

He lifted his coat, saw where the coffee stain had been, and decided it blended in sufficiently with the brown of the coat so that no one would notice. He shoved his cell phone into his pants pocket. Holding his coat by the collar, he tossed it across his shoulder and started working his way back to the *Denebola*. He was happier than when he walked down this way before.

The sound of the hangar door leading from the pier into the aft hangar bay drowned out the hydraulics of the two cranes lifting containers. The air was thick with the fumes trapped in the artificial valley between the ships.

His eyebrows wrinkled, causing the sweat caught between the folds of skin to roll down his eyelids. Maybe all of these supplies on the pier weren't for the ships. He wiped away the stinging sweat and picked up the pace. The aft crane repositioned over the ramp leading into the forward section of the *Denebola*. Merchant seamen scrambled around the container, connecting the heavy cables to the eyes. Sailors scurried along the pier, lining up near the bullocks where the *Denebola* lines were tied. As he passed the stern of the USNS *Denebola*, a bullhorn blared, "Single up all lines."

Along the side of the ship he was supposed to be on, sailors lifted the top lines off the bollards and dropped them immediately. Merchant Marines on board the USNS *Denebola* began pulling the lines up, hand over hand, quickly moving them out of the way. Zeichner wasn't sure exactly what "single up" meant, but from watching them cast off the top lines, it meant something seriously related to getting underway.

His breathing was heavy when he reached the bottom of the gangway. Glancing up, he saw one of the officers—a third mate, Zeichner thought the man called himself—motioning for Zeichner to hurry up. Zeichner wanted to catch his breath, but he didn't want to get left behind.

"Excuse me," a merchant sailor said, shoving by Zeichner.

Zeichner moved aside as the man and several others dashed up the gangway as if they were out for an easy stroll. He looked up. Four stories, he estimated. He wondered if CPR could be done on a gangway.

He started up the steps, slowly taking one step at a time, giving his breath a chance to catch up with the effort. His thoughts turned to the telephone call. Zeichner imagined the chagrin if he had to call headquarters back to tell them he missed the boat because he had a heart attack while boarding it.

It would be the last nail in what had started as a great career and turned mediocre, and stagnated further sometime a decade ago.

He needed both hands to go up the ladder. He stopped at the midway point and put on the coat. If he didn't, he was going to drop it over the side. He needed both hands. He looked up, feeling the heat increase with the coat on. Shaking the sweat from his face, Zeichner grabbed both railings and continued upward, using his hands to help pull him along. The metal railings swung slightly, left and right, with each step. He bit his lower lip, releasing it quickly so he could breathe.

To hell with calling them and telling them he missed the boat—what if the boat called them and told them he'd died of a massive coronary from trying to board it. They'd never understand and his death would be one great joke for the office for years to come. Zeichner vowed to lose weight on this trip. He really was going to get into some sort of exercise program.

It was the pain in the legs and knees that drew the breath from him. His lungs were fine; it was the weight he carried. And for the second time going up the gangway, he promised himself when he reached the mid-platform that he was going to come home several sizes smaller.

"Hurry up, Mr. Zeichner!" the third mate called through cupped hands from above. "We're getting under way!"

He lifted an arm and waved, unable to speak as he caught his breath.

Hands grabbed him as he stepped off the ladder.

"Mr. Zeichner, take that coat off, sir. It's too hot for suits."

Hands helped him off with the coat.

"Someone get him some water."

Other hands guided him to a nearby seat. His shirt was matted to his body. He looked down. His stomach draped across his beltline, nearly hiding the crotch of his pants. That did it, he promised himself. He was going to come back from these six months at sea a new man. Or at least a thinner one. His breathing was heavy, and from the looks of Captain Boxford, Master of the *Denebola*, he knew the younger man was weighing whether to keep him on board or send for an ambulance to offload him.

Zeichner forced himself to stand. "Thanks, Captain," he gasped out. "Not used to those long ladders," he said in a normal voice, his lungs screaming for him to take deep, deep breaths.

"Get below, Mr. Zeichner. We'll be pretty busy here for the next couple of hours. If I were in your place, I'd sneak in a nap. Now, if you'll excuse me; I have a ship to get under way."

Richard nodded. "Thanks, Captain. I think I'll heed your advice."

"Good idea, Mr. Zeichner," Boxford said, then turned as Zeichner headed toward the ladder leading up. "Oh, Mr. Zeichner. It's going to be hot on the sea. I would recommend you consider something along the lines of short sleeves, no tie, and short pants like the rest of us."

Zeichner nodded, and continued toward the ladder.

Behind him he heard the captain tell the first mate he was heading to the bridge. When the tugs arrived, he wanted the *Denebola* to follow *Pollux* out into the channel. Zeichner heard someone comment that every tug in Pearl Harbor was out here getting them under way. He let out a deep breath. A nap sounded good. This "going to sea" shit was enough to knock the wind out of anyone.

Zeichner climbed the ladder and opened the hatch. The cold air struck him fully in the face, making it seem as if he had stepped into a freezer. He breathed in the cooler air deeply as he turned and shut the hatch. He walked slowly toward the ladder that lead below to his stateroom, grateful for the chill of the cool air on his wet body. He saw no one in the passageways, so he braced his movement with his hands along the bulkhead.

It took two ladders and twenty-five minutes for him to reach his stateroom. Zeichner was senior enough that he didn't have to share with anyone else. That was good; he didn't want anyone to witness his discomfort. His girth was his embarrassment, but when he came back, he wasn't going to have that girth. He reached down and lifted the fat that was hanging over his beltline, letting the cool air of the stateroom touch beneath the roll. "No siree, Bob," he said. "You and I are going to part company."

Zeichner flopped down into the huge recliner between the wooden desk and the tall wrought-iron lamp. He grabbed the liter-and-a-half bottle of spring water—nearly dropping it as he unscrewed the cap—and drank almost half of it. He pushed against the back of the chair, the footrest rising. Five minutes later he was asleep. He slept through the armada of huge Fast Sealift Ships easing away from the piers amidst the myriad of blasts, whistles, and shouts needed to shift the colors of the United States from the stern to the main mast.

When he woke four hours later, the ships were outside Pearl Harbor and Hawaii was fading on the horizon. He was still tired.

Too many years behind a desk and too many inches around the middle had stolen much of his stamina for physical effort. He went to the bathroom, then returned to the recliner. He lifted the clock from the desk and checked the time.

He had done more physical activity this morning than he had done in the past six months. He felt the slight roll of the state-room, almost like a cradle, and his eyes shut and he dozed off. He slept through dinner, on into the evening, never rising from the brown synthetic leather recliner. For the first time in many months, the REMs of deep sleep kept his eyes shifting beneath the eyelids. No one saw the slight smile cross his face as he slept and enjoyed his first peaceful sleep in months.

FIVE

Richard Zeichner leaned back, his chair creaking from the strain. He grabbed the arms and leaned forward quickly, afraid it was going to roll backward against the bulkhead again. The back of his head still ached from earlier when the chair had rolled about two feet and hit the metal bulkhead. What kind of sadist would buy office chairs with wheels for shipboard use? Probably someone such as himself with little or no experience at sea. He winced slightly when the chair steadied and his stomach pressed against the desk. One of these days he would lean back and there would be no bulkhead to stop the chair. He was going to find his overweight, fat self trapped beneath this heavy metal chair, suffering the indignity of having his deputy Gainer free him.

"Tomorrow," he said aloud of the unspoken promise to start walking the topside deck of the *Denebola*. The chair rolled away from the desk a few inches. Zeichner reached forward, grabbed the edges of the metal desk, and pulled himself forward. He spent as much time trying to stay in position as he did rolling away. He let go of the left edge and grabbed the center of the desk to pull himself the last few inches. Only he inadvertently grabbed the drawer instead of the desk, startling himself when the drawer shot out and stopped three inches later when it hit his stomach, which was the only thing that kept the drawer from falling out and dumping the contents over the vinyl deck.

"Damn." He slammed the drawer shut, the force causing it to bounce back open. Zeichner grabbed the desk correctly this time, holding both sides and pulling himself up to the desk, moving so forcefully that his stomach hit the underside of the slightly opened drawer. "I can see we're going to get along fine on this trip," he whispered irritably to his stomach. "One of us has got to go, and it's gonna be you."

Zeichner pushed the drawer shut and picked up the message that had been laid on the desk earlier. The new yeoman had stamped SECRET in large red letters at the top, bottom, and across the center of the sheet several times. Either something had changed in the couple of weeks they'd been at sea about how classified material was marked with a simple stamp at the top and bottom of the page, or the yeoman was showing her irritation over baby-sitting a couple of NCIS agents. *Now, why would he think this?* he asked himself. Could it be her *too low to hear clearly* muttering that was always in the background? Or maybe the grunts she used to acknowledge his requests?

His professional eye noticed there were no declassified lines at the bottom telling the reader who had classified it or when the classification was eligible for downgrading to a lower classification. Ever since the Navy, in its rush for efficiency, did away with the Cryptologic Technician Administration rating, security procedures had suffered. He sighed. If you stayed in government long enough, you soon learn that narrow-thinking bureaucrats and sycophants never allowed logic, common sense, or better judgment to stop a headlong rush toward the cliff of oblivion.

He gripped the one-page message by both sides and read the message twice more, each time hoping some new tidbit of information would leap off the page. Zeichner lacked the experience his bosses credited him with earning over the years. But he had learned a lot during his career in regard to investigating. One was to always weigh first impressions. First impressions, like first reports from the battlefield, are seldom accurate. Regardless, when you don't have anywhere to go, you need to pick a destination until something new comes along to change your direction.

When he received the heads-up e-mail a week ago—the same day the Sea Base convoy sailed from Pearl Harbor—he immedi-

ately reached a preconceived idea that whoever the person was, he
or she had to be Russian.

An older agent, now retired, once told him that NCIS agents
weren't much different from intelligence officers: Both start
making assumptions based on available facts. It was the good
ones who never tied their ego to their conclusions because it
made it easier to allow the facts to change the course of their
analysis.

His own self-assessment convinced him that he never assumed
his analysis was accurate until every logic trail was tracked, scru-
tinized, repudiated, and nailed to the board. Of course, a couple
of times in his career he'd been wrong, but those were the times
you never mentioned.

He held the message in his left hand and slapped it lightly with
the right. "How the hell do they know this?" he asked aloud. "If
they know this much, then how come they don't know . . . ?"

Glancing at the clock above the doorway, he saw it'd been
nearly thirty minutes since the Information Technician from Ra-
dioShack had delivered it. His yeoman had made him sign for the
message because she had had to sign for it from the IT. One thing
about the Navy—they had the custody string down pat. He'd
signed for messages throughout his twenty-seven-year career
with Naval Criminal Investigative Services, but each time he
signed, it meant trouble.

Zeichner scanned the message again, looking for the name of
the analyst or a point of contact. Someone he could call to get an
informal read on the information. You could learn a lot from talking with the agent who developed the information. A lot of things
that could not be proven so didn't make the cut. Things that could
be useful to the agent in the field, but because of the "chop chain"
in a message, some desk jockey supervisor had weeded it out.

It would be nice to have more raw data. Agents hated to give
away raw data, preferring their own analyses be used. But, seeing what this agent based his or her information on could provide Zeichner with a logic trail. After all, he and Gainer were on
the scene and there was no substitution for the person on the
scene. A good logic trail from the raw information may even
help him better focus his investigation. It would also tell Zeichner a little about the analyst's personal biases and professional
depth. No one ever lied in conclusions, but personal biases, po-
litical pressure, and personal ambition could change conclu-

sions. It wasn't done with malice. It wasn't done with purposes of evasion. It was just a fact of Washington life. Here he was, hundreds of miles from Hawaii, away from the intrinsic pressure of Washington, and he would dearly like to have his own personal biases included.

He pulled his laptop forward, hit the e-mail key, and quickly sent an e-mail to headquarters asking for the raw data used to determine they may have a foreign agent onboard Sea Base. Satisfied, he pushed the laptop to the side. It would be tomorrow before he received a reply because of the time difference. The request for the data on an espionage case would be decided on at a higher level and, even then, the lawyers would be involved. They'd want to be sure that anything given to him didn't violate future prosecution or endanger any agents the United States or its allies might have involved.

Zeichner reached for the telephone and lifted the handset off the cradle. Holding it to his ear, his eyebrows bunched as he pushed a button in an attempt to dial, swore twice, pushed another button, and repeated the same sequence of button smashing. After several attempts, he slammed the telephone back in its cradle. He could send an e-mail half a world away, but couldn't even dial a stateroom two decks away.

He leaned back—carefully—and crossed his arms behind his head, letting the cool air dry the moisture beneath them. The Russians had the most to lose by Sea Base moving into their sphere of influence. Even though the Russian Federation was considered a close ally of the United States, the xenophobic history of this half-world size country still permeated their government. It wouldn't be the first time Zeichner had been involved in the tracking, identifying, and secret arrest of a Russian Foreign Intelligence Service—commonly referred to as the SVR—involved in espionage on American soil. His eyebrows bunched: *What do you call American territory when it's a ship at sea?* He doubted the importance the message from headquarters placed on the idea of having a foreign espionage agent embarked. It would be nice to know if the agent was there to gather information or to blow up Sea Base. As a rule, if there was a rulebook for espionage, foreign agents want to stay covert—unnoticed— and gather information. Then, of course, there were the North Koreans. Who in the hell knew what they wanted to do? Zeichner sighed, letting out a huge breath. Just another example of how far the intelligence services had deteriorated since the CIA was torn apart in the early 2000s and replaced with politically astute individuals.

The worse the scenario, the better the government liked it. It's easier to back off of a worst-case scenario than to poo-poo something only to have it become a massive casualty event, such as the train station bombings of Baltimore, New York, Washington, Philadelphia, and Los Angeles a couple of years ago. Someday, everyone will learn that you can't afford security for every contingency. Who was it that said, "Those who would give up essential liberty to obtain a little temporary safety deserve neither liberty nor safety"? His eyebrows furrowed for a moment until he recalled it was Benjamin Franklin. But then old Ben wasn't heading out to sea on a massive never-before-tried experiment to set up an eighty-one-plus-acre metal island.

Zeichner took a deep breath, stuck his hands up in the air, and twisted them back and forth, enjoying the cool feel of the air-conditioning blowing against him.

Like everyone else, he had been a firm supporter of the Patriot Act after 9/11, but now, twenty years later, he was a closet card-carrying member of the American Civil Liberties Union. He wondered how many other moderates such as he joined the ACLU and kept their membership a secret because of the conservative-type job they did? No way would he put the bumper sticker on his car—just no way.

He lowered his arms, leaned forward, and lifted the paper once more. After reading it again, he laid it back on the desk, and with his right hand holding it down, used his left to straighten the creases. Zeichner pushed his chair away from the table, grabbed both arms to stand, thought against it, and stayed seated. He never considered the Chinese or the French espionage services as possible candidates because both were more interested in gathering industrial information and intelligence. Their motto should read something like, *Never blow up something we might want to steal, copy, or claim later for the greater economic might of our nation.* Of course, China could buy anything it wanted from America.

He looked at the closed door across the compartment. Maybe Gainer was here and not in his stateroom. "Kevin!" he shouted. "Come here!"

The door burst opened and Kevin Gainer, Zeichner's deputy on this deployment, scrambled into the compartment. "Yes, sir," Gainer said, his arm bumping the door as he stepped toward the desk. He stopped in what could only be described as a position of attention—feet at a forty-five degree angle, heels touching.

"Kevin." Richard sighed. "You're not in the Army anymore. You're a civilian. You don't have to knock my door off the hinges and you don't have to stand at attention."

"Thank you, sir." Gainer relaxed his stance, his brown eyes shifting from one side to the other. His arms started to go behind his back before he dropped them to his side.

"And don't act uncomfortable. We're civilians, you and I. We can be informal and all that shit." Zeichner pushed away from his desk and stood. He handed the message to Gainer. "Here's some more information on that telephone call two weeks ago." He shrugged. "Not much new information, but it provides a little more insight."

Zeichner waited a couple of minutes for Gainer to finish reading the message.

"Sir, does this mean our ship, or someone on these ships—including the warships with us?"

Zeichner nodded. "Good question, Kevin. I would say somewhere out there, within this convoy, is someone who wants to gather as much information as possible on Sea Base."

Gainer looked at Zeichner, their eyes meeting. "Sir, you've heard of the two explosions in Pearl Harbor before. . . ."

Zeichner nodded and shrugged. "I know. Within the last few weeks the number of explosions at banks, abortion clinics, and government offices has increased."

"I read an FBI notice where they suspect it to be a homegrown terrorist organization going under the name of God's Army."

"At least we're safe from them here. You can't have a homegrown terrorist organization in America without someone turning you in."

Gainer's lower lip pushed against the upper. "Pisses me off when I hear of Americans doing this. It isn't someone with a non-government organization, like those assholes in al Qaieda. I hope when the FBI catches them, they throw them in prison and throw away the key."

Zeichner agreed and changed the subject by taking the message from Gainer. Let the FBI worry about this fanatical religious group. He had a spy on board. "Kevin, this message tells us we have a real-life spy from another country in our deployment." He leaned against the edge of the desk. The compartment was too small for both of them to stand in front of the desk; the desk took up nearly a third of the space.

"Do you know how long it's been since we've truly had to chase another country's spy?" Zeichner asked, shaking his head. The fluorescent light reflected off the shiny spot at the back of his head.

"No, sir."

"Well, let me tell you—" he started to reply and abruptly stopped himself. "Don't try that."

"Try what, sir?" Gainer asked, his face betraying his confusion.

"Try to distract me. Whoever is on board can have several objectives."

"Sabotage?"

"Could be one, but I doubt it."

Gainer's eyebrows rose to accompany the questioning look he gave Zeichner.

"Could be just a spying expedition?"

"Bingo," Zeichner agreed, crossing his arms. "If he's reporting, then he'll have to use a radio or something. Then again, if he is on a technology-gathering expedition, he'll have an array of cameras."

"Do you want me to check the manifests?"

"Manifests are one thing we'll have to check. I want you to start with the special security officers. Have them review everyone's security records and see if there are any who may fit the profile."

"Profile?"

Zeichner waved his hand at Gainer. "You know: foreign connections, interim clearances awaiting final adjudication from one of the approving authorities. Something in a record that shows a foreign connection should be there."

"That's assuming whoever we are looking for has a security clearance, sir. What if he—"

"Or she."

"—doesn't? What if it is some young sailor who just joined?"

Zeichner nodded. "You're right, Gainer, but we have to start somewhere. My experience with foreign agents—and it isn't that much—is that either: one, they are foreigners themselves or, two, they have foreign connections. They've traveled to foreign countries. They need money. Or they are so dissatisfied with our government that they are ready to turn traitor because of ideological beliefs." He shrugged. "I would submit our guest is a foreigner, so check and see how many of our 'trusted allies' we have on board. And do what I asked with the special security officers."

"This will require a lot of work while we are under way."

"Damn good thing, too, Kevin. Otherwise we'll be cooped up in these three rooms until we dock six months from now. Manifests." Zeichner nodded and uncrossed his arms to take the message back from Gainer. He held up three fingers. "Third thing is to do what you recommended, Kevin. Get a complete roster of everyone who has sailed on this convoy, if such a thing exists."

"Yes, sir. When do you want all this?"

"Yesterday would have been nice, Kevin."

"If you don't mind me asking, sir, how could this person have gotten on board?"

"Most likely walked aboard as casually as you and I. Spies are covert sons-of-bitches, which is why they're spies in the first place. Our guest may be anyone from the captain on down to the sailor working in the bilges pumping out the bilge water."

Gainer's eyebrows curved inward. "Boss, I have no idea what a bilge is, but even the words "bilge water" make my stomach churn."

"It's the water collected in the lowest level of a ship. Kind of like a maritime version of a sump pump in a house."

"I'll get busy, sir."

"Make sure you get the names of the merchant marines who joined for this trip. When I was talking with the master of the *Denebola*, he told me they have forty-some-odd merchant marines on board the ship. In port, they have a crew of fourteen."

Gainer shook his head. "Hard to believe, boss. This ship is almost as big as an aircraft carrier, and an aircraft carrier has over three thousand people on it."

"Kevin, the *Denebola* is launching and recovering helicopters off her stern constantly—night and day since we came on board. Every one of the ships in this convoy is doing the same thing. People going from one ship to the other as they prepare to raise Sea Base. If I was a spy, I'd be taking advantage of these undocumented trips."

"Then, whoever this is, has free reign of the convoy. He could be on any ship at any time, taking photographs—"

"Or planting explosives, which I don't think he or she is. Worst case is how we play this, Kevin. We will treat this as an espionage-only investigation until something tells us different. I've sent e-mails to the other agents on the other ships, to include the NCIS team on board the USS *Boxer*."

"You think he may be Chinese?"

"No, I think he or she is Russian. Why would the Chinese want to screw with the very market making them rich?"

"But the plan calls for us to set up near Taiwan."

Zeichner bobbed his head from side to side a couple of times. "Well, you could be right. But you know what I've discovered in my years of this type of work, Kevin?" He continued before Gainer could answer. "I've discovered that most times it isn't whom you think. Did you know the United States has never had a naturalized citizen apprehended as a spy? That's not to say that maybe one or two didn't sneak by, but we've never discovered one. Usually they are citizens of the country from where we apprehended them; or they've been true-blue American-born American citizens. Go figure," he finished, shaking his head.

"So you think he may be an American citizen."

"He—or she, Kevin—most definitely will be an American citizen. You have to be an American citizen or trusted ally to be part of this convoy; an American citizen to be part of the military."

"That's not exactly correct, sir. When I was in the Army, we had everything from illegal aliens to green-card holders to true-blue American-born American citizens. Most joined because they—"

"You know something, Kevin," Zeichner interrupted. "We'll get along much better if you will remember that even when your boss is wrong, he's right."

"Sir!" Gainer seemed to snap to attention.

"Kevin," Zeichner said. "I'm kidding, son. I want you to tell me what you think. I don't care if I'm wrong, but I will care if I'm wrong and you know it and you don't tell me. You understand?"

Gainer relaxed. "Yes, sir. As I was saying, Mr. Zeichner—"

Zeichner held his hand up. "Right now, I don't care about the citizenship laws that permit non–U.S. citizens to apply early for American citizenship if they serve in the U.S. military. Was that what you were going to tell me?"

"Yes, sir."

"Kevin, get busy on gathering the information needed. Try to get the manifests on disk. Don't accept a paper run from anyone. That'll make it easier for us to run data pulls on everyone out here—and I mean everyone."

"Data pulls?"

"We'll want the pull divided into three columns: one column, non–U.S. citizens; a second, naturalized U.S. citizens; and the last column, 'born in the U.S.A.' citizens," Zeichner ordered, holding up his fingers one at a time as he told Gainer what he wanted.

"Yes, sir," Gainer replied, turning toward the door.

"Wait a minute, Kevin. Not so fast. I'm not done."

Gainer turned.

"Along with their names, I want to know their security clearance level, what organization they are from or with, and what their assignment is on board Sea Base. Right now we're eight Fast Sealift Ships, the USS *Boxer*, an amphibious something-or-other, and a couple of destroyers. Go for the Fast Sealift Ships first, followed by the *Boxer*. I don't think the destroyers are going to be major players in this, but run them anyway to see if anything leaps out at you. We've got three-thousand-plus possible candidates. Let's eliminate as many as we can."

"Mr. Zeichner, the message said whoever this person is may have experience with explosives."

"You're thinking of the bombings in Pearl Harbor again?"

Gainer nodded. "Eight dead. Fourteen wounded."

"Nine dead as of this morning. The young girl died last night."

Gainer's lips visibly tightened. "Someday whoever did that will pay for it."

Zeichner nodded. "Always seems to be those who think a higher authority gives them leave to kill their fellow human beings. God's Army wants to hurry Armageddon along by bringing on another world war. Go figure."

"I'll also look to see if any of the personnel records have anything in them about being trained in explosives. Out of three-thousand people, a few must have some Army or Marine Corps experience in explosives."

"And they may have experience with driving a car or having illicit sex." Zeichner touched the message on the desk. "For once, I wish the authors of this shit would just state the facts and their analyses of those facts without a bunch of conjecture."

"If they have access to explosives . . ."

Zeichner shrugged. "Kevin, this entire gaggle of ships is made up of explosives. My fifteen-year-old son could get explosives out here and he wouldn't even have to try. First, I don't think we have a saboteur on board. Blowing up things dumps them in the drink just as it would us. We'll stick with the espionage angle for the time being." He saw the dejected look on Gainer's face, stopped for a moment, and then continued. "Okay, check for anyone with explosives experience. That way, if we need it, we'll have it. It might be the third fact we need in doing good old-fashioned analysis." Zeichner grimaced. "But right now, what we have is a good old-fashioned information-gathering spy whose only weapon is a camera."

He motioned Gainer away. "Go run the data pull and then we'll go over the names. Something has to leap out at us."

Zeichner waited until the door shut behind Gainer before he sat back down. Breaking in a new deputy is rough enough at shore, but in the middle of a convoy it was something else. Doing it on what was supposed to be a secret test wasn't going to be easy. A secret test that made the *New York Times* the day after they sailed.

He glanced around the small compartment. Why in the hell he had volunteered to lead the NCIS contingency aboard this trip was beyond him. This was supposed to be a secret deployment. Designed to shock the world when eighty-one acres of floating American territory showed up in the middle of the Pacific—or wherever they wound up. This damn thing had been so secret that now—two weeks later—nearly every major newspaper in the world had it plastered all over in headlines. The last great secret in America was probably John F. Kennedy and Marilyn Monroe, and even that little fling was published eventually. But at least they didn't do it in the Oval Office. They did it somewhere at some out-of-the-way rehab center in Maryland.

SIX

The explosion shook the ship. It also shook Naval Criminal Investigative Service agent Richard Zeichner. His eyes flew open, the gray metal bottom of the rack above filled his vision. If this were one of the classier staterooms on this ship, he'd hate to see where the junior ratings slept.

The ship shook again. The vibration rolled with the long muffled sound of the second explosion. Zeichner instinctively grabbed the sides of the rack, riding the tremors as the explosion eased. He released his breath, not realizing he had been holding it. He took several deep ones, feeling adrenaline starting to race through his body. His body wanted to run. His mind held it in check.

"What the hell . . ." he mumbled, hearing the slight tremor in his voice. Scared? Damn straight, he was. He slid his huge body across the Navy bed everyone called a rack. His lower back hurt, but it wasn't because of the explosion. One thing he'd learned during these two weeks at sea: The word *rack* was the appropriate nautical term for the flimsy mattress slapped on top of an unbending aluminum frame.

He grabbed the edge of the top bunk and pulled himself around so his feet touched the deck. The back of his head bumped the frame of the top rack.

"I've got to lose some of this gut," he said for the umpteenth time, renewing a continuum of promises. No galley for him today.

The sudden *bong-bong* sound of general quarters, vibrating the bulkheads and shocking the eardrums, caused Zeichner to jump. Those two explosions may make his vow of "no galley today" a mute testament to his lack of willpower. Goose bumps raced up his spine and down his arms.

"What the shit is happening?" he said, nearly shouting. He leaned forward, his hands searching the deck in the dark for his sneakers. They were here someplace.

Outside the closed stateroom door, the sound of running feet increased his sense of urgency. Faint light from the outside passageway filtered through the small space at the bottom of the door. It wasn't as if he was a sailor like these merchant marines who made up the bulk of *Denebola*'s crew. What if this old tub was sinking? He shook his head back and forth as his fingers searched frantically for his shoes beneath the bed. Zeichner had no intention of going down with it.

Not finding them, he stood, reached over beside the door, and flipped on the light. He jerked his trousers off the back of the lone chair in the stateroom, grimacing at the sound of cloth ripping—as long as it wasn't the crotch, he didn't care. The shirt lying on top of the pants fell to the deck. *On second thought, when the ship you're on is sinking, who cares if the family jewels are hanging out?* Shit! He was going to get off this bucket of bolts before the ocean swept . . .

The thought gave new impetus to his dressing.

Hopping on one foot, he stepped into the right leg, bracing himself with a hand against the metal desk as he nearly toppled to the side. He belched, heartburn quickly following, but he didn't have time to think about that right now. *Do they have antacids on life rafts?* He shoved his other leg into the remaining pants leg and quickly pulled them up. He grabbed his shirt off the deck and slid it over his head. His sneakers were beneath the shirt. He turned the chair around, sat down, and a minute later his sneakers were tied. They may be sinking, but damn if he was going into the water without shoes, though common sense told him shoes weren't going to keep sharks from ripping his legs off at the hip. He didn't want to think about the family jewels as dangling bait.

He reached up, lifted his gun belt off the top rack, and quickly strapped it over his shoulder so the holster hung beneath his left arm. Zeichner took a deep breath, expecting at any moment to feel the ship heel over and start zooming toward the bottom. A lesser man would have already run screaming from the metal coffin they called a stateroom, but Zeichner told himself he wasn't a lesser man, though his legs moved him quickly toward the door of his cabin. He grabbed his suit coat off the hanger, slipping it over the shirt and the gun. Even sailors had a problem with someone carrying a "piece"—the Navy term for any type of gun. He was learning a lot about Navy terminology while out here.

He should have gone to sea in his earlier years with Naval Criminal Investigative Service instead of waiting until he was a senior agent and have someone more senior saddle him with this. Everyone thought he'd had lots of sea time, which was one reason he'd been chosen. He stopped at the door and pulled out the .38 Colt revolver, slipped the catch on the left side of the chamber, and swung the cylinder out sideways. It was loaded. What use was a gun if it wasn't loaded? It was hard enough to shoot someone with a loaded pistol; it was damn impossible with an empty one—not that he had ever shot anyone.

Just because he had never shot at someone didn't mean he wouldn't. It was just that opportunity never gave him a chance to shoot at anyone. But Zeichner kept his gun loaded and ready, for he never knew when circumstance and time might call on him to use it. And he wanted to be ready.

He wondered briefly how effective a .38 would be against a shark. The idea of carrying a .45 suddenly appealed to him. The other agents can have their .45s. For him, it had been a macho-thing to throw out to the younger agents, *You can have your .45s, but real men carry a .38*. He'd take his double-action "small boy" over the wrist-wrecking .45 any day. Satisfied, he slid it back into the holster. No way was he going to destroy the myth of his sea time perpetuated over his career. Guess if you look old everyone thinks you aged by going to sea or dodging bullets. He had done little of either until now. Bombs were a different matter. He'd spent his time in Iraq, and even did two weeks in Indonesia. His piece spent as much time in his hand as it did in the holster.

Zeichner opened the door and stepped into a deserted passageway. The ship seemed level. He shifted his weight a couple of times from right to left. "Yeah, it's level," he mumbled.

Zeichner turned left and several feet later climbed the ladder leading to the main deck. He wasn't sure where the explosion had originated, but being topside on the open deck was better than being below. He'd have a better picture of what was happening once he was topside. He'd also be in a better position to figure out how severe the damage to the ship was. He may never have fired a shot in anger or self-defense, but he'd spent enough time attached to the Department of Homeland Security and fighting terrorists in Iraq to know an explosion. Someday he might write a book about some of the clandestine things they do from Nebraska Avenue or one titled something like *Duct Tape and the Art of Interrogation.*

He twisted the three-foot-long handle to the right, opening the watertight hatch someone had closed when the ship sounded general-quarters. Before the door opened, the change in pressure sucked the unmistakable odor of cordite into the passageway. Smoke sailed past Zeichner as he pushed the hatch open and stepped into the maelstrom of damage control parties fighting a fire at sea.

He was standing at the rear of the forward forecastle where the bridge was located.

Smoke roiled from an opening above the main cargo hole of the USNS *Denebola*. The forward forecastle bracketed the main cargo hold with the slightly taller aft forecastle over six hundred feet away. The deck over the main cargo hold took up nearly two-thirds of the overall ship length of 946 feet and 1½ inch. Zeichner had a thing for numbers. He never thought about how he was able to do it—recall numbers hours after seeing them or how he could figure calculations in his mind. He even knew months in advance what day a date fell on. He did know it was a neat game to play with some of the mentally challenged agents with whom he spent his daily routines. Little things, such as reciting license plate numbers, upwards of twenty in a row, without missing a beat.

He wasn't sure exactly where in the main cargo hold the computers and servers that controlled Sea Base were located. If the explosion destroyed them, then this deployment may be over before it had fully begun. The backup servers on the USNS *Pollux* were designed to cut in and take control if something happened to the information technology suite on *Denebola*, but that was after Sea Base had stood up.

From the look of the thick, impenetrable column of smoke curling upward through the opening, he didn't see how any electronics would survive.

"Damn," Zeichner said, stepping back quickly as two men pushing an AFFF mobile foam machine raced by screaming, "Make a hole! Make a hole!" He flattened himself against the bulkhead, letting them go by as they raced to the ladder and quickly tugged the heavy equipment down to where other fire teams were already fighting the conflagration. He noticed at least two other AFFF systems lining up around the opening. He turned and followed in their wake as those ahead moved aside to allow the fire party access. The merchant seamen set up the AFFF system. AFFF stood for Aqueous Film Forming Foam (AFFF). It was as old as the modern Navy. Designed to fight liquid fire, it would smother any fire upon which it was used and because it was foam. It rode atop burning liquids wherever they flowed, breaking up the fire-triangle by keeping oxygen away from the hot flammable liquids.

At the bottom, a couple of able-bodied seaman met the two men, grabbed the metal handholds on the AFFF machine and moved it toward the open hatch where the dark smoke continued to pour out. Zeichner thought he caught a glimpse of flame in the center of the smoke.

The wind shifted slightly and the smoke encompassed the men on the main deck for a second. When it rolled away, they wiped their eyes. Some bent over coughing out the smoke that filled their lungs during that unexpected shift. Four men now carried the AFFF machine, those ahead of them moving aside to allow them access. Zeichner stepped up on the ladder to the second rung for a better view and to stay out of the way of those fighting the fire.

He figured they knew what they were doing since AFFF had water as a component; someone, somewhere must have secured the electrical circuits in those computers in the main cargo hold or they were going to have one God-awful shock when they poured that foam down on it.

Across on the port side of the main cargo hold, a damage control team held a twenty-foot nozzle over the open hole, spraying a fine water mist into the conflagration. So much for wondering if the electricity had been secured.

Several sailors mingled excitedly off to one side, bumping into each other as they hurriedly put on protective gear and breathing apparatus. Zeichner shook his head slightly. Standard Navy Oxygen Breathing Apparatus—OBA, they were called. Fires contained toxic fumes and smoke; the OBAs allowed the sailors to enter burning spaces so they could fight the fire. It also allowed them to search for survivors—or non-survivors. They were braver men than him. A woman tossed her ball cap onto the deck and slipped an OBA over her head. *And women, too.*

Shooting it out against a band of *I wanna die* terrorists was one thing he knew he could do. Jumping into the absolute darkness of a smoke-filled compartment at sea . . . Blind and knowing the only way out was to follow the hose backward . . . It terrified Zeichner to even think of it. Two merchant marines gave a thumbs-up to the sailors helping them. Zeichner watched them march off, disappearing behind the thick smoke. Others followed the two, heading into the fiery furnace of the hanger bay.

Zeichner watched the AFFF team change directions and start approaching the burning hole from the starboard side, where the slight wind was blowing the smoke up and away from the opening. He silently wished them well.

"Hold off on the AFFF!" someone shouted.

It was the first mate. The tattoos on both lower arms made him easy to recognize. Zeichner had shared dinner with the man several times since they had left Pearl Harbor. Tommy Parks was the man's name, from Savannah, Georgia. Parks's statistics rolled through his mind as if Zeichner was reviewing a criminal record. Over twenty-five-years as a merchant marine. Married, two teenagers in high school. Worked his way from able-bodied seaman to first mate. Hoping to get his Master's license and his own ship sometime in the future, but well aware the American merchant fleet was small—nearly nonexistent—and mostly Navy owned.

The teams with the AFFF machines set them down at the edge of the open hole.

"Move those sprays up here and fill this compartment!" The first mate turned and pointed at the nearest AFFF teams. "As soon as the rescue parties are out, we'll—"

Another explosion rocked the ship. The first mate and one of the nozzle teams were knocked to the deck, dropping the open fire hose. The force of the spray coming from the twelve-foot extension sent the hose whipping back and forth like a wild, angry snake. Flames blew up through the open hole, reaching twenty feet above the opening before disappearing beneath the smoke.

"Get that damn hose!" the first mate shouted, climbing back to his feet. "Keep that water—" he started to say, but the other nozzle teams were doing it already. Parks turned to one of the other officers of the *Denebola*. "Get someone down there and get the rescue team out! Now!" Parks started speaking into a walkie-talkie.

Zeichner stepped onto the main deck, keeping close to the bulkhead to stay out of the way of those fighting the fire. He worked his way to the starboard deck edge of the ship, stepping over the hose running from the risers along the rear of the forward forecastle.

Shouts drew his attention. Several sailors and merchant marines appeared through the smoke, their arms helping to hold up rescue team members and guiding them to the edge of the main deck. The OBA masks hung by their hoses, bouncing off their chests.

"Make way! Make way!" came shouts from behind the first waves of people. Two men carrying a rescue team member by her arms and legs appeared through the smoke, shouting, "Make way!"

Behind these two came another pair of sailors carrying a second rescue team member, the OBA mask dangling beneath the man's head, flopping back and forth with each hurried step the two sailors took. The injured man's eyes opened, darting everywhere, as if regaining consciousness; the man was trying to figure out where he was.

Behind them, stumbling into the open air and ripping their masks off came the remainder of the rescue team. One of them slapped his ears, trying to regain hearing that had been shocked away by the explosion.

More sailors appeared down the forward starboard passage of the ship, forcing Zeichner to step back until they passed. Zeichner looked back at the first mate. Parks was ordering the AFFF teams closer to the hole. No chance to rescue anyone, if anyone still remained in the belowdecks inferno. Zeichner may have had little experience at sea, but he knew the attempt had been made to save anyone belowdecks, and now it was time to ensure the survival of the ship.

"Now hear this," bellowed a voice over the ship's announcement system. "If you are not involved in fighting the fire, then clear the area."

Zeichner shaded his eyes from the brightness of the sky. The morning sun was a quarter of the way up on its trip across the cloudless sky. He looked up toward the starboard bridge wing. The captain of the USNS *Denebola* stood there, leaning on the solid metal barrier that encircled the bridge wing. The gray strands of the neatly trimmed beard on this thin reed of a captain stood out in the clear weather surrounding the bridge area. Down the center of the gray was the fading red hue from the man's youthful years. The sectioned beard made Zeichner think of small streams weaving their way through a thick forest. It gave the man a look of Viking fierceness, though Zeichner knew from the few times he had dined with Captain Boxford that the man claimed Scottish heritage. He also knew the captain was married, lived in Norfolk, and had two children he saw every six months or so, whenever the *Denebola* wasn't "underway, making way," which wasn't often. Forty-four, graying, with a face weather-beaten by salt spray from every ocean in the world. Why would someone choose this profession, he wondered?

Boxford looked down, spotted Zeichner, and frowned.

Zeichner saw Boxford say something to someone inside the bridge area.

A few seconds later, "I say again," boomed the announcement system. "If you're not involved with fighting this fire, then clear the area."

Zeichner looked away from the speaker back to the bridge and saw a questioning look on Boxford's face. That last announcement may have been for him.

Other than the dining experiences, their paths seldom crossed on this behemoth of a ship. He recalled asking Boxford what they called a civilian captain on a Navy ship. The man had replied, "They call me Captain, unless they're pissed off at me, and then they call me Master. Either is acceptable as long as they do what I ask."

Captain Boxford straightened, standing ramrod straight on the starboard bridge wing, looking aft at the activity. The ship was turning. The vibrations of the engine and the strain on the ship changing direction sent a steady beat vibrating through the metal decks of the *Denebola*. The forward forecastle hid the bow of the *Denebola*, but as the ship turned, first the bow of a Navy warship appeared, and seconds later enough of the ship came into view to show it was the destroyer, USS *Gearing*.

The sea churned behind the destroyer as the Navy warship raced across the bow of the burning ship. The *Denebola* was in a left turn, causing the approaching destroyer to drift right as the bow of the Fast Sealift Ship turned to take advantage of the wind.

Zeichner grabbed the railings of the nearby ladder and started up. If he stayed out for the entire six months, he'd know so much about port, starboard, bearing drifts, decks, and overheads that when he returned he'd have the terminology to go with the myth of his sea time. If only he could take the physique of one of those sailors with him, then the Frederick American Legion would be a lot more fun on ladies' night.

Zeichner stopped at the top of the first deck. Looking up, he caught the Master glancing down at him. He cupped his hands and shouted, "Captain!"

Captain Boxford looked at him, shook his head, and motioned Zeichner away.

Zeichner ignored the motion. He understood the captain had a lot of things to do right now, but he was the by-God senior NCIS agent in the Sea Base project and an explosion at sea was in his jurisdiction unless it was accidental.

Confidence returned to Zeichner now that he had left the immediate vicinity of the fire. The smell of smoke still surrounded him, but he was in clear air. The ship wasn't in danger of sinking—*yet*. Confidence was something Zeichner possessed in abundance—once he grasped enough of a situation to understand its severity. He was sure some thought of him as arrogant. He wasn't above throwing both his authority and physical presence around when the job called for it. Beneath that veneer of confidence, or arrogance, existed a low level of self-doubt on his ability to do the jobs that came his way. He sometimes thought his rise through the ranks of the Naval Criminal Investigative Service was more sheer dumb luck than having anything to do with competence. But doubts are something most people learned to keep to themselves. Those knives of doubts sticking out of his back, where other agents had gleefully placed them, were deep.

He hurried across the third deck to the next set of ladders, stopping for a moment to catch his breath. After a couple of minutes, Zeichner started up toward the bridge wing where Captain Boxford stood. A conversation was going between Boxford and the second mate, who stood just inside the bridge, one leg protruding through the open hatch onto the bridge wing.

The *Denebola* was turning so the speed and direction of the ship would increase the wind across the main deck in such a direction that it would blow the smoke away from those fighting the fire.

Zeichner stopped again to catch his breath. This ladder thing of going up and down everywhere you went on a ship would be good for his health, if he didn't have a massive heart attack first and drop over the side. He glanced over the side, glad that no dark shapes flickered by. A .38 wasn't going to stop a shark.

A fire at sea was worse than flooding. At sea, sailors could always dewater or refloat a sinking or sunk ship, but they couldn't rebuild one burned to the waterline. The golden rules for damage control was fight fire first and keep flooding under control. Once the fires were contained or out, then turn your attention to pumping the water overboard. It was a curious mixture of benefits that braced the damage control parties from the various repair lockers of a ship.

THE smoke now blew across the deck off the port side of the ship, clearing the starboard side where most of the fire parties were fighting the fire. Kiang stepped along the front of the aft forecastle, keeping close to the bulkhead and at the edge of the smoke. He glanced several times at Zeichner, breathing a little easier when he saw the NCIS agent start up the ladder toward the bridge. He raised his small camera and took several photographs of the fire, the sailors, and the merchant marines fighting it. His handler may find the photographs interesting, even if they were of little intelligence value.

Reaching the part of the forecastle where the starboard passageway cut through the edge of it, heading toward the aft helicopter pad and aft cargo holds, Kiang stopped. Nothing to do now but wait for the helicopters to start ferrying additional fire parties to the blaze. He'd hitch a ride off with one of them.

"Excuse me," a sailor said, heading toward to the aft portion of the ship.

He'd blend in with those who had come to *Denebola* for varied reasons and head back toward his own ship, hopefully via a different ship enroute. He lifted the camera and aimed it toward Zeichner, who was standing on the third level of the ladder, catching his breath. Not much danger of this agent outrunning him, but it mattered little how fast you could run or dodge at sea. At sea, there was only so far you could go. He pressed the tele-photo lens button, feeling the whirl of gears vibrate through his cheek as he focused on the NCIS agent. At least his handler would appreciate a small tidbit of photo intelligence. Some of his training by his hereditary countrymen warned him to always suspect that someone was closing in on him. Never underestimate the other side. Always believe that someone suspects you.

Kiang had taken the advice seriously, so he continuously watched his "six," referring to his back. He had heard the term on the television series *JAG* and had grown accustomed to using it. He bowed slightly toward Zeichner as he lowered the camera. The NCIS agent began to climb the last set of ladders toward the bridge. He had to believe that someone would be doing whatever was necessary to trap and catch him. The *someone* for this trip was Zeichner. It was this overweight man he would keep watch. As long as Kiang kept Zeichner off his butt, the safer Kiang would be, for with his safety rested the lives of his parents.

ZEICHNER glanced at the bridge wing above, took a deep breath, and started the last leg of the ladders leading to the bridge wing. Halfway there, he looked up and saw the second mate standing beside Boxford, glaring down at Zeichner. Their eyes locked for a moment before the second mate turned and went back inside the bridge, relaying a new set of Boxford's orders.

"*Denebola*, this is *Gearing*!" came the bullhorn call from the destroyer passing to the right of *Denebola*. "Intentions are to circle back after you complete your turn and take position on your starboard side. Request confirm!"

The master disappeared from the starboard bridge wing. A moment later, as Zeichner reached the bridge wing, a voice boomed through a bullhorn.

"*Gearing*, this is the captain of *Denebola*. You are cleared to position yourself on my starboard side. Be advised I am maneuvering to clear the smoke. You may find yourself blinded."

"Roger, understand."

Zeichner reached the bridge wing, bending over at the top of the ladder, his hands on his knees, to catch his breath. He was going to lose *forty*-pounds while he was out here. This had to stop.

A loud wheezing sound reached him, causing him to first touch his chest, thinking it was coming from him. But he quickly realized the sound was behind him. He turned and look aft. The noise came from several AFFF systems that had activated simultaneously to pour foam onto the raging fire. From this vantage point he could see the flickering flames licking upward in the center of the smoke, tens of feet above the open hole. It looked worse up here than down there. Turning back, Zeichner caught a glimpse of the stern of the American destroyer as the bow of the *Denebola* uncovered it.

"Mr. Zeichner."

He straightened.

"Captain Boxford, I wanted . . ."

"Now is not the time, Sir," Boxford said, irritation showing in what was usually a calm voice. "I have a fire to fight and a ship to keep afloat. There is nothing more important than this. When the fire is out and the reflash watch is set, then you can start your investigation."

"My investigation?"

"Yes. I presume that is what you want to do."

Zeichner nodded. "Yes, that is what I wanted to do," he gasped out. He grabbed his handkerchief, reached up, and wiped the sweat from his face, bringing away a soaked cloth.

"Good. I don't want to sound rude, but you're to stay out of the way until then."

KEYLAND pulled the new sonar technician, Smith, to the edge of the deck and leaned him against the safety lines. The dark-haired Smith turned and rested the side of his face on the middle line. A long, choking cough caused him to straighten up. Keyland slapped the petty officer on the back.

"What the shit were you thinking, Smitty? What the hell were you doing down in the main cargo bay, you stupid shit? The senior chief is going to be one pissed-off mother when he finds you."

"Don't curse," Smith coughed out in reply.

"Don't pull that Holy Roller crap now. You could have died."

Smith nodded. "I know. One moment I was walking along the makeshift corridor near the bulkhead, and the next thing I knew, I was waking up as they carried me up onto the deck." He paused. "It is true that God reached down, enveloped me in his arms, and guided me to safety."

Keyland leaned away, his face displaying his anger. "You better hope God is keeping your ass safe, Smith, because when the senior chief gets a hold of it, it's going to be one bruised mess."

"I am untouchable," Smith mumbled.

"What did you say?"

"What?"

"I asked what did you say. I didn't hear you."

"Nothing. I am just grateful—" Coughing interrupted him and sent him into another spasm.

"Damn good thing those firefighters found you," Keyland said, slapping him on the back. "You might want to lay down on your side. Squatting on the deck is putting too much pressure on your lungs."

"It was God watching over me."

"Well, damn good thing God was wearing an Oxygen Breathing Apparatus when he found you."

Smith shook Keyland's hands off him, grabbed the top safety line, and pulled himself up. "Someday, Keyland, God will punish you and those like you for your blasphemy. One day you will regret words that offend Him. God is—" Coughing erupted anew.

"Oh, shut the fuck up, man. That's all we hear from you day in and day out: God this and God that. Man, you gotta quit thinking you got a monopoly on the Big Guy. America ain't about monopolies on religion."

Smith sneered, pointed at the fire, and started to say something, but another fresh wave of coughing caused him to lean over the safety cables. He vomited, his stomach heaving repeatedly. Thankfully, the wind was blowing from the port side.

"Here, Smith," Keyland said, putting his hands on the man's back. "You either sit down or lie down, or you're going to fall down. We gotta get you to medical and have the doc look you over."

Smith allowed himself to be helped to the deck. A trace of vomit ran from his mouth to the edge of his chin.

Agazzi ran up beside the two sailors and crouched down on his haunches beside Smith. "Smitty, you okay?" he asked, touching the man on the shoulder.

"Yeah, he's okay for a stupid shit. He was down there when everything went to shit."

"In the main cargo hangar?"

Smith nodded. "I was walking back from the galley to the for-

ward control room when it exploded. I don't recall too much—"
A couple of deep, rasping coughs choked off his explanation.

"I told everyone to stay out of the server farm area unless the
diagnostics showed otherwise. It's a classified area."

"Ah, Christ, Senior Chief," Keyland objected. "It's only a classified secret. It ain't as if it's really classified."

"Classified is classified."

"Stop using the Lord's name—" Coughing stopped Smith
from continuing.

"Smith, what were you doing down there? You can reach the
galley from the main deck."

Between coughs, Smith answered, "Senior Chief, I was bringing some breakfast biscuits from the galley."

"You could have done that on the main deck. No reason for
you to be belowdecks in an area that is off-limits." Agazzi turned
to Keyland. "Let's get him to the rear of the aft forecastle, out of
the way of the firefighters so we're not clutter they have to worry
about. I saw a couple of helicopters circling, so they're going to
start running the helos now that the ship has maneuvered so the
wind clears the smoke. Where are Taylor and Bernardo?"

As if hearing their names, shouts from the entrance to the passageway running through the aft forecastle along the starboard
side caught their attention. Bernardo had fingers jabbed into
each side of his mouth, whistling, while Taylor motioned for
them to come.

"There they are, boss," Keyland said.

"Glad to see you've kept track of everyone, Keyland." Agazzi
was upset. He was responsible for these sailors. Keyland was the
leading petty officer he entrusted with this responsibility.

Agazzi stood. He and the others came here to discuss their requirements with the Information Technology team in charge of
the computers. The senior IT team had been with Agazzi in the
conference room below the forward forecastle when the explosions went off. Keyland and the others were supposed to have
been with the network technicians, reviewing the optical and electronic connections. Instead, two explosions later he discovers his
four sailors scattered across the main deck. A main deck of several acres. He should be grateful they were all alive and, except
for some smoke, the new guy Smith seemed to be none the worse.

Keyland acknowledged the waves and shouts from Bernardo
and Taylor. "They're waving us to them, Senior Chief."

Agazzi reached down and put his arm under Smith's right arm. "Give me a hand," he said to Keyland.

When Keyland tried to take the sailor under the other arm, Smith jerked away. He pushed Agazzi's arm away. "I can walk by myself," Smith said, accentuating each word. The smoke and coughing left the man's voice hoarse and raspy. Smith touched his throat.

"Sore, isn't it?" Keyland asked, with no pity in his voice. "Serves you right for being where you shouldn't."

"Good," Agazzi said. "Let's get back nearer the heli pad so we can leave as soon as they can take us." Agazzi looked at the sky. More helicopters had joined the original two, orbiting counter-clockwise off the starboard quarter. Toward the horizon there were other helicopters, some lifting off the other ships, others flying between them beginning to fill the air. Even with this calamity, the work of the fleet continued with the helicopters making their transit rounds between the ships of the convoy. Until Sea Base was implemented, the only way between ships were either the notorious Boatswain Chair, a ship's boat, or by helicopter.

"Senior Chief?" Keyland asked.

Smith stumbled in front of them. Agazzi reached out, but the older sailor caught himself and continued walking toward the other two crewmembers.

"What's he saying?" Agazzi asked softly.

"He ain't saying nothing, Senior Chief. He's praying because he thinks God reached down, patted his skinny ass with love, and guided him to the main deck."

"Well, if God didn't do it, then the man was awful lucky. You saw what happened to the rescue team, didn't you?"

"Yep. Nearly lost them, they did."

"When we get back on board the *Algol*, Petty Officer Keyland, have Smith go see the doc. I want to make sure he's okay."

As they neared the entrance to the enclosed deck edge passageway of the aft forecastle, a man dressed in a white shirt, tie, and slacks moved aside so they could pass. Agazzi gave the man a hard stare. When you're fighting a fire at sea, you don't need uninvolved observers. The man needs to move away from the scene like they were doing. Out of the way and out of the confusion.

Agazzi glanced back at the man, who had stepped back into

the shadow of the enclosed passageway. "Hey!" he shouted. "If you're not involved in the fire, then you need to get out. . . ."

Without acknowledging Agazzi's shout, the man turned and headed toward a nearby ladder.

"Guess you told him, Senior Chief," Keyland said with a tinge of sarcasm. "What a way to go, boss."

They reached the passageway.

"Wow, Smitty," Taylor said. "What the hell happened to you?"

Smith held up his hand for a moment and, without replying, walked past the two men.

"He looks like shit," Bernardo said.

"He was in the cargo bay when the explosion went off. Bernardo, go check with the flight deck officer and see when they're going to start landing helos."

Bernardo walked toward the merchant marine who was dressed in khakis and holding a radio, and braced against the safety lines.

"Then how in the hell did he survive?" Taylor asked.

"It was the grace of the Lord," Keyland said, holding up his hands toward the sky.

"Stop it," Agazzi said. "Smith is one lucky devil. I don't know how he managed to get out of that inferno."

"Ah, Senior Chief," Taylor said. "We don't mind Smith having his religion; we just don't want him to keep preaching it to us." Taylor turned to Keyland. "He makes me nervous with his *holier than thou* routine. Let the Holy Rollers . . ."

Bernardo returned.

"Enough," Agazzi said, holding up his hand. "Bernardo, what's the situation with the helicopters?"

"They're going to start allowing them to land soon. Other ships are gathering their own firefighting teams together to come here to help. If we're at the helipad when the first one lands, we can hitch a ride to another ship on it. From there we can reach the *Algol*."

At the end of the passageway, clear sky and clean air greeted the men. Smith bent over, leaning against the bulkhead, coughing. Bernardo walked over and touched Smith on the back.

"Hey, I can walk myself," Smith said, jerking his shoulder away from the man's touch and breaking into light coughing. "Father, you were right."

"Right! And, yo momma, too."

"Talks to his dad all the time," Taylor whispered to Bernardo.

"I've seen him on the fantail staring off as if debating whether to jump into the sea or walk on it."

"Wish I'd been there to give him the encouragement to try."

KIANG Zheng stopped at the foot of the ladder, watching the two sailors trailing the one coughing. Once they were inside the covered passageway, he stepped off the ladder, walked around it, and stopped beneath it, hidden slightly by the shadows while he watched the firefighters. He touched his shirt pocket, feeling the small camera inside the pocket. A couple of minutes more and he could have been one of the bodies in the explosion. He lifted the camera and took some more photographs of the firefight and damage.

A fresh wave of smoke poured out of the main cargo hold, the volume briefly expanding to cover the whole main deck before blowing off to the port side. Flames burst through the smoke, reaching up past the main mast. Roiling upon itself, the wind from the starboard side blew the smoke to the right and out to sea, lifting it above the low-riding destroyer coming alongside the starboard side of the ship.

"This is *Gearing*," came the bullhorn from the destroyer.

He didn't see how the destroyer could provide much help. The masts of the small warship barely reached the main deck of this Fast Sealift Ship. Only the tips of the main mast showed above the main deck of the USNS *Denebola*.

Kiang took more photographs as merchant marines rigged lines between the two ships. The AFFF teams continued to pour foam into the main cargo hole, with little effect, from what Kiang was seeing. The flames licked up from the cargo hole as if laughing at the feeble effort by those trying to stomp it out.

Belowdecks, the fire was fighting to spread, heating the metal bulkhead walls that kept it at bay. Watertight doors exposed to the heat inside the main cargo hold had begun to buckle; smoke seeped around the edges. The nearest passageways had over a foot of smoke covering the overhead; the smoke inching downward threatened to fill them completely.

Nothing could survive this conflagration, Kiang told himself. Miracles sometimes happen, but if the smoke told the story, then nothing would escape the damage being done in the main cargo bay. The computers and servers Kiang had sought to photograph were the core of Sea Base. Without them, he didn't see how the exercise would continue. What Kiang didn't know was that if the ship's crew failed to control the fire in the next few minutes, it was in danger of sinking.

He breathed a sigh of relief. At least he had the photographs; his handlers would be happy for them. If Sea Base failed to deploy it would be a setback for the United States in trying to reassert its influence in an area China now considered its lone domain.

He shut his eyes for a moment and bowed his head, thinking of his parents and wishing them happiness. He knew their happiness and well-being would last as long as his usefulness to the colonel remained fruitful. Once the colonel decided Kiang was of little use, his parents would disappear. He also knew *he* would disappear, but it was for his parents that he betrayed the country of his birth, or so he told himself. He knew all of this. How could someone with his intellect not know otherwise? But he held tenuously to the promise that when he had served faithfully until he could serve no more, then his parents would be released. He also knew that if his parents died, then he would have no reason to continue to work for the colonel. He shivered for a few seconds over what the colonel would do to him if he ceased to earn the man's favor.

Two firefighters lugging barrels of AFFF bumped into him as they passed.

"Hey, buddy, didn't you hear the captain say to get the hell away from here?"

Kiang smiled and nodded, stepping back against the bulkhead, noticing the heat from the bulkhead, and attributing it to the sun.

"Fucking Chink!" the other merchant marine muttered as the two hurried toward the other fire teams.

All along the sides of the opening, portable foam machines pumped foam into the large open hole. These machines could never make enough foam to put out the fire, Kiang told himself. He glanced up and saw the helicopters circling in a counterclockwise pattern off the starboard side of the ship.

At the main deck, fire hoses from the USS *Gearing* were quickly being pulled through the bottom gaps of the safety lines and secured. Barrels of AFFF from the destroyer were appearing farther down the deck nearer the forward forecastle.

Kiang's face remained an emotionless mask even as he felt relieved that his mission was over before it had begun. Without the server farm responsible for Sea Base, the only way they could implement the concept would be the mirror-image servers on-board the naval vessel *Pollux*. He had taken steps to slow the daily electronic updates from reaching the machines on the *Pollux*. Once the Office of Naval Research realized they only had the baseline software programs for Sea Base, he doubted they would implement Sea Base. He wouldn't. His business calculation esti-mated a less than thirty percent probability of success. But then the Navy wasn't a business; it was an arm of national security. Win percentages mattered little when the safety and influence of the nation guided its missions.

The hard work of two years was gone. Destroyed by a fire at sea in manner of minutes. As a scientist, in the back of his mind there would be the fear of no safety backup if what happened on the *Denebola* happened to the *Pollux*. The concept was dead on arrival—DOA, as they say on *Law and Order*. His bosses couldn't ask for anything else when he told them how this fire destroyed everything. He had done his job; or, at least he'd tried. He patted the camera once again, then reached into his pants pockets and felt the CDs. Proof of his words. The Ministry of State Security believed in having proof.

He turned toward the covered passageway. Already he had been noticed twice. He squinted as he glanced toward the bridge wing where he had last seen Zeichner. He wasn't there. But when Zeichner began his investigation someone would recall him being there. Someone would recall how he watched the fire burn. Someone would reach the conclusion that Kiang seemed happy even despite his propensity for keeping an expressionless face. Those with whom he worked kidded him about it. It wouldn't do for him to be noticed a third time. It was time for him to return to the USNS *Regulus*. He still had his "real" job and that was supporting the standup of the Combat Information Center. After all, he had to earn his American paycheck because the colonel thought keeping his parents alive was payment enough.

ZEICHNER had been hidden by his turn around the first level of the ladder as he worked his way back down toward a mid-level wing where he would be out of the way of Boxford and the fire-fighters. He would stand here until he decided what to do next.

From that vantage point he could hear the captain and watch the firefighters at the same time.

"Is everyone out of the main cargo hold?"

Zeichner turned at the question. Boxford was speaking to his second mate. On a Navy warship, the executive officer was the equivalent to a first mate on a merchant marine ship. He hadn't quite figured out what the second mate was; probably like a XO in waiting.

"The rescue team only had time for a small sweep, sir, before the fire exploded. They brought out three people. One was pretty badly burned. He's been carried to medical. The other two were able to walk. Our rescue team got caught when the fire blazed outward, but for the most part, they're fine. Burns and smoke inhalation."

"Good."

"Captain, the fire is spreading. I know you're waiting, hoping for others to escape, but the heat is too intense. There can't be any survivors left in the hole."

Boxford nodded. "How many lost?"

"Won't know for sure until we put it out, but according to the work manifest, there should have been nine to ten down there. We've accounted for twelve who escaped. Some were passing through, so . . ." The second mate shook his head. "We don't know for sure."

"Give me an estimate."

"Ten to twelve dead."

"Supposed to be ten max in the cargo bay and twelve came up. Let's hope ten of them were those assigned down there."

"I gave the team leader permission to send a team back into the cargo bay once the fire was contained. He has two teams belowdecks, starting to spray the bulkheads around the main cargo bay. We have buckling and paint melting already."

"Tell the first mate to bring everyone topside, away from the main cargo bay, and to report when he's done that. Keep the fire watches at the perimeter. I don't want this fire spreading. What does the chief engineer say about the deck directly below the main cargo bay?"

"Hot, but no spread. He's got water spraying on the overhead, hoping to keep it from buckling. Fire is contained—right now—within the main cargo bay."

"What are you doing?" Zeichner shouted up at Boxford.

Boxford looked down. His lower lip pushed against the upper one. Zeichner could tell the man resented the question. Most questions asked by NCIS agents were resented.

"I'm going to put out the fire, but first I want to make sure we have everyone topside where there is plenty of fresh air. I don't want anyone belowdecks except those sealed into engineering."

"Why?"

"Mr. Zeichner, you ask a lot of questions and you ask them at the wrong time."

He shrugged. "Part of the job, Captain."

Zeichner and Boxford's eyes met and held.

"Derrick!" Boxford shouted.

"Yes, sir," the second mate replied, sticking his head out of the hatch from the bridge.

"Sound the halon alarm, but don't give engineering permission to activate the system until I give the okay. Mr. Zeichner, for your information we have a halon system in the main cargo bay."

"I've heard of halon, but I'm unfamiliar with it."

Boxford jerked his head, reluctantly motioning Zeichner back up onto the bridge wing. "If I'm going to explain this to you, I don't want to have to shout."

As Zeichner started up the ladder again, the announcement system squeaked, sending goose bumps up his spine. A long siren followed, accompanying him the remainder of the way up the ladder. At the top, it stopped.

The familiar sound of the hydraulics that drove the crane reached Zeichner. He turned, trying to see what was going on. The arm of the crane came into view. Merchant seamen scurried toward the far end of the main deck.

"Listen up, everyone."

Zeichner recognized the voice of the first mate on the announcement system.

"We are going to close the main cargo hold. Everyone belowdecks with the exception of engineering is to come topside immediately. Those not involved in the firefighting effort are to muster on the forward and aft decks. Ensure Condition Zebra is maintained behind you as you work your way topside. Officers are to ensure the watertight hatches to the main cargo bay are closed and sealed. Report when ready."

Zeichner looked up at the taller Captain Boxford.

"Here, Mr. Zeichner," the second mate said, taking Zeichner

by the arm and positioning him to the captain's left side and behind him. "Stand here where you're out of the way. Don't speak. Just listen and save your questions for later."

Zeichner nodded at the man. His lips pursed outward for a moment. If he could work up a physique like this man's then he'd need a whole new wardrobe. The second mate stepped off the bridge wing and into the bridge.

"Mr. Zeichner, halon is what mariners call a halogenated extinguishing agent. It starts out as a carbon-based liquid combined with one or more halogen agents such as fluorine, chlorine, bromine, and iodine. In our case it is Halon 1301, the most common shipboard halon for the U.S. Navy. Along both outer bulkheads of the main cargo bay and overhead on the portions that don't open are huge tanks of this stuff. The tanks are built to withstand the heat of the fire we're fighting. When we activate it, this liquid is going to spew out of those tanks, turning into a gas when it hits the air. This gas has no oxygen in it. It will smother the fire out almost immediately, unless there is something down there I don't know about, like magnesium, which only stops burning when it's completely gone."

The second mate stepped halfway onto the bridge wing. "Captain, forward bulkhead sealed."

"Thanks."

The second mate shrugged his shoulders. "There may be others down there, but . . . As we both know, Captain. We may have missed someone, but we brought more up than should have been in there. I don't think anyone could still be alive in this."

"Let me know when the aft bulkhead has been confirmed."

"Aye, sir," the second mate replied, stepping back into the bridge.

Boxford continued, "Basically, Mr. Zeichner, once the halon fills the space, it replaces the oxygen the fire needs to burn. Without oxygen the fire triangle of fuel, oxygen, and heat is broken. We can remove any one of those elements and fire stops burning. As it is, halon is the only thing I have left to put out the fire."

"So, the fire will be out."

Boxford nodded. "Oh, yes, the fire will be out, but it'll be a couple of days before we can get in there to assess the damage and to discover if we've lost anyone. It'll take one day to ensure there is no heat down there to cause the fire to reflash before we can open the vents and holes. Going to be hot in the staterooms for a couple of days. It'll take a third day before people can reenter and, even then, we'll send an outfitted team to check the air; make sure it's toxin-free and can support life. Wouldn't want to send a bunch of people back into the space only to have them die from lack of air."

"Captain!"

Boxford faced the open hatch to the bridge. "Yes, Derrick?"

"Aft bulkhead secured. They're sealing the main cargo hold now."

"Sound the alarm for a second time."

Zeichner stepped past the captain, nearer the ledge of the bridge wing for a better view aft. He noticed the smoke diminishing as the cargo holds were sealed. Firefighters moved toward the deck edge, wiping soot from their eyes. Some squatted. One squatted for a moment and then laid on the deck, only to jump up, shouting something about how hot the deck was.

The loud alarm drowned out the few shouts from weary team members below. After several seconds, the alarm stopped.

"This is the Captain."

Zeichner looked back. He was alone on the bridge wing.

"I am about to activate the halon system in the main cargo bay. Once I've done that, no one . . . *and I mean no one* . . . is to go into the space until I say you can. No one is to open any hatches belowdecks that lead either forward or aft. If you have to move about my ship, then do it on the main deck. For those of you who are riding the *Denebola* on this deployment, halon is an odorless, clear gas that will kill you just like a car exhaust in a closed garage. If you aren't sure how to get from one part of this ship to another for the next couple of days, then you'd better ask someone. You die on my ship and I'm going to be one pissed-off sailor." The captain paused. "One minute to activation. There will be one more alarm. Now is the time to report anything to stop this."

A minute later, Zeichner heard the captain call the chief engineer on the bridge telephone and tell her to activate the halon system in the main cargo bay. The last alarm sounded, resonating across the topside of the ship to be heard as far away as the USS *Boxer,* sailing nearly fifteen-nautical miles away along the horizon.

Zeichner sighed. Nothing he could do here. He ambled down the ladders to the main deck, walked across to the ladder leading up, and made his way to the hatch leading down to his room. He stopped at the top of the ladder and looked at the scene below. Once he washed his face, he'd go to his office in the aft forecastle of the ship.

The sound of helicopters drew his attention as he reached the main deck. CH-47 Chinooks, still around after all these years, started approaching the stern of the *Denebola*. Zeichner could see faces in each of them pressed against the small round windows. Fire teams from the other ships were arriving. They'd arrive in time to relieve the fatigued teams of the *Denebola*. In one fell swoop, Captain Boxford had put out the fire.

Now, what would happen to Sea Base? Was the backup server farm on the USNS *Pollux* capable of functioning alone? Guess it wasn't his problem. His problem was to discover what had caused the explosion in the main cargo bay. Computers and servers don't just up and explode. They need help. On board warships, there were a myriad of things that could go *boom*. Auxiliary ships like these Fast Sealift Ships were designed to carry warfighting supplies such as explosives. It wasn't inconceivable that *Denebola* had more than computers and servers in its main cargo bay. The thought of the message that still lay on his desk caused Zeichner to consider that this could be the result of a saboteur, but sabotage was something from the past. It didn't happen between nations today; or did it?

He sighed leaned against the bulkhead, looking at the firefighters sitting on the hot deck, drinking water, wiping their faces. Several had their knees drawn up, arms crossed over them, heads resting on their arms.

The growing sound of the rotating props of the first helicopter approaching the *Denebola* drew his attention. The CH-47 flew along the port side of the huge Fast Sealift Ship and disappeared behind the aft forecastle. It was almost as if the convoy took time out for this emergency and, as soon as it was over, returned to normal routine. Little ever upset the routine of a Navy ship, and less could be allowed to upset the routine of a convoy moving together in the same direction at a speed determined by the slowest ship. No zigzags like he'd seen in old World War II movies because there was no submarine threat. At least none that he could think of. The only countries with an appreciative submarine force in the West Pacific were Japan, who was our ally; China, who was no one's ally; and Russia, who couldn't figure out whether they had allies or not.

The helicopter disappeared completely behind the forecastle. Across the open deck, movement caught Zeichner's attention. A man stepped from under the ladder near the enclosed starboard passageway.

For a moment Zeichner thought the man looked familiar. His eyebrows arched inward as he tried to recall where he had seen the man. The face was Asian, but a lot of Americans were of Asian descent. Asian-Americans were expected to become the second largest minority in the United States within the next five years; right behind the Hispanics. He shrugged. Just another observer. When the man stepped into the starboard passageway and disappeared down it, heading toward the aft section of the ship, shouts from below caused Zeichner's momentary interest to disappear.

Zeichner stepped away from the bulkhead and peered down at the firefighters. The supervisors were rearranging the firefighting gear, setting up the fire re-flash watches. Through the soles of his sneakers he felt the warmth of the deck and wondered if it was from the fire or the sun.

Wisps of smoke rose from around the closed main cargo hold. How did the server farm here update the mirror-image servers on the *Pollux*? Maybe it didn't. If it did, then it would have to have been through wireless communications. There was no other way. Otherwise, whatever servers waited on the *Pollux* to assume Sea Base control would be missing the data destroyed since they sailed from Pearl.

He walked to the deck edge and grabbed the safety lines so he could scan the masts of the *Denebola*, looking for a satellite antenna. He found several and figured that maybe one of those provided the mechanism by which the server farms exchanged information, but then he shrugged, making a mental note to find out. There was a chance Sea Base might continue. He wiped the sweat from his brow, surprised to find soot covering the back of his hand.

More shouts from below drew his attention. From the port side, two fire teams sprayed water across the metal deck, cooling it off. He turned away, leaving the professionals to their duties.

Zeichner opened the hatch leading below and closed it behind him. Surely it wouldn't hurt to open the hatches leading forward.

AGAZZI reached down from the door of the CH-47 and pulled Smith on board. Keyland piled in behind them. Bernardo and

Taylor were wedged between two others farther down the fuse-lage. Several other technicians crawled aboard. Usually they had to fill out a flight manifest before the helicopter took off, but emergencies always shoved administrative requirements aside. Four other people crawled aboard. Two of them had slight burns and, like Smith, had soot covering their faces and hands. The man who Agazzi had ordered away from the fire climbed aboard and shoved into a space alongside Agazzi.

Six minutes later, the helicopter lifted off *Algol* after dropping off Agazzi and his two sailors. Hunched over to avoid the rotat-ing props, the three hurried to the aft forecastle. Agazzi turned and watched the helicopter take off, wondering for a moment on which ship the Asian person was staying. Shielding his eyes, he watched the helicopter for a few more seconds before dropping his hand and working his way toward his stateroom. The man must have been one of those Office of Naval Research types, he thought, as the now much-better Smith argued against following Keyland to sick bay.

Agazzi never made it to his stateroom. Before he entered the aft forecastle, he changed direction, walking along the main deck toward the hatch leading down to the ASW control center. It might be best to check out the backup systems while everyone's attention was on the fire.

Which reminded him; he'd have to schedule a trip to the USNS *Bellatrix* to confirm the operational software programs for the Unmanned Underwater Vehicles. Maybe it should be *Under-manned* Underwater Vehicles? After all, the Navy with its "human capital strategy" had decided he only needed ten sailors, and then the Bureau of Naval Personel manning math had as-signed him eight. In the old Navy, he would have had the eight-een to twenty sailors really needed to fight a split anti-submarine division. He smiled. At least the Navy in its infinite wisdom had recognized that a senior chief was more than capable of being a division officer.

Agazzi bit his lower lip, his head down as he headed toward the hatch leading down to the ASW control center. He'd need to check out the top-secret discs in the radio shack safe for the trip. If they got to the *Bellatrix* and discovered the program was cor-rupt, he wanted to have the master programs so he could load them right then.

"Alistair, you asshole!"

Agazzi grinned. How in the hell did Jacobs get over here? he asked himself, turning to see the master chief approaching from the post side. In the man's left hand dangled an unlit cigar, and grease coated Jacobs's right hand—outstretched toward Agazzi. He shook his head, his grin widening farther. He knew Jacobs was going to put that greasy palm in his whether Agazzi wanted him to or not.

Jacobs lowered his hand as he neared. "Christ, man. You're covered in shit."

"Fire . . ."

Before Jacobs could stop him, Agazzi hugged him.

Jacobs pushed away. "Hey, man! Stop that shit." Jacobs's eyes looked both ways. "We ain't been out to sea that long." Jacobs looked down at his khaki uniform, spots of soot now stained the shirt and trousers. "Shit, Alistair, look what the hell you've done to my clean uniform."

"Master Chief Petty Officer Jacobs, that's the same uniform you've had on since we left Hawaii. I recognize the dried egg above the right pocket."

Jacobs shook the cigar at him. "Dried egg matches the khaki color. Soot doesn't. Now I'm going to have to put on my other set, and I was saving them for something important." He brushed at the soot with his right hand. "Damn! Now look what you've made me do. I've got grease all over them now." He looked up at Agazzi. "You must have been over on *Denebola*."

The two turned and walked toward the starboard side, looking at the diminishing trails of smoke rising from the *Denebola*. Agazzi told Jacobs about the fire. Jacobs was listening intently until the boatswain mate had heard all he wanted. Then he changed the subject to how his khakis probably looked more like a working uniform with soot and grease on them.

SEVEN

Agazzi, Keyland, Taylor, and Smith stood on the top deck of the *Algol* watching the eight Fast Sealift Ships maneuver into position. Agazzi smiled. The tests on the *Bellatrix* had gone off without a hitch. All they needed now was to connect the UUV compartment with the ASW control center on the *Algol*.

"I'm here," Bernardo said loudly as he joined the four.

A gust of wind swept over the men, bringing a smile to Agazzi's lips. A near cloudless day with a hot sun burning down with a slight breeze sufficient to mitigate the heat. Any day at sea was a good day, he thought, knowing the sailors' mantra was anything but true. North Atlantic gales; riding destroyers through long, high, slow rolling waves; riding out a hurricane by going through it. Nope, not every day was a good day to be at sea, but then the days like today overshadowed every bad day he had ever experienced in his twenty-two years. As far as he could see, in any direction, gray ships of the United States Navy rode. How could one photograph ever capture the might that stretched across the sea from horizon to horizon? Over fifteen miles of visibility in whichever direction he looked and a U.S. Navy warship or auxiliary was there. He wished every day at sea could be like this. He sighed.

"I know, Senior Chief," Keyland said from beside him. "It's boring when you don't have anything to do."

The wind shifted slightly, bringing the smell of burning fuel from the stacks of the ships off the port side of the *Algol*. The odor was just enough for Agazzi to sense it and dissipated so fast it didn't burn his eyes. The sea rode easy beneath the ships of the Sea Base convoy and though there was no land in sight, it made Agazzi think of April in Newnan, Georgia, with the trees blooming, the sun yet to reach the humidity-heat intensity of summer. Just a fine day. And here he was with his sailors rolling across the eternal Pacific with only the smell of burning fuel to remind him of the cities.

"What are they going to do with the *Denebola*?" Keyland asked.

Agazzi shrugged. "Not sure. I heard because of the damage, she'll trade places with the *Pollux*. Should know shortly," he said, pointing toward one of the huge ships separating from the convoy pattern, kicking up speed, and heading to the center of the formation. "That's *Pollux*."

"For old ships, these things can put on the speed when they want to," Taylor offered as he flicked his cigarette over the edge of the deck.

"Hey, Taylor!" Agazzi said. "If you're going to smoke then either use the butt kits around the deck or don't smoke. We're up too high to be flicking those things overboard."

"Yeah, asshole," Keyland joined in. "And get downwind from us. I don't want any of that secondhand smoke ruining my lungs."

"Okay, okay, okay," Taylor said, waving his hand at the two of them. "You don't have to be an anti-smoking Nazi for me to get it. Besides, Keyland, you remind me of my mother."

"I don't," Keyland replied. "I remind me of *my* mother."

"The Navy is going to ban smoking in its entirety, you know," Smith added. "It's a filthy habit. The Navy is going to—"

"How's the hand, Petty Officer Smith?" Agazzi interrupted.

Smith held up his bandaged hand. "Better, Senior Chief. Doc says the bandages can come off in a couple of days," he said, not looking at Agazzi.

"Yeah, you're one lucky mother, you know."

"Taylor," Smith snarled, "why don't you—"

"Eat me," Bernardo finished for him.

"Naw." Taylor shook his head. "You're not only too old, but you're the wrong sex."

Smith turned red, his face twisting angrily. "I never said that, nor would I *ever* say something as offensive as that."

"Bite me," Bernardo said to Taylor, both sailors ignoring Smith's indignation.

Smith turned and walked away, heading down the starboard side of the main deck, away from the others.

"Knock it off," Agazzi said. "Watch the show. It's something you can tell your kids when you're sitting in your rockers at some German-run assisted-living facility."

"Yeah, Taylor. 'Here *ve* asks the questions!' "

Taylor elbowed Bernardo in the ribs, nodding toward Smith. "Good riddance," Taylor said quietly.

"Man's a nutter."

"Yeah. A religious nutter, as if we don't have enough."

"You can say that again, but I thought they were forbidden from coming to sea."

"You wish," Taylor said.

"I thought we left them on shore when shoved off."

"Don't we wish."

Smith stopped near the forward forecastle. He turned, watching the *Pollux* maneuver.

"Why in the hell did he join the Navy?" Taylor asked.

"Said his father made him."

"His father! The man has to be in his early thirties."

Bernardo shook his head. "Naw. He's twenty-nine. Just looks thirty. Comes from someplace in the west—Wyoming or Utah or Montana, I think."

Master Chief Jacobs walked up. Several sailors followed about ten feet behind the number-one boatswain mate of the convoy.

"Here comes the head duck with his ducklings," Taylor said in a low voice.

Bernardo shushed him. "Don't, Mort. You want the master chief to hear you?"

Taylor shrugged. "What's he going to do? Throw me overboard?"

"This one would."

Keys and tools dangled from the key chains fastened to the boatswain mates' web belts. Jacobs's squad of boatswains mates—the last vestige of the sailors who could trace their heritage to the days of sail.

Agazzi knew each boatswain mate had a set of keys, a lone marlinespike, pliers, and a knife attached to long key chains made from line woven into fancy macramé. Jacobs demanded everyone who worked for him carry the accoutrements of their trade. Each key chain was a little different—Jacobs's deference to a little individuality. Agazzi knew it must have hurt a lot for him to give his people this little bit of individuality.

It was the macramé of the key chains that drew the admiration of others. Each was created by the owner to display their marlinespike seamanship—an all-encompassing term dealing with the art of tying knots. They were an unorganized nautical band of walking chimes, clinks, and clangs—small metal objects bouncing against each other and soft swishes of swinging bundles brushing against dungaree trousers. And all of them walked with a slight sway of arrogance. Their heads searched both ways as they followed in Jacobs's wake—much like the ducklings trailing their mother. Agazzi laughed, having overheard the exchange between Taylor and Bernardo.

"What you laughing about, Alistair?" Jacobs asked as they approached.

Agazzi's eyes turned to Jacobs. "Nothing, Master Chief," he said, a smile remaining on his face. "Just thinking to myself what a fine bunch of sailors you've got with you."

Jacobs glanced back at his boatswain mates. Six men and two women, who stopped when the master chief turned, keeping a notional ten-foot distance from him. "Of course they're a fine bunch, but I don't need a sonar-tech to tell me that." He paused. "I make them tell me that at evening quarters." Then, quieter, Jacobs said, "So watch your mouth. If they hear you say that shit, their heads will be so big there won't be a hatch large enough for those empty, swollen heads to fit through."

"Ah, fuck, Master Chief! We can hear you, you know. Why don't you say something nice about us?" one of the women piped up, her hands on a set of broad hips that were wider than her chest. Her left cheek seemed swollen and bruised.

"I just did, Petty Officer Schawzernitz."

"It's *Showdernitzel*, Master Chief! Not . . . not . . . whatever it is you keep calling me," she said, irritation showing as she shook her head and held her hand up, palm out. She turned and slapped one of the sailors near her.

"Why in the hell did you hit me?"

"You were laughing."

"I wasn't," the sailor said, rubbing his cheek.

"Well, you were thinking about it."

Jacobs turned back to Agazzi. "If they'd only send me some-one who had a name I could pronounce, I'd feel better."

"She slapped him, Jerry."

"A little physical contact between shipmates is good for bond-ing."

"But . . ."

Jacobs waved him away. "He likes it."

The two men ambled off to one side. Agazzi noticed the boatswain mates congregated to one side of the deck edge while Keyland, Bernardo, and Taylor edged closer to the aft forecastle. Smith was the only one of the sailors who remained where he had been—alone and leaning against the safety lines, nearly a hundred feet forward.

Even in the Navy different ratings had different social stand-ings. Where you fit within those standings depended on which rating you wore on your left shoulder. Jacobs thought all ratings envied the boatswain mate rating—"*It ain't as if any rating other than us boatswain mates have any history,*" he liked to say.

Agazzi knew he could never keep up with a team of boatswain mates bent on *real* traditional Navy liberty, though he knew his friend Jacobs could. Agazzi gave up trying to out-drink, out-party, and out-smoke Jacobs years ago when they were both first class petty officers. And there was no way he and Frieda could out-argue and out-fight Jacobs and his wife, Helen. There was a book somewhere in the relationship of Jacobs and Helen, but he pitied the author who might try to write it—though he was sure it'd be a bestseller and the writer would be on *Oprah*.

"What do you think?" Agazzi asked, pointing toward the USNS *Pollux*.

"I would be surprised if our clothes are still dry by this time to-morrow. I think we're all going to find ourselves trying to swim a long way up from the dark depths of the Pacific."

"You don't know if things will work until you try them."

"Some things aren't meant to work." Jacobs pointed at the sea, motioning from left to right, encompassing all the ships in sight. "You see those Fast Sealift Ships?"

"Hard to miss."

"The United States Navy has eight of them. Those eight Fast

Sealift Ships belong to the United States Military Sealift Command. Every one of them is forty-five years old, with two of them over fifty." Jacobs pulled out a cigar, unwrapped it, and bit the end off of it. "They were built in the 1970s in Germany and Netherlands—makes them one of the few things in this world not built by China. Each one is over 946 feet long—"

"Nine hundred forty-six feet long?"

"Agazzi, why do I even try? What is it about sonar technicians that makes them want exact everythings? Christ, I could never be a sonar tech. Hidden belowdecks all day. Sneaking above decks at night. Never feeling the salt breeze on your face; never seeing the luminescence of the sea."

"Never having flying fish knock you down."

Jacobs shook his head, his lips pursed. "I pity the other ratings of the Navy." He pulled the cigar along his lips. "Well, if you want exact, the book measurements are 946 feet, one and a half inches."

"You can tell they're big."

"Big? You ask for exact. I give you exact and you say they're *big*. I give up," Jacobs replied with an exaggerated sigh. "Yeah, they're big. Each is over 105 feet at the beam. For you 'exact' types, that's 105 feet six inches wide. The reason some ride lower in the water than others has to do with what they're carrying, but each one of them has a draft of thirty-six-feet when fully loaded, and displays nearly thirty-thousand long tons when empty and over fifty-five-thousand long tons when full."

"Where you learn this shit, Jerry? And, what's a long ton?

"British measurement. A long ton is 2240 pounds. We"—he pounded his chest—"Americans use two thousand pounds to the ton. Means a Fast Sealift Ship can carry around sixty-two-thousand tons when fully loaded.

"And, as for knowing this shit; it ain't shit, Alistair. Us boatswain mates are expected to know this stuff. This is stuff that really keeps ships afloat so they can bore holes through the water and sail safely into port." He lifted the cigar and flicked on his small Bic lighter. Conversation stopped for a few seconds as Jacobs moved the lighter around the end of the cigar he was rotating round and round, the other end resting between his lips. He turned slightly to put the wind to his back.

"Hey, Slowersnitzel! What's the beam of the *Algol*?"

"One hundred five feet, six inches, and it's Showdernitzel!"

Satisfied, Jacobs turned back to Agazzi. "Did you know the USS *Abraham Lincoln*—United States Navy nuclear aircraft carrier number seventy-two—is only 1092 feet in length? That's only slightly less than 150 feet longer than any of the Fast Sealift Ships. Of course, the *Abraham Lincoln* is four and a half acres of United States territory capable of taking out most small countries in the world. Including the city of Washington, which might improve the efficiency of government."

Agazzi looked around quickly. Seeing everyone was engaged in watching the maneuvering ships, he leaned down, and in a soft voice warned, "Jerry, you're going to get yourself arrested one day, voicing things like that."

"Fuck them if they can't take a joke."

"The Patriot Act doesn't have a sense of humor."

"You know, what kind of country do we have where we can't joke, can't bitch, and have to worry about how we'll explain why we checked out certain books from the library."

Agazzi straightened. "Either way, my friend, you know there are those who would enjoy phoning in a hot-line tip for no other reason than to get a little attention."

Jacobs blew a puff of smoke that softly rolled across Agazzi's face.

"They'd never find anything on me. I don't go to the library and I don't buy books, so the FBI would have to look elsewhere."

"Internet."

"What's that?" Jacobs asked, blowing a smoke ring.

"Hey. Stand downwind from me, if you're going to do that."

"Then quit worrying about what I say. I've reached the age of cantankerousness and I intend to enjoy it."

"Well, write me letters from prison signed by all the other cantankerous Americans twiddling their fingers and smacking their lips every so often, waiting for someone to charge them or bring them to trial."

"Helen wouldn't let them keep me in prison."

"She may not have much say in it."

"Then you don't have an appreciation of her good side."

Agazzi walked behind Jacobs, taking position on the master chief's left side.

Jacobs pointed at the *Pollux*. "She's slowing."

"What happens now?"

"Well, if those mad scientists are right, once the *Pollux* steams into position, her captain will pass control of the ship to those computers in her main cargo bay. Then we watch the ballet of man against the sea become one of computers against the Pacific." Jacobs flicked a large ash over the side, watching it drift downward a few feet before the breeze wisped it along the side toward the ocean to disappear within the waves lapping against the side of the *Algol*. "My money is on the sea."

"It's pretty calm right now."

"Nothing is ever as it seems, my boy. Beneath these calm seas are raging rivers of current, springboards of tides pulling and jerking against each other, and things down there past the sunlight no one has ever seen. A calm sea is misleading. It only wins for a while until another of nature's whimsy ways takes charge of the sea. Without warning those so-called calm waters can go from the tiny licks against the hull to a bitch in heat."

Agazzi shook his head. "You sure have a way with words, Master Chief Jerry Malone Jacobs. Tell me again why you've never been convicted of harassment."

Jacobs grinned. "First, I have never harassed anyone. Second, if I did, they deserved it. And third, the English language is the best one I know for developing the fine art of expletive-deleted's."

"You only speak English."

"There! Proves my point." Jacobs nodded toward the USNS *Pollux*. "I would say the *Pollux* is doing about four knots. Just enough to be making way; just enough so she has control of the sea."

Jacobs could revert to nautical-speak as soon as the man's feet touched a pier, a dock, and most definitely a ship. "Making way" meant the ship was moving through the water. Didn't matter if the ship was barely moving or zooming along at the top speed of these Fast Sealift Ships, which Agazzi knew was over thirty knots. "Making way" was a term he seldom heard except from Jacobs, though he suspected the boatswain mates secretly fought the current Navy idea of turning officers and sailors into business executives by using nautical-speak in every aspect of their profession. He wondered fleetingly if, in the throes of passion, Jacobs would refer to making whoopee as "making way"?

"I don't like the way your mind works, you know," Jacobs said, waving the cigar at him.

"What? *Moi?*"

"Yeah, you—*moi!* I can tell when you have that expression on your face that you're up to no good. You're standing there thinking shit when you should be watching this for your own safety."

"My own safety?"

"Yeah, your own safety. The *Algol* is going to be the fifth ship to hook up to Sea Base."

On board the *Pollux* from the forward and aft forecastle, huge cylinder-shaped columns began to rise. Along with the deployment of the columns, three ramps emerged from the starboard side of the *Pollux*. Though he couldn't see them, he knew three identical ramps were extending on the port side of the ship.

It took nearly an hour for the columns to reach their maximum height. When they did, they towered over the masts. Agazzi estimated the thick columns were a good thirty feet higher than the navigation light at the top of the main mast on the *Pollux*. For the next twenty minutes, the two men stood silent, watching, waiting for the next event in the stand-up of Sea Base.

"Amazing, ain't it. Once those ramps connect all the Fast Sealift Ships, their cranes will start the hard work—lifting the top of Sea Base. Sea Base is supposed to fit across the top of those columns," Jacobs continued, using his cigar as a pointer. "Long tentacles of carbonized steel will emerge from each of the columns, fitting underneath the airborne causeways to hold it in place." He shook his head. "From a ship to a floating spider web just because some chief of Naval Operations decided to read a business book and some chief scientist—whose exposure to the ocean is probably limited to the *National Geographic* channel— came up with this Darwinian idea. It would've been safer for us sailors and kept our Navy from—" Jacobs took a puff on the cigar. "Yeah, you're right, Alistair. Some day those men in black suits are going to bust my door down and haul me away for being so pessimistic."

The sound of metal grinding against metal rode the air from somewhere within the convoy.

"What was that?"

"That was man's way of challenging the sea. The dark Pacific is going to wonder what the hell type of contraption she is when Sea Base hits bottom. You and I won't be around for the underwater pictures when *National Geographic* publishes them, but at least the chief scientist can see what happened."

Another ship approached on the port side of the *Pollux*.

Agazzi wished it were the starboard side so he could see the lash-up. The concept of this floating island had the eight Fast Sealift Ships joined by a series of ramps and by steel mesh overhead; braced by columns on each of the ships would be a series of steady but slightly flexible causeways. Those causeways were the top part of Sea Base. This top part was where the weapon systems would be deployed and the place where aircraft could land and launch.

Causeways normally referred to sections of floating piers linked together on the surface of the ocean, slightly off shore, or even connected from the ship to the shore. Causeways were like floating bridges. World War II, Desert Storm, and Operation Iraqi Freedom would have been lost without causeways to allow transport ships to offload their cargo. Causeways let soldiers and Marines drive tanks, armored personnel carriers, and anything with wheels directly from the ship to the beach. During Desert Storm, troops waiting to go ashore climbed aboard transports as drivers left the ship, driving fully loaded trucks directly to the front.

Though each Fast Sealift Ship carried portable causeways, the floating causeways were useless for Sea Base. They weighed too much, had no flexibility, and would come tumbling down at the first sign of sea state. It took a new metal for Sea Base. Office of Naval Research scientists had come up with the idea of using a molecularly-combined carbonized steel–aluminum web construct that was light enough to be supported by the eight ships, but strong enough to support the aircraft and weapon systems envisioned on top of her.

"Alistair, I'm as much for working with the other services as the rest of the Navy, but there's something about having Air Force squadrons riding Sea Base that just bites my ass."

Agazzi nodded. "I don't think they care what we think, Jerry."

"At least the Air Force will put in a golf course."

"You don't play golf."

"No, but I drink, and if they put in a golf course, they'll have to put in a nineteenth hole, and for that hole I am always par."

"Sea Base is going to be one phenomenal example of American ingenuity and technology."

"If she works," Jacobs added.

Agazzi nodded. "If she works." His thoughts turned to the concept of Sea Base, recalling the words of the professor back in

Pearl Harbor, mentally reconstructing the drawings displayed on the screen.

Once Sea Base was fully deployed, it would be over eighty-one-acres of American territory floating in international waters. Capable of going anywhere and setting up operations even while en route. Agazzi doubted it would go anywhere fast. Even with computers controlling and synchronizing every ship movement, there were still the ever-changing sea anchors the ONR had developed. How do you move ships through the sea when they were designed to operate independently, not as a unit? His eyebrows furrowed.

"It will be phenomenal, as you say. For me, it shows that in Washington, someone, somewhere just didn't have enough real work to do. Man's ocean follies feed the deep."

Agazzi sighed. "Good thing I've got you to keep a cheerful eye on this."

"Ain't nothing cheerful about this."

"What are you and your boatswain mates doing over here?"

Jacobs winked. "Well, I've got teams on every ship; just thought that my old friend Alistair Agazzi could use some pep talk from his dear shipmate, Jerry Jacobs. At a time like this, people like you need to hear the truth from people like me who know it. That way, you'll feel better."

"I think I felt better when I wasn't worried I was going to be fish food in the dark Pacific."

"It's only dark past the first mile down."

"See. I feel better already."

Jacobs jerked his head down in a single nod. "See. I told you, you needed me. Now you'll be able to sleep better tonight."

"It'll be hard, wearing a life vest."

The sound of metal meeting metal rode the air within the formation. The two men looked toward the *Pollux*.

"That's the *Regulus* linking up to her, ramp to ramp. My boatswain mates are probably already inside the new passageways, checking the locks, the flexible rubber fittings, and the breakaway guards."

"What are the rubber fittings for?"

"Well, I call them rubber fittings. About every thirty feet inside those ramps . . . I know, I know," Jacobs said. "You want the exact distance between each one. This time, you're lucky. The distance is exactly thirty feet. Each ramp is one hundred feet long. Once connected, you've got a two hundred-foot-long ramp. The rubber fittings run completely around and through the ramp." He waved his cigar in a circle. "This gives the connected extensions some give and take with the changes in the sea."

"So plans are made for us to break away, if things go bad."

Jacobs frowned. "Don't bet your life on it." His eyebrows went up. "Sorry, we are betting our lives on it." He shook his head, took a puff on his second cigar. "Alistair, if those ramps fail and break away, what do you think is going to be happening to those airborne causeways riding on top of these eight ships?" He paused for a moment, then in a quiet, solemn voice continued. "They are going to come falling down. They're going to fall on the ships. They're going to fall on the ramps. And they're going to fall on us. Many will die. Some may live. But when it is over . . . there will only be the surface of the Pacific masking the race of metal and flesh zooming toward the bottom."

Agazzi took a deep breath. "Jerry, I want to thank you for deciding to spend this time with me. I don't know what I would have done without your reassurances."

"Maybe I needed some," Jacobs said, not looking at Agazzi. "I do have a bad feeling about this. I've had them before."

"I know. Every time we go to sea."

Jacobs turned, grinning. "And every time when I have to break the news to Helen that I'm leaving."

Agazzi laughed. "You've never broken the news to Helen about leaving. Someone else has always had to do your dirty work."

"I'll make it up to her. I'm told that on board Sea Base the contractor who owns and operates the maritime sealift ships has made arrangements to have a mini shopping mall. I'll find something in there that she'll like. She's collecting purses now."

"How many collections does she have?"

"Collections are hard to define. When Helen has three or more things of a kind, she calls it a collection."

"Well, good luck. I don't know why she's stayed with you this long."

"I don't, either," Jacobs said wistfully.

They turned their attention to the two ships. The two men had failed to notice that every ship in the formation had slowed to the minimum speed needed to maintain their position. Another ship made its approach, this time to the starboard side of *Pollux*.

""'That's the USNS *Capella*. Means we'll get to see it this time," Agazzi said.

"That may be good because you're going to get to experience it after two more ships."

The second cigar and an hour later the three ships were linked. The distance from the port side of the *Regulus* to the starboard side of the *Capella* was slightly over seven hundred-feet—four hundred-feet of extended ramps and three ships, each 105 feet wide. From the bow and sterns of the three ships, single ramps emerged. Agazzi wondered what would happen if the bow of the three ships hit waves at this time, but watching the hundred-foot ramps emerge captured his attention and he forgot for a time the warnings of his "good buddy" Jerry Jacobs. Jacobs stood silently watching the unfolding of Sea Base.

"Where will we be?" Agazzi asked.

"You mean the *Algol*?"

Agazzi nodded.

"You should be astern the *Capella*."

"And, *Bellatrix*?"

"The USNS *Bellatrix* is supposed to be outboard-port side of *Antares*. . . . Now, listen, if you're going to be asking me these questions, you know the next thing you'll want is for me to draw you a diagram, and I'm not doing it. I came up here to enjoy my cigars, watch the birth of a major disaster at sea, and give you some encouragement."

Jacobs unwrapped another cigar.

"Wow! I am one lucky shipmate," Agazzi replied, and then added, "Well, you've enjoyed two, and that makes three. Don't you think three cigars are a little too many, my friend?"

Jacobs waved his cigar, ashes falling off the end. "Yes, three are too many, but I'd better enjoy them while I can. And, yes, you are one lucky shipmate. Don't forget—I don't charge you anything for being your bestest friend."

"I doubt I could afford the cost, if you did."

"Damn straight."

Behind the center ship, the *Pollux*, another Fast Sealift Ship approached.

"That's the *Antares*," Jacobs said.

"The *Bellatrix* will steady up on the port side of *Antares*. You're going to be on the starboard side."

Agazzi thought about the distance between the Anti-

Submarine Warfare Center on board *Algol* and the UUVs compartment aboard the *Bellatrix*, which was going to be two ships away. If he had to go from *Algol* to *Bellatrix*, he was going to have to walk up six decks; walk across open ocean inside a two hundred-foot-long ramp to the *Antares*. Another 105 feet across her main deck; then, another two hundred-foot-long extended ramp to the *Bellatrix* before walking down six decks to the UUV compartment. Shit! He might as well pack a lunch and carry an overnight case. He shook his head.

"I know. I feel the same way," Jacobs said, shaking his head. "It ain't gonna work."

The tableau in front of them drifted to their right. The USNS *Algol* was turning. Agazzi knew they were maneuvering for their connection to this floating Sea Base concept, and the confidence he had in this idea hours earlier was dented by the leading boatswain mate on this voyage. The very person who had more practical nautical sense than anyone embarked in this convoy, including the airdale admiral on USS *Boxer*, who was figuratively in charge of this modern day Aesop's fable.

The sun had set by the time the eight Fast Sealift Ships were tethered to each other. The critical part would be the next three days as cranes hoisted into place the parts that constituted the top half of Sea Base. Once connected and secured, the United States would have a floating piece of territory capable of reaching anywhere in the world. The United States would be announcing its return to the Asian theater in a dramatic way—a theater from which American forces had packed up and left over six years ago.

ZEICHNER patted his stomach. He was proud of himself. He had eaten a small bowl of oatmeal for breakfast, passed up hamburgers and hotdogs at lunch for a small salad, and in about thirty minutes he was going to reward himself with a great big dinner. This first day of his diet was going well. He looked down at his beltline. Still couldn't see his belt, but he felt skinnier.

The ramp leading from the bow of the *Denebola* to the stern of the *Antares* had taken time to connect. The *Denebola* ramp would only open about two-thirds of its one hundred-foot length. This meant the *Denebola* was only 175 feet from the stern of the ship in front of it. Zeichner didn't realize how huge these ships were until he discovered how close the *Denebola* seemed to the

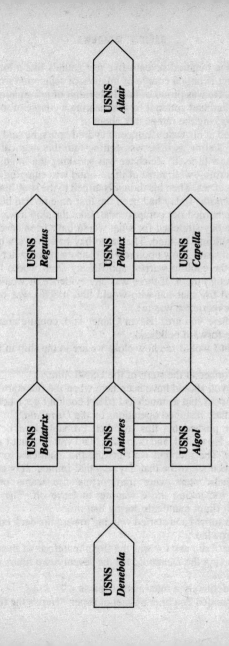

Figure 1. The Sea Base foundation.

USNS *Altair*

USNS *Regulus*

USNS *Pollux*

USNS *Capella*

USNS *Bellatrix*

USNS *Antares*

USNS *Algol*

USNS *Denebola*

Antares. One hundred seventy-five feet sounds like a lot, but at sea, 175 feet is only a couple of minutes of separation to a collision at sea. He was proud of that little tidbit of information, even though he had had gotten it by overhearing a couple of merchant marines working the ramps talk about it.

He looked at his watch. nineteen hundred hours, he said to himself, really feeling as if he was getting into this nautical role in which he saw himself. Zeichner was speaking the lingo, understood the terms—well, most of them—and was enjoying the fact that he was at sea. Then his thoughts turned to the soot-black hole in the *Denebola*. Today had been the first time he had been able to enter the burned-out compartment. Like the ship it was in, the main cargo bay stretched for what would have been several stories of a building on land. The cargo bay had over six hundred feet of open space. Row upon row of blackened computer servers sat silent, the cabling warped and flaking from where fire had burned through them. If there was any evidence, it would be an experienced fire marshal who would find it. This was one area where *his* experience was nil.

"Boss, there you are," Kevin Gainer said, coming around the edge of the forward bulkhead.

"Thought I would see how close we are to the ship in front of us."

Gainer looked at the stern of the USNS *Antares*.

"Kevin, you should have been here when the fire started."

"I know boss, but as much as I tried I couldn't get a helicopter back until they resumed operations on the *Denebola*."

Zeichner pushed his lips together. Probably best he hadn't been there. He sighed, and then said, "Did you do what I asked?"

"Yes, sir. The problem isn't getting the manifests for movement between ships for that day; it's that immediately after the fire, the helicopters were transporting fire teams onto the *Denebola* and taking those wanting to leave off. They didn't bother with flight manifests during that time."

Zeichner turned and started walking toward the deck edge. His stomach growled.

"So, what I did ask for was the flight manifests of those coming and leaving the *Denebola* for the seventy-two hours prior to the explosion."

"It was definitely a man-made explosion."

Gainer handed Zeichner a sheet of paper. "Here's the fire marshal's draft for his report. I talked with him. He's back on board the *Boxer*, but if you read this . . ." •

"Can't read it out here; too dark."

"I know, sir," Gainer said, his voice showing no reaction to Zeichner's sarcasm.

Why am I doing this? Zeichner asked himself. The man was doing his job and here he was acting like a spoiled two-year-old who had to share a toy with a new playmate. *Get your act together, Zeichner,* he told himself. *You keep doing this to Gainer and you're going to discover one day the man doesn't share anything with you because you're an asshole.*

"Sorry about that," Zeichner said as he opened the hatch.

"Sorry about what?"

"Oh, nothing, Kevin. It's been a long day and I'm kind of snappy."

Gainer pulled the hatch shut behind them. When he turned around, the former soldier had a big grin on his face. "Mr. Zeichner, I've been ignored, insulted, shouted at, and cursed by the best the United States Army has to offer. If you think you're cranky, then you haven't been around soldiers much."

Zeichner grinned. "So, what did you find out?" he asked as they turned and started down the ladder. The galley was aft, but he wanted to walk through the burned cargo bay on the way.

"I haven't found out anything, sir, but I do have the manifests—except for the one from the air crew on board USNS *Regulus*. They'll get us copies by tomorrow."

Zeichner stepped over a knee-knocker, grinned at knowing that was the nautical term for those metal portions of the deck that curved up where hatches would normally be. Knee-knockers also identified where separate portions of the ship joined. They were called knee-knockers because if you didn't step over them, you could bump your knee, though Zeichner didn't see how. Most were only ankle high.

"What I wanted to do was to start going through the manifest to see who arrived on and who left the *Denebola* during the past seventy-two hours. We're going to compare their names with the security run you did the other day. If any of them match, then we can start following up on why they were on the *Denebola*."

Zeichner opened the hatch leading into the main cargo bay.

"Good job, Kevin. But get some sleep. Tomorrow, we're going to walk across to the *Pollux* and see how the main cargo bay is configured. It should have the same layout as *Denebola* before the fire. When the fire marshal determines where the explosive device or devices were planted, it may give us an idea of why the perp planted the devices where he or she did. Bring a camera."

Zeichner took a couple of steps into the main cargo bay. The huge overhead hatch to the main cargo bay had been removed to increase the circulation of air. The blackened space seemed to meld with the stars above, making it seem almost as if they were walking through air. Across the bay, a faint light from a single bulb gave them direction. Tomorrow, portable lights were to be rigged around the main cargo hold. For now, only faint starlight coming through the open hatch and two single bulbs jerry-rigged over the hatch where he stood and the far one at the other end provided any light.

A member of the *Denebola* merchant crew sat in a folding chair, a fire extinguisher leaning against the starboard bulkhead as he watched for any signs of a reflash. The fire marshal told him yesterday that most likely anything burnable had already burned and the chances for a fire to spontaneously combust were practically nil. Zeichner had learned that sailors always viewed fire as their worst enemy and they treated it with respect. He could understand why, days later, Captain Boxford wasn't going to take chances.

Zeichner and Gainer exchanged greetings with the merchant sailor as they passed. When the hatch shut behind them and the two were in the aft forecastle of the ship, the smell of dinner whiffed through the passageway, stealing the odor of burned wiring and paint from their nostrils.

"Guess I'll have dinner now," Zeichner said, expecting Gainer to join him.

Gainer pointed down a nearby ladder. "Then I'll be going back to our offices and get busy on the manifests. I have a copy of the fire marshal report, so you can keep that one, sir."

"You're not going to eat, Kevin?"

Gainer shook his head. "I've done nothing but eat all day, boss. Besides, I want to finish these manifests before tomorrow."

"Don't overdo it." He tapped his head. "This is what we use to do our job. It needs a lot of rest."

"I'll make sure I get enough sleep, but I need to do this so we can determine our next step, Mr. Zeichner."

Zeichner watched the young man turn, grab the railings of the ladder leading down, and quickly disappear.

Zeichner took a deep breath. Roast beef, mashed potatoes, biscuits . . . his sense of smell never failed. He wondered whether it was apple pie a la mode tonight or pecan pie with whipped cream. He grabbed the doorknob leading into the galley. Zeichner thought he was going to drown as saliva filled his mouth. This dieting was harder than it looked, and this was only his first day. It should get easier now that he had begun. His body trembled with anticipation. Food was the nearest thing to a sexual orgasm, and right now he would have batted any woman out of his way to get to the food calling to him . . . waiting for him . . . begging him to hurry. What size plates would they have?

EIGHT

"Where have you been?" Agazzi asked Smith.

Smith shut the hatch behind him. "Went to the head, Senior Chief," he replied, shrugging his shoulders. He continued as he walked toward his console, "But popped up on deck for a minute to see how far along they are lifting the outer pieces of Sea Base." He walked past Agazzi's desk, down the few steps to the console area of the ASW operations center, and slid into his seat in front of the SQR-25 console: The latest anti-submarine sonar. "Amazing."

"What's amazing?" Taylor asked from the maintenance desk.

"Amazing the Lord—"

"Amazing the Lord don't make the fucking thing fall down and kill every soul on board," Bernardo interrupted, grinning and staring at Smith. "Ain't it Smitty."

"You are going to hell, you know," Smith said, his voice low. "You and every—"

"Cut the shit!" Petty Officer Keyland said.

Smith spun around in his chair, his face a mask of anger. The man's hands gripped the arms of the chair, tightly for a few seconds, then Smith's face as well as the muscles in his arms visibly relaxed. "Sure thing, Petty Officer Keyland," he said, turning back to the console.

Keyland leaned down so only Smith could hear him, "Smith, glad you came to your senses, but don't you ever look at me like that again. This isn't a cruise ship. It's a fu— It's a United States Navy warship." He pointed around the room. "Every person here, including you, is going to be cramped together for six months," he added, his voice rising slightly.

Taylor and Bernardo exchanged winks.

"Yeah, a warship shaped like a Chinese game board," Bernardo offered.

"You, too, Bernardo," Keyland said, straightening. "Every one of you is going to have to get along, work together, and function as a team. If someone doesn't like the kidding, then stop it. Does everyone understand?"

"We understand, Petty Officer Keyland, but does—" Bernardo said.

"Stop! You all heard me. Now do it."

Agazzi waited about ten minutes and then called, "Keyland!"

When Keyland looked from the far side of the Anti-Submarine Warfare operations center, Agazzi motioned him to his desk near the hatch, away from the proximity of the others. What was he going to do? Before they cut his division in half, he had one smooth group of sailors. Now it seemed the longer they stayed out, the more they grew apart.

He opened his drawer and withdrew the division officer file on Smith, reading the name *Charles Alonzo Smith* followed by the man's service number. He opened it to the counseling section. He glanced down the personal data page on the other side of the opened notebook, noticing an error on it. Agazzi picked up a mechanical pencil and made a tick mark beside the race category. Smith was Caucasian, not Afro-American as this indicated. Things such as this happened.

Back to the counseling page, Agazzi read the two transgressions by Smith since the convoy had departed Pearl Harbor. He was late for muster the day they sailed; he had walked through the main cargo bay of the *Denebola* after Agazzi had told everyone to avoid it; and now the sailor had disappeared for nearly an hour while they were in the middle of activating the Anti-Submarine Warfare operations center. Lots of things you overlook when people perform their job well or are working hard to "square away" as they say in the Navy. Some things people tried to overlook. If you weren't the top operator, but were trying, or you had myriad personality quirks, but kept them to yourself, sailors were known to overlook those things. But you had to be able to depend on your fellow sailor to be in the right place at the right time for the right reason.

"Ankle-biter," Agazzi said to himself. Ankle-biters were those little disruptions and small crises that seldom did more than slow down routine.

Smith was an ankle-biter right now, but his small irritants were disrupting routine. More than that, it was contributing to low division morale. Christ! He hated ankle-biters. If you didn't take care of them, they had a habit of growing into full-blown body blows.

"Yes, Senior Chief," Keyland said upon reaching the desk.

"Look here, Petty Officer Keyland," Agazzi said in a low voice.

Keyland shut his eyes for a moment. When the senior chief started a sentence with "look here," Keyland knew it was going to be a one-way conversation.

"I believe you're allowing your sailors to get a little lax in the area of timeliness. We're not a bunch of boatswain mates and we sure as hell aren't wannabe business leaders. You need to take a tight turn on Smith—and the others—so he understands the meaning of the words *reliable* and *dependable*. For the others, tell them to knock off the shit they're putting on the man. Okay?"

Keyland's eyes narrowed. Agazzi knew his orders offended the leading petty officer's sense of professionalism and impinged on the shorter man's leadership. "You want me to put him on report?" he asked with a deep sigh. "Boss, I'll do it, but we got so much to do—"

"Petty Officer Keyland," Agazzi interrupted. "I'm not telling you to put anyone on report. I never will. That's a leadership decision. If I believe someone needs to see the 'old man,' then *I'll* put him on report." Agazzi knew Keyland would never wait until Agazzi had to put someone on report. He'd do it first.

He sighed.

Keyland sighed also.

Agazzi cocked his head at Keyland. "You mocking me?"

Keyland put his outstretched hand on his chest. *"Moi!"* he exaggerated. "Senior Chief, I would never do that."

Agazzi waved him away. "Take care of Smith and take some tight turns on our team, Keyland. I don't want a dysfunctional bunch of sailors more intent on stacking shit on each other than protecting Sea Base."

A few seconds of silence passed and Keyland dropped his eyes. "I'll take care of it, boss," he said. "Smith knows better. He's old enough and been around the block a few times."

They both looked at Smith.

It never hurt to every now and again to remind everyone they were part of a fighting team. Different methods produced similar results. Sometimes cajoling worked; sometimes humor yielded the same results; but a little show of displeasure most times worked quicker and more effectively. This was one of those times in Agazzi's self-taught lessons of leadership. Some would argue that being an hour late was not a big thing. But even a second could be the difference between life and death in a combat situation.

Agazzi ran his hand across his chin, feeling the slight growth of stubble, but then it had been over eight hours since he shaved.

He loved being a senior chief. He'd love being a master chief even more. Right now though, he hated the responsibilities shoved on him even though everyone in the Navy that knew the higher you went on the rank ladder, the more important your responsibilities became. He also knew the higher you went on that ladder, the more your butt was exposed.

Agazzi knew, as everyone else did, that this trip was supposed to be only to test new concepts and technology in an at-sea environment. At the classified level, it was to show the world that America could be a presence anywhere in the world whenever it chose.

Sea Base was an opportunity to meet both objectives. Even the Army had players coming aboard later to show the versatility of Sea Base as a staging point for special forces. Agazzi turned his chair so he could see the array of consoles across the compartment. He crossed his arms as his eyes swept the bank of consoles. Regardless of why they were at sea, they were still warfighters. They may lack the broadswords of the nineteenth century, but his sailors wielded enough firepower under Agazzi's control to clear thousands of square miles of ocean surface and subsurface. With such great destruction capability came an even greater need for appreciating their responsibilities. A professional team must be professional at all times. And right now, he wasn't happy with what he was seeing.

Smith sat at the SQR-25 console, going through the diagnostics of the passive sonar. The man was unhappy about being assigned the passive sonar watch. His argument had been that as the manual operator for the UUVs in the UUV compartment, he should be the remote operator here. Keyland had finally brought the argument to Agazzi, who refused to change the watch assignments. Launching weapons meant he had to have someone he had confidence in on the console. Smith was an enigma. He was older than his fellow petty officers, with the exception of Keyland. Agazzi respected everyone's right to worship their God as they saw fit, but it worried him when God started talking to his sailors.

Smith had worked the manual console the other day when they loaded the UUVs into the firing cradle. Smith failed to appreciate that any member of the ASW team could operate the manual console. For the remote operation, Agazzi wanted his best information technician on the console. He shook his head slightly and smiled.

His best information technician was also the bane of liberty hounds, Pope Bernardo. If he wasn't being brought back by the shore patrol, a woman was bringing him back. In every port it was the same. First day the booze and the second day the sex. Decades ago, he'd be a chief by now. And he'd have his priorities reversed. In today's Navy, he was lucky to still be in uniform.

Agazzi looked at the back of the man from New Jersey. Bernardo was bent over the opened diagnostics book. Pope Bernardo came from one of the small cities along the coast. Dark black hair with a natural sheen accented by brown eyes. A mustache, like his hair, always pushing the perimeter of Navy regulations. Agazzi recalled the man had worked his way up through his junior year in college as a city trash collector.

Keyland had told him the story. Bernardo would have graduated if it weren't for an unfortunate day when the trash truck clipped a small dog. Thinking the dog dead, Bernardo picked it up and tossed it unceremoniously into the back of the trash truck about the same time the elderly lady in a bathrobe ran out shouting at them for killing her dog. It was at the same time Bernardo pushed the lever that activated the crusher. The other men were apologizing and trying to calm the lady. From the inside of the truck, a small bark erupted only to be abruptly cut off in the middle of the second bark.

Bernardo joined the Navy the following day when he learned the woman was the mother of the chief of police. Bernardo's stories kept even the chief's mess abuzz. Bernardo was good at computer games. No one could beat the sailor once he had learned the rudimentary rules of the game. He was a natural information technician, plus while Smith spent his time God knows where, Bernardo was taking college courses via the Internet and on board the ship. He was intent on completing his college degree. He may only be twenty-four, thought Agazzi, but the man was well on his way to obtaining a commission—if he could keep his dick in his pants. Allowing the little head to think for the big head had cost many a promising leader his career.

As Agazzi watched, Bernardo looked up from the book he was reading, pressed several icons, and the screen filled with code. Bernardo was running functional diagnostics. The petty officer had already reported the ASW Center console was up and fully operating. Agazzi couldn't see over the man's broad shoulders, but he knew the next step involved checking the flow of information on the optical coaxial cables running between the *Algol* and the *Bellatrix*. These cables passed through the *Antares*. If there was any chance of a malfunction in this dispersed ASW concept, it would be in the cables. Regardless of how much these scientists depended on their computers to keep Sea Base steady and immovable, those who had spent their lives at sea knew the folly of such thought.

The *Algol*, *Antares*, and *Bellatrix* would have different motions from the ocean impacting their stability. Agazzi knew even the minute motions on the three ships would be stretching, pulling, and pushing the cables in many different directions at once. The reliability and availability promised by the manufacturer had better live up to expectation or they were going to find themselves having to work remote via sound-powered telephone. That is . . . if they ever got the sound-powered telephone systems up and running across the eighty-one-plus acres of American territory called Sea Base.

KIANG reached up and clamped the small box onto one of the security video lines running along the overhead of the passageways of the USNS *Bellatrix*. He pushed the new ball cap down off his eyes. He'd pick up the box when he returned.

He continued down the ladders, heading toward the lowest level of the *Bellatrix*. Once at the bottom, he glanced up, confirming the red light on the video camera was off. A few steps and he stood in front of the UUV compartment. Kiang reached up, pushed the top part of the hatch, and heard the faint suction as the airtight seal loosened. While in port, he had jimmied the hatch so he could open it without biometrics. His handler had given him a crash course on how to defeat biometrics and obtain the four-digit combination for the door. Kiang was a scientist. Anything high tech left signatures and pointing fingers. Old watertight hatches on old ships always needed maintenance. It had been risky, but he had fixed the hatch so it never fully closed.

Kiang glanced both ways up and down the passageway, seeing no one; he slipped the long blade from his pants leg, slipped it through the door, and hit the electric contacts. The hatch slid open. He only had a few minutes, but a few minutes were all he needed.

AGAZZI'S attention wandered back to Smith. The man was working through the checklist displayed on the left of the SQR-25. A digital rainfall worked its way down the SQR-25 thirty-six-inch high-definition display. Passive sonar rainfall displays played the primary role in identifying threat submarines and surface ships. They mapped the noises of the ocean environment, revealing all that sailed on top of or beneath the waves. The SQR-25 rainfall was even now turning the sounds of the ocean into a series of digital bits inching down the screen. Those sounds would be refined as more sensors entered the water. The ocean was like a thick atmosphere capable of transmitting sounds for hundreds of miles. Interpreting those sounds was the work of the sonar technicians in the Navy.

Unlike the black and gray screen of the older models, the SQR-25 was a cascade of different colors accenting the sounds from the ocean. A bank of five servers lined the forward bulkhead of the compartment.

"Got a problem here, Mort," Bernardo said. "Can you check the server connector?"

Taylor tossed his screwdriver onto the maintenance table. "Yeah, if I have to, I have to."

"I think that's all it is."

"Senior Chief," Taylor said. "Whoever designed this layout ought to have their heads examined. There's barely enough room to squeeze by between the servers along the bulkhead and the consoles here, much less for me to contort myself around so I can do any real work."

Agazzi nodded. Engineers designed systems to work; the idea that one of their systems might fail or need maintenance was a foreign concept to most. "It's something we'll try to have them correct next time."

"But, right now, Mort, I need someone to check the server connections."

"I heard you, Pope."

Taylor, the maintenance man, hated the arrangement. To get to the servers, he was forced to squeeze his muscular frame between a narrow space at the end of the row of consoles and the port bulkhead. Taylor never did anything happily, but the "squeeze" would start a nonstop row of bitching and moaning about stupid engineers who never had to work on anything they designed. Working with three feet of space between the back of the operator consoles and the servers created its own dynamics. Taylor would lie on the deck, twisting onto his side to punch codes, run diagnostics, and check connections.

Taylor walked to the end of the consoles and disappeared around the edges. Agazzi could hear the grunting and mumbling coming from Taylor as the man wormed his way along the back of the consoles toward the one that served Bernardo's UUV console.

Stamped across top of both the operator consoles and the server racks were the words TOP SECRET in bright red letters. The same words were also across the bottom of the racks. Within those classified servers resided the Office of Naval Intelligence database of underwater sounds.

"You there yet, Mort?"

"When I'm there, I'll tell you," came a sharp reply.

"Thanks."

"I'm there."

On Smith's console, the rainfall display of underway sounds inched down the display. He sat one seat to the left of Bernardo.

The security console with the television cameras and detection lights was located beside the Taylor's maintenance console. Taylor was both the maintenance person as well as the security person. A red light over the UUV hatch came on, telling whoever saw it that the hatch to the compartment on the *Bellatrix* was open.

Agazzi enjoyed watching the passive sonar display. The new varied colors highlighting the various sounds that rode the ocean helped the operator in his rainfall analysis.

Varying shades of green highlighted surface ships to help the operator differentiate between screws, own-ship noise, and contact machinery noises. Miles away from a contact, the SQR-25 could tell you the number of screws on a ship, whether it was coming toward you or sailing away, and provide design characteristics of the target. It would give the operator a continuous update of a contact's course and speed, refining it as more data was collected. A brilliant blinking red alerted everyone to the presence of a submarine. If the operator failed to manually stop the blinking in thirty seconds, the speakers would emit an alarm. No one wanted to hear the alarm. The color blue identified friendly submarines. Submariners refused to believe the SQR-25 would ever show the color blue.

Pale gold highlighted ambient noise, which included everything from sea state to sea life. If the ambient noise level was too high, the operator could tune it out so no ambient noise was reflected.

From his console, Smith could integrate signals from huge sonar arrays waiting to be lowered from the ships *Altair*, *Regulus*, and *Capella*. These sonar arrays dropped beneath Sea Base to depths ranging from several hundred feet to several thousand. These arrays provided the noise input from sound trapped beneath what ASW'ers called the layer. The layer was where warmer temperatures of the upper ocean collided with the cooler temperatures from the bottom. This layer was never constant, always changing, depending on the collision of temperatures convoluted by currents, winds, and salinity. Submarines preferred to sail beneath the layer so sounds would bounce off the layer above them and ricochet down to become lost in the vast depths of the Pacific. Sometimes there was more than one layer and when that happened, sound trapped between the two layers would oscillate outward—sometimes for hundreds of miles. When this happened, ASW-ers called it the convergence zone.

"There, Mort! There!"

"What the hell is a 'there'?"

"Whatever you did cleared the console."

A few seconds passed and Bernardo's console blinked a couple of times and then steadied.

"Stop! Whatever you did cleared it up, Mort."

More mumbling and cursing tracked the maintenance man to the edge of the consoles where he appeared, shaking his hand. "Senior Chief, those f'ing engineers are going to have to redo this arrangement. I can't get any room back there to work on things."

KIANG stepped into the UUV compartment, glancing at the camera mounted near the door. No lights showed on the camera. He spotted the small camera on the computer suite near the UUV firing cradle. Kiang eased the hatch shut. In the ASW operations center, the UUV hatch status light turned to green.

Kiang raised his camera and began photographing, checking the digital images for the first three, then continuing without further checks. He moved quickly along the bank of UUVs stored along the bulkhead, careful to stay out of the viewing area of the camera on the computer. That camera had not been on the schematics he had obtained from the Office of Naval Research. At the end of the row, Kiang stood behind a huge hydraulic lift to photograph the UUV firing cradle. Several minutes passed before he checked his watch. Taking a chance, he leaned forward and photographed the computer with the camera.

"WHAT'S wrong with the hand?" Keyland asked Taylor as the man stood at the end of the consoles.

"He stepped on it," Bernardo offered.

"*Fun-ny*. I sprained it unscrewing and resetting the connectors." He shook it. "Ain't bad, just a little sore. It'll be all right."

"Which one was it?" Bernardo asked.

"It was this one," Taylor said, holding up his hand.

"Not your hand. I don't care about your sex life. Which connector was it?"

Taylor shrugged. "Don't know. I just reconnected all of them. You got control now?" He eased over to Bernardo's console and looked at the display. "Looks okay now."

"Yeah, it's okay."

"What's this little photo in the upper left-hand corner?"

Bernardo tapped the area Taylor was referring to. "It's the picture from the camera on the computer above the UUV firing cartridge."

"I didn't know we had that," Taylor said, glancing at the security console across the compartment and seeing all the lights glowing green. "I thought we only had the video cameras for security."

"It's not for security. It's so we can have a video conference if we need one."

"Don't have enough people to have a video conference," Keyland added. "Barely have enough people to man the watch here."

"What was that?" Bernardo asked.

"What was what?" Keyland said.

"Mort, you sure you fixed the connection?"

Taylor reached around Bernardo and tapped the screen. "You see any hiccups echoing across this?"

"Well, I just had a bright flash go across my screen."

"Well, it ain't . . ." The screen brightened for a second.

"There! There it is," Bernardo said.

Taylor shook his head. "I saw it," he said quietly, walking back toward the end of the console row. "Let me reconnect them again."

KIANG walked between the lifting gear and consoles surrounding the UUV firing cradle. Near the hatch, he lifted the camera and took photographs of the overhead track system for moving the UUVs from storage to the firing cradle. Finished, he opened the hatch swiftly and closed it quickly behind him, hearing the click of the security mechanism. He reached up and checked the block, ensuring that if he had to return, the hatch would be easy to jimmy. He smiled.

TAYLOR disappeared behind the operator consoles. Muttering and cursing once again tracked his movement. The security light for the UUV compartment hatch blinked red for a second before returning to green. Agazzi was looking at where Taylor had disappeared around the edge when the UUV hatch light blinked red. He blinked a couple of times, assuring himself he saw the light change. Walking over to the security console, he tapped the light a couple of times, but it remained a steady green.

"IT'S working fine now, Mort," Bernardo said.

"I'm still going to reset the connections, Pope."

The screen blanked out for a few minutes as Taylor disconnected the cables. Then, as suddenly as it blanked out, it came back on. "How's that?"

"Looks picture perfect."

The cursing and muttering tracked Taylor as he bumped his way to the end of the small opening and reappeared.

"Petty Officer Taylor," Agazzi said. "You done diagnostics on the security console?"

"Yeah, Senior Chief," he replied, shaking the injured hand.

"I thought I saw a light go from green to red, back to green."

Taylor shrugged. "Maybe the system was resetting itself."

"Senior Chief," Keyland said. "The UUV system is back on line."

The UUVs were new technology; this would be the first opportunity Agazzi and his team would have to see how they performed in an open ocean environment. With the exception of Petty Officer Charlie Smith, who joined them a month ago, and Seaman Calvins, who tramped aboard the day they sailed, the others had been with the supersecret program for over a year. These were Agazzi's babies. They were going to change how anti-submarine warfare was done.

Agazzi walked back and sat down at his desk, his back to the consoles and the maintenance desk. He leaned forward, pulled out a pad of yellow-lined legal paper. From the inbox he lifted the message from Naval Postgraduate School that highlighted the predictive sound layers and currents of the Pacific where Sea Base was operating. He had seen fellow chiefs who could read the complex string of numbers and symbols and mentally form the sound-carrying properties of the ocean in their minds. He could, but not as quickly as drawing it on a sheet of paper. He should use the computer program, but he was old Navy and the mental skills taught when he first became a sonar technician gave him enjoyment.

Minutes later, Agazzi had a good mental picture of how sound would travel and act for the next couple of days in his part of the ocean. His lips tightened slightly as he turned in his chair to watch the men continue preparations, run diagnostics, and flip through the hardcopy pages of the user manual when needed.

They would launch the UUVs from here. Weapons located three ships away!

Once the UUVs were in the water, he was going to show the United States Navy what a bunch of enlisted ASW-ers could do. The underwater data gained here from the passive sonars beneath Sea Base and other sources would be piped to the UUVs, which would also be providing their own data return to the ASW operations center.

The remote UUV signals would become part of the integrated ocean profile. Another piece of the underwater profile—the protective undersea umbrella protecting Sea Base—would be sonobuoy barriers. SH-36 anti-submarine helicopters on board the destroyers *Gearing* and *Perry* would deploy barriers over a hundred miles from Sea Base. These barriers would be early warning devices—their detection of ocean noises would be the first part of the overall ocean seascape.

Agazzi took a deep breath. This was going to be the best encompassing profile of the ocean any sonar operator had ever seen.

A twinge of excitement caused him to smile. He was surprised at being excited over anticipating the drop of the first UUV. The first-anything in life is usually exciting.

But before he could do all this, Agazzi had to be assured the equipment functioned properly and the control of the Unmanned Underwater Vehicles worked. All the information in the world on what was within striking range of Sea Base was useless to the admiral if Agazzi couldn't launch weapons when so ordered.

Keyland walked down the three-step ladder to the lower portion of the compartment where Smith and Bernardo sat silently going through diagnostics.

Petty Officer Taylor was stooped forward on his stool, hunkered over the workbench on the far side of the compartment. The sailor was unpacking tools, setting up electronic measuring devices and the myriad of other things maintenance-types need to ensure computerized systems remained up, running, and functioning properly. Seaman Tom Calvins, a new member who joined the crew just before they sailed, stood to the left of Taylor. He'd be Taylor's gofer until the new addition to the Navy family learned the basic skills needed to man a console. A gofer was an apprentice, called that because when something was needed, this was the person to "go for" it.

The irritation with Smith passed. It was hard for Agazzi to stay angry. Anger was never monumental with him. Anger was a tool used when people needed a prod in the right direction; when an incentive to do what was expected of them was needed. In his twenty-two years as a sailor, Agazzi had taken six sailors to Captain's Mast. Six sailors before the mast. He didn't think that was too bad. Six sailors whose problems Agazzi couldn't solve himself.

The masts of sailing ships had long ago given way to gigantic metal towers reaching toward the sky, filled with radars and communications antennas. In today's Navy, a sailor going before the mast did so in a ceremony held wherever the captain of the ship wanted to have it. Most times, the captain stood behind a wooden lectern while the master-at-arms marched the accused before him. With his or her best scowl, the skipper would listen to the sailor's excuse as to why he—*the captain*—was wasting his or her time standing there in dress uniform listening to this hogwash. Then the captain would render awards to the accused. Awards in the Navy had many different meanings, and awards at Captain's Mast usually consisted of fines and extra duty. For the more egregious acts, a skipper could award confinement in the brig for thirty days and, after a doctor's evaluation, three days on bread and water. Here the Navy was into the third decade of the twenty-first century and sailors at sea could still be confined for three days with nothing more than bread and water.

No, he wasn't ready to take Smith to mast. Mast was the last recourse for an effective leader. That was his opinion. Others preferred to get the culprit before the captain at the first opportunity and then have no further problems.

Jacobs had told him that when he was a chief petty officer he served a tour as the leading chief at the Navy brig in Charleston, South Carolina. The story Jacobs found amusing, and Agazzi viewed with disbelief, had to do with Jacobs picking raisins out a loaf of bread for a sailor confined to bread and water. *"Raisins weren't allowed."* Jacobs had cackled. "And, I did it seated on a stool in front of the man's cell so he could see me doing it. It was a great summer day in the southern port of Charleston. God! I miss that duty."

It wouldn't surprise Agazzi if Jacobs carried "report chits" in his back pocket already filled out. A report chit was the term for the paperwork that moved through the system showing the legal-beagles what dereliction the sailor was charged with. It also showed where the accused *willingly* signed the papers acknowl-edging his or her rights to a court martial. When at sea, the ac-cused had no rights to a court martial. Everything was at the behest of the captain.

Smith was twenty-nine years old. With the exception of Agazzi and Keyland, Smith was the next oldest sailor on the ASW team. There were others like him. Agazzi scratched his chin. *Wonder what his story is?* Every person has a story. Some more interest-ing than others. The decline of the American economy after the excesses of the second Bush administration had been a great time for the military. The economic collapse had propelled thousands of older men into the service, even with the ever-shifting war against terrorism.

The Army and Marine Corps benefited more than the Navy and Air Force. They needed soldiers and Marines to fight on the ground in Somalia and Indonesia. With their reduced budgets, The Navy and Air Force provided the money for the two primary fighting forces to chase terrorism around the globe.

How did Smith get into the Navy? Agazzi had reviewed the man's service record when he checked on board a few months ago. Nothing spectacular. High school graduate, no family, no children, and no next of kin. From some place in Montana. Go figure! Whatever had happened to the man, there was no one waiting for him out there. Agazzi had questioned the new arrival on his goals and objectives, encouraging him to pursue an off-duty education. The Navy wanted all its enlisted to have an asso-ciates degree by the time they were first class petty officers, with chief petty officers having a bachelor's. Agazzi was nearly fin-ished with his Master's, which he figured was a checkbox for a master chief. Mentally he crossed his fingers. He'd find out by the end of this cruise if he'd made master chief.

Jacobs laughed at the idea of degrees for the enlisted and was quick to point out that he only had a high school degree. He was glad he had made master chief before academic arrogance had settled on the Navy.

Agazzi's story was that he had graduated high school, and though his parents could afford college, he wasn't interested.

Growing up, he cut grass in the neighborhood to earn spending money. A unique customer was a nearby neighbor, his front door bracketed by a red light and a green light—a retired sailor. In winter, the man wore a watch cap. Every trip to cut the man's grass was memorable. Each time the retired sailor brought some knick-knack from his navy days onto the front porch, along with the obligatory glass of lemonade made by the man's wife. As Agazzi sipped lemonade, the retired sailor relived his career. Others would have found the sea stories befuddling or boring, but Agazzi looked forward to them. The adventures the man told filled the young Agazzi with fantasies of faraway places and open seas.

He didn't recall ever giving it serious thought. One day after his eighteenth birthday he just up and walked down to the Navy recruiter, signed the papers, and walked into a family maelstrom when he proudly showed them to his parents. His mother cried. His father shouted. When he left two weeks later to go to boot camp, they had come to terms with his decision. The U.S. was at peace at the time and 9/11 was two years away. Twenty-two years later and the religious wars were still ongoing, shifting from a shaky but democratic Iraq to Indonesia and Somalia. America had its own homegrown terrorists blowing up things. This God's Army radical religious cult seemed to be untouchable by the FBI.

Raised voices broke his revelry. Keyland was leaning over Smith, his voice low enough Agazzi couldn't understand what the leading petty officer was saying. But from Keyland's hand motions and Smith's head motions, he knew the wayward sailor was receiving some direct counseling. Maybe it would get through to the older man. Maybe it was because Smith was older that they were having these challenges with him. Agazzi shivered slightly. For some reason Smith caused him more concern than he should—but why? He shook his head. There was something . . . he didn't know what . . . but he would.

Agazzi dismissed the thought. It never occurred to him to be uncomfortable taking orders from someone younger. It happened all the time. The Navy sent its young officers to sea as soon as they were commissioned. They wanted the officers to learn seamanship; not only how to handle a ship, but how to fight it. Which was one of the reasons he and other chiefs, senior chiefs and master chiefs, found themselves subordinate to young men and women whom they were tasked with training at the same time they were obligated to obey their orders.

"Senior Chief," Petty Officer Bernardo said, catching Agazzi's attention. "All systems check out." The dark-haired Romeo glanced back at his console. "Contact between here and the UUV compartment is a-okay. No anomalies on the cables. I've started the UUV checks." Bernardo glanced at the clock mounted on the starboard bulkhead behind Agazzi. "Give me about twenty minutes and we'll do the button-smashing."

"Senior Chief," Keyland added. "Smith has good readings on the passive sonar arrays."

Keyland was going to be a good chief petty officer. Chew them out first and then bring them back into the team. Agazzi uncrossed his arms and moved to the railing running along the top portion of the compartment. "Do we have good data flowing from the three dipping sonar arrays?"

Smith turned. "Only from one, Senior Chief." He looked back at his readout display. "The *Altair*, at the front of the formation has its sonar array lowered. Stats show array is at the two-hundred-foot mark. The *Altair* array is marked for eight hundred-feet, Senior Chief," Smith said.

"What do the underwater conditions look like?" Agazzi asked, already knowing the answer. He enjoyed competing against the computer.

"I've got that, Senior Chief," Bernardo said, raising his hand. "The layer is at approximately one thousand feet. Smitty should have good pickup above the layer."

Agazzi glanced down at his figures. Nine hundred eighty-four feet was the layer depth he had calculated.

Passive sonar, the choice of professionals, was designed to eavesdrop on the noises in the ocean. Water conditions determined the range in which passive sonar picked up signals.

His eyebrows bunched as he thought of those three arrays dropping beneath the keels of three ships, capable of reaching eight thousand feet; more than sufficient depth to penetrate the layer. He had approached the ONR scientists about his concern of those arrays trailing aft and wrapping about a ship's prop. ONR told him it was very unlikely. *Very unlikely* wasn't the same as *can't happen*.

The SH-36 LAMPS helicopters weren't scheduled to deploy sonobuoy barriers for another three days. Three days from now, the admiral had scheduled a test of Sea Base sensors and weapons systems to function as a whole. Until then, Agazzi had the towed arrays beneath Sea Base, and soon he would have his UUVs in the water.

The Office of Naval Intelligence also believed the Russians and Chinese might send a submarine out to look over Sea Base. The Russians may be America's ally, but America was in their backyard now. The Chinese depended on America for their economic growth. The admiral pooh-poohed the ONI report. Said it was written by a bunch of desk jockeys who had never seen a ship.

Agazzi thought the ONI report had merit, but what the hell did he know? He was just a senior chief. But if the Chinese were America's allies, then why did they have such an aggressive submarine construction program? That's what he should have said, but . . . he didn't. It's hard to disagree with an admiral, even when everyone in the room knows he or she is wrong.

Bernardo shifted his headphones over his ears for a moment and then lifted one side. "*Capella* is deploying its array." He turned, hit a couple of icons on the screen, then announced, "It's down, Senior Chief, and descending. We've got two sensors in the water. What depth you want this one?"

"I have signals from the *Capella* array," Smith added. "I recommend putting it below the layer."

Agazzi glanced at the back of Smith's head, bit his lower lip for a moment, then said, "Leave the *Altair* at eight hundred. Take the *Capella* array below the layer. Petty Officer Keyland! Initiate an underwater profile. I want to know what sounds we have out here. I want every one of us so familiar with our territory sounds and what the displays show that anything—*and I mean anything*—out of the ordinary is recognized instantly. I want our team to beat the computer in determining what we have out there."

"We can do it, Senior Chief," Smith replied.

"Of course you can do it. You're the best."

"We're the best!" shouted Seaman Calvins, turning red when no one else shouted, but everyone turned and looked at him.

"Keep it under control, dickhead," Taylor said good-naturedly. "This ain't a football rally and you ain't in high school."

"I'm running diagnostics on the UUV sonars, Senior Chief," Bernardo said. "Only the ones in the firing cradle. I can check those in the UUV storage cells if you want, Senior Chief, but I'd have to go there to do that."

A lesson-learned to be passed along to the Naval Research scientist, Doctor Malone, was that a capability to remote check the UUVs in the storage cells was needed. Having Taylor or Bernardo or one of the others go from UUV one to another, remove the nosecone, hook up test equipment, and spend a whole week checking them was a loss of valuable, limited manpower. It had to be done electronically, so checks and rechecks would take seconds and minutes; not hours, days, and weeks. Otherwise, he wouldn't know if a UUV was nonfunctioning until it was loaded. Then it would be another long process to trade it out.

"The SQR-25 is working on every one of the loaded UUVs," Smith said, his voice low but easily audible. "Request permission to test the active mode."

"No!" Agazzi shouted. He turned to Keyland. "Who do we have in the UUV compartment?"

"MacPherson and Gentron are on their way, Senior Chief. I told them to finish lunch and then check in when they reached the compartment."

KIANG passed two sailors hurrying down the ladder from the main deck as he climbed upward. He glanced at his watch. He had been inside the UUV compartment for under four minutes. Next time—if there was a next time—he'd have to cut his time to less than three minutes to ensure he had a measure of safety. He sighed. If he had stayed longer, the two sailors rushing to check the security alarm might have stumbled into him while he was inside the compartment. He lightly touched the electronic device in his pants pocket. He would need it again to disrupt the security cameras, if he had to return.

"TAYLOR, why are those cameras off?" Agazzi asked, pointing at the security console.

Taylor shrugged. "I don't know, Senior Chief. We have been having problems with them." He got up off his stool and walked over to the nearby security console. He flicked the on–off switch a couple of times and the cameras came on line. "There they are, Senior Chief. Must have been a glitch."

Agazzi walked over to the security console. Six television

screens displayed views of the UUV compartment from their cameras. He reached down and took hold of the toggle switch to camera number six mounted on the bulkhead inside the entrance to the UUV compartment. He flicked it off, then on again. The picture came back on.

"Petty Officer Taylor, when you get a chance, run a diagnostics on the security console. Can't have the cameras malfunctioning and I thought I saw the light to the hatch blink red a few minutes ago."

"Maybe Jenkins and Mertz have arrived," Bernardo said, using MacPherson and Gentron's first names.

Agazzi tapped the status light of the UUV hatch. It changed from green to red.

"Look! It's done it again."

In front of the camera, the backs of MacPherson's and Gentron's heads came into view as they entered the compartment. The light blinked back to green.

"I think that's why it blinked red, Senior Chief," Taylor said with a smile. "Though I think you tapping on the light helped."

"Cut it, Taylor," Keyland said.

FIVE minutes later, Gentron had a sound-powered telephone headset on.

"We got comms with MacPherson?" Agazzi asked. He turned to Keyland. "The sound-powered telephone system working? I thought it was still being connected?"

Keyland reached over and slapped Bernardo on the shoulder.

"Hey!"

"You got comms with MacPherson?" he asked, tapping the camera picture on Bernardo's screen.

"Yeah," Bernardo said, "But not on sound-powered telephone. Gentron's just adjusting straps and headset. The damn thing doesn't work yet."

As if hearing the comment, Agazzi saw Gentron remove the headset and set it down on the deck.

"I'm talking to MacPherson now," Bernardo confirmed. "Or, rather, he's talking to me."

"What's he using?" Agazzi added.

"He's got the telephone on speaker." Bernardo pointed down to the telephone on the ledge of his console. The handset had been removed and the enterprising sailor had patched in his headset to the base. "Works as well as sound-powered phones."

"Tell them to do a quick check of the compartment and get out. We want to test the active component of the sonar and I don't want them getting fried when we do it."

Agazzi watched MacPherson pick up the sound-powered headset, set it on top of the UUV manual control console, and say something to Gentron.

"I got them on the cam," Bernardo said, pointing to the small moving picture in the top left portion of his console screen. "The cam mounted on the computer near the manual control console also shows the firing cradle. It lets me see the UUV drop through the well deck into the ocean."

"Good, good, Bernardo," Keyland said with a sigh. "Now, just pay attention to the test."

Agazzi stood near Taylor's maintenance table, following the movements of MacPherson and Gentron as they walked toward the hatch, both looking up and waving as they passed the camera. When he saw the handle shift down, securing the hatch, Agazzi glanced at the security light. It flashed to red for a few seconds, then switched to green.

"Okay. One ping and only on one UUV."

"Senior Chief, why all this?" Keyland asked. "We've done active testing before."

"Yes, but we usually do it when the sonar is in the water. I don't know what the impact will be when we do it on a UUV hanging out in free space."

"One ping done. System secured."

And, it was over. That quick. Agazzi looked at the camera images. MacPherson and Gentron stood outside the UUV compartment in the passageway, their images on two cameras. One camera showed the passageway to the left while the other transmitted a constant picture of the passageway from the right. "Tell MacPherson he and Gentron can go back inside. Tell them to check the compartment again."

A minute later, Bernardo took off his headset. "Senior Chief, Mac is saying some wires are smoking near the manual console. It looks as if the high frequency from the active sonar did something to them."

Taylor leaned back from his workbench and slid off the stool. "I'll take it, Senior Chief." He lifted his work belt, tools dangling from it, and strapped it around his waist. "Damn, it's one thing after another. Day in and day out."

"Diagnostics show no effect on our capability to remote launch and control the UUVs," Bernardo offered.

"Might be safer if I'm over in the UUV compartment when we launch, Senior Chief. I could do it manually if it doesn't work," Smith volunteered.

"I'll go with you, Taylor," Agazzi said, ignoring Smith's offer while he mentally cursed himself for not taking into consideration what high frequencies could do. They acted like an open microwave. He needed to be thinking ahead of everything. He had done this all wrong. First, he should have told the captain of Sea Base he was going to test the active sonar. If it had been in the ocean, it would have been standard operating procedure. Second, he should have told the captain of the *Bellatrix* what he was doing. After all, it was on the man's ship. And, third, whether he had done the first two or not, he should have had a fire team standing by while they tested it. These were all lessons-learned he would capture. UUVs would require the ASW teams to rethink how they prepare to fight an underwater war. He mentally kicked himself. The good news was no one was hurt; no fire had occurred—yet. And diagnostics . . .

"Bernardo, run diagnostics again while I head over to the *Bellatrix*. Let me know how it goes."

Diagnostics was information technology at its finest. It existed in the virtual world where anything could be true. The real truth was in the things you felt and touched, like the UUV firing cradle over a closed hole that opened into the sea.

"Senior Chief, once we finish the diagnostics, you want to start the launch sequence for the UUVs, or you want me to hold until you finish your on-site inspection?"

Agazzi shook his head. "No, Keyland, let's keep running diagnostics. I don't want to do anything with the UUVs until we see if our single ping did any damage."

"How about the *Regulus* array? You want to go ahead with its deployment or hold it also?"

Agazzi thought for a moment. "No, go ahead and deploy it, but if you see any signs of trouble, cease immediately and call me."

"What depth?"

Agazzi looked at Bernardo, who exchanged glances with Keyland. Everyone knew he had screwed up. And every one of them would avoid mentioning it. It was the *way*. "Petty Officer Keyland, work with Bernardo and Smith to determine best depth and set it to that depth. We can always change it later."

"Senior Chief, can I go with you?" Smith asked. "I know the manual console and if it's not working and Taylor has to fix it, then I can help."

He looked at Smith, opened his mouth to say no, and instead said, "Okay, come along. You might be able to help." Turning to Keyland, Agazzi said, "Holler if you need Smith to come back."

"I'm hollering now," Keyland mumbled.

A moment later, Agazzi was out the hatch, rushing to keep up with Taylor and Smith as they ran up the ladders. *Damn youth*, he thought. They were out of sight by the time Agazzi reached the first deck. Still no sign of them when he turned into the enclosed passageway that stretched from the *Antares* to the *Algol*. This was only the second time he had been inside the enclosed passageways that linked the ships and held up the massive acres of Sea Base above him.

He didn't like it the first time and he didn't like it this time. The passageway was nothing more than a metal coffin stretched between two ships. It reminded him of those shaky native-built bridges seen in jungle movies strung by rope and old planks across a raging torrent of water hundreds of feet below. He knew it was nowhere near the same, but if this passageway fell into the ocean, the results would be the same. Every creak and groan echoed inside the passageway as it adjusted continuously to the minute changes between the two ships, giving Agazzi impetus to cross the chasm before it fell.

He glanced up as he hurried along, thinking of Jacobs expounding on the nightmare of the whole thing disappearing suddenly into the dark Pacific. He was running by the time he reached the *Antares*.

NINE

Zeichner stood on top of the newly raised Sea Base. The warmth of the deck beneath radiated through the thin soles of his dress shoes. Gainer moved slightly on his left, stepping into his peripheral vision. Zeichner wiped the back of his hand across his forehead. The platform stretched unbroken in every direction; the gray metal island was a myriad of activity. Sailors, engineers, and contractors moved across the top, preparing for the next phase of hoisting the operations tower and, eventually, the new-age weapons systems to defend this floating island of American territory.

"I know, boss. It's this constant sun. Then, when it sets, every particle of heat captured by this deck is released, so you sweat during the night, too. I can understand why people die so quickly if abandoned in the middle of the ocean."

"I just hope they know what they're doing." Zeichner sighed. This heat was atrocious. A man wearing docksider shoes, blue jeans, and a short sleeve shirt walked past them. Maybe he should take a lesson from the contractors and go casual. Ditch the white shirt, tie, and slacks. But he was the senior NCIS representative on board Sea Base and as such he had an image to project. He had already quit wearing his suit coat except on special occasions and interviews.

Zeichner twitched. Why in the hell should he feel uncomfortable about not wearing his coat? Maybe it was because NCIS was a security blanket for the Navy and it was important to look confident. Looking confident meant dressing correctly.

Others in better physical shape would have been less interested in the Pacific heat and the moisture running down from the top of the head, the armpits, the cracks and crevices of overlapping fat bunched around the middle, eventually finding homes around the waistband of the underwear, between the legs and thighs, and in the socks. They would have enjoyed watching an historical event unfolding on this hot summer day, with the steady light breeze rolling across the expanding deck of Sea Base. Hundreds of people hurried about the broad, flat plain of Sea Base, seemingly with little direction and no supervision. Most moved as an entity, a part of a working group accomplishing tasks to secure the top.

Speckled across the deck were khaki clad chief petty officers and officers wearing yellow long-sleeved shirts identifying them as the supervisors and leaders. If the observer knew enough about aircraft carrier operations, he or she would have smiled when they realized those long-sleeved shirts and the cranial helmets being worn topside came from that common background.

Sea Base was always expected to emulate a super-super carrier. It would evolve its own set of operational principles and guidelines that, like aircraft carrier operations, would become more like suggestions than directives. The colored long-sleeved shirts of the aircraft carrier deck apes had been carried to Sea Base.

Green-, purple-, white-, red-, and yellow-clad sailors sped about the evolving top of Sea Base. If the person watching knew what the shirts meant, then they would have an idea what each sailor was doing. Green shirts handled aircraft, driving small tractors, chocking wheels, and shifting aircraft from one parking space to another. The few purple-shirted sailors moving about the deck were responsible for fueling everything. If it involved fuel, the purple-shirted sailors were all over it. A smattering of red-shirted sailors decorated the top. These specialized individuals were the ordnance handlers, and right now Sea Base had no weapons systems deployed or aircraft on board requiring shells, missiles, or bombs. So the few red shirts glided across the deck as if enjoying the pleasure of being topside on the largest man-made island ever built.

A bunch of individuals wearing blue jumpsuits congregated around where the tower was to be raised. Beards, long hair, and constant chattering amongst them identified the scientists from the Office of Naval Research. They wore the same jumpsuits Navy engineers did, but no one expected scientists to understand what a Navy engineer did down in the bowels of the engine room.

A couple of sailors wearing white shirts walked by the two men, saying *excuse me* as they passed. White shirts were worn by the miscellaneous sailors of the carrier. The observer had to look at the cranial helmet worn by the white-shirted sailor to determine the person's function. Corpsmen wore white shirts with a bright red cross on the white cranial helmet.

"We could go below," Gainer offered.

Zeichner shook his head. "Not yet. We need to get a feel for Sea Base. Know where everything is going to be and know where we can gain access at any time."

He stepped out, walking about a hundred feet from the edge. Gainer fell in on Zeichner's left.

It had taken nearly half a day longer than expected to raise Sea Base above the masts of the eight Fast Sealift Ships.

Zeichner should have been impressed with this instead of working furiously to keep the sweat from his eyes. Sea Base would easily rate as one of the top one hundred scientific achievements in human history.

"Quite an accomplishment," Zeichner said.

"If it doesn't sink. This could go down as one of the top ten catastrophes at sea, if it does."

Zeichner cut his eyes at Gainer, who was staring straight ahead.

The afternoon sun had reached the edge of the port side of the forward extension. Zeichner took a deep breath. Not a cloud in the sky and here he was, with his prone-to-sunburn skin, standing topside without a hat. Even Gainer had been smart enough to bring a ball cap.

The sound of an aircraft drew their attention.

"Now hear this," an announcement echoed across Sea Base.

Zeichner's eyes searched for the source, quickly finding it. Speakers rose from the edges of Sea Base, pointing inward at forty-five-degree angles, focusing announcements toward Sea Base and away from the sea behind them.

"Sea Base has a P-3C inbound. FOD walkdown completed.

Everyone is to clear the runway." The announcer paused, and then continued, "This is the first aircraft to land on Sea Base. It is the first aircraft to land on anything man-made at sea that was not a ship."

Sailors rushed to clear the pair of marked runways running down the center of Sea Base. The ONR engineers stopped what they were doing to watch, and as Zeichner looked around Sea Base he saw everyone was waiting for the aircraft to land, even Gainer and himself.

A couple of minutes later, a P-3C four-engine turbo-prop maritime reconnaissance aircraft flew over Sea Base, wiggling its wings in greeting. Applause erupted across Sea Base.

A couple of miles later, the aircraft turned left. Topside, everyone turned with the aircraft, raising hands to shield their eyes from the setting sun. As the aircraft made its circuit, heading toward a fourth turn miles behind the stern of Sea Base, the audience turned with it, watching this momentous occasion when the first aircraft would land on this floating piece of American territory in the west Pacific.

Ten minutes after the P-3C Orion aircraft had flown over Sea Base, little puffs of smoke whiffed across the deck from the friction of the aircraft wheels touching down on Sea Base. People started applauding again. Sea Base was now truly operational.

Even Zeichner was awed over watching the landing. He took a deep breath and nodded in appreciation, only to erupt into coughing as the exhaust fumes from the aircraft blew across them.

"Wow! That was something wasn't it?" Gainer said.

"Guess so. It was amazing."

"You're right there. It hit so hard, I expected Sea Base to collapse." Gainer shook his head. "Wonder how long you can tread water?"

Small yellow tractors manned by green-shirted sailors wearing helmets made Zeichner think of soldier ants as they led the aircraft to the parking apron. About a dozen other sailors walked alongside the aircraft. Zeichner presumed their job was to make sure the aircraft didn't run over anything. Right now that shouldn't be a problem.

"That was the fourth," Gainer said.

"That's the first aircraft to land. Probably had to fly all the way from Hawaii—with only a brief stop for refueling in Guam."

"That was the fourth if you count the helicopters. It is amazing, isn't it, boss. Eighty-one-acres floating around here on top of the Pacific where three days ago there was only a bunch of aging ships."

Zeichner nodded and started walking again, keeping clear of the parking apron marked off by the aviation boatswain mates for the aircraft. "Tomorrow, or the next day, the Air Force fighters start arriving."

"Should be something for them to land on an aircraft carrier."

Zeichner agreed. "I wouldn't call Sea Base an aircraft carrier, but I guess you're right. It's essentially one. At the morning brief, the admiral said two squadrons of F-22 Raptors would be arriving. They're flying all the way from the States, being refueled enroute by huge KC-135 tankers. Quite an accomplishment. Kind of buggers my mind though."

Gainer slowed his pace to stay even with Zeichner.

"How's that?"

"Well, you're ex-Army, so you're probably not aware that the Navy and Air Force have a decades-long argument over whether the Navy should even have aircraft carriers. The Air Force argument is they can deploy anywhere at any time and conduct warfighting missions. The Navy's counterargument is the Air Force needs permission to use another country's landmass to do their mission. The Navy can stay offshore and conduct air operations incessantly without another nation's permission. So the argument continues."

"So, who's right?"

"Both of them, if you want my opinion. If we needed to have fighter or bomber aircraft somwhere immediately, then I'd turn to the Air Force expeditionary concept—aircraft take off; tankers align along their flight path to keep them fueled; and, after their mission they land at the nearest friendly location."

"What if there are no nearest friendly locations?"

"There is always a friendly location, if enough dollars are involved."

"And the carriers?"

"An aircraft carrier may take a few days to reach its area of operations, but once on station, a lone carrier can conduct five days of 'round-the-clock missions using the same aircraft. Air Force would have to set up some sort of rotation to fly a long-distance mission from its stateside bases." Zeichner tripped, catching his footing with skip. "Whew! That was close."

"Then it would seem to me they complement each other. And if this is such a hot issue, then why is the Navy allowing the Air Force to be the service to use Sea Base?"

"If you want Congress to give you the money to do something spectacular such as Sea Base, then you've got to give up something parochial. So the Navy is allowing Air Force squadrons to man Sea Base. Navy gets to keep its eight aging aircraft carriers."

Grainer smiled. "Everyone's a winner, I guess."

Zeichner shook his head. "Not that it matters much to me, but if I were a senior Navy admiral and I wanted to keep my aircraft carriers, Sea Base is the last warfighting concept I'd agree to build."

"Why?"

"Because Sea Base is a floating island. It doesn't have the versatility of an aircraft carrier. Once up and running, moving Sea Base will be a logistical and scientific nightmare. An aircraft carrier, you can just throw the wheel over to port or starboard, crank up the engine speed, and be on-station anywhere in the world within days—a couple of weeks at most. Sea Base is built to do everything from flying offensive missions to landing Marines ashore to repairing damaged ships. But in the argument between Air Force and Navy air power strategies, it proves the Air Force is more than capable of doing the mission of the aircraft carriers. The eight the Navy has now won't be eight in another five years, if Sea Base works." He made a sweeping motion, encompassing the large expanse of Sea Base in front of them. "And it appears to be doing just what Navy scientists said it would do."

"The Navy used to have twelve aircraft carriers, didn't it?"

"About seventy-five years ago, it used to have over a hundred, but that was World War Two. It's been a downward trend ever since."

A beeping sound caused both men to look right. One of those yellow tractors that made Zeichner think a World War II jeep was approaching. The sailor driving it, goggles mounted on his scuffed white helmet, waved as he passed several feet in front of them. Exhaust fumes blew into their faces, bringing tears to Zeichner's eyes.

He pulled a handkerchief from his back pocket, wiped away the tears, and ran it across his forehead to catch the sweat.

"Where did that come from?" Gainer asked as they continued their stroll.

The sound of large hydraulics drowned out any answer, bringing both men to a stop. Off to their left, a giant elevator loaded with yellow aircraft-handling equipment rose level with the main deck of Sea Base. That elevator could be dangerous during air operations, thought Zeichner. He turned and looked across the runway to a mirror image spot on the aft port side where another elevator operated. If an aircraft veered off the runway and either of those elevators were down, then the aircraft could roll right off Sea Base and into the ship beneath. A quick vision of Sea Base slowly cascading down in an ever-expanding cacophony of destruction brought a quick chill down his spine.

"I guess that is going to be the tower?" Gainer asked, pointing across the four thousand-foot man-made runway.

The runway ran straight down the middle of Sea Base. It stretched from the bow of the *Altair* to the stern of the *Denebola*, bringing up the rear. Sailors had already metaphorically divided the floating eighty-one acres into ports-starboard sides with the center of the runways acting as the dividing line. During the middle of the night some enterprising sailor had painted, quite nicely, *Mason-Dixon* on the centerline of the runway. So far, no one had acted to remove it.

Zeichner's keen analytical mind immediately postulated the sailor was from the south—probably from some small town like Crewe, Virginia. But then that's why they paid him the big bucks to be a NCIS agent—to draw these analytical conclusions. He smiled.

"Is it going to be the tower?" Gainer asked again.

Zeichner shrugged and looked to where Gainer was pointing. On the port side—or southern side, if you observed the etiquette of the Mason-Dixon designation seriously—Seabees were shifting prefabricated material around. Zeichner noticed the gaggle of blue-suited scientists had moved away, leaving the hands-on work to the Seabees while they congregated nearby, watching the action.

The base for the tower was about two hundred feet from the runway.

"I think it's the only reason the ONR crowd would be there," Zeichner said. "They're supposed to have the bottom floor as their center of operations. On the second floor the combat information center—or CIC, as the Navy calls it—is going to be acti-

vated. The third floor will be the skipper's deck, and above that
will be the aircraft tower. Should be impressive."

"I was told there were going to be several buildings put up on
Sea Base."

"The tower is the primary building. I believe they're going to
put up something called a transient quarters with some bunks and
bathrooms in it. I also believe they're going to put some sailors
in a prefab somewhere up here and double it up as a ready-room
for the watches."

The P-3C Orion had turned around and was slowly taxiing
alongside the runway, following a small pickup truck that had replaced the yellow tractor. A huge blinking sign with the words
FOLLOW ME was mounted on the top of the pickup. The Air Force
was definitely going to feel at home.

The sound of approaching aircraft drew their attention. Even
as large as the vintage C-130 transport aircraft were, the three
were less than a mile from Sea Base when Zeichner spotted the
first one.

Zeichner and Gainer stood and watched the three C-130s land.
They came straight in to land, not entering the racetrack pattern
the P-3C did. The noise of their propellers drowned out all conversation as the two men continued their walk around Sea Base.
Zeichner had ridden in numerous C-130s during his time in Europe, sitting in the web passenger seats, shifting constantly, trying to get that metal bar down the center out from the middle of
his butt.

On the port side of Sea Base, helicopters occupied the forward
quarter of the main deck. Zeichner wondered if that was inten-
tional, or if some enterprising helicopter commander had acqui-
sitioned the space. It had been his experience that in large
concentrations of force, or the more complex or complicated the
task, those with the enterprise to make decisions without waiting
for directions achieved success. The person in charge determined
the definition of success.

Gainer was talking, but Zeichner was only half paying attention. It seemed to him Gainer never breathed. To breathe would
mean interrupting his talking.

"They're going to deploy the railgun systems sometime
today," Zeichner heard Gainer say, and nodded in agreement.

"Then they'd better do it soon. It's already eight o'clock."

Zeichner's mind was back on the explosion on the *Denebola*.

The fire had been so intense that whatever evidence there was had been destroyed. The fire marshal told him there were three explosions. Three explosions that happened in tandem. The first explosion had set off the second, which had set off the third. The fire marshal had been able to identify the three separate locations where they occurred. None of the locations had anything that would have spontaneously blown up simultaneously. Multiple fires and explosions in different locations that occur simultaneously are never accidental. They are always man-made.

Zeichner no longer believed he was dealing with a spy. He was dealing with a saboteur, but he didn't know if he was dealing with one person or a group of people. Perversely, he hoped it was a group. It gave better odds on catching them. You catch one, it's like a leak in a weak dam. In his years of working law enforcement, he had learned that criminals were stupid. They ridiculed the police among themselves into where they actually believed what they were saying. They convinced themselves they were smarter than the law. And they're so impressed with their illegal acts that most only need the opportunity and they'll bubble over with enthusiasm telling you how smart they are. The prisons were filled with "smart" people. Even the few who refused to talk told you something. When putting together a crime scene and looking for leads, every little clue helped—even silence.

". . . runs on electric current one of the scientists told me last night when we were jogging . . ."

Another reason, thought Zeichner, *as to why I find it hard to like you, Gainer.* Joggers were like reformed smokers. They thought everyone ought to be one.

I guess the question is, Zeichner said to himself while Gainer continued telling him how railguns operated, *why would anyone want to blow up Sea Base?* If he figured that out, it would lead him to the culprit or culprits. Home base believed the sabotage was linked to the suspected foreign agent on board. Most foreign agents in today's information age didn't go around blowing things up. They sat in front of computers and sucked the data they needed from open sources like university papers, technical magazines, and government documents posted to the Internet. When the day is finished, they go home, grab little Johnny, and take him to his soccer, baseball, basketball, or whatever practice. Blowing things up was more the modus operandi of the idiots living behind the cloak of a peaceful Islam. Or the white supremacists calling themselves God's Army, running around America trying to convince everyone Armageddon was coming.

". . . uses something called a DeLorean or DiLorenzo force . . ."

"That's Lorentz force, Kevin," Zeichner said, his mind keying on the misinformation. "Lorentz is some sort of electromagnetic force; a DeLorean is a vintage twentieth-century car they used to make in Northern Ireland." He paused for a moment, and before Gainer could continue, Zeichner added, "I think there're only twenty of so of them still in existence today."

"You're right, boss. And DiLorenzo is the medical center inside the Pentagon." Gainer grinned and bent down toward Zeichner. "Must be a Freudian slip." He leaned away as they continued walking. "Anyway, what the scientist told me is the electromagnetic current drives the explosive shell in front of it, picking up speed, until the shell is fired. When it comes out of the barrel, it is going at speeds much higher than any explosion could create. Made it sound as if the shell reached the speed of sound before it left the barrel."

Maybe he was dealing with two different elements here, Zeichner thought. Maybe the foreign agent didn't create the explosion. It's an easy conclusion. A conclusion that would make headquarters happy, but maybe, *just maybe*, he's dealing with a malcontent.

There are always those who don't want to go to sea for six months. It wouldn't be the first time he'd dealt with someone trying to stop a ship from getting underway, or doing something to turn a ship around, causing it to head back to port, and mamma-san. The odd wrench tossed inside a turning shaft; the odd fire in the engine room; the explosion on *Denebola*? Most cases of malcontent sabotage involved some damage to a vital piece of engine-room equipment. Damage elsewhere in the ship most times could be easily fixed without returning to port—either while underway or once they reached their destination. But engineering casualties meant being tied up pierside or in dry dock. Serious engineering damage like a bent shaft meant at least a week tied up. Couldn't be a malcontent, he decided. The explosion was designed to destroy the computer backbone of Sea Base, not cause the convoy to return to port. But then again, maybe the malcontent figured destroying the servers would cause the Sea Base experiment to be canceled—

in which case they'd return to Pearl Harbor. Zeichner tripped again.

"What are those things?" he asked aloud as he quickly regained his footing.

"Gotta be careful of those, boss. They're tie-down something-or-others. The entire Sea Base is covered with them. It's so they can tie down an aircraft or tie down anything else to keep it from being blown overboard." Gainer squatted, running his fingers through the slightly raised metal X covering the tie-down.

The list was growing as to why Zeichner should dislike his deputy.

"This X-shaped tie-down protrudes slightly above the floor—"

"Deck."

"—protrudes slightly above the deck to allow the person doing the tying down to put the chain through it, or slip a hook onto it." Gainer stood. "It's amazing the things I'm discovering out here. Being a soldier is a lot easier. All you do it point the weapon and fire. Of course, the downside is that sometimes you've got people firing back at you. I remember once when I was deployed to Somalia . . ."

Zeichner dipped his head slightly so he could watch his step. They walked in step, continuing their trek around Sea Base.

Zeichner had handled several malcontent cases during his career. With the exception of one, all had been sailors on their first enlistment who were dissatisfied with the Navy; wanted out; were refused; and decided to act out their anger. He was sure by now some had finished their sentences to join the ranks of dishonorably discharged Americans.

The case that had taken longer to solve and caused him a number of sleepless nights involved a senior chief whose wife decided to leave him the night before the ship set sail. Somewhere that former senior chief was sleeping as a former Navy seaman with the dishonorable discharge sheet hidden somewhere. The man had had eighteen years of service when he was court-martialed. He had no sympathy for any of them.

". . . with better accuracy. They can do close-in protection against inbound missiles and aircraft, or reach out over a hundred miles to support the Marines ashore. Know the biggest technological hurdle they had to solve?"

Sometime in the past five minutes, Gainer had switched subjects back to railguns.

"Sufficient electrical power," Zeichner replied, even as his mind whirled with the possibility that they might be complicating their work by trying to force the explosion and the perceived presence of a foreign agent into one-size-fits-all category.

Gainer frowned. "How did you know that, boss?"

Zeichner didn't answer. If he had a malcontent on board who didn't want to be at sea, then obviously the man knew that throwing a wrench or disabling one ship wouldn't stop the deployment. With new technology brings fresh waves of crime. *Oh, he's smart*, thought Zeichner, *very smart indeed*. Blowing up the servers was the critical nexus. Without those servers to keep the ships operating as a single unit, Sea Base could never deploy; it would have to return to Pearl Harbor. So it could be a malcontent anyway.

The two men turned slightly, taking their walk toward the forward edge of the main Sea Base deck and away from the four-engine turbo-prop P-3C turning into parking position. The three C-130s were being parked near the end of the runway where they had landed.

This place was going to get crowded with two squadrons of Air Force F-22 Raptors tied down topside. The admiral had mentioned this morning the one thing lacking on Sea Base was a hangar bay where aircraft could be worked on round the clock. The way it was arranged now, bad weather would curtail most maintenance and nearly any major repair.

The lower left side of Zeichner's lip turned up in a half-smile when he recalled how the lead ONR scientist had taken this as a complaint against his team. How could anyone find anything to complain about such a technological advancement? All good ideas have blemishes.

"He said they'd have their two lasers up and operating by this weekend. This is going to be a well-defended place."

Zeichner nodded. One foot from the deck edge, four-foot-high removable beams were being installed in holes around the edges. Boatswain mates were running safety lines from one to the other starting a foot above the deck to the top of the metal beam.

"I would hope it's well defended. I understand the Chinese aren't happy about Sea Base being only a thousand miles northeast of Taiwan."

"Guess they don't want you walking off the deck on a dark

night?" Gainer asked, shaking the top safety cable. "Not much movement. They got them on tight."

"Hey!" a female boatswain mate shouted. "You want to keep your fucking fingers off the line?"

"Sorry," Gainer said sheepishly.

She waved her hand in dismissal. "S'alright. You ain't the first one to check out the work."

"Hey, Slowermetzil, what the hell you doing?" A man wearing master chief stars shouted at the female petty officer.

"Master Chief . . . What did you say your name was again?"

"You know my name, Showdernitzel."

"Wow! God must be looking down, Master Chief Jacobs. You actually said my name right."

Zeichner and Gainer continued walking, moving farther away from the unenclosed edge of the Sea Base deck, leaving the Navy working party behind them, their voices trailing off.

"Then again, if you're tall, you could trip over them, knock yourself out on the edge, and fall overboard." He looked up at Gainer. "If I were you, I'd be careful up here at night—especially jogging."

Gainer pointed at the forward end of the runway extending outward twelve hundred feet over the USNS *Altair*. "You can see the *Altair* from this vantage point," he said.

Zeichner leaned forward. It was quite a sight. Slight waves rode up the bow of the ship. He estimated the ship was drawing a draft of about a hundred feet. The weight of Sea Base, distributed across the floating power of eight Fast Sealift Ships, caused a large displacement.

"What was that?"

"What was what?"

"You said something about displacement?"

He didn't realize he had spoken aloud. "I was just thinking how low the USNS *Altair* is riding in the water," he said, pointing to the ship. "It is my understanding these ships ride nearly a hundred feet out of the water when empty. Look at it. I would say there is only about thirty feet of distance between the ocean and the main deck. The difference is called the *displacement*."

Gainer shook his head, his lower lip pressing against his upper. "Boss, you are one fantastic walking book of nautical knowledge."

If you only knew.

Gainer grabed the top safety wire that was slightly above waist-level on him and tried to shake it. "I noticed last night that they don't have those where the runway ends, begins, or protrudes out. Instead there is a series of metal nets around the edges. I guess that's to catch the aircraft if it tumbles off." Gainer pointed in the direction of the *Altair*. "See them above the Altair? Just big metal nets. No safety line. Guess if you fall overboard there, you'd land in the nets."

"Or something like that. They have those on aircraft carriers. You are right. It allows sailors to leap into them away from trouble."

"It's not for catching aircraft?"

"Aircraft have been caught in them. If nothing else, it slows the aircraft's fall to the ocean and gives a few more seconds for the pilot to eject."

"Glad I don't fly."

"Kevin, when you were gathering the data about who had been coming and going on the *Denebola*, did you separate them into military and civilian like I asked?"

"Sure I did. You asked me this once before, Mr. Zeichner."

Zeichner saw Gainer looking at him, the man's left eyebrow raised.

"You know something you're not telling me? I get the distinct impression that you haven't decided whether you can fully trust me or not, Mr. Zeichner."

Zeichner's lower lip pushed against his upper. After a few seconds of thought, he shared his conjecture that maybe there was more than one hostile on board. Maybe there was a spy and maybe there was a saboteur also. Maybe there were two people or two groups. And, maybe they had a malcontent or several malcontents who had decided they enjoyed the pleasures of Pearl over the beauty of the Pacific. It was up to Zeichner and Gainer to narrow down the investigation.

"Look at that," Gainer said, suddenly, pointing down at the *Altair*.

Several dark shapes rode in the shadows of the ship and Sea Base. Fins broke the water.

"Looks as if we have sharks," Zeichner said, recognizing them from his visits to the Baltimore Aquarium.

Aircraft engines revving up drew their attention.

The doors opened and rear ramps dropped. Working parties were already rushing up the ramps to unload supplies the vintage workhorse aircraft of the twentieth century had brought on board this twenty-first-century marvel. The engines of the C-130s wound up, then started down, before winding to a stop.

The whine of the P-3C engines winding down eased the decibel level topside. Within a minute, the Orion was chocked, tied down, and the engines whirled only on momentum. The left rear door opened and the interior ladder descended. Crewmembers in green flight suits with scuffed black flight boots tramped down the rickety ladder to the deck of this gigantic aircraft carrier called Sea Base. Zeichner always wondered when he saw Navy fliers why they always looked as if their flight suits, gloves, and boots came from a second-hand charity shop. They were always wrinkled, looked as if they needed washing, and many times you could smell the crewmember downwind.

On the other hand, Air Force pilots seemed to have ready-press flight suits. They always looked as if they could walk out of their planes and do a recruiting photo-shoot.

THE bonging of general quarters woke Zeichner, causing him to sit up abruptly, bumping his head on the rack above him. He was edging his way off the bed when the general announcement system on *Denebola* broke through over the alarm. "Listen up," the civilian Officer of the Deck said. "There's been an explosion topside. Set condition Zebra throughout the ship and report to the bridge when set."

He hadn't felt any explosion. Where was the explosion? What exploded? Dozens of questions rattled through his mind as he hopped around on one foot, shoving his legs into his pants. He heard the rip of the hem. "Damn," he said aloud. He jerked his pants up, buttoned the belt, and sat down, pulling his shoes to him. That left him with three sets of pants to wear now, knowing he'd never find anything to fit him out here.

Topside, the announcement said. What could explode topside? The railguns weren't deployed topside when he came belowdecks. Earlier, the flight deck supervisor had moved the P-3C alongside the three C-130s. If one of the aircraft had exploded, the others would have gone also.

It took less than two minutes for Zeichner to dress, stumble out of his stateroom, and move his hefty self up the ladder toward the main deck and the column leading to topside. Zeichner grabbed the handrails and started up the hundred feet to the main deck.

Fifteen minutes later, Zeichner reached the top of Sea Base, having stopped twice along the way to catch his breath. He could hear the pounding of his heart in his ears. Safety lines enclosed three sides of the deck-level hatch. Zeichner moved to the side, away from the open hatch.

He stood on the port side of the runway about a hundred feet from the center of Sea Base. A C-130 burned in the distance. Smoke whipped down every few seconds to obscure the raging fire burning through the aircraft.

Zeichner leaned over, putting both hands on his knees as he gasped for breath. *Now is not the time to have a heart attack,* he told himself. *Wait until later.*

Tractors moved back and forth, hurriedly moving the unaffected P-3C and the two other C-130s away from the aircraft engulfed in flames. This was a deliberate act. The burning aircraft was in the middle of the row. This was not the work of a malcontent. He shook his head. Fire teams encircled the burning aircraft, showering foam over the conflagration.

No, malcontents wanted to return to port. They knew what they were doing was wrong, but they didn't want to get caught and they didn't want to kill anyone. The servers were one thing; they were belowdecks where most malcontents concentrated their small acts of sabotage. But no malcontent he'd ever dealt with had ever done anything such as this. They usually just wanted to go home.

Whoever did this expected the explosion to engulf the two aircraft on both sides of the C-130, spreading the fire to the others. Whoever did this wanted to destroy Sea Base.

Regardless of whether it was a saboteur or a foreign agent—or whether they were one and the same—he had to find out who was setting these explosions. And that meant whoever was doing it had access to explosives.

Zeichner straightened, using his handkerchief to wipe the great drops of sweat running off his forehead, down his neck, and soaking an already saturated shirt.

"Shit! Everyone on this floating island has access to explosives."

"Looks as if he struck again."

Zeichner raised his head slightly and looked over at Gainer, who stood there without a speck of sweat on him, his clothes neat, and for the first time Zeichner noticed the man's belt hung loose. He wondered how long it'd be before he regained enough strength to toss him overboard.

"You want to get closer, boss?" Gainer asked, starting to cross the runway to the starboard side.

Zeichner raised himself and, still wiping the sweat from his face, followed the younger man. His breathing was nearly back to normal. He was going to start walking. With eighty-one acres of American territory floating northeast of Taiwan, he could walk forever. He wanted that half inch of loose belt in front of him. He wanted Gainer's half inch of loose belt. Glancing down, he decided he'd best set his goals low. First, he'd settle for just being able to see his belt.

"Looks as if they're getting the other aircraft out of the way without them catching on fire."

"No other explosions," Zeichner said, gasping out the three words.

"I was wondering . . ." Gainer started, then his voice trailed off.

After a few seconds, Zeichner said, "Go ahead. What are you wondering?" His voice was returning to normal.

"Well, what I was going to say was it doesn't appear whoever is doing this wants to injure or kill anyone. I think whoever is doing this wants Sea Base to be somewhere else or wants to sink Sea Base. That supports what we discussed earlier today. We have someone who doesn't want to be out here. I don't think it's the foreign agent person, if we have one on board. I think it's someone with either a vendetta against the Navy or the government. Or some person in a leadership position out here." Gainer looked at Zeichner. "Maybe you should talk with the admiral and the captain to see if they know of anyone on board who has it in for them."

Zeichner nodded. "I can do that . . . and I will. But I've never had a case where the primary reason for sabotage was a vendetta against someone. It was always someone with a personal issue. Something directly affecting them. And I've never had nor heard of a malcontent doing such . . ."

". . . so much damage?"

Zeichner nodded. "Yeah, so much damage. Usually it's limited to a piece of critical equipment."

"The aircraft are critical."

"Yes, but destroying the aircraft won't turn Sea Base around and head us home."

"But it could severely damage Sea Base and make us go home."

Zeichner shook his head. "A malcontent is now on the bottom of my list of possibilities."

Another fire team appeared from the other side of the C-130. Sailors scurried around the three undamaged aircraft now on the port side of Sea Base. The aircraft were not in any sort of alignment. They were being tied down where they were. Widely dispersed from each other and facing different directions.

Zeichner hoped none of the three had explosive devices on them. The thought sent a chill racing through him. He took two more steps before stopping.

He grabbed Gainer's arm. "The other aircraft," he said, his voice loud. "Tell me! If you wanted to destroy something as large as Sea Base or cripple it so it had to return to port, would burning one aircraft do it? Sea Base is designed to fight." Zeichner stomped his foot a couple of times on the metal deck. "This deck is designed to handle crashes. But, what if you blow up one aircraft, rig the others to go later, and let the firefighters disperse the—"

"Jesus Christ."

"Let's go!"

Gainer quickly left Zeichner behind. Zeichner ran nearly to the center of the runway before slowing to a quick walk.

Five minutes later, he reached Gainer who was talking to one of the firefighters—the man had a chief petty officer insignia on his helmet—and pointing at the P-3C in front of him. Zeichner walked past the two men, and as he neared the front wheel well, the two came up on both sides of him.

"I was just telling the Chief what—"

"Search the wheel wells, but don't touch anything you find. If he rigged the aircraft to explode, then the devices may have a fail-safe switch that will trigger them if handled improperly."

Zeichner reached the nose wheel. "Give me your light, Chief." Taking the flashlight from the chief, Zeichner shined it around the inside cavity where the nose wheel resided when the aircraft was in flight.

"Go ahead!" he said, concentrating on the inside of the wheel well. "Go look at the other two wheel wells." He looked at the two men. "Hurry! This joker will have estimated how long it would take to shift the aircraft."

He pulled his head out of the wheel well. Gainer was heading toward the left wheel while the chief took the right. He hoped he was wrong. His hope was shattered when the chief started shouting and motioning him to the right wheel well.

Zeichner surprised himself by how fast he moved. He shined the light inside. A large square brick of C4 was mounted on the uppermost portion of the wheel well. The firing cap ran from it to a digital mechanism, counting down the time in bright red numerals.

"Looks as if you're right, boss."

"And it looks as if we're wrong, Kevin. This joker does want to kill people." He turned to the chief. "Chief, you need to tell the control center we need the bomb disposal unit up here ASAP."

"They're already up here, sir." He pulled his brick from the holster, hit the transmit button, and told everyone on the circuit about having found the bomb.

"How long do we have?" the chief asked, reaching over and tilting Zeichner's hand with the flashlight upward so he could see the explosive better.

Zeichner pointed with the other. "If the read-out is right, then you've got forty-five minutes to disarm this device." He let out a deep breath as the chief passed along the information.

Zeichner put his hand on the man's arm. "Chief, stop! Move it away from the aircraft. We don't want to accidentally trigger the device. Kevin," he said, pointing to the farther C-130. "You're in better shape. You take the far C-130 and I'll take the one off to the right."

Gainer nodded. "Jesus Christ, boss."

"Not yet, but if the timers on the other two are less than this one, we may get to meet Him."

Gainer took off in a dead run toward the C-130 parked several hundred feet away. Only a few sailors were around it, checking the tie-downs.

Two minutes later, Zeichner found a similar device on the main wheel well of his C-130. This guy knew what he was doing. The main wings of the P-3C and the C-130s held fuel tanks. The detonation would have created similar explosions to the first one. Whoever did this knew the fire team would move the unaffected aircraft away from the burning one, moving them across Sea Base and expanding the damage the next series of explosions would have created. The second set would have exploded along the entire length of Sea Base. Glancing to the side, Zeichner saw where the Seabees had completed the first floor of the tower.

The chief was walking toward him. He heard his name being shouted. A couple hundred feet away, Gainer had his hands cupped as he shouted something. He couldn't make out what Gainer was saying, but he knew that Gainer had found the same thing on the far C-130. This search for the saboteur or agent—or both—had now become a race for survival. Every day more weapons were going to be deployed and more aircraft were going to arrive.

It was no longer a question of whether there would be a next time; it was a question of when. He had to find the person or group planning the next explosion. This time whoever did this had misjudged the amount of time it would take the damage control teams to move the aircraft. The bomber also misjudged how quick NCIS could react. Next time, there would be no forty-five-minute grace period for them to disarm the explosives.

TEN

"Kevin," Zeichner said as he sat down at the conference table. He tossed a bunch of loose papers onto the table. "Time we go through this again and narrow down our suspects." He didn't mention the nasty e-mail he got this morning from NCIS headquarters chewing his ass and blaming his lack of progress on bringing in the foreign saboteur as the cause of the two explosions. Back at headquarters they'd already be discussing his relief. The two explosions would be catalysts for those young animalistic wolves who were nowhere to be found when they needed a volunteer to take this deployment, and who would now be campaigning with vigor to replace him. He grunted.

"What was that, boss?"

"Nothing. Just thinking." Thinking how six months ago his NCIS comrades had more important things to do, so "Old Zeichner" had been ordered to take it. Well, "Old Zeichner" had it. He was going to keep it. He was going to catch the bomber. And he was going to have a lot of enjoyment when he did. Especially if the bomber turned out to be someone other than this elusive espionage agent some analyst thought was on board. His challenge would be to act gracious while they shook his hand.

"There're nearly seventy, boss."

"What?" Zeichner asked, Gainer's words jerking him back to reality.

"I said we have nearly seventy suspects."

He nodded. "That's seventy out of three thousand." He handed a sheet of paper to Gainer. "I've gone through and eliminated all the active-duty military visiting *Denebola* the day of the explosion."

"But . . ."

"But what? Supervisors watch the military day and night. If any are involved in this, I'll eat my shorts. No, our saboteur is a single individual—not a group. He's about my height and your weight. He's in good physical shape because he has to carry explosives, keep a low profile, and be able to get somewhere else by the time the explosions happens. He has to blend in with the crowd."

"Then, Mr. Zeichner, I would say we can't eliminate the sailors. They blend in because that is what Sea Base is about: the Navy. Most of the three thousand people on board Sea Base are sailors. The sailors would blend in. I do think you are right on target with the supposition that he is young enough to still be in good physical shape, but why do you think he's your height? I would submit he is around six foot two, and yes, he probably has my profile."

"Why six foot two?"

"The height of the wheel on the P-3C where he planted the bombs either required him to climb up into the wheel well, or stand on the tire and reach it. I measured the distance from the deck to where the explosive device was mounted. It was over six feet. If he was around six foot two, then he could stand without stretching and easily mount the improvised explosive device."

"Someone must have seen him plant the IED."

"Someone may have." Gainer opened his green notebook. "I interviewed a Petty Officer Leary—member of the flight deck crew. He recalls someone working on the wheel well of the P-3C around seven P.M. He didn't pay it much attention because there were a lot of sailors and contractors on the flight deck doing a lot of different things."

Zeichner set his cup on the table, lifted the coffeepot, and refilled it. "Why did this Petty Officer . . ."

"Leary."

". . . Leary remember this guy? Did he recall the others on the flight deck, or is he one of these 'too helpful' types."

Gainer shrugged. "Could be, but his story fits where we are going with the profile. The person he saw was alone. Nondescript. Leary said the impression he got from his glance was the man was lean. The individual was stretching up with both hands out of sight inside the wheel well. Ergo—in good shape, young."

"Young. Why couldn't he have been old?" Zeichner lifted his cup and took a sip. A slight smile escaped. Gainer was smarter than he thought. No one enjoyed seeing their plan dented or destroyed, but Zeichner wanted to find the culprit and if Gainer was the hero, so was he. Catch the bomber, regardless of how the two of them did it.

"To recap, Mr. Zeichner, you said this is most likely an individual—not a group. The individual has to be young enough to still be in reasonably good shape and being in good shape onboard a military installation makes it easier to blend in with the crowd. Plus, an older individual would most likely be senior and less likely to be pulling a solo maintenance act. If he looked like . . ." Gainer stopped.

Zeichner's lips pursed for a moment. "If he looked like me, everyone would have noticed. Is that what you were going to say?"

"Boss, I didn't mean it that way," Gainer said, holding his hands out to the side. "I just meant . . ."

"I know what you meant, and you're right." Zeichner smiled, waving the protestations away. "If he was out of shape and carrying a few extra pounds"—*A few? Try a lot*—"then he'd stand out and this Leary would have noticed."

"You've lost some weight since we've been out here, you know."

Zeichner took another sip, slid the chair out from under the conference table, and sat down. "You're too late, Kevin. Flattery is only good when there's no reason to give it. So quit trying to recover and go on. You're doing good, so far."

Zeichner saw the man swallow. *Have to admit, there is a perverse pleasure in making him uncomfortable. I need to stop that.* Sure, he was overweight. He was more than overweight—he was fat. *There: fat, fat, fat.* But this morning he had buckled his belt in a hole he had never used. Still couldn't see his feet or anything immediately below the waistline, but by the time he finished six months here, he was going to be *one thin mother*. All he had to do was steer clear of the mess decks. Some were open twenty-four hours a day.

"Leary said this guy drew his attention because he was working on the P-3C alone. He figured the man had a partner somewhere who had sauntered off to the head or to get some drinks, or bring something back from the chow hall. He didn't think much about it at the time because he was driving a deck tractor with a tow filled with—" Gainer glanced at his notes "—tie-down chains."

Zeichner drummed the fingers of his left hand on the green plastic that covered the top of the metal table as he cradled the coffee cup in his right. He looked at Kevin. "So the man was working alone. Why would Leary remember that?"

Gainer turned in the chair, put his arm on the table, and crossed his legs. A big grin spread across his face. "Safety regulations. Leary said it's standard operating procedure for work to be done in pairs around aircraft or other machinery that had the potential to cause serious harm. This guy was working alone." Gainer held up one finger for a moment. "Petty Officer Leary is a trained and certified safety supervisor."

"Then, why didn't this 'trained and certified' safety supervisor stop and say something to this guy who was working alone? Plus, why does he think this person is a guy?"

Gainer nodded. "He said the man—"

"Was he sure it was a man?"

"That's what he said, boss. He kept calling the individual 'a sailor' until I asked him what the guy was wearing and Leary said it looked to him that the man was in a flight suit."

"Nearly everyone on Sea Base wears some sort of jumpsuit. Jumpsuits look like flight suits. Even civilians wear them. Even you and I were issued a couple of sets when we embarked."

Gainer nodded as he pulled his handkerchief from his pocket and blew his nose. The noise filled the small conference room.

Zeichner involuntarily leaned back. *Wonder how many pounds I'd lose with a little seasickness or a bad cold?*

"It might be a good idea to wear them."

"We're NCIS; not Navy, not contractors, and sure as hell not academic professors. We'll keep to our shirts and ties, at least while we're out here." He lowered his head slightly so his eyes peered from beneath raised eyebrows. "You still haven't told me why this petty officer thought the suspect was working with someone."

"He said there was a large toolbox sitting near the right wheel where we found the device. The toolbox, he believed, would need two people to carry it."

"That supports the young and fit supposition," Zeichner said, then continued. "It doesn't complement our one-person theory. Still doesn't tell me why this petty officer didn't stop and say something."

"Said he knew he should have, but while standard operating procedures call for two people to be there, the real truth is this happens a lot. So Leary made a mental note to swing by the aircraft on the way back and say something."

"So, when this petty officer drove back by the aircraft . . . ?"

Gainer laid his notebook on the table and shut it. He uncrossed his legs and leaned forward, putting both elbows on the table as he clasped his hands together. "He doesn't recall. He thinks he looked at the aircraft, but Leary had a run-in with his chief when he got to the elevator. He didn't return immediately as he expected to do, but about an hour later. He doesn't recall anyone working on the Orion when he passed it. By then, the sun would have been on the horizon. I walked along where I thought Leary might have driven. At that time, the light would have been behind Leary and the plane would have been in the shadows. Plus, Leary was late for chow. So Leary's mind was on getting the tractor parked and secured."

"So no toolbox, either."

"Boss," Gainer said, holding his hands up in a questioning gesture. "He didn't even recall the sailor working in the wheel well until I questioned him. It took some effort to help him recall his trip back across the deck." Gainer flipped open the notebook again and glanced at the page in front of him. "I'm estimating, of course, but based on the timeline Leary provided and from talking with him, the individual he saw had plenty of time to plant the IED. By the time Leary drove back past the P-3C, the individual could have already done the other three aircraft and been gone. If Leary had returned as he expected, then there is a good chance he would have seen this person working on one of the other rigged aircraft."

Zeichner leaned back. "Eighty-one acres filled with people

walking every which way they want and only one person saw this person working on the aircraft. It's a little hard to believe. There must be others out there who saw this guy."

Gainer nodded. "I'm hitting the decks again. I spent this morning stopping those working near where the P-3C and the C-130s were parked. When we finish here, I will return to the flight deck."

"Flight deck?"

"Yes, sir. The sailors have christened the top of Sea Base the 'flight deck.' They're starting to use the terminology of an airfield."

"Or an aircraft carrier."

"You're right, boss, about others seeing this guy. Somewhere someone should be able to add more to what Petty Officer Leary saw."

Zeichner nodded. "I hope you're right."

"I hope so, too."

"Kevin, good job." He shoved the sheet of paper back across the table to Gainer. "While you're doing the search topside for more witnesses, I'll try to match the height, body fat, and profile against these names and see if we can narrow it down further."

"I think we should add the military suspects back on the list."

Zeichner nodded. "You win. But I want to eliminate as many suspects from the prime list as soon as possible. We need a more refined list for our second sweep. If our angle doesn't pan out, then we'll include everyone."

Gainer smiled. "Thanks, boss." He stood. "By the way, I ran into the skipper topside. He asked how the investigation was going. I told him we were interviewing people. He said *talk* was fine, but he needs *action.* The captain intends to hold a unit-wide sweep and space inspection. Figures if nothing else, maybe it'll cause the bomber to make a mistake. . . ."

"Or go to ground or decide to take Sea Base with him in a grand display of fireworks. It could make it harder for us to find him. Or the explosion will be last thing we see." Zeichner shook his head. "Wish the warriors would leave this stuff to us."

"I did suggest he talk with you before he took action. He said our job was to find the person responsible for the explosions. His job was to protect Sea Base and if a massive search caused the bomber to stop, then he'd done his job."

"Well, he has his job and we have ours. I don't want either one of us making it harder on the other. I'll swing by the tower"—

Zeichner looked at his watch—"after this and see if I can per-
suade him to wait on the unit sweep." He leaned toward Gainer.
"Kevin, let's look at the women, also. See if we have any who are
five-eleven or taller."

"Leary was adamant the suspect was male."

"How could he tell?"

"He said, 'No tits.'"

"JESUS Christ!"

Agazzi's head jerked toward Taylor, who was dancing around
the maintenance table, holding his right hand and cursing.
Smith's eyes narrowed as he looked at the maintenance technician.

"Smitty," Keyland said, his voice low.

"Blasphemy," Smith muttered. "This whole—" the man
paused searching for the right word to describe Sea Base
"—thing is full of people who abuse the Lord's name."

"Cut the words, Taylor," Agazzi said loudly.

"Senior Chief, it's the damn security box again. Thing hasn't
worked right since they hoisted Sea Base."

"It didn't work at all before they hoisted it, Petty Officer Taylor," Seaman Calvins added.

Taylor let go of his hand, shook it a few times. "Calvins, when
I want shit out of you, I'll squeeze your head."

"What happened?" Agazzi asked.

Behind Agazzi, Smith turned away from those around him. He
hunched forward, over the huge SQR-25 rainfall display, so close
his lips nearly touched it. Keyland touched the sailor's shoulder,
who shook it off. Keyland's face turned red in the soft white desk
light.

"I was trying to unscrew the cover plate to the fuse box and the
screwdriver slipped causing my hand to slam against the metal.
It's the warning light, Senior Chief," Taylor said. He leaned close
to the security console and began pushing icons. "I'm going to
have to bring it down and run diagnostics again." He tossed the
screwdriver onto the metal worktable.

Smith jerked, his eyes squinting, but he kept his mouth shut.

Keyland shook his head and walked behind the operator consoles to the small ladder leading to the upper level where Agazzi
and Taylor stood.

When Keyland reached Agazzi and Taylor, he said, "That's the fourth time since Wednesday this thing has locked up. It's a piece of shit built by some sandcrab at the lowest cost to the government."

"What's a sandcrab?" Seaman Calvins asked.

"I can still see the firing cradle, Senior Chief," Bernardo said, pointing to a small cam view on the upper left-hand side of his screen. "Everything looks A-OK from the camera mounted on the computer in the UUV Compartment."

"Well, I'm glad someone can see something," Taylor said sarcastically.

"What's a sandcrab?"

"Calvins," Taylor snapped. "A sandcrab is a term for a contractor."

"Why?"

"How the hell should I know?"

Smith leaned toward Bernardo's console, looking at the cam image of the UUV compartment.

"That camera doesn't focus properly. You have to be directly in front of it to be seen," Taylor said. "It's just a cheap—"

"I didn't expect a lecture on the utility of the son-of-a-bitch, Mort. I just said I could see the firing cradle from the cam."

"Don't get your bowels in an uproar, Pope," Taylor said.

"Well, I didn't stab you with the screwdriver. You stabbed yourself."

"That's enough," Keyland said.

Agazzi leaned forward, putting his hands on the metal railing separating the upper portion of the anti-submarine operations center from the lower portion. "Kind of a small picture isn't it, Petty Officer Bernardo."

Bernardo shrugged. "I can see it all right. Guess you can have it small and off to one side; or, you can fill the screen with it and not worry about controlling the unmanned underwater vehicles or keeping an eye on the feedback data."

"Calvins!" Taylor shouted. "Bring me that Phillips screwdriver. I'm going to take off the front panel and check the circuits."

Bernardo laughed. "Right tool for the right job is what a former girlfriend once told me."

"Pope, eat my shorts."

"Damn good thing that screwdriver only hurt you a little. I bet you'd be a real joy if it had broken your skin."

"It did break my skin."

"Mort, swing by sick bay later and get something for it. Don't want an infection or anything," Keyland added.

Taylor grunted in reply. "I think my hand will last, my dear leading petty officer."

"What'd you say?" Keyland asked tersely.

"Not a damn thing, Petty Officer Keyland."

"And, a damn good thing you didn't."

The maintenance technician pushed the power button. The noise level crept lower as the security console powered down. Without the security console they were unable to visually monitor the UUV compartment or the passageway running outside of it. All they had was Bernardo's cam, but at least it worked.

As Taylor went about his business, Agazzi glanced at the small image on Bernardo's console. Using information technology to reduce manpower was a great idea on paper—if you were back in Washington, wearing a bunch of gold and you didn't have to go to sea again.

Minutes went by as everyone continued their individual diagnostics and checklists, preparing for the upcoming launch of the first UUV. Agazzi glanced at his watch and then the clock on the bulkhead. He had expected Office of Naval Research scientists to be swarming over this compartment. After all, this was going to be the first test of a UUV in open ocean under near-operational conditions.

"Thanks. Now, bring me the voltmeter," Taylor said to Calvins.

Bernardo swung around in his seat. "I could expand the image, Senior Chief, so you could see it better. But the larger it gets, the smaller other things I need to operate the UUVs become." He shrugged. "I was going to shut it off nearer launch time." He looked over his shoulder and nodded at the image. "I don't know how the computer in the compartment is going to take the vibration and noise when we launch."

"Senior Chief," Keyland interrupted from his left. "Smith has incoming signals from the three dipped sonars. Steady signals. One of them is below the layer," he finished, referring to where the salinity, temperature, and depth of water formed a sound layer that caused most noises above it to bounce back to the surface.

Sounds that penetrated the layer, for the most part, were caught in a physics game of Ping-Pong, bouncing back and forth

between the top layer and the next lower layer, or the bottom of
the ocean, escalating outward from the source.

It was below the layer where anti-submarine forces did their
best work. Signals could travel for hundreds of miles, but passive
sonar detection depended on being in the noise path and connecting with one of the oscillating waves as it passed your sensor.

"What you got?"

"We're mapping it now," Keyland said.

Smith worked quietly, his right hand resting loosely on a
large-ball mouse to control the cursor. When the cursor blinked
directly on top of the noise event trailing down the digital rainfall, the system compared the parameters with its database. Red
digital numbers and letters sped through the readout as the Office of Naval Intelligence database searched for a match.
Smith's left hand rested on the knob that controlled the intensity
of the display. Other digital controls mounted around the edges
of the display allowed Smith to change the speed of the digital
rainfall traveling down the display to focus the frequencies of
the SQR-25.

"You satisfied, Petty Officer Smith?"

Smith raised his head and looked directly at Agazzi for a few
seconds before turning back to the SQR-25. "It's working, Senior
Chief," he said curtly. Smith leaned closer to the display, his actions not inviting further questions.

If he had other sailors, Smith would be in First Division working for the friendly, people-person Jacobs. Agazzi shook his
head.

Keyland glanced down at Smith and then looked at Agazzi.
Keyland shrugged—arms wide, hands open—and shook his
head.

Agazzi wasn't the only one who failed to understand this loner.
The man wore religion on his shirtsleeve. The least little thing offended Smith, and Agazzi was getting tired of it. There was a
limit to how much diversity a division could accept.

Agazzi wondered why he had even joined the Navy if so much
of it offended him.

Keyland had told Agazzi of the few times anyone had drawn
the taciturn man into conversation; Smith soon found reason to
discuss a deep religious faith—one that made Agazzi nervous
and uncomfortable. Smith wasn't the first fervent religious per-

son Agazzi had run into during his career. Unlike younger sailors who look for, reach out, and grasp the advice of their senior petty officers and chiefs, Smith didn't. It was the exact opposite. Smith took exception to anyone "prying" into his personal life, as he told Keyland when the leading petty officer checked Smith into the division. *"Everything you need to know about me is in my personnel record, Petty Officer Keyland."*

"Petty Officer Smith, what's the status of that contact?" Agazzi asked.

"Just ambient noise, Senior Chief. It's gone. Probably shrimp doing their thing." Smith leaned to one side so Agazzi could see over his shoulder.

The wide white-green smudge that had minutes before flowed down the rainfall display was gone. The screen had returned to the normal uninterrupted green pattern. The database readout had ceased searching and returned to its waiting status.

It was easy to believe that beneath the surface of the ocean it was a world without sound, but the ocean bubbled with noise. Noise created by wind, waves, and ships whose propellers churned the waters as they moved along the surface of the ocean. Noise from the myriad of sea life living beneath the waves, from whales to sharks to things as small as shrimp. It was a cacophony of sounds roiling beneath the waves. The ocean was not a quiet, sleepy world of soft water lapping at the beaches. It was an uncoordinated orchestra of misaligned strings riding on and through each other, filling the waters with ambient noise.

Ambient noise to an anti-submarine team meant every non-man-made sound beneath the waves. Ambient noise was as common to the ocean as the sound of birds chirping on a spring day. Agazzi thought of the sharks filling the waters around and beneath Sea Base. Even they used ambient noise to detect the death throes or thrashings of a wounded meal. A person swimming reproduced the sounds of both.

"Let me know if it comes back."

Smith didn't reply. Agazzi shook his head. The man was going to be a third class petty officer for a long time, or a very short one.

Keyland climbed to the upper level, heading to where Taylor had leaned the front panel from the security console against the worktable. Agazzi stayed out of the way of the petty officers as they did their job. Unlike Jacobs, he didn't feel the need to lean over the shoulders of his sailors.

The six seventeen-inch color televisions of the security console were hardwired to cameras inside the UUV compartment and along the passageway outside. Black and white static filled each screen.

The green light at the top of the panel glowed, showing Agazzi the hatch to the UUV compartment was secured. At least something was working. The hatch to the UUV compartment was identical to the one leading into the ASW operations center. To obtain entry, you placed your hand on a biometrics hand reader. Once the biometrics database recognized your handprint, you had to know the right set of four numbers to activate the legacy combination lock that served as the final entry security feature. The biometrics reader guarded against someone using a lifeless hand, flopping all over the place, to fool the database. The biometric reader checked body temperature and listened for blood movement. Wrong temperature, no detectable blood movement, and all the combinations in the world wouldn't open the doors.

A terrorist could stand outside in the passageway to the UUV compartment, slapping the dead hand onto the biometric reader all day. All he'd do was scatter blood on the bulkhead and make his arm sore.

The hatch opened to the ASW operations center. Agazzi's ears popped as air pressure equalized with the passageway. Another defensive measure for those compartments with lots of sophisticated technical equipment was to have inside air pressure slightly higher than the normal day-to-day air pressure outside—this way anything airborne was pushed away. It protected against a bio-chemical attack.

"Rest assured, my fellow sailors. MacPherson and Gentron are here," MacPherson said, as the two stepped into the ASW control center.

Gentron followed.

MacPherson set his cup of coffee on Agazzi's desk near the entrance. "Well, Taylor, what's wrong? You find another piece of equipment that's working too perfectly?"

"No, it's not working good," Seaman Calvins said as he took a fuse from Taylor. "But now that he's using—"

"Calvins, seaman are to be seen, not heard," Taylor asked.

Bernardo turned, a frown across his face. "Taylor! Was your brother an only child?"

"Very funny, asshole."

Keyland pointed at Taylor, started to say something, thought better of it, and let the hand drop.

"Wow, Senior Chief! Someone die while we were gone?"

"No one died," Calvins interjected. "It's just—"

"Calvins! Shut up."

"Wow! Leave him alone, Mort. I don't think I've heard Calvins say three words since we left Pearl," MacPherson said. "And, about time, too, Calvins."

"Three words! The sailor hasn't shut up since he came aboard," Taylor said.

"Looks as if he's coming out of his shell. Feeling good about being with his fellow sailors," MacPherson said as he tossed his ball cap at the hooks along the bulkhead. He turned and picked up his coffee cup, taking a sip. The ball cap hit the bulkhead and fell onto the deck.

"Well, he picked a hell of time to come out of his shell. So don't encourage him," Taylor piped up. "He's got enough problems. . . ."

"I'll say. He's working for you. Calvins, when it gets too much and life seems to hold no future for ya, you come see me. Don't cut your throat or jump overboard like the last seaman who worked for Mort."

"If you decide to cut your throat, come see me. I have this new knife that is fantastic," Gentron added.

Calvins took a couple of steps away from Taylor, drawing laughter from MacPherson.

"Just what we need. Two comic seamen," Taylor muttered. "Calvins! You gonna help me or stand there shooting the shit with everyone."

"Okay, MacPherson, cut the grab-assing and get to your position."

"Sure, Senior Chief, but seriously, Mort," MacPherson said to Taylor. "Why are you fucking around on the security console again?"

Taylor stopped and turned. He picked up a rag from the worktable and wiped his hands. "It's still acting up. It's the televisions," he said, tossing the rag at Calvins. He picked up the screwdriver and waved it at the bank of green lights aligned across the top of the console. "Just the cable television. Sometimes going off, sometimes not displaying anything, and other times displaying static or a bunch of colored lines and distortions."

"Funny. On board *Bellatrix*, we weren't having any problems seeing here."

Taylor turned back to his work. "That's why I think it's something here. If the security console in *Bellatrix* was having the same problems, then I'd be looking at the connecting lines. But . . . it must be something internal here. If this doesn't work, then I'm going to have to go over to the UUV compartment and do some checks there."

Agazzi stepped down the short ladder to the lower compartment. He glanced over Smith's shoulder, watching the digital rainfall for a few seconds. Nothing. Not even ambient noise disturbed the display. Along the left side of the display was the important detection quadrant. When you started seeing noise in that decibel level, then you were seeing something non-U.S.

MacPherson headed to the consoles, bumping Agazzi as he slid into the chair beside Bernardo. A grin spread across MacPherson's face. "Excuse me, Senior Chief," he said with a wink. "My! You're looking great today, Senior Chief. I can't tell you how seeing you has made my day," MacPherson said, his voice loud and the words exaggerated. "Yep, Senior Chief, my day isn't great until I've seen you."

"I'm going to be sick," Bernardo said.

Agazzi grinned. The daily MacPherson greeting made him feel good, even though he and everyone knew the exaggerated worshipping from MacPherson was a comic routine. Every team needed a MacPherson: a person with gregarious good humor. It brought a contagion of high morale. Morale was something his division could use right now.

MacPherson reached over and tugged on Bernardo's belt loops. No belt. "I just love your fashion statements, Pope."

Bernardo looked down. "Shit!" He looked up at the Senior Chief. "I'm sorry, Senior Chief. I really did think—"

"Pick it up when you have your break."

Bernardo held up three fingers at MacPherson. "You read cipher, Jerkings MacPherson?"

"Don't you mean Jenkins?"

Bernardo touched his chin, his eyes squinting as if in deep thought. Then, he shook his head. "Naw! *Jerk*-ings is the right word."

MacPherson slapped Bernardo on the shoulder, bringing a smile to both of them.

"One of these days, Jenkins . . ."

"Better men than you have tried."

Bernardo always forgot something. His belt one day; his T-shirt the next; and two days ago he showed up with a black and a brown sock. The man's professional competence made up for his lack of military appearance. Which reminded Agazzi to mention Bernardo's haircut—or lack thereof—to Keyland.

"I don't know, Senior Chief," Taylor said in a loud voice. "This piece of shit worked fine a week ago. It checked out perfectly ashore, but now, it just doesn't want to work properly. We may have to depend on the lights," he said, pointing at the row of lights below the security televisions, "to tell us if anything is malfunctioning in the compartment." The man shrugged. "Besides, the televisions are only supposed to be a visual backup. It's the bells, lights, and whistles that really tell us when something is not as it should be."

Agazzi climbed to the upper level and walked over to the security console. "If we have to we will, but I prefer to have the televisions on line. Otherwise, we'll find ourselves running back and forth between here and the *Bellatrix*."

One of the lights turned red.

"It's the hatch."

"MacPherson! You were just in the UUV compartment. Did you secure the hatch?"

MacPherson stood, looking toward Agazzi and Taylor. "Sure did, Senior Chief. Not only did I secure it, I jerked it a couple of times to make sure it was locked."

"Well, the light says it's open."

"MacPherson, you win the lottery. Get your ass over to the *Bellatrix* and check that hatch."

"Ah, Senior Chief, I just came from there."

"Which is why you're going back." Agazzi jerked his thumb to toward the hatch. "Now, beat feet. Get over there and check that hatch."

MacPherson laid his headset on the small operator shelf in front of his chair, and in a couple of seconds was at the hatch.

"And, when you get there, MacPherson, you're going to have to do a security check inside the compartment. Give us a call before you enter."

"Aye, Senior Chief."

The hatch closed behind the man.

"Nearly seven hundred feet," Keyland added. "Nearly seven hundred feet we have to go every time we head to the UUVs. And that's just from main deck to main deck. It doesn't include the six flights of stairs up and down when we leave here and arrive there."

"Just think what good shape we're going to be in," Bernardo added. "You want to feel my muscles?"

"Here," Taylor replied, "feel this muscle." His hand tugged his crotch up and down a couple of times.

"Stop. We are on watch now," Keyland said to Bernardo, including Gentron and Smith. "Focus on your consoles. Smith, keep training Gentron on the AN/SQR-25. Now, the rest of you, keep quiet and keep focused."

Several *aye ayes* acknowledged the leading petty officer's orders.

"Taylor," Agazzi said. "Keep working on it. I want those on line before we launch this afternoon." He turned to Keyland. "Have you heard anything about the sea anchors?"

"E-mail told us the sea anchors were out and functioning properly." He pointed to the dark display screen at the back of the compartment. "When they hook up the distribution servers to Sea Base, we should be able to see their status on the common-screen."

"Ain't this information world great?" Taylor muttered.

Each of the eight Fast Sealift Ships had been outfitted with two inflatable devices designed to be flooded with seawater to act as anchors. Each sea anchor was seven hundred feet in length. Sea anchors helped compensate for the influence of the ocean currents, sea state, and winds, giving the computers better control over the integrity of Sea Base. The same computer servers keeping the ships in a near-constant pattern of separation, course, and speed while holding aloft Sea Base also controlled the sea anchors.

For Agazzi, sea anchors were another hazard to avoid. As long as the UUVs were maneuvered out to sea off the port side of the *Bellatrix*, they could avoid the maneuvering horror of sixteen sea anchors rising and falling, inflating and deflating. Never constant—always in a state of flux. Regardless of what the ONR scientists believed, those sea anchors were going to get a workout. He didn't want to think what would happen to Sea Base if those sea anchors ceased to function like the security console had. Of course, the scientists said Sea Base could survive with only half of them operational.

Master Chief Jerry Jacobs had been quick to point out that the computers would have little choice but to constantly change the depth of the sea anchors, for the ocean was never constant itself. Jacobs pointed out, *with glee*, that sea anchors were another reason why Sea Base was going to be sitting on the bottom before this deployment was finished. One area where Jacobs had been wrong was his belief that if Sea Base started the long descent downward, they'd all be drowned by the suction. Since the sharks showed up, Agazzi doubted few would have an opportunity to drown.

"The sea anchors are working properly." Keyland clenched his lips together for a moment. "You know, if they come loose, they're going to fall like a rock. It would make our underwater hazard problem less."

Agazzi shook his head. "It that happens, the UUVs are going to be the least of our problems. They'd only fall until their weight reached a compensatory depth. Then they'd float there, waiting."

"Waiting for what?"

"Until the rest of Sea Base caught up with them," Bernardo said.

"Thanks, I needed that."

Agazzi looked at the clock. It had been ten minutes since MacPherson had departed. Though MacPherson complained, Agazzi knew the man would hurry to *Bellatrix*. He'd have a good timeline for the distance between the center and the UUV compartment once he heard from MacPherson.

"Senior Chief, I got a request from the CIC," Bernardo said, tapping the bottom of his screen. "Combat Information Center wants to know if the UUV launch is still on target for this afternoon."

"Tell them yes."

The telephone on Bernardo's console rang. He hit the speaker button. "That you, Mac?"

"Tell Elvis and the senior chief. I'm here at the UUV compartment. The hatch is secure, so it must be a loose sensor."

"Damn!" Taylor exclaimed, hearing the explanation. "One more thing to fix."

"Oh, Mac," Bernardo said in a singsong voice. "You're on speaker phone."

"Oh," came a weak response. "So, I guess . . ."

"You guessed right. Petty Officer Keyland would like to talk with you when you return."

Agazzi leaned forward. "MacPherson, have you completed a security walk through of the compartment."

"Not yet, Senior Chief, I just got here."

Agazzi looked up at the clock—it took MacPherson seventeen minutes, but MacPherson was a runner. His eyes narrowed. It'd take him about twenty minutes—if he hurried—to get from here to the UUV compartment.

"I see him!" Bernardo shouted, tapping the cam view on his screen.

Agazzi and Keyland leaned against the metal railing. They could make out the man walking near the firing cradle. If Agazzi didn't know the figure moving in the picture was MacPherson, he'd have a hard time determining who the person was. MacPherson disappeared out of camera view, turning toward the canisters where the armed UUVs were stored.

Five minutes later the intercom blared. "Everything is fine here, Senior Chief. Watch the light, I want to try something."

Everyone turned their attention to the light that reflected the status of the UUV compartment. It shifted from green to red to green back to red, and just as quickly back to green, and stayed there.

"Did you see anything?" MacPherson asked.

"It's green!" Taylor shouted.

"But, it keeps going from red to green and back again. What did you do?" Agazzi asked.

"Senior Chief, the hatch has some wiggle room. I have the lever down and it's supposed to be locked tight, but when I jerk on the hatch, I feel a bit of movement."

Agazzi grimaced.

"Think we should put a watch down there until we can get the hull technicians to fix it?" Keyland asked.

Agazzi thought for a moment. Every time the light switched to red, they were going to have to send someone to check the compartment, even though every one of them would know it was nothing but a poor connection. Damn, he didn't have the people or the time to do this. Nor did he have the people to man both the UUV compartment and the ASW control center twenty-four hours a day, seven days a week.

He shook his head. "No, let's live with it for a while and see how bad it is."

"You want someone to check it every time it goes red?"

"Of course. Even though it will mean someone out of the spaces for nearly forty-five minutes, we will check it every time it goes red."

"But, boss . . ."

"I know, Petty Officer Keyland. It isn't going to make life easier if we have to do this a lot, but we've been connected for a week and this is the first time the hatch has given us trouble. Unless we hit weather or some poor sailor bumps into the hatch, it should hold."

"You're the boss, Senior Chief. I would hate for us to have to jump through a bunch of security hoops because of a poor connection."

AN hour later, MacPherson was back in his position, giving Bernardo a hard time while Taylor, shaking his head and muttering beneath his breath, put the front panel back on the security console.

"I take from the lack of pictures on the screens that it's broken," Agazzi said.

"The thing is a piece of shit, Senior Chief. I've done everything I can to it and it still doesn't work." Taylor looked down where Smith was sitting. "It's a fucked-up Jesus Christ piece of shit."

"That's enough, Taylor."

"Aw, Senior Chief, the man's weird," Taylor said, his voice low.

"And you're not?"

"Of course not. I'm just your normal fucked-up maintenance tech whose parents changed on a monthly basis. You hear that, Smitty? The thing is goddamned fucked up."

"Taylor, you put the thing back together and watch your language. I'd hate to lose you for harassment."

"Senior Chief—"

"He doesn't bother you, Taylor. You don't bother him."

"Okay, Senior Chief," Taylor said with a shrug. He turned his back to Agazzi, picked up a screw, slipped it into a hole, and began to turn. "Before you ask, Senior Chief, what I'll do now is pull the schematics for the whole shebang. First thing we'll do is inspect the most logical places for where the foul-up can be. Since I've checked the security console on board the *Bellatrix* yesterday and this is the second time here, I want to look at the electronic connections between *Algol* and the *Bellatrix*." He picked up the second screw. "If that doesn't work, then I'll figure something else to do."

The conduits between the widely separated compartments ran on different lines. This was going to take Taylor a few days because he would have to go hand-over-hand, following the cabling from this console to the *Bellatrix*, stopping at every connector to verify a good circuit. A few days were an optimistic estimate because if any other equipment suffered a casualty, Taylor would have to redirect his energies.

Taylor grabbed another screw, stretched, and put it into a hole at the top of the panel. "If checking the connections doesn't work, then we'll have a lot of fun. We'll start here"—he pointed to the overhead lines with his screwdriver—"and visually follow every line between here and there to see what we can see." He returned to his work with the screwdriver. "Until then, Senior Chief, we'll have to rely on the cam device on Bernardo's console and the lights up here. I think that should be sufficient. It ain't like nothing is going to happen in there we can stop from here."

"You know, Senior Chief, rather than having our people running back and forth between here and the *Bellatrix* every time the light goes from green to red, maybe Taylor . . ." Keyland started.

"I'm an electronic repair–type person. I don't do doors, hatches, and windows. I do connections." Taylor held up his hand. "When I reach the *Bellatrix* and the hatch, I will look at it. If it's something simple and something within my skills, I'll fix it."

"Why don't you do it now?" Keyland asked.

"Why don't I forget about fixing the security console or doing preventive maintenance on the SQR-25 or the other things that one man is supposed to do?" He looked at his watch. "It's already one o'clock—or thirteen-hundred for you career lifers. I haven't had lunch, and we're going to launch the first UUV later." He looked at Keyland. "You want me fiddling with the hatch or around here in case something goes tits-up?"

"Okay," Agazzi said. "When you reach the *Bellatrix*, check the hatch. In fact, Petty Officer Taylor, why don't you start at the *Bellatrix* and work your way this way?"

Taylor shook his head. "Won't work, Senior Chief. I need to start at this end. This is where the circuit originates that controls both this security console and the smaller one in the *Bellatrix*. Besides, I can't start this before tomorrow anyway. I have some stuff that has to be done before we launch and it'll take time to gather the gear I'll need to trace the cabling. We've got too much going on and you only have one maintenance man."

"HEY, can I have a break?" Smith asked.

Agazzi raised his head from the paperwork on his desk, eavesdropping on the conversation a few feet behind him.

"You're supposed to be training Gentron on your position."

"Petty Officer Keyland, he knows enough to run the thing without me. Besides, he's got an entire room full of sonar technicians if he has a question, if a fleet of submarines show up."

"Probably a good opportunity to let our people take a break, Petty Officer Keyland," Agazzi added without turning around. He looked at his watch and then the black-rimmed Navy clock mounted on the bulkhead. "It'll be another couple of hours before we launch the UUV. Everyone's been cooped up here all day."

"Wait until Taylor returns and you can go."

Ten minutes later, Smith stepped out of the hatch.

SMITH walked into the passageway, stopping long enough to push the lever down on the watertight hatch. The light above the biometric hand reader mounted on the left blinked from red to green. He looked both ways, saw no one, and turned to the ladder leading up. Six flights to the main deck of the *Algol* and another hundred feet or so to the main deck and fresh air. At the oh-three level, Smith turned away from the ladder and disappeared down the passageway running along the varied staterooms that filled the two forecastles of every Fast Sealift Ship. Several minutes passed before he returned and continued his climb to the top.

In the ASW control center, the security televisions suddenly returned to life.

"Hey, Taylor, great job," MacPherson said, pointing at the

screens. "If you'd worked another couple of hours, we could have had color."

The pictures turned from black and white to color.

"Wow! Good job. Magic."

Taylor stepped back from the workbench so he could see the secure televisions. "Damn, I hate gremlins."

"Gremlins, hell! You owe Smitty credit for that. I heard him praying for the things to come back on. You need to add prayer to your tool set."

"Here, add this to your tool set," Taylor said, holding up his middle finger.

"Whoa!" MacPherson said, laughing and shaking his hand back and forth. "That burned."

Agazzi turned in his chair. All six screens were back on line. Must have been a glitch in the connections between here and the *Bellatrix*. He turned and picked up the ship telephone to see if the lines worked between there and the tower. He flipped through the brochure distributed yesterday with the complete list of telephone numbers for Sea Base. The book was organized alphabetically by organization. Tower had its own set and within the raised tower on the second floor, the Combat Information Center was coming to life much as the ASW center was.

Finding the number for Operations, Agazzi punched it in. After several minutes of waiting and explaining, he received permission to launch one UUV at nineteen-hundred hours. That gave him two and a half hours. All they could do now was wait.

He glanced at the screen and saw the firing cradle suspended over the closed hatch. The checklists for launching the UUVs lay on the small shelves in front of each console. The closed hatch would be opened when the time came to launch the UUV. He wondered briefly if the lights from the UUV compartment would draw sharks to the opening.

The firing sequence called for the cradle to lower the UUV until it was a foot from the surface of the water, and then drop it. They could open this hatch from here, but if he were the skipper of the *Bellatrix*, he'd want to know if someone was going to open the bottom of his ship to the Pacific. He thumbed through the telephone numbers again. Five minutes later, he hung up.

The master of the *Bellatrix* seemed unconcerned. Agazzi was slightly amazed until the master told him that the doors had been opened during open-ocean testing off Pearl Harbor.

"It worked then and the ship didn't sink," he had said. "It'll work now, and the *Bellatrix* will still stay afloat. Besides, even if something goes wrong, all we're talking about, Senior Chief, is a small compartment on board a ship that, when full, can carry over 55,000 tons. A ton or two of sea water won't even change the draft of the *Bellatrix*."

When Agazzi hung up, he stared at the telephone for a moment. *But what if those UUVs with their warheads go up?* he asked himself. *That would change the draft of* Bellatrix.

"What are you doing?" Keyland shouted.

Agazzi turned. Keyland was reaching over Seaman Gentron's shoulders.

"I was just fiddling with the knobs, Petty Officer Keyland."

Keyland didn't say anything. His eyes were locked on the solid gray-white line that had suddenly appeared along the outer edge of the rainfall display. Even from his chair, Agazzi could see the difference in color. He was out of the chair and in the lower compartment in seconds. As the rainfall continued to flow down the console, the line grew in length. The database readout scrambled through red numbers and letters as it searched for a match. The line changed to red, but the database continued searching. The red meant unknown and would remain red until the database found a match. If the match were non-U.S. or nonfriendly, then it would remain red.

When the line began to curve to the right, Agazzi stopped in his tracks. A slight chill rode up his spine. The chill always happened when he first recognizeed the presence of a submarine.

"That's . . ."

"A submarine," Agazzi finished.

"And, it's not . . ."

The database base stopped. It had a match.

". . . One of ours." Agazzi reached over and flipped the sound-powered box before he remembered the sound-powered intercoms only operated within the individual ships. The technicians were still working the sound-powered telephone connections for the watches, but last he'd heard, walkie-talkies were the mode of communications between the topside watch standers.

"Start tracking it. I want a time-motion analysis on the contact now."

The line steadied up again, riding straight down the rainfall display.

Keyland reached for the icon, but Gentron's finger was faster.

Agazzi dialed the number to the combat information center, slowed by having to look it up again.

"Contact bearing 330, speed ten knots; increasing noise-decreasing range. No bearing drift."

Translated, the data told Agazzi the contact was heading toward Sea Base, and if Gentron hadn't changed the contrast, the submarine could have reached Sea Base without them ever being aware. He should never have allowed Smith the break. Bernardo and Smith were both gone and he had the second team on the watch.

"Estimated range is between sixty to one hundred nautical miles, Senior Chief. Contact is below the layer."

"Identity?"

"Not yet, but if you run a line through the bearing, it goes straight through to China."

The telephone rang on the other end. When answered, Agazzi started to explain about the contact, but the officer on the other end told him to wait because they were very busy. Raising his voice, Agazzi explained about the closing contact. The officer's tone changed as she understood what Senior Chief Agazzi was telling her. Only a few seconds passed before the captain was on the line. When he hung up, the timetable for launching the UUV had changed. He no longer had two hours to launch; he had minutes.

The ship jerked slightly as if pushed down for a moment and released. Agazzi glanced up, his stomach tightening for a moment; Jacobs's dark Pacific rushed through his mind.

"What the hell was that?" Keyland shouted.

"Air Force fighters landing," MacPherson said. "Read your e-mail alerts. They're landing two at a time. Bet *Denebola* felt that. They're touching down right on top of it."

"Contact constant on bearing 330," Gentron said, his voice shaking.

Keyland touched him on the shoulder. "You're doing fine. Stay calm. This happens a lot among warships. Other countries want to know what we're doing. We want to know what they're doing. What better way to find out than using a submarine? It happens all the time. We're part of the game. Once it sees we're on to it, it'll most likely turn tail and scurry away until we lose contact."

"What if it doesn't scurry away?"

"Then the captain will have to make a decision." Agazzi turned to Keyland. "Where are Smith and Bernardo?"

"Smith just left for his break. Bernardo should be back soon, Senior Chief. You want me to go find them?"

Agazzi shook his head. *You fight with what you have.*

"You think they're going to do more than just try out our defenses and see how close they can get—"

"Before we show our hand?" Agazzi finished. "I think as soon as we launch a UUV, they'll collect data on how we did it; how close they were when we did it; and how long it was between the time we detected them and the time it took for us to launch. If they get within torpedo-launch range before we launch the UUV, then they'll go away believing they can attack us whenever they want. They'll just stay the hell out of our detection range and launch torpedoes."

ELEVEN

Zeichner wiped sweat from his brow, beads of it joining the soaked shoulders and collar of his white shirt. The heat, sun, and sweat finally convinced him the tie looked better hanging beside the coat in the stateroom closet. Zeichner touched his belt buckle—it was buckled back in the old hole. So much for yesterday's elation. Looking both ways along the starboard walkway of the *Regulus* he saw no sign of Gainer. He glanced nervously at his watch. Thirty minutes he'd been waiting for his deputy to return with the team promised by the skipper of Sea Base. Zeichner stepped back into the shadow provided by the ladder well leading up to the next level. He leaned against the bulkhead for a second before the sun-heated metal caused him to move away. Even the air-conditioning inside the *Denebola* was unable to keep up with this constant heat. Zeichner tugged the matted shirt away from his chest and let it go, taking a deep breath in appreciation to the momentary coolness. He'd be glad when this was over and he could return to what little coolness his room provided. He shut his eyes, seeing himself in the recliner, overhead air conditioner blasting across his body, and stealing a few minutes of a power nap.

The sound of voices from the forward part of the ship snapped him back to the deck of the *Regulus*. He turned, twisting his knee slightly, bringing a fresh wave of pain across it. The throbbing in his left knee drew a moan. When he returned to Pearl Harbor, he was going to invest his retirement account in those little painkillers the ship's doc gave him. He did sleep better and the knee throbbed less in the morning. He ran the handkerchief across his face, pushing beneath the double chin to swipe the sweat burning beneath it.

Shipboard life was shit. Why in the hell did these sailors do this and enjoy it? Day after day, pounding up and down metal ladders. Jerking their heads from side to side as they hurried through metal passageways, dodging bits of low-hanging stuff some engineer designed for ship survivability. A design capable of decapitating the unwary person. The vision of a sailor running down a passageway while his head bounced on the deck behind him caused Zeichner to shake his head. Metal floors everywhere—or decks, as these denizens of another century called them. It's a wonder any could still walk after a twenty-year career, much less carry on an intelligible conversation with a civilian. Head: bathroom. Port: left. Starboard: right. Overhead: roof. Bulkhead: wall.

Zeichner patted his pants pockets, feeling the small tube of cream the surgeon on the *Algol* had given him. Told him to rub this stuff on the knee before he went to bed and *voila*, the heat would soothe the joint. He'd try anything.

"Boss!"

"Finally! Gainer and his permanent smile," Zeichner mumbled. He stepped to the starboard safety lines of the *Regulus*.

"Kevin, where's the team?" Zeichner asked as the young man reached him.

"Four master-at-arms. They're going to meet us—"

A loud splash interrupted Gainer, causing both men to look down at the water. They stared for several moments.

"They're all over the place," Gainer said, breaking the silence. "I was on board the *Antares* earlier this morning and it looked as if hundreds of them were swimming in the shade of Sea Base."

A dark shadow swam from beneath the *Regulus*, its shape weaving back and forth as the fin of the great white cut through the surface of the waters, the smaller sharks flicking their tails and scurrying out of its way. In the ocean, the depths belonged to the meanest, not always the biggest. But most times the great whites were both. Almost like the streets of Washington, Zeichner shuddered.

"I know how you feel, Boss. I'd hate for this thing to go down."

"Yeah."

"You wouldn't have to worry about drowning. Of course, that depends, I guess, on which half they ate first. If they ate you from the waist down, then . . ."

"You really have to find more things to do, Kevin," Zeichner interrupted.

The sharks had appeared within a couple of days of Sea Base's deployment. Since then, it seemed their number grew daily. Zeichner heard one sailor tell a couple of shipmates that Sea Base was near where the World War II cruiser *Indianapolis* went down after being torpedoed by a Japanese submarine. His interest was piqued; he had eavesdropped as the petty officer told the story of hundreds of survivors, huddling together, and being picked off one at a time by sharks. A visit to the ship's library branded the story as untrue; Sea Base was nowhere near where the *Indianapolis* had been sunk.

The sound of sharks fighting over something in the water drew their attention toward the stern of the *Regulus*.

"It makes the water look as if it's boiling."

Zeichner grunted, watching the spectacle silently.

A few seconds later, only the soft lapping of the surface covered what had been a twisting, churning cauldron of gray shapes fighting over whatever had peaked their interest.

Once it had been empty blue water lapping against the sides of the ships. Within a day of Sea Base being raised above the eight Fast Sealift ships, the ocean beneath the man-made island was filled with the ocean's eating machines. It was the shade, he figured. Not only the shade, but the permanency of Sea Base and the thousands of pounds of garbage Sea Base tossed overboard every day: a magnet to the eating machines of the sea.

The captain had immediately banned swimming. No one attempted to ignore the ban. The sea had its own way of deterring those foolhardy enough to ignore its perils. It'd be the shortest, most exciting swim they ever had. Unfortunately, they'd never be able to share their experience.

"It is something that's with us now."

Zeichner nodded. "It's something no one thought about, but as long we're up here and they're down there, I'm happy."

"Some sailor on board the *Denebola* caught a great white yesterday."

While swimming had been banned, fishing was growing as the favorite off duty pasttime. Contests abounded between ships, between departments, between intramural teams set up by the Morale Welfare and Recreation crews. T-shirts appeared almost overnight, each identifying specific fishing teams. Of course, the most-caught fish was the shark.

Zeichner guffawed. "I'm sure the stupid shit tried to bring it on board."

"How did you know?" Gainer asked, but continued before Zeichner could answer. "The whole team was helping him pull the thing up the side of the *Denebola*. They had this twenty-five footer nearly to the open cargo hatch on the side. You know the hatch these Fast Sealift Ships open so a ramp can be put on the piers to allow cars, trucks, and tanks to drive aboard or drive off?"

"Yes, I know what hatch you're talking about, Kevin. Plus, I doubt the shark was fighting to get away."

"They had it nearly to the lip of the open hatch and—"

"What happened?" Zeichner asked. There has to be a point to this story.

"The shark wasn't fighting until it reached the lip of the open cargo hatch and then nearly pulled the sailors into the drink with it."

Zeichner looked down at the sharks swimming between the *Regulus* and the *Pollux*. "They're smarter than we think. That shark probably thought he had caught the sailors. If the thing had waited another few seconds until the sailors pulled him on board, it would have done more than thrash around among them. Those sailors would have been a group of footless, legless, screaming . . . No, sharks are smarter than we think. You know sharks have been here since the age of the dinosaurs and they'll be here when the age of man passes."

"Maybe they know something we don't."

Zeichner shook his head. "Let's hope you're wrong and its just the shade and garbage that keeps them here." He pointed over Gainer's shoulder. "Those our MAAs?"

"Here they come," Gainer said, glancing down at his watch. "Right on time." He gave a short laugh. "I have to admit, boss, I wondered if they would show. The senior chief didn't want to send anyone. Said he had no orders from the captain to do it."

"The captain is the one who promised them."

Gainer nodded. "I told him that, but he was adamant he had no orders to provide NCIS with a working party."

"I wouldn't call this a working party."

The work shoe of the Navy is called a boondocker: steel-toed, heavy soled, unshined leather, hanging loose around the ankle, issued in boot camp and seldom replaced. The sound of boondockers pounding on the metal deck of the *Regulus* was as uncoordinated as the movement of the MAAs.

If they had been Marines, which were Zeichner's first choice, there'd be twenty of them, running in formation, each foot slapping the deck in symphony, each weapon cocked and loaded with their fingers on the triggers. Marines were always pegged to the fight. A good day for a Marine was enjoying that after-combat cigarette with the bodies of his enemies lying all around him.

Sailors didn't walk or run if they could get a ride. But he had developed an appreciation for the life of a sailor after being out to sea for one month, two weeks, and five days. Didn't mean he understood why they chose the life they did, but he understood it was hard to march inside the skin of a ship.

"I guess you convinced him."

Gainer nodded. "I called the operations center and had the officer-in-charge tell the man to get his head out of his ass and send the MAAs."

Zeichner glanced up at Gainer. "Mr. Gainer," he said, the broad smile causing the sweat to trickle around the edges of his lips. "I am thoroughly impressed."

"They didn't only teach me tact in the Army."

"Mr. Gainer," the young man wearing second-class stripes said. "We were told to report to you."

They look so young, Zeichner thought, his eyes canvassing the four sailors. Each sailor carried a CAR-45 semiautomatic rifle. Zeichner eyes traveled from face to face of the three men and one woman who stood before them. This second-class petty officer couldn't be more than twenty-five, and the woman . . . *Girl must just be out of high school*, Zeichner thought. Here he was about to raid a stateroom where a "mad bomber" could be waiting to blow all of them up, and they send him a high school cheerleader with a semiautomatic rifle. Why didn't that surprise him? The

Navy never took NCIS seriously. Most thought of them as wannabe policemen. *But, by God, they were their wannabe policemen.*

"Glad you're here, Petty Officer . . ."

"Dickens, sir. Petty Officer Dickens."

"This is Mr. Zeichner. He is in charge of this raid."

The sailor's eyebrows curled into a deep *V*. "Raid? I don't understand. We were told you were going to arrest someone and we were to take him into custody."

Zeichner ignored the statement that was more a question. "We're going to a stateroom where there is a person of interest to us. Fact is we"—he swept his hand across Gainer and the four-man squad, stopping by placing it on his chest—"are going to conduct six raids. We want to make sure there are no problems. That's why we asked for you."

Dickens turned his head to look at his team and then back at Zeichner. "I guess I don't understand why you need four armed MAAs to search a stateroom, unless you're expecting trouble?"

Zeichner took a deep breath and let it out through his nose. "I hope not, but we're investigating the explosions—"

Dickens's eyes widened. "Jesus Christ, sir. Is this guy the bomber?"

"I didn't say that—"

"This is the bomber," the tall, lanky MAA behind the Dickens said loudly. "I'm ready. I'm ready," the sailor continued, his hands clenching and unclenching on his carbine.

"Can it, Labeau," Dickens said irritably. Then the leading petty officer turned back to Zeichner. "Sir, I'm going to have to call the senior chief. He said for me to call him if it seemed dangerous."

"Let's get this first one done, before we stand out here lollygagging and let the suspect get away. Then you can call your senior chief." Zeichner was getting irritated. A reluctant petty officer; this Labeau must be some sort of psychopath, and a cheerleader. *Damn!*

"Sir, we're in the middle of the Pacific Ocean. The suspect ain't gonna go nowhere."

Zeichner's lower lip pushed against his upper. A drop of sweat ran between the lips into his mouth. "Son, I know he isn't *gonna go nowhere*, but he might decide to take all of us with him in a explosive cloud if he thinks we're on to him. Now, your captain has assigned you to me, right?

"Yes, sir, but the senior chief said . . ."

"I don't care what your senior chief said. I don't care what your mother thinks. What I care about is keeping Sea Base afloat and operating. Come here." He motioned the four sailors to the safety lines. "Look down there." He placed his hand on Dickens's shoulder.

Beneath them, gray shapes weaved in and out among themselves, disappearing beneath the ships while others appeared to take their place. He felt the petty officer shiver, knowing how the man felt. Sailors hated sharks. Every day hundreds of thousands of shivers probably went through the crewmembers of Sea Base. Probably the only relief they got from this heat. He moved his hand.

Dickens turned around. "They're everywhere," he said in a soft voice.

"I would rather not be down there with them. To help keep them down there and us up here, we need to catch this son-of-a-bitch, rather than swimming among them." He pointed over the side. "We're trying to find him, if you get my drift."

Dickens let out a deep breath. "Yes, sir." His knuckles turned white where the sailor gripped the carbine. "We're ready, sir."

"Wait a minute," the young girl said. "I can't find the safety on this thing."

"Stella, leave the safety on," Dickens said, turning to the youngest member of the team. He looked back at Zeichner. "This is her first week with us, Mr. Zeichner. She arrived on the C-130 last week." He turned back to young woman. "See this here," he said, touching the safety. "Just flip it forward if you need it."

"Stella, why don't you go in front of me?" Labeau said.

"Why?"

"Labeau, she is going to bring up the rear."

"The rear?"

"Yes, the rear," Dickens said.

Just what I need, thought Zeichner. A dysfunctional raiding party that may shoot all of us in a panic if anything happens.

"Listen, Dickens," Zeichner said. "I just need you for a few hours. We're wasting time. Mr. Gainer and I will take care of entry. All you have to do is stop anyone who tries to bolt and get away. You're to place your men—*sailors*—at each end of the passageway. You should leave one member up here and put another member inside the cargo bay, in the event our person of interest decides to head through the ship."

Dickens straightened. "Sir, we're fully prepared to go with you. I've been trained in forced entry."

"Is deadly force authorized?" Labeau asked, his lanky frame twisting with anticipation. "I hope it is. I've always wanted to be able to shoot someone and say stop."

"It's 'halt or I'll shoot,' " Gainer corrected.

"Shut up, Labeau," Dickens said. He turned to Zeichner. "Deadly force isn't authorized, is it?"

Zeichner's head bounced a couple of times in disbelief as to where this conversation was going.

"Don't we need a search warrant?" the remaining member of the team asked, pushing his glasses back on his nose.

Zeichner rolled his eyes, ignoring the comment, and looked at Dickens. "I'm sure you have experience in entry, Dickens, but I don't think the rest of your team is the right squad for this. So, post someone here. Have someone go with us so he can go to the other side of the ship to stop anyone from disappearing that way."

"Okay, sir," Dickens answered.

Zeichner heard the disappointment in the man's voice. "And, call your senior chief and tell him to send you a team that knows how to take someone down. This isn't the time for training new people." He looked at the man called Labeau. "And it isn't the time to be killing someone just because you've never done it before."

"That's not what I meant," Labeau whined. "I just—"

"Ah, shut up, Labeau," Dickens and the fourth member said in unison.

FIVE minutes later, with the MAAs deployed and the replacement MAAs rushing to augment the team, Zeichner and Gainer stood outside the stateroom of Kiang Zheng.

Zeichner had pulled the man's file. Kiang was a first-generation American of Chinese descent working for a non-profit defense institute in San Antonio: unmarried with a Ph.D. in systems engineering from Johns Hopkins University. What had moved him to the top of the list was that the man was a marathon runner and had spent four years in the United States Army as an explosives expert. The man also had parents who had immigrated to America, lived there for twenty years, and then one day packed up and returned to China. Kiang Zheng had taken them and returned alone.

Everything any police officer would want had been laid out in this man's history. The man barely managed to keep an impressive security clearance because his parents were in China. The military service credentials were probably what had convinced the security reviewers to give the man some of the highest security clearances in the government. Zeichner wouldn't have given the man a confidential-level clearance, much less the top-secret mumbo jumbo shit they blessed this man with. Any man with parents in a foreign country couldn't be much of an American in Zeichner's book.

The fact that Kiang was a late addition to the contingency from San Antonio was the cherry on top. The other item that raised an eyebrow was the discovery that Kiang Zheng wasn't even supposed to be on this deployment. The person selected had died in a car accident two days before the deployment, so Kiang had volunteered. Pretty mysterious, if you asked him. Go figure.

Zeichner crouched right of the closed door. Gainer poised on the left. Both had pistols pulled. Both grasped with two hands and both pointed up. Zeichner looked behind him.

Dickens stood watching him.

At the other end of the passageway squatted Labeau, his fingers curling and uncurling off the carbine pointed in their direction. Zeichner felt an uncomfortable itch in the small of his back.

Zeichner looked back at Dickens. The petty officer had slid into a crouching position, his carbine held loosely, pointing away from them. The man nodded as their eyes met.

"You ready?" Zeichner asked quietly.

Gainer nodded.

Zeichner reached around and twisted the knob slowly. It turned, but the door didn't open. "Locked."

Gainer reached over and knocked a couple of times, waited, then knocked again.

"Doesn't seem to be anyone home."

Zeichner dropped his gun to his side, stepped away from the bulkhead, and walked in front of the door. He took a couple of steps back and leaned against the bulkhead. He raised his foot.

"Wait, boss." Gainer grabbed the doorknob, put his shoulder against the door, and shoved. The door snapped open. He stepped back quickly.

Zeichner burst into the room, his pistol grasped firmly with both hands. The stateroom was empty. Zeichner hurried to the door leading to the head, threw the door open, and jerked the shower curtain back. Empty. He tucked his pistol into his holster. "Looks as if our man is elsewhere."

"Well, it is lunch time."

Zeichner's stomach growled. The air inside the compartment was cold from the high settings of the air-conditioning, bringing an involuntary shiver as the colder air swept across his wet shirt.

"Looks as if our man is neat," Gainer said, pushing down on the made-up rack, his hand leaving a small imprint.

"Let's go through everything. Don't make it too obvious. If we don't see anything that leaps out at us, we'll come back later. I want to roust all six suspects before Sea Base sounds 'stop work.'"

Sea Base integration had begun as soon as the Fast Sealift Ships raised the main platform and one way the Navy captain commenced this sense of unity was to put every ship, every crew, and everyone on board, regardless to whom or where they were assigned, on the same time schedule. The loudspeaker system had been one of the first things activated. Every announcement reached every nook and cranny of Sea Base, including security areas that required a hand scan and a combination to enter.

Every morning started with a boatswain piping reveille and every evening ended with taps. There were boatswain whistles for meals, whistles for muster, whistles for when to dump trash, and even whistles for when to start and stop work. If Zeichner never heard another whistle when he left Sea Base in four months, two weeks, and two days, he would be a happy man.

"He's brought his own radio," Gainer said, nodding toward the desk.

Zeichner picked it up off the metal desk and turned it on. Music from a Sea Base radio station came from the speaker. Zeichner turned the radio back and forth, reading the *Made in China* sticker on the bottom. It was one of those with long-range reception capability. Zeichner turned the volume up. Music filled the stateroom. Elevator music, he would call it. He turned it off and set it back where he found it. Looked at it for a moment and then turned it slightly to the original angle.

He moved and nearly tripped over Gainer, who was on his hands and knees, looking under the rack. "Nothing down here, boss, unless you like shoes."

"Pull them out and make sure there's nothing in them."

Zeichner stepped into the bathroom and opened the cabinet. "Toothpaste, razor, antiacid, vitamins, some Band-Aids," he mumbled aloud as he inventoried the contents. Nothing here but stuff he'd find in his own cabinet. He heard Gainer stand up.

"Look in his desk," Zeichner said. "But leave it as you find it. It would be nice if Kiang didn't suspect we had been here when he returns." He heard Gainer pull one of the drawers open.

"What if he returns while we're here?"

"Then we'll go back to plan one and interview the suspect."

"I found something.

Zeichner shut the cabinet door and stepped back into the main part of the stateroom. "What is it?"

Gainer held up a framed document. "It's his honorable discharge."

Zeichner took it. He turned it around, examining the sides, the back, and running his hands across the glass. He sighed and handed it back to Gainer. "His records show he was honorably discharged. Guess you can't hang someone for being proud of it."

Gainer slid it back into the bottom drawer. "Suspicious, if you ask me."

"You're right. Why would anyone have their honorable discharge framed and be carrying it with them?"

Gainer shook his head, his nose wrinkling. "People don't carry their discharge papers with them. They leave them at home, stored in the basement with their other military paraphernalia, so when they get old and have grandchildren, they can impress them with it. They don't carry it with them."

Zeichner stepped to the door. "You may be right, but he's first-generation American. He might have some sort of immigrant pride. . . ."

"Immigrant pride? Never heard of that," Gainer said as he lifted the edge of the mattress. "Looks as if he hides his money the way everyone else does."

"How much?"

Gainer pulled the bills out, dropping the mattress. "Ummm. One hundred dollars exactly." He looked at Zeichner. "One hundred dollars."

"Put it back."

Gainer lifted the mattress and pushed the money under it.

Zeichner stepped into the passageway. "Think you can close it like you opened it?"

Gainer gave him a questioning look and nodded. He stepped into the passageway, reached inside the door, pushed in the lock, and pulled it shut. "Easier this way, boss."

Zeichner waved at Dickens. "Okay, get your team together. We're heading to *Denebola* next."

KIANG stood near one of the large ventilation shafts on the stern of the *Bellatrix*, smoking a cigar. A black satchel sat on the deck near his feet. His watch showed it was a little after five. He glanced at the satchel. This was the most dangerous time for him. Caught now, he would have little argument as to his intentions.

He took a puff, nearly coughing. He didn't smoke, but he had to have a reason for being where the other smokers came to relax. The *Bellatrix* had nothing that concerned his area of expertise. The destruction of the servers had removed it from his list of interests. He was a systems engineer and a contractor. Contractors were like ghosts. No one really saw them until they were needed. They walked along the periphery of Navy operations, providing technology to win wars, training sailors on the latest gear, sometimes even writing the damn training manuals for them. When something went wrong, it was miraculous how the contractor became an integral member of the team. Until then, they were ignored and treated horribly, disappearing once again into this ghostly vestige of experience flickering around the edges of operations.

Minutes later he glanced at his watch—five thirty. The smokers were starting to drift away from the stern area, tossing their butts in the red-painted butt can sitting alongside the bulkhead. Twenty minutes later, the area was empty with the exception of Kiang. He squatted and quickly unzipped the satchel, looking both ways before pulling out a long, dark cylinder about two feet long. Quickly, he walked over to the security lines and dropped the cylinder. He glanced both ways to see if anyone had seen him.

Then he glanced downward just as the cylinder hit the water. A couple of sharks turned sharply, and in a burst of speed dove toward the cylinder. For a moment he thought one of them would swallow it, but at the last second, the two sharks turned aside.

With both hands he grabbed the lifeline, leaning forward to watch the cylinder. His intellectual mind wondered briefly if they turned aside because they recognized the cylinder wasn't edible or if they turned because of their proximity to each other. He watched another moment or two until the cylinder disappeared from sight.

Releasing the lifeline, he turned around. A first-class sailor stood there, smoking a cigarette and watching him. His knees felt weak.

"Lots of them down there," the man said, smoke curling around the words as the first-class spoke. "I find myself watching them a lot, too."

Kiang smiled weakly. "I've never seen sharks."

"I've never seen this many. Almost as if the Pacific wants us to know it doesn't like us being here."

Kiang nodded and picked up his satchel. "I think it's more the shade and garbage."

"It's always about shade and garbage when you're at sea."

Kiang walked away, leaving the man to his deep philosophical dribble. *Shade and garbage? What's always about shade and garbage?* He walked along the port side of the *Bellatrix*, glancing out to sea every now and again. The top of Sea Base ended a hundred feet out from where he stood, strong steel-alloy beams holding up the extension protruding out to sea. Light dancing in the gap between the sea and the bottom of Sea Base played on the soft waves of the ocean, the ripples always a constant change of blues. He found it soothing.

TWO hundred feet beneath the keel of the *Bellatrix* the cylinder started to change shape. Two small fins shaped like wings emerged from each side. The front end of the cylinder fell away, creating a huge funnel that quickly filled with water. On the other end, four covers were ejected from small openings. From a distance, someone seeing the cylinder might mistake it for a barracuda. The changed cylinder drifted downward and slowed as the weight of the water above and the pressure beneath began to equalize. Internally, a small turbine came to life, and in the next instant, two tiny propellers started turning.

Like a barracuda, one moment it was motionless except for its slowing descent, and the next, it was shooting away as if fired from a cannon.

KIANG opened his stateroom. His nose twitched. It was the odor of perspiration. He sat the satchel on the floor and shut the door. He walked around, surveying his stateroom. Careful not to touch anything yet. He stepped into the bathroom and saw where the shower curtain no longer touched both ends of the shower. Stepping back into the main stateroom, Kiang walked to the desk, flipped on the light, and bent down to look at the radio. It was a good three inches from the faint pencil marks on the dark gray desk. He looked at the framed Honorable Discharge certificate and saw it was canted in a different direction.

He lifted the radio and ran his fingers along the edges until he felt the minute protrusions. Then he pinched the sides together. A small drawer snapped open. With his fingers he pulled on it. The side of the radio clicked out a couple of inches before stopping. Twisting the radio to the side and holding it to the lamp, Kiang saw where the thin strand of string was still attached. He pushed the side shut. Whoever had come into his stateroom had touched the radio, but hadn't found the communication device within it. He leaned against his desk, tapping the radio lightly against his right hand as he surveyed the room. Looking down, he could see the writing on the shoeboxes. When he left this morning, the shoeboxes had been pushed farther back, out of sight, the way he preferred it.

He sat the radio down on the desk. At his bed, he lifted the mattress. The money was still there, but folded to the right instead of the left. He grabbed the money and put it into his pocket. He would have preferred to find the money gone. The money was his tripwire to let him know if he'd been discovered. If the radio, money, or other valuables were gone he would have attributed the break-in to theft.

With nothing gone and a half-hearted attempt to hide their search, it meant they suspected him. If they were sure, he'd already be arrested. He pulled the desk chair out and sat down, his mind analyzing the event. There was nowhere to hide on Sea Base. If and when they wanted him, they'd come for him. Most likely, because no one was waiting when he had returned, the searchers were in the information-gathering phase of their investigation. With the thought of investigation, he quickly focused on Zeichner. The man was smarter than Kiang gave him credit for. What had Kiang done to make this man suspicious? Their paths had crossed twice: once along the pier and the second time on the *Denebola* during the explosion. No doubt Zeichner saw him on the pier, but did the NCIS agent see him on the *Denebola*?

Somewhere Kiang had tripped up. Where and how, he wondered? He thought he knew more about Zeichner, but it looked as if the agent also had something on him.

He knew Zeichner's routine and habit. The overweight pig got up every morning, ate a huge breakfast, and soon disappeared into the spaces allocated for NCIS. Seldom did the man come out except to eat, sleep, sweat, and eat some more.

Kiang's nose wrinkled. The smell of sweat must be Zeichner's. He smiled at how easy it was to analyze the event, to even name the person who had been in his stateroom. If Zeichner was here, then his dandy shadow Gainer had tagged along. Gainer was probably the one who searched the shoe boxes—it was too low for Zeichner to reach without the fat man having to lie on the floor.

They probably weren't too sure about Kiang, otherwise they would have had someone waiting for him when he returned. They may be searching Sea Base for him now, but since no one was waiting for him, Kiang wondered why.

He breathed easier. They may be looking for him, but they weren't sure whom they were looking for. Therefore, when they failed to find him in his stateroom, Zeichner and his team must have gone on to others on his list. He was chasing the bombers.

If he was wrong in his assumption, it mattered little to Kiang. He had given his handler what he wanted. The colonel would live up to his promise—or so Kiang told himself. The information was on its way. In this day and age of information, the old fashioned way of photography, written code, and handoffs was even more secure than trying to use the Internet or, Lord forbid, sending it over the airways.

No, they'll come back to him eventually. It would be easy to find someone on Sea Base. You announce to everyone you were looking for him and you'd find him. He smiled. His name was on a list. A list with others on it. If others were on it, then they were looking for the bomber. He laughed. Anything to connect him immediately with what he was doing went over the side of *Bellatrix*. He looked at the radio. *With the exception of the radio,* he thought.

Kiang stood and lifted the radio. He thought a moment about throwing it over the side, but it was the only means of communications he had with his handler. Zeichner and Gainer didn't find it the first time; he'd chance them finding it when he finally talked with them.

He stood and started undressing, glancing at his watch as he laid it beside the radio. A quick shower and then back to the operations center to check on that faulty radar sensor. He'd fix it now. As he stepped into the shower, he thought of the sonar team six decks down on the *Algol*. Even if they detected the approaching contact, no one would do anything. How could you attack a submarine from a country that owns your country's debt?

THE tiny propellers of the small projectile churned the water as it followed the directional beacon toward its destination. Riding inside Kiang's device were photographs no spy satellite or outside intelligence agency could ever produce. It took a man on the scene with a Chinese camera purchased at an American discount store. A small CD keyed to the photographs carried written and verbal explanations.

KIANG stepped into the shower, confident Zeichner would never prove anything. He'd scream racial prejudice and watch the multitudes back off. The real proof was hundreds of feet below the water and probably already a couple of miles out.

Kiang knew little of what he did really mattered. In the People's Republic of China, everyone was suspect. So every tiny bit of intelligence was checked, double-checked, and compared with other tidbits of information from other agents who knew nothing about each other. The process reminded him of those machines where you threw in rough rocks and the continuous motion of the machine bounced the rocks around, polishing them until, when done, they emerged smooth to the touch. Those smooth rocks were the truth as the Chinese saw it.

He lathered the washcloth and began a rough scrub of his arms, followed by his feet and legs, working his way up his body. He twisted the hot water tap, increasing the temperature.

How could his handlers not know everything about Sea Base? The Shanghai University had people on nearly every major U.S. information technology board of directors. They even owned some of the IT firms in California's Silicon Valley.

Chinese students and professors worked in nearly every major U.S. defense industry. The same could be said for every industry that would be considered a major element of national security. Each had some link with the PRC, from electric to financial to water to the military-industrial complex. They didn't need people such as him, but the xenophobia and paranoia caused the communist government to trust no one.

He squirted shampoo into his hands and washed his hair, his eyes squeezed shut from the hot water hitting the top of his head.

Over the years of providing information to his handler, he watched the global economic scene change. He watched during the Bush years as China built up its economy by being smarter than the Americans in economic warfare. Even today, the People's Republic Bank of China owned the bulk of the American debt. China already had a weapon so powerful that it rendered America impotent to oppose China militarily.

When China decided it was time to invade Taiwan, would the will of America be able to stand the economic warfare that would accompany it? He turned off the water, reached outside the shower stall for his towel, and dried himself off. It was something to consider, he thought. Kiang enjoyed thinking through complex issues such as economic warfare.

Over the years, he had provided information so his parents would be allowed to live and thrive on the mainland. He looked at his reflection in the fogged mirror and nodded. At the same time, he had even destroyed some information he believed would be so damaging to the United States it would change the balance of military power. Those isolated instances, few and far between, were Kiang's way of proving his loyalty to the country in which he was a "born in America" citizen. It never occurred to Kiang that not providing this extremely sensitive information made him suspect to the very handler who held the life and death decision over his parents.

TWELVE

As Kiang was stepping from the shower, the underwater espionage vehicle that had been dropped thirty minutes earlier was almost four miles from Sea Base.

The logic head inside it detected a change in headings from the beacon it was following. Small wings along the sides twisted up slightly, causing the nose to turn downward. The small but powerful propellers drove it deeper. Minutes later, Kiang's vehicle broke through the sound layer separating the upper part of the ocean from the lower, colder depths. The churning of the water behind the propeller began echoing off the upper layer.

The noise of the propeller blades trapped by the sound layer above and a second one below it started an oscillating journey, traveling farther, amplified by the reverberations.

"SHIT, Senior Chief!" Keyland shouted, pointing at the rainfall pattern flickering down the SQR-25 screen. "I've got revolutions in the water. We got a torpedo here!"

Agazzi leaped from the upper level to the lower. "Where!" he shouted even before he reached the console.

Seaman Gentron leaned away from the display so Agazzi

could see. A faint trail paralleled the larger passive display of the approaching submarine.

"It's faint, but those are not 'big boy' propellers. That's a torpedo rev. I can't tell if it's coming toward us or how far out it is, but I know a torpedo when I hear one."

"They must have launched one from way out and—"

"They? Who is they?" asked MacPherson.

"Chinese. The submarine has to be Chinese," Keyland said sharply. "Their torpedoes aren't designed for a long-range launch. They are designed to blow up when they reach the proximity of the target."

"Looks as if they do have long-range capability and they can still blow up when they reach our proximity." Agazzi reached down and changed the intensity slightly.

The green background flickered a second before settling down to the new intensity, an intensity that highlighted the faint red streak that Keyland identified as a torpedo. The faint pattern remained on a constant bearing.

"It's not traveling fast," Gentron mumbled.

Agazzi and Keyland exchanged glances.

"Senior Chief, a characteristic of a long-range torpedo is slower speed. Slower speed means fuel lasts longer; it can travel farther," Keyland said.

Agazzi touched Gentron on the shoulder. "Hit the database and see if ONI has anything on this."

"Aye, Senior Chief," Gentron said, reaching over and pushing in the intelligence database icon.

A small computer window appeared in the bottom right-hand corner of the screen and a series of numbers began rapidly cycling through the digits. The numbers stopped periodically for a fraction of a second before shoving off for another round of rapid cycling. The Office of Naval Intelligence was key to keeping ahead of possible adversaries' technological advances. It was the lone remaining outpost of Navy experts capable of exploiting these advances.

"Can we tell if it is heading toward us or away?" Seaman Gentron asked, his voice quivering.

"Oh, it's coming toward us," Keyland said emphatically. "Otherwise it would have been us who fired it. The only way we can fire a torpedo is with our UUVs, which are fancy torpedoes themselves, or . . . Senior Chief, our destroyers have SH-36 helicopters embarked."

Keyland and Agazzi looked at each other.

"They'd be piss-poor anti-submarine platforms if they didn't," Taylor said from across the room.

"You keep tracking," Agazzi said. "If it's coming at us, it doesn't look as if it's coming at a fast speed. I'll alert the Combat Information Center and see if we can get the helos in the air."

Keyland nodded, leaned forward, and touched the database icon again. "This thing should have identified it by now." He turned and shouted to Agazzi. "Senior Chief, it may be coming at us at a slow speed, but I have no idea how far out it is. It could be one mile or it could be twenty."

"What's wrong with the database?" Agazzi asked as he quickly climbed the ladder to the upper deck.

"Something's wrong with it? Should I start it over again?"

"Gentron, I didn't say anything was wrong with it, I just said this database should have identified it by now."

"Then I shouldn't start it over again?"

"No, don't do anything. Keep your fingers away from the controls unless I tell you to do something. The water and the other ambient noise in the ocean may be masking the signature," Agazzi offered as he lifted the handset of his telephone. "At least it doesn't seem to be heading this direction fast."

"Okay, Senior Chief, but slow torpedoes do more damage," MacPherson offered.

"Why?" Gentron asked.

Agazzi offered an explanation as he jerked his chair out and sat down. "They're slower because they're heavier. They're heavier because they're carrying more explosives." He shook his head. "I can't believe the Chinese would fire on us."

"Yeah," Taylor said. "Who'd buy their shoes if they started a war with us?"

He ignored Taylor's comment as he dialed the Combat Information Center in the tower. He passed on the new information. Two minutes later he was back down at the consoles, standing alongside Keyland.

The database quit searching, a large flashing ERROR message on the readout drew their attention.

"What the fu . . . !"

Gentron hit the database file. Where the diagnostics that morning had shown nearly a petabyte of data, they now showed none.

"The database is gone. . . ." Keyland said, his voice trailing off.

"How in the hell . . . ?"

Gentron pushed the database status icon again. The same ZERO was reflected. "Nothing there."

"Impossible."

"Forget it," Agazzi said. "The database is nice to have, but it doesn't change the fact that the inbound is a long-range Chinese torpedo."

"What did CIC say?" Keyland asked.

"They're launching two SH-36s. One from the *Gearing* and the other from the cruiser off our port sides."

"No change, Senior Chief. It's still coming toward us," Gentron said.

"You could be right," Keyland added.

"Turn off the database, Keyland," Agazzi said. "Let the thing power down, then reboot it. Maybe the glitch will go away with a reboot."

"Hit it," Keyland said."

Gentron pressed the SHUTDOWN icon.

"And continue recording the signature of the torpedo, Gentron," Keyland ordered.

"Should I forward the signature to ONI?"

Keyland leaned down. The icon flashed recommending the acoustic recording be forwarded electronically to Suitland, Maryland. "Yeah, send it."

Keyland turned to Agazzi. "Well, that sure as hell narrows it down," Keyland said. He reached over Gentron's shoulder and pushed the MUTE button on the volume. The short beeping stopped and the warning sign reduced to an icon at the bottom of the screen.

It continued to pulsate as the acoustic signature was saved into a file for transfer. Later, they would download the entire scenario with the new signal and send it along with this initial request to the Office of Naval Intelligence in Suitland. There, professionals who had spent their lives working on underwater acoustics would analyze, probe, and extract what type of propeller and propulsion system made this signature. Right now, that knowledge was unavailable, so Agazzi and his team were left to their own professional depth and biases.

"Senior Chief," Taylor said, "What if it's one of those self-propelled mines instead of a torpedo?"

Agazzi said, "It's a torpedo. If it was a self-propelled mine, it would have launched closer and we'd already be fighting to stay afloat. If it's a UUV, then we'd see a lot of turns and deviations. Turns would break any wire guiding a torpedo. And, if it does a 'U-ey' then it can definitely be classified a UUV." He tapped the top of the SQR-25 display screen.

Gentron lifted one side of his headpiece. "It sounds like it's fading."

"You can hear it?" Agazzi asked, his eyebrows bunching.

Gentron nodded.

"Why didn't you tell us?" Keyland asked.

Gentron shrugged. "I figured you knew," he replied softly.

"Were you able to hear the revs when the pattern appeared," Agazzi asked.

Gentron shook his head. "No, Senior Chief. It was a couple of minutes later."

Though Agazzi knew that sound in the water could play tricks on distance and direction, this news only served to further convince him the torpedo was headed toward Sea Base.

What if Jacobs was right? There were a lot of targets holding up Sea Base. It wouldn't matter which one the torpedo hit, the whole synchronized ballet of ships, connecting passageways, and overhead platforms would start crumbling. Would Sea Base take the hit and stay afloat or would it cascade into the ocean like toppling dominoes as it self-destructed? He thought for a moment of the sharks beneath Sea Base, shook his head, and returned his full attention to the display.

Agazzi turned to MacPherson. "How are we coming on positioning the UUV?"

MacPherson pointed to the cam. "I have one in position, Senior Chief." He tapped the picture a couple of times. "See, the deck is opening. One minute—two, tops. How long do I have?"

"Gentron?"

"Senior Chief, the sound hasn't changed."

"It's at layer depth, Senior Chief," Keyland said. "Or riding beneath the layer." His eyes squinted as he looked at the console. "It has to be. What we're seeing is the noise riding the layer sound path."

"Means it's a few miles out," Agazzi concluded.

"How far out?"

"Gentron, if the Senior Chief or I knew that, we'd be in Washington working for some commercial contractor pulling down megabucks."

"Means the acoustics are riding beneath one layer and bouncing off a second one beneath it," Agazzi explained. "When it gets within a couple of miles of Sea Base, we'll see the noise it's making appear above the layer."

"Senior Chief, the well deck of the *Bellatrix* is nearly open. One more minute, then I'm only a checklist away from launch," Gentron said.

"Damn," Taylor said. "I hate gremlins." He turned to Agazzi who was watching the camera on MacPherson's console. "Senior Chief, I've just lost two security cameras; both of them located outside the UUV compartment. One covering the passageway and one on the hatch leading into it."

"Keep working it," Agazzi said, waving Taylor away. "Anything on that checklist we can do while we wait?"

MacPherson shook his head. "Already done everything I can do, Senior Chief. We can always launch without doing the checklist, but if we screw it up, the master of the *Bellatrix* is going to be one pissed-off soul when we pluck him from the water."

"Keyland! Any change?"

"No, Senior Chief. Constant bearing." Keyland leaned down to Gentron. "Keep it coming, Gentron. Keep up a steady report on bearing and noise intensity so we don't have to ask."

"Aye, Petty Officer Keyland. Bearing 220, level—"

The ship shook again as another pair of Air Force F-22 fighters landed on Sea Base.

The telephone rang on Agazzi's desk.

"Senior Chief!" Taylor shouted. "I got a red light on the UUV compartment hatch. Damn to hell water! I hate this fucking system. Even when they don't mean to, the Air Force screws with us sailors. That last landing must have shook the hatch away from the contacts."

"Bearing 220, no change in intensity," Gentron reported.

Agazzi picked up the handset and answered the call. A few seconds later he hung up and headed back to the consoles. "That was CIC. One SH-36 LAMPS airborne off the *Gearing*. The other one is being loaded with a torpedo. How's that well deck coming?" he asked as he stepped down to the console level.

"It's coming, Senior Chief."

Agazzi and MacPherson watched the deck continue to slow roll away. The darkness of the ocean peaked through the opening. The cam blinked a couple of times and suddenly blacked out.

"What the hell?" MacPherson said, hitting the cam icon. He even reached up and tapped the black square where moments before the cam image had been of the UUV compartment.

Agazzi leaned back. Too many bad things happening at once, he thought. He had expected a few hiccups for Sea Base operations, but this wasn't the time for them.

"Hey, Taylor," MacPherson moaned, "Your gremlins just ate my cam."

"Wadda you mean?"

"I just lost my camera."

"That damn cam on the UUV computer isn't on my circuits, Jenkins MacPherson. So don't blame me."

MacPherson turned to Agazzi. "Senior Chief, I need that camera. I can launch this thing on the red and green lights, but safety says we have to have a visual."

"I told you not taking a full complement to sea was a dumbshit act," Keyland added. "If we had more people, we could have some in the UUV compartment like the manual calls for. But no, we've got to save manpower at the expense of operations. Every officer a warrior, but every officer a businessman. If the Navy—"

"Keyland," Agazzi snapped.

Keyland waved his hand down in frustration. "I know, I know, boss. I'll go. Someone has to be in the UUV compartment when we launch."

Keyland was needed to manage the consoles and oversee the launching of the UUVs. MacPherson was better than Agazzi on the UUV launch console. Gentron barely knew his way around Sea Base, and he couldn't be depended upon to make the right decisions if sent. Taylor had to remain in the ASW control center until the UUV launch. *Damn! Where in the hell are Smith and Bernardo?*

"No, you stay here. I'll go. I know the consoles and manual launch sequences for the UUVs."

"But, Senior Chief, you're the *jefe* here. The boss. You should—"

"Make the right decision. You can handle it."

It took two steps for Agazzi to reach the top level, another second to grab the telephone, and fifteen seconds to ask the Combat Information Center to pass the word for Smith and Bernardo to lay to the ASW control center.

Agazzi looked at Taylor. "The light still on?"

"Senior Chief, the open hatch light is still on."

Agazzi stood. His place was here. He could order someone else to go, but of the ASW team, he was the only one expendable to take over the UUV compartment. With these technology gremlins running rampant through his circuits, he needed to man both compartments. At least he knew how to manually launch the UUV from the local console inside the compartment. A flick of the safety clasps, a hard slap against the large red release button on the UUV firing cradle, and gravity did the rest. The only thing he'd have to do would be to change clothes because he would be soaked when the UUV splashed into the ocean with him standing near it.

"Petty Officer Keyland, you have the watch. I'll call when I reach the *Bellatrix*. Then we'll coordinate the launch."

"The open-water light should be green, Senior Chief," MacPherson said. "The well deck should be fully opened by now, but according to the lights, it's either still opening, stopped, or closing. I have no hell of an idea what the condition is. I can't launch." MacPherson leaned back. "Shit! Senior Chief, I don't know what in the hell is going on."

THE laser beacon tweaked the logic head of Kiang's projectile. The port fin changed its arc slightly. The projectile, with its data, photographs, and charts stored on small CDs, changed directions. It wasn't a big change. A few degrees to starboard, but the change brought the propeller around so it pointed directly back toward Sea Base. The small UUV continued away from Sea Base, the small but powerful propellers churning the water behind them. The ambient noise bounced off the layer overhead, riding the sound channel back to the passive sonar arrays designed to warn Sea Base of underwater threats.

GENTRON jerked his earphones off. "The noise is louder," he said, his voice shaking.

Keyland grabbed the earphones, jammed them down on his

ears, and pressed the earpieces firmly against his head. "Damn, damn, damn. Senior Chief, we're gonna need someone inside the compartment before we launch." Keyland looked up at the rainfall display. "That torpedo or whatever has changed its direction of travel and the noise has increased. You can see it on rainfall. It's definitely coming toward us."

"Jesus Christ!" MacPherson said, leaning over to look at Gentron's console.

"I'm on my way. Keyland, call the CIC and bring the officer of the deck up to date. Tell them I recommend general quarters. I'll call when I get there!" Agazzi shouted as he burst through the hatch into the bottom passageway of the *Algol*. Damn, he was going to have a sore set of knees tomorrow. He grabbed both railings, using his hands to move quickly up the ladders, hurrying as fast as he could toward the main deck and the connecting passageways leading to the *Bellatrix*.

Agazzi burst through the hatch onto the main deck of the *Algol*. His legs ached slightly and his breathing was deep, regular—the sign of a man who worked to keep his body in shape. He turned left, running. A bunch of boatswain mates were chipping rust away from the paintwork on the *Algol*. He saw Jacobs about the same time the master chief saw him.

"Hey, how's my asshole buddy doing?" Jacobs shouted, raising his coffee cup aloft in salute.

"Can't talk right now!" Agazzi shouted, hurrying by his friend. "Got to get to the UUV compartment on the *Bellatrix*—electronic problems."

"That's why the boatswain mate way of life is a hell of lot better than what you geeks have!" Jacobs shouted after him.

His friend's voice faded as Agazi ran down the connecting passageway.

JACOBS watched his friend disappear. Something was wrong. Though his friend had had a lot of reasons in the past four years to be one big basket case, Agazzi never seemed fazed. Jacobs let out a big sigh. What are master chiefs for if not to check up on these young senior chiefs?

"Hey, you! Showdernitzel! You're in charge of the working party."

"Why me, Master Chief? Let Jaime do it. I was in charge yesterday."

"Don't give me any of your lip. Potts can be it tomorrow." He hefted his cup and drained it, then set it on a nearby ledge. "And don't peterwhip my cup."

"Master Chief, you're a gross pig," Showdernitzel said. "First of all, I'm a lady and ladies don't have peters to whip anything."

Jacobs smiled. "It's been my experience that ladies are more ingenious than men when it comes to revenge." He looked down the connecting passageway.

Showdernitzel held up three fingers and saluted.

"Showdernitzel, put yourself on report. I'll sign the chit later. Potts! You're in charge. Give that paintbrush to Showdernitzel. You come hold my cup," he said, picking it up and handing it to the short young man from Pennsylvania. "This is the official symbol of your authority: my coffee cup. If anything happens to it, I'm holding you responsible. You understand?"

Jacobs smiled when he saw the young third-class petty officer's hand shake slightly as he took the coffee cup. "Yes, Master Chief, I understand."

"Where are you going, in the event something important comes up like free cake or candy?" Showdernitzel asked, slapping the paintbrush onto a cleared section of the deck.

He pointed down the passageway. "Think I'll mosey over to the *Bellatrix* and see what this newfangled UUV compartment looks like."

"You know, Master Chief, there's a lot of scientific equipment and technology things in there."

"I know."

"Then maybe you should take a camera so when you get the pictures, we can explain to you what you saw."

"Showdernitzel, pick a charge from the UCMJ and add it to the list of things for your court-martial. I'd throw you overboard, but it wouldn't be fair to the sharks."

They watched as Jacobs disappeared down the passageway. Showdernitzel pushed herself up off her knees, walked over to Potts, and jerked Jacobs's cup away from him.

"Don't—"

"Oh, hush up, you wimp." She walked over to the edge of the deck and tossed the cup overboard.

"Christ, Mad Mary! He's gonna kill me."

She shrugged. "Oh, Potts. Don't be a wimp. The master chief loves us. Besides, he's just a big old teddy bear."

"He's gonna kill me."

One of the other boatswain mates looked over at Potts. "Dude, as we say in Augusta, Georgia: It sucks to be you!"

AGAZZI stepped through the passageway onto the deck of the *Antares*. He had been through earlier this morning and the deck had been clear. Now, stacked pallets on the main deck blocked direct movement to the connecting passageway to the *Bellatrix*. They weren't secured to the deck, so Agazzi knew it was a temporary arrangement, but he couldn't wait for them to be moved. Agazzi glanced both ways and saw what looked like a small opening near the aft forecastle. He inched his way toward the opening. When he reached it, he saw it went inward for two pallets before stopping. Turning sideways, he worked his way down the narrow opening. At the edge of the two pallets, another small opening led forward. He slid through it for a couple of minutes to another channel about twelve inches wide. He could see the port safety lines.

It was one hundred and five feet from the starboard side of the *Antares* to the port side. Minutes later, Agazzi stepped out onto the port side to find the path to the connecting passageway blocked by four pallets stored one on top of the other. The pallets were pushed against the safety lines, blocking his path.

Agazzi looked up. Only one way to get to the connecting passageway without going back to find another way. He grabbed the tie-down strap on the nearest pallet and started climbing. Probably should have thought of that earlier. Grunting from the strain, he pulled himself up. A minute later he was on top of the pallets running across the top of them.

"Hey, you!" a voice shouted from the aft forecastle. "Get the hell off my stores!"

Agazzi reached the edge of the pallets near the entrance to the connecting passageway. He eased himself over the edge of the pallet, holding on to the tie-down strap. Agazzi glanced down. He was a few feet above the deck. He let go, landing upright on the balls of his feet. Pain shot through his knees. Agazzi fell to his hands on the deck. Pushing himself up, breathing heavily, Agazzi ignored the pain and started a hobbling run down the metal passageway connecting the two ships.

By the time he reached the end of the passageway the pain had ebbed and he was back to a full sprint. He raised his left arm and glanced at his watch. Fifteen minutes since he'd left the *Algol* and no way to tell Keyland and the others where he was. Internal communications on Sea Base were crap.

Agazzi emerged onto the main deck of the *Bellatrix*, turned left to the hatch leading down, and moments later was grabbing the ladders with both hands and sliding down, feet raised. Sweat poured down his neck, soaking his shirt.

One would think that under the shade of Sea Base, it'd be cooler, but the facilities design for taking heat and smoke from the ships to the edge of Sea Base had been flawed. Most of it escaped along the sides of the above platform, but because of the volume, if the ocean breeze dropped below a couple of knots, heat and exhaust queued beneath Sea Base.

He grabbed the two metal handrails on the last ladder, lifted his feet, and slid down to the metal deck. Bending his knees, he hit the bottom. Rising up, Agazzi walked hurriedly toward the hatch leading to the compartment. The white lights in the lower passageway had changed to red. Red lights were the norm for nighttime to protect the night vision mariners needed to sail safely. Agazzi didn't think too much about the change of lighting. Neither had he heard the sounding of general quarters, but maybe the red lights that bathed the passageways now were part of the *Bellatrix*'s checklist for battle stations.

Rounding the corner, he breathed a sigh of relief. The hatch leading to the UUV compartment was closed. When this was over, his number-one priority was going to be to have someone fix those contacts. He'd be damned if he were going to do this every time the red light blinked.

He placed his hand on the biometric reader, watching the red symbols above it cycle through until the word APPROVED appeared in bright red. He moved his hand and quickly punched in the four-digit combination. Hearing the click, he pushed against the hatch and was surprised to discover it slid open effortlessly. The hatch had been open. His lower lip pushed against his upper. Agazzi shook his head.

MacPherson was the last person here and he had forgotten to check the hatch. The sailor had left it unsecured. Here they were, thousands of miles out to sea with someone running around blowing things up, and MacPherson didn't check the hatch to an area in Sea Base that held enough explosives to sink the damn thing. He hated what he knew he would have to do. But he couldn't let this go unpunished.

It was dark inside.

Agazzi stepped inside. The master light switch was on the computer console. The faint red of emergency lights filled the compartment. He was more disappointed with MacPherson than angry. Sometimes the rules of the sea forced you to do things you would prefer not to do; punishing a good sailor was one of them.

Rules were rules, and rules at sea were meant to keep you dry, alive, and afloat. The rules also included leaving the lights on in the UUV compartment.

Otherwise, why in the hell have security cameras . . . even if they weren't working properly. Maybe MacPherson had a good excuse, but it only took a shake or two on the hatch to tell if it was properly secure or not. Obviously, MacPherson hadn't done that.

The door slid shut behind Agazzi. As it closed, Agazzi's eyes widened. Wait a minute! When he left ASW control center, the last scene on MacPherson's cam showed a lighted compartment. Unnoticed, the hatch hit the seal, stayed shut a few seconds, and then bounced slightly ajar. In the ASW control center, the light shined green for a couple of seconds before turning bright red again.

Just what they needed, Agazzi thought as he waited for his eyes to adjust to the red light—another technology gremlin to figure out. Satisfied that his night vision was all it could be, Agazzi started moving toward the main console that overlooked the UUV firing cradle. There, he would telephone Keyland and turn on the overhead lights. The sound of metal hitting the metal deck startled Agazzi. He stopped. The echo of noise filled the compartment. That was no accident. Someone was in here with him.

Agazzi looked around for something—anything. He shivered slightly as the thought that the bomber might be in here with him and he had no way of communicating this to anyone. The nearest telephone was on the manual control console and that lay in the direction of the noise.

He stood motionless, listening intently for any other sounds. Then, he heard it. Footsteps, soft, barely audible, but nevertheless footsteps. Agazzi took a step backward, thinking of easing outside the compartment and calling for help. He stopped. A torpedo

was headed their way and they needed the UUV in the water to
stop it.

Plus, if this was the bomber, by the time he could get anyone
here, the torpedo would already be at Sea Base. Even if the torpedo missed, the bomber could send this place up in a massive
explosion and Agazzi, along with everyone else, would be heading for the dark Pacific.

Agazzi inched forward; the intruder must be unaware of his
presence. The red lights of the passageway would have masked
him opening the hatch. He listened to the person moving and
heard him on a ladder. The only ladder in that direction was the
one leading down to the lower compartment. The lower compartment held the firing cradle, and waiting in the firing cradle
were eight UUVs primed and armed for launch, each with over
five hundred pounds of high-grade explosives.

Agazzi edged to the end of the long row of stored UUVs.
These, too, had the same amount of explosives. It mattered little
where the explosion started; once ignited, it would seem like one
gigantic blast regardless of the microseconds separating each one.

He peered around the edge of the row. In the red light of the
compartment, the intruder squatted alongside the bottom UUV in
the firing cradle. To Agazzi's right was the manual control console. Farther right, he saw the cam on the computer. Something
dark was draped over the lens.

Agazzi looked at the computer and the manual control console. If he could hit the light switch on the console and climb to
the level with the computer, he could jerk the covering off the
cam. MacPherson would see what was happening and call for
help—he hoped.

"Damn," the intruder said, metal dropping onto the well deck.

The well deck was nearly closed. The intruder must have tried
to close it and been partially successful, for about four feet of
open ocean separated the two sides. Not enough room to ensure
a successful launch. If MacPherson launched the UUV *thinking-
hoping-praying* the well deck was open, the UUV would drop
onto the metal deck of the *Bellatrix*. By itself, it wouldn't explode, but Agazzi knew the man down there with the UUV had
to be the bomber. There was no other reason for anyone to be
here.

He stepped around the edge of the row, grabbed both metal
railings of the ladder, and, lifting his feet, let gravity slide him

silently down to the second level. He stepped in front of the manual control console. It was dark. Someone had turned it off. Safety rules called for it to remain operational at all times. This was so the safety observer, of which they had none, could intervene and override the remote controls of the UUV operator.

When he hit the power switch beneath the console, there would be a slight humming sound as the equipment warmed up. Agazzi squatted, his hand reaching beneath the console, feeling for the power button. It was there somewhere. He found it, visualized the red color of the ON–OFF switch, and pushed it forward. His eyes squinted as the faint hum of power surged through the console.

Agazzi stood, expecting to find himself staring directly into the eyes of the intruder. Down below, the intruder seemed intent on what he was doing, oblivious to the new sound added to the normal noise of a ship at sea.

The green light of the display suddenly glowed as the system booted up. Agazzi watched the display, waiting for the familiar operating icons to appear. Several seconds passed before he looked in the direction of the intruder, but there was no one there.

His head jerked back and forth as Agazzi searched for where the man had disappeared to. What if the man had finished laying the explosions and was at the hatch? The change on the display drew his attention. The operational icons glowed into existence.

He hit the compartment light switch. Bright white fluorescent lights flickered on. Agazzi turned toward the computer, keen on completing his original plan. The intruder stood there.

"You!" Agazzi shouted.

The intruder swung a long metal pipe at Agazzi's head. Agazzi swerved at the last minute, taking the blow on his left shoulder. The force of the blow sent him tumbling backward, knocking him into the ladder that led from the second level down to the well deck.

Bright white dots of pain clouded his vision. He rolled to the left, a short scream escaping as his shoulder took his weight. Agazzi couldn't move his fingers on his left hand.

He glanced back. The intruder, grinning, stepped around the console and raised the metal bar above his head.

Agazzi kicked out, his boondocker connecting with the intruder's knee, knocking the man backward into the console. The metal rod dropped to the deck and rolled away. The sound of metal on metal echoed through the chamber. Agazzi grabbed the nearby railing with his right hand and pulled himself upright.

He scrambled down the ladder to the well deck area. *Why, why, why?* he asked himself. He glanced at the computer. The cloth or rag of whatever had been thrown over the cam was still there.

The telephone rang. That would be Keyland calling to see if he had arrived.

The sound of the rod being lifted off the metal deck caused him to snap his head back toward the intruder.

"Senior Chief, you should have stayed in the control center. A few more minutes and I would have been gone."

"Why are you doing this, Smith?"

"Name's not Smith." The intruder laughed. "Name's never been Smith. The Smith on my ID card died years ago. Died as an infant in Boise, Idaho." He laughed. "I think every one of the infants who have died in Boise, Idaho, have been resurrected for God's Army."

Agazzi searched for something, anything nearby to use as a weapon. He saw the explosives arrayed against the nose cone of the lower UUV. Three blocks of C4 packed nicely together, wires trailing from firing caps jabbed into each; the wires were wrapped tightly together, and led to a digital timer. A digital timer that slipped from four digits to 9:59 while he watched. Seconds continued to run off it.

"Pretty good, even if I do say so myself, but then God expects us to do His work with meticulous care."

Smith, or whatever his name was, slung the metal rod over his shoulders and started down the ladder toward him.

"Smith, they'll kill you for this."

Smith laughed. "Senior Chief, I intend to die with Sea Base. I am a messenger of Armageddon. I will ride with you on the trip to the bottom of the ocean."

"I don't understand," Agazzi said, stepping toward the wired UUV.

"I wouldn't touch that if I were you; and I'm not you, so if you want to fiddle with my work go ahead. It's just that if you screw with it, the digital arm will immediately drop to zero and our next meeting will be in the afterlife as you head to hell and I pass gracefully into God's arms."

Smith jumped from the second level to the well deck a few feet from Agazzi.

"Then, if it's foolproof, why are you trying to kill me?"

Smith shrugged, then grinned. "God always demands a sacrifice for doing his deeds."

Smith's eyes widened as the he gazed upward as if seeing something Agazzi couldn't. Smith's mouth opened and his breaths came in deep, long draughts. "You can never know the ecstasy of serving the Master. Of knowing His approval of you doing His work." Smith sighed. "But His vision given to me by Ezekiel is to be in the ASW control center when the *Bellatrix* goes down. I'm to ride Sea Base down, blessing the religious among us as we become part of the Master's plan to hasten Armageddon."

Agazzi took a step backward; only a few more steps, and his back would be against the bulkhead. He bent his left knee slightly, shifting his weight onto it.

Smith's gaze jerked back to Agazzi. Smith's knuckles turned white as he tightened his grip on the metal rod.

"Now, Senior—"

Agazzi leaped, closing the few feet between them in one jump, hitting Smith in the chest with his right shoulder. Pain shot through his body as the blow rattled his injured shoulder. The metal rod fell, bouncing several times on the deck, filling the compartment with echoes.

"Uggg." Smith gasped as he tripped backward, the breath knocked out of him. The man grabbed the metal railing running along the top of the well deck as he fell, stopping his fall, and coming to a halt on his buttocks. He looked at Agazzi lying on the deck and smiled. "God protects me. He is great in His righteousness."

Agazzi pulled himself to his knees. His good hand reached up and touched his left shoulder. He moaned.

Smith ran forward, drew his foot back, and kicked.

Agazzi saw the blur of the foot though his clouded vision and pulled back as Smith's foot barely missed his face. He reached up and grabbed the foot, pushing Smith away. Off balance, Smith fell on top of the half-closed well deck, rolling toward the open edge.

The well deck dipped toward the center where the two edges had met. Unlike decks with nonskid installed on top so people could walk on them without slipping and sliding all over the place, the well deck had no nonskid. It was slick, non-rough metal designed to open into the ocean.

Smith knew this. He spread-eagled himself. "Good hit, Senior Chief. How's that shoulder?" Smith laid his head on the well deck for a moment, then his hands and legs started moving in unison as the man began to crab-crawl up the slight incline toward the lower deck.

Pressing his back against the rise between decks, Agazzi pushed himself upright. He walked to the ladder, grabbed the railing with his good hand, and climbed to the next deck.

He ran to the manual control center. The power was still on. He hit the OPEN icon beneath the well deck symbol. The sound of hydraulic gears grinding into action filled the compartment. Smith was shouting at him. He could even make out a few of the words such as *God* and *wrath* and *hell*. The well deck started inching apart as the doors retracted.

Smith's movements increased as he fought to stay ahead of the opening. It looked to Agazzi as if there might be a lip where the two edges came together, a lip Smith could brace his boondockers against and ride the retraction to the well deck.

Agazzi moved toward the computer, reached up, and jerked the cloth off of the cam. In the ASW control center, Keyland and the others could now see what was happening. Help would be coming soon, but would he be alive when it arrived? Would any of them be alive when it arrived?

What he didn't expect was for MacPherson to see Smith about to fall into the ocean and override the opening of the well deck. As soon as Agazzi heard the hydraulics winding down he realized what had happened. Around the edge of the well deck opening were protruding metal eyes designed for tying down the UUV firing cradle during maintenance and loading. Smith grabbed one, working his fingers for a better grip.

Agazzi lifted the telephone. He punched in two numbers, then couldn't recall the last two. The telephone number for the Combat Information Center flashed into memory. He dialed it.

"Senior Chief, I'm coming!" Smith shouted. "You cannot stop God's work."

Someone answered on the other end. "Get someone to the *Bellatrix*!" he shouted. "The UUVs have been rigged to explode. The man who did it is Smith."

On the other end, Agazzi realized the voice was a recording—a recording advising him he was in queue to be answered. Then music filled the earpiece. When too many users were on the telephone, efficiency meant queuing. Without sound-powered telephone, the sound to general quarters had sent everyone racing to the telephones. He wished they had also devised a way to identify priority.

Smith picked up the metal rod and started up the ladder. "Senior Chief, you are messing with God's plans," he said, venom in every word.

The sound of hydraulics rose again, drowning out Smith's continuing tirade. Agazzi knew he couldn't fight the man with this injured shoulder, but neither could he run. He was going to die either stopping Smith or when the explosives went off. Glancing at the explosive-rigged UUV, he could see the red digital read-out continuing to count down. Beneath it, the well deck continued to retract. He hung up the telephone.

"Seems your team is efficient, Senior Chief. They waited until I was safe before starting to open the well doors." Smith shrugged. "I'm not sure which is better for the explosion: having them open or shut." He looked up at Agazzi. "I guess with them open, the ocean will race in sooner. With the hatch rigged to stay open, there's nothing to stop the water from leaving this compartment." Smith smiled and worked his way up the ladder. "Of course, that assumes, Senior Chief, the explosions don't rupture the ship in half. After all, they did put the UUV compartment in the center of the ship."

"Smith, you need to think about what you're doing."

"Oh, I have, Senior Chief. I nearly bungled the one on the *Denebola*, nearly found myself engulfed in the explosion, but God protected me and guided me through the smoke and flame to the ladder that took me topside. If I needed more proof of my divine purpose, that first time showed me His plan."

Smith hefted the metal rod over his right shoulder, took two steps toward Agazzi, and swung.

Agazzi pulled back as the rod swung by, barely missing him.

The telephone rang, causing Smith to glance at it.

Agazzi scrambled backward, aware he was inches from where the walkway ended against the forward bulkhead.

Smith turned back to Agazzi and raised the rod again. "Senior Chief! It is God's will."

"What if you're wrong, Smith!"

"My name's not Smith. I've told you that."

"Whoever you are, what if you're wrong. What if God meant for you to stop Sea Base, but not sacrifice innocent lives to do it?"

Smith shook his head, pausing with the rod held high. "You've never read the Bible, Senior Chief. God accepts the innocents for what they are: innocent. They are His children. If they are truly innocent, then they will join me at God's right side."

"What if you've interpreted God's will wrong? What if God is angry with you for doing this?"

Smith's face turned red with rage. His voice trembled, but he still held the rod motionless above his head, gripped with both hands, knuckles white from his grip. "I have talked with God. I know what He wants. He is unhappy with the world. He wants Armageddon and me—God's Army; we are His messengers." He lowered the rod to his side. "America and this thing here are only pawns. When Sea Base sinks, America will think the Chinese or the North Koreans, maybe even the Russians did it. It will be a little more pressure on the trigger finger of global anarchy. With anarchy comes the Lord. With anarchy comes Armageddon."

The hydraulics stopped as the well deck reached full open status. The sound of the firing cradle shifting position caused Smith to stop and look at the UUVs.

Keyland and his team were moving the rigged UUV into the firing position.

"No. No," Smith mumbled.

Agazzi kicked out, his foot catching the man between the legs. Smith stumbled backward, the metal rod tumbling onto the deck as the man grabbed his crotch. The rod bounced twice before rolling halfway off the edge of the walkway. Agazzi reached down to grab it. Smith tackled him, grabbing Agazzi around his shoulder, squeezing the injured shoulder and holding him upright as they twisted along the walkway.

Agazzi screamed, his vision clouding over for a moment. He reached up, and with his right hand clawed at Smith's eyes. Smith squeezed his eyes shut, releasing Agazzi. The man stumbled back against the safety railing.

Released, and without Smith holding him up, Agazzi fell to his knees. Barely conscious, pain was overcoming the adrenaline. Agazzi tumbled to side onto the deck, fighting to stay conscious. He heard Smith say something, but Agazzi didn't understand what the man had said.

He lay on his side on the walkway, waiting for the metal rod to swing down and finish the job, and nothing happened. He forced his head up and his eyes open. Smith was at the manual control console. The metal rod lay braced against the side of the console.

Agazzi looked at the firing cradle. The UUV rigged with the explosives was directly over the open well deck. The outer edges of the well deck appeared as Smith sought to close it before the ASW team on the *Algol* could release it.

Breathing heavily, Agazzi reached out and wrapped his fingers on the bottom stanchion of the security railings. He pulled himself into a sitting position. Grabbing the second stanchion, he pulled himself upright. He climbed the ladder to the second level and stumbled toward the computer console. He stopped in front of the cam and mouthed the word *Fire* several times. He then held up five fingers and slowly began to pull the fingers down one at a time until he pulled the index finger down last.

Behind him he heard the splash of the UUV as it hit the water, disappearing beneath the surface.

A long, mournful cry came from Smith. Smith reached down and jerked the metal rod up. Screaming at the top of his voice, he rushed at Agazzi.

Thoughts of Frieda and how she would take the word of his death flashed across Agazzi's mind. He didn't fear his own death as much as the grief of how she would cope without him. He was about to die. The rush of events in the last few minutes had been a rush toward his death. But he had saved Sea Base and those who rode on her. He raised his arm to deflect the blow.

THIRTEEN

"Look!" MacPherson shouted, tapping the cam picture. "Something's wrong with the senior chief."

Keyland threw the telephone down and slid down the ladder rails to the lower deck. On the screen was the face of Senior Chief Agazzi, blood running down both cheeks.

"Wow! He must have taken a fall or something."

"Why in the hell doesn't he answer the telephone?" Keyland asked.

"He's saying something."

"Expand the picture."

The cam picture filled the screen. Behind the senior chief, the UUV appeared properly positioned for launch, hanging above the open well deck."

"What the hell is going on?" Taylor asked, sliding down the ladder to stand alongside Keyland.

"Senior chief's hurt."

"What's he saying?" MacPherson said.

"He's saying fire," Taylor offered. "I don't see no fire."

"He's lifting his hand. Five fingers. He's pulling them down, one by one."

"It's a countdown!" Keyland shouted. "MacPherson! Launch the UUV."

A red light replaced the green one, reflecting the status of the well deck.

"The well deck is closing. I can't fire if it's closing. Safety—"

"Something's wrong. You see him looking toward the manual control console."

"Three fingers. What do you want me to do?"

"He's the *jefe*," Keyland said. "When he makes a fist, you release the UUV."

"If I release the UUV and it hits the side of the well deck—"

"Then we'll explain everything to the investigating board. Reduce the picture so we can see the UUV."

Agazzi's profile slid to the upper left-hand corner of the console. Behind him the edges of the well deck could be seen closing.

"I don't think we'll have to worry about a board," Taylor said. "We'll be more worried about those damn sharks."

"One finger."

MacPherson reached up and put his hand on the launch button. Behind him, everyone except Gentron crowded around MacPherson's console watching the senior chief.

"Launch!" Keyland ordered.

MacPherson hit the release button. Agazzi disappeared from in front of the cam. They watched as the UUV disappeared beneath the surface. Water splashed up and into the compartment before flowing back down the open well deck into the ocean.

"Senior chief needs help. I'm going down to the UUV compartment," Taylor said.

Keyland waved him away. "Yeah, Taylor. Call me when you get there. MacPherson, go intercept that torpedo and let's scare the shit out of the Chinese."

THE UUV fell past the keel of the *Bellatrix*. Several dark shapes sped away from it with quick, sharp snaps of their fins while others attracted to the light above swam toward the open well deck.

MACPHERSON activated the battery-driven turbine engine of the UUV, and in moments the UUV emerged from beneath the *Bellatrix*, heading southwest. At ten knots, MacPherson maneuvered the UUV onto a collision course with what they believed to be a

long-range torpedo heading their way. Keyland leaned over
MacPherson's shoulder, watching the tableau in the UUV compartment while giving directions to the two men.

"We're still above the layer," Keyland said. "The Chinese torpedo is below it."

"I will lose contact for a few moments when we pass the
layer," MacPherson said. "Increasing speed to twenty-five
knots."

"We won't be able to hear anything passively at twenty-five
knots," Keyland objected.

"New technology, LPO," MacPherson said with a shrug.
"Once we break the barrier, I can slow it down, if we lose contact."

"You will regain it, right?"

MacPherson shrugged. "We're supposed to be able to, but
nearly everything on this floating bucket of bolts is new technology built by the lowest bidder."

Keyland looked toward the hatch as Taylor opened it. "Taylor . . ." Keyland said with concern in his voice.

Taylor threw a short salute back at the leading petty officer as
he stepped into the passageway and pulled the hatch closed behind him.

"Okay, it's passing the layer. We're a mile out."

"I think I'd feel better if we had a wire attached to it like a
wire-driven torpedo."

MacPherson nodded. "I would, too, but those ONR scientists
say this AT&T laser communications technology is better."

"Studebakers used to be better, too."

"What's a Studebaker?"

"Never mind," Keyland said. "Just concentrate on intercepting
that torpedo."

The telephone rang.

"I got it," Keyland said, hustling up the short ladder to the
upper level and jerking the handset up. "Hello."

It was the Combat Information Center asking for the status
of the launch. He brought them up to date only to discover CIC
tactical action officer shouting at him for launching without his
say-so. Keyland explained that the senior chief was in the
UUV compartment and injured. The TAO demanded the senior
chief call him, and then put a chief on the telephone to talk
with Keyland.

"What's going on?" Gentron asked, jerking his head toward Keyland.

"He's getting his ass chewed out," MacPherson replied, staring at the back of Keyland's head.

Gentron shook his head. "Wow. Someone's always getting their ass chewed out. Is that a Navy phenomenon?"

MacPherson let out a huge guffaw. "Naw, man, it's a phenomenon of life." He jerked his thumb at Keyland. "Shit, you want to see ass-chewing, you should have been in the old Navy."

Keyland argued for a few seconds with the chief on the other end who wanted him to remain on the telephone so CIC could keep in touch. Keyland agreed and then hung up. The chief was right. The TAO was right. But, by God, they were saving Sea Base; they didn't have enough sailors to do the job, and they wanted them to do more. *Go fish*, he thought. He glanced at Calvins, who was standing and watching everyone from near the maintenance table.

"Calvins! Get your ass over here and man the telephone. When it rings, you start talking and keep talking. You tell CIC everything we're doing and put some color into it."

Calvins nearly tripped and fell as he hurried to Agazzi's desk just as the telephone rang. Keyland lifted it and handed it to Calvins.

"What do I do, Petty Officer Keyland?" Calvins asked in a whisper.

Keyland was already hurrying down to the lower lever. "Tell them you're the sound-powered phone talker and then just keep talking. As long as you talk, they can't ask questions."

Moments later Keyland was alongside MacPherson.

"Who was it?" MacPherson asked.

"Combat Information Center."

"What'd they say?"

"They said the USS *Gearing* and one of the cruisers have launched their SH-36 helicopters. CIC is directing a sonobuoy pattern ten miles out. They have two ASW helicopters on board the USS *Boxer* being outfitted with Mark 45 torpedoes."

"That's good news. No way we could have controlled the helos from here and fight the UUV at the same time." MacPherson smiled. "Glad someone is happy with us."

"Happy? Did I say they were happy with us?" Keyland shook his head. "They're pissed we launched without them giving the

final go-ahead and they're pissed because we haven't been keeping them up to date on what we're doing and they're pissed because everyone else in CIC is pissed."

"Hey, man, how in the hell can they pissed with us? We're the
ones who told them the submarine was out there and we're the
ones who told them the torpedo was inbound. What the hell more
do they want?"

Keyland shook his head. "I'm not worried about it. It's their
own goddamn fault. If the sound-powered phones were up and
operating, we'd be exchanging information in real-time. Instead,
we've got a hosed up telephone system as the interim."

A beep on MacPherson's console drew their attention.
MacPherson reached up and changed the intensity control of the
laser beam. "We have contact."

Keyland stepped over to view the rainfall pattern when the
hatch opened. Bernardo stepped into the ASW control center.
"You been looking for me?"

"Yeah, get your ass down here and help MacPherson," Keyland said, jerking his thumb toward the UUV console.

Keyland leaned over Gentron's shoulder. On the right side of
the rainfall pattern a wider line ran parallel to the smaller enemy
torpedo pattern. "Gentron's got the UUV on sonar."

"Where's Smith?" Bernardo asked.

On the telephone above them, Calvins cupped his hand over the
mouthpiece and kept a running commentary on what was happening in the ASW control center. He had the mouthpiece pressed
close to his lips with the earpiece hanging beneath his chin.

"Haven't seen him since he went on his break over an hour
ago."

"He should have been here now, if they sounded general quarters," Taylor added.

"I didn't hear anyone sound GQ. Did anyone hear it?"
MacPherson asked.

"They said they sounded general quarters when we told them!"
Calvins shouted from the telephone. "They said they're having
problems coordinating all the ships to sound GQ."

"We didn't hear it."

"We're a mile out," MacPherson said, referring to the UUV.

Keyland moved back to the UUV console. "You got telemetry?"

"Telemetry? Man, I got television," MacPherson said, joy in
his voice. "Look at this." He slid the mouse symbol down to the

line of icons running along the bottom of the screen, clicked, and replaced the cam display of the UUV compartment with the combined display coming from the two cameras mounted close to the skin of the launched UUV near the fins. The dark blue of deep water filled the screen. Small bubbles bounced off the lens as the UUV sped through the water.

"I can't see anything," Keyland said.

"You're looking at water," Bernardo offered. "And that's all we'll see until we near the torpedo or the submarine. Man-oh-man, this laser shit works great."

"We recording this?" Keyland asked.

MacPherson and Bernardo exchanged a glance at each other and then in unison said, "We can, if you want."

With irritation, Keyland replied, "Record the son-of-a-bitch. What are you thinking? We're going to have these new Navy warriors with their business degrees all over our asses wanting to know why we did one thing and why didn't we do something else. Shit! I know more about return on investment than any self-respecting sailor ought to know—"

MacPherson and Bernardo looked at each other.

"Is that a yes?" MacPherson interrupted.

Keyland stopped and grunted. "Yes, that's a goddamn yes."

Bernardo reached beside MacPherson and pressed a lighted icon on the side of the console. "There, Petty Officer Keyland, we are recording the visual. The system automatically records the telemetry from the time we activate the UUV for launch. And, like a black box on an aircraft, the system also records our actions. Kind of an ASW black box for those investigators."

"They want to know where the UUV is!" Seaman Calvins shouted. The sound of someone shouting over the telephone could be heard at the consoles.

"Tell them it is on a course of 220; two thousand yards and separating."

"I've lost audio on the torpedo, Petty Officer Keyland," Seaman Gentron said, pulling his earphones off.

"It must have gone between convergence zones," Keyland said. As underwater sounds oscillated outward, bouncing between layers, there were moments when the sound disappeared. When the submarine or torpedo creating this ambient noise moved between oscillating wave fronts, the passive sonar array could lose contact. The rainfall display ceased to track until the noise reemerged on its next bounce. The null spots were determined by the locations of the platform generating the noise and the sensors tracking it.

"When we will pick it up again?" Gentron asked.

Keyland shrugged. "When it reenters the convergence zone."

"When will that be?"

"When you put on your earphones and you hear the sound of propeller revs again," Keyland snapped. "Jesus Christ! I can't be training you now!"

"I have detection on my sonar," MacPherson said, referring to the passive detection devices in the nose of the UUV. "We are closing. Think we ought to go active?"

Active was the bane of sonarmen. Once the torpedo or sonar went active, the adversary could immediately determine course, speed, and location. Within seconds of an active contact, you knew what the torpedo was doing.

"Ummm," Keyland said. "I don't know. Can't you steer the UUV toward the torpedo without us letting the submarine know we have something in the water?"

Bernardo nodded. "We can, but if the submarine sonar team is worth any salt, they already have our UUV on its plotting table."

"Gentron, you still have the submarine on rainfall, don't you?"

"It's still there, Petty Officer Keyland."

"Let us know if it does anything like change course or increase or decrease speeds."

"Aye aye."

"The passive sound is increasing," MacPherson said, tapping the passive sound meter on the left of the console. "In fact, decibel level is increasing rapidly."

"How far out are we?"

"UUV is passing four miles out."

ON the UUV, the digital read-out attached to the explosives rigged to the UUV was speeding toward zero.

THE picture from the UUV went blank.

"What the f . . . !"

Gentron screamed, "Jesus!" He pulled his earpieces off and threw them on the shelf.

Simultaneously, MacPherson shouted, "Holy hell," also pulling his earpiece off.

Both men rubbed their ears.

"What the hell?" Keyland asked.

MacPherson moved his lower jaw back and forth. "I can't hear anything," he said.

"Gentron, what happened?"

"CIC wants to know what happened!" Calvins shouted.

Keyland waved Calvins away. "Tell them, wait one."

"I don't know," Gentron said. "One moment I was hearing nothing and the next, this loud noise—"

"Explosion," MacPherson interrupted, his hearing having returned. "Something blew up.

Keyland straightened. "They've blown up our UUV."

FOUR miles out the concussion from the explosion of the UUV hit the spy UUV, tossing it around in the water, twisting one of the propeller blades. When the concussion passed, the small vehicle had lost contact with the Chinese submarine. It went into a circular pattern, searching for the directional beacon so it could continue on to its destination.

THE blast wave hit Sea Base, sending a shudder through the platform. The ASW team looked around the compartment as coffee cups rattled and the overhead fluorescent light blinked a couple of times. Then everything returned to normal with the exception of the strange quietness that descended over the men.

"We're unarmed and helpless," Calvins said softly.

Keyland jumped. "Bullshit!" He slapped MacPherson on the shoulder. "Launch the next UUV."

"Boss, it's not that easy. I've got to position it; check the list . . . The senior chief is going to have to visually check the well deck. I don't think we can—"

"Quit thinking, Sailor, and launch that next UUV."

MacPherson hit the button to open the well deck. On the small camera screen the edges of the well deck reversed direction and started withdrawing.

*   *   *

THE concussion from the explosion reached the Chinese submarine. On board, a similar act with the earphones occurred. Within minutes, the commander of the submarine abandoned the pickup of the material and dove deeper, passing a second thermo-layer before turning toward the deeper waters off the coast of China. His report would tell the Shanghai Red Army Navy headquarters of how the Americans had warned him away by launching a torpedo and exploding it near him. A warning; nothing more. His instructions had been explicit. Pick up the material being delivered via a miniature unmanned underwater vehicle and bring it back, unopened, to the Ministry of State Security.

The second part of his orders came directly from his admiral. It was to avoid confrontation with the Americans and, if detected, abandon the mission and return.

His ASW team detected the UUV when it had launched. The Ministry of State Security database identified the noise as belonging to an experimental UUV. His sonar team also determined the American UUV was heading toward them. Further calculations showed they could retrieve the data and be out of the area before the UUV reached them.

The explosion occurred moments after his sonar team realized the UUV had accelerated to twenty-five knots. He had already decided to abandon the mission when the explosion shook the waters. He nodded, coming to the conclusion that the explosion had been the American Navy's way of telling him they were preparing to attack.

His submarine passed the third sound layer. The ambient noise from Sea Base faded. If he couldn't hear them, they couldn't hear him.

"THE submarine has disappeared," Gentron said.

"Shit!" Keyland said. "If we've blown up a Chinese submarine, there is going to be holy hell to pay."

"But we couldn't have been that close to it," MacPherson said.

"Yeah, that submarine is running," Bernardo added smugly. "We scared him away."

"You sure?" Keyland asked.

Bernardo and MacPherson exchanged glances, then shrugged at Keyland. "You can never be sure, LPO, but that's our story and we're going to stick to it," MacPherson said.

"The Chinese had to be miles away when the UUV exploded," Bernardo added.

"But why did it explode?"

"We don't know. It wasn't supposed to," MacPherson said.

"I know," Gentron volunteered. "It hit the inbound torpedo. They both went off rainfall at the same time."

"Yeah, Petty Officer Keyland. That's what happened. The UUV ran smack into the inbound torpedo."

"We didn't see it."

MacPherson shrugged. "We didn't see much of anything with the cameras. . . ."

"But the pings were coming closer together," Bernardo finished. "It's the only logical explanation."

Keyland hung his head down. "Secure all logs. Make sure the recordings are safe." He climbed up the ladder. "Calvins, hand me the telephone." Keyland spoke to the CIC chief for a few seconds before hanging up. Then, he lifted the handset again. "I think I will call the senior chief."

"We got the second UUV positioned," MacPherson said.

Keyland looked down at the sailors staring at him. "Don't launch it."

THE metal rod came toward him. Agazzi scrambled backward, his feet and good hand pushing him along the walkway. The rod hit the metal deck, drawing a laugh from Smith.

"You look like some crab sliding sideways along the beach, Senior Chief."

"Smith, you don't have to do this. Think of your family."

"Who do you think sent me on this mission?"

Smith hefted the rod up with his right hand and slapped it a couple of times into the palm of his left hand. He walked slowly toward Agazzi. "Senior Chief, this isn't against you, you know. It's necessary. It's a grand design in which our lives mean little. You think death is the end of everything. It is only the beginning."

Agazzi raised his hand. "At least, if you're going to kill me, tell me why. I deserve to know, don't I?"

Smith raised the rod, his eyes wide. Spittle ran from the side of his lips. He paused for a moment, then stepped back, shaking his head. "You're just trying to save yourself."

"Of course I want to save myself. Tell me the plan—or are you even sure you understand it?"

Smith stepped forward, raising the rod. "You're not interested in God's plan. You're only interested in saving your life."

"If you're going to kill me," Agazzi gasped out, "then, I deserve to know why."

Smith shrugged. "Senior Chief, I was chosen for this mission. I kneeled in the cradle with a pistol pressed against my temple and God reached down, touched the weapon, and commanded it not to fire. Of the six men who went through this selection, I was the one God chose." Smith took a deep breath. "Armageddon is the reason. Armageddon will bring God among us. When Sea Base sinks, America will blame the Chinese or the North Koreans. It doesn't matter who they blame. The destruction of Sea Base is a high visible message to the world. By itself it won't ignite Armageddon, but it is part of the plan."

He stepped closer to Agazzi. "If I didn't do this, someone else on board would. Eventually, everything will fall in place and the cascading effect of anarchy will escalate us toward a world where the Lord must return."

"Are you telling me there are others on board Sea Base working with you?" Agazzi asked, glancing to his side, calculating if he had enough edge to slide between the bottom safety rail to the well deck area.

The well deck stopped closing. Then the sound of the hydraulics of it reopening filled the compartment.

"I don't think you could make it, Senior Chief."

"Make what?" Agazzi asked. He ran his tongue lightly over his dry lips.

"You know," Smith smiled. "Rolling off the walkway onto the well deck." He moved forward raising the bar.

"You would kill everyone here for that?"

Smith drew the rod back and moved toward Agazzi. "Enough, Senior Chief. I've got work to do here and you're stopping me. Besides, you are a nonbeliever. You wouldn't understand. Nonbelievers never understand."

"But your plan is already dead, Smith. The UUV is gone."

"That's not my fault. That's yours. You have messed with God's plans!"

With both hands grasping the metal rod, Smith hefted it farther above his head, stretching as if to get as much power as possible behind it. All Agazzi could do was watch. He thought of shutting his eyes but couldn't.

The rod started down. From the other side of the computer console a scream startled Smith, causing him to glance toward the upper level as someone leaped over the edge of the railing and hit Smith on the right side. The blow knocked Smith to the deck, sending him tumbling over the top safety rail toward the opening well deck.

The metal rod tumbled out of Smith's hands, coming down on top of Agazzi left thigh. A fresh wave of pain shot through him, causing him to involuntarily squeeze his eyes shut for a moment.

Agazzi watched as Smith flailed, trying to grab the rails before his feet hit the smooth sides of the half-opened well deck. "Help me!" Smith shouted as he slid toward the gaping hole. Smith threw his arms wide, trying to stop from falling into the ocean. As his feet slid into the water, the friction of his arms and upper torso stopped his slide.

He looked up, his eyes meeting Agazzi's, and smiled. "I'm coming," he said before his eyes widened and a deep, bestial scream filled the compartment. Behind the man, Agazzi caught a glimpse of several gray fins. The next moment, Smith disappeared beneath the *Bellatrix*, the water in the well deck turning red.

AGAZZI turned.

Squatting beside him was Jacobs. "What in the hell is going on here, Alistair?"

He couldn't help it. Tears flowed down his cheeks. "I never thought I'd be so glad to see you."

"Bullshit. You cry every time you see me." Jacobs pulled his handkerchief from his pocket and ran it over Agazzi's face, wiping away the blood. "Man, you look like shit, you know." Jacobs stood.

The telephone rang. "Wait here," he ordered.

"Isn't as if I could move if I wanted."

Jacobs climbed to the top level to the manual control console and lifted the handset. "Hello." He listened to the voice on the other end.

"Shut up, Keyland. Get medical and get the MAAs down here ASAP." There was a moment of silence.

"Who is this? You know who in the hell this is. This is Master Chief Jacobs. Now, get your ass moving. Yes, he's okay."

Agazzi looked over at the well deck.

He then looked up at Jacobs, who came back and slid down to the desk beside him.

"You're crying," Agazzi mumbled.

"Fuck you," Jacobs said, his voice trembling. "Boatswain mates don't cry. It's just when we're this far belowdecks, our eyeballs sweat from the pressure." He lifted Agazzi's head up. "You okay?"

Agazzi tried to nod. "I think I'm okay."

"Then you're more fucked up than you look." Jacobs saw the cloth that had earlier covered the cam hanging half off the upper deck above him. He pulled it to him, rolled it into a loose ball, and stuck it under Agazzi's head.

"I do feel like shit," Agazzi said, his low voice betraying the pain.

"Good. If you can feel like shit, then you're going to live. If you're going to live . . ." the man stopped, his voice breaking.

"Your eyeballs sweating again?"

"Hey, Senior Chief!" Taylor called from the hatch. "Where are you?"

Jacobs looked toward the hatch but didn't reply to the call. He turned back to Agazzi. "Eyeballs sweat a lot sometimes. Besides, what in the hell do you expect? If you go and die on me, I'm going to have to be the one to explain to Frieda and she is going to be one pissed-off old lady." Jacobs slapped his chest. "She'll blame me; she'll tell Helen, and two things will happen. One, Helen will cut me off; and two, I'll never have a chance to get in your wife's pants."

Agazzi's lips twitched as he tried to smile. His eyes felt so heavy. The throbbing of the pain. The exhaustion of the fight. He closed his eyes.

"Alistair, stop that shit. Don't you go to sleep on me, Alistair."

"What the hell!" Taylor said, looking down at them from above.

"I just wanna rest my eyes," Agazzi mumbled, his voice trailing off.

"You!" Jacobs said, pointing up at Taylor. "Make sure that hatch is open so the medics can get in."

"What happened?"

"Never you mind. You just get your ass over to the hatch and make sure the medics know where to come. And turn on that passageway light before someone kills themselves."

Jacobs looked back down at Agazzi. "You keep those eyes open. You hear me? You stay awake until those medics get here, then you can rest all you want!" Jacobs shouted.

Agazzi's eyes shut. His thoughts tumbled as his consciousness began to fade. One moment Agazzi was in the UUV compartment, the next he was driving his '57 Chevy, and the next hovering above Frieda—a crying Frieda. No kids—they'd always regretted that. His falling stopped. He could hear his name being called as if someone on top of a great cliff was beckoning him to climb up from the valley. He climbed. He fought. And as he got higher the words were recognizable. His name—followed by the word *asshole*, and he knew it was Jacobs. His eyes opened.

"They're sweating again."

"Not as much as yours are. If you do that shit again we won't need the doctors. I'll kill you myself."

The sound of racing feet pounding through the hatch of the UUV compartment drew their attention.

"Down there!" Taylor shouted, pointing over the edge of the upper level.

"How did you get in?" Agazzi asked faintly.

Jacobs shrugged. "Your security is shit, Alistair. The hatch was open."

The blurry vision of several sailors and someone in white was the last thing Agazzi remembered as he slipped into a deep sleep.

Turn the page for an exciting preview of

DARK PACIFIC:
PACIFIC THREAT

Available from Berkley in January 2007

"Captain's in Combat," the tactical action officer, Commander Stan Stapler, announced as Captain Hank Garcia stepped through the hatch leading from the two floors above Combat.

"What you got, Commander?" Hank asked, setting his coffee cup on a nearby chart table. He looked up at the LCD display mounted on the forward bulkhead.

"Those bogies seem to be growing in number, Captain. When I briefed you a couple of hours ago satellite reflected them leaving the North Korean land mass. At that time, all they did was establish a racetrack pattern about twelve miles off the coast. Satellite radar and intelligence reports all indicate a combat air patrol. I think it could be because Sea Base moved into the SOJ," Stapler said, referring to the Sea of Japan. "Original estimates indicate no more than ten formations of two aircraft each."

Garcia picked up his cup and took a drink. "I take it that has changed?"

"Since fifteen hundred hours when we briefed you, Skipper, over and over again, we watched the North Koreans fly the same figure eight pattern. Every now and then, a formation breaks off and returns to North Korea; probably to refuel. For every formation that breaks off, a two-plane formation replaces them in the pattern. I should mention that over the past hour, the number of formations increased from the original ten to eighteen."

"Yes," Garcia answered morosely. "You should mention it, Commander. You should have told me fifty-five minutes ago instead of now."

"Yes, sir. My apologies, Skipper. It won't happen again," Stapler apologized, and then quickly changed the subject with a laser pointer, highlighting the returns on the bulkhead LCD display. "Since they continue doing the same racetrack, I didn't think too much of it. They're 400-nautical miles away."

"In the future, Commander, keep me up to date on things as they change," Garcia said, a hint of displeasure in his voice.

"Aye, sir. I didn't want to bother you."

"Bother me, please. I enjoy it."

"A few minutes ago, the formations started having hiccups."

"Hiccups?"

"Yes, sir," Stapler answered. "When aircraft fly close together it is hard to distinguish how many aircraft actually make up a formation. The radar returns one blimp, meshed together because of the proximity of the aircraft within the formation."

"Okay. I think I know where this is going."

"Look at this, sir. Chief," Stapler called to the chief petty officer standing nearby, "Take us down."

On the LCD screen above the radar and weapon consoles images started collapsing until only two radar returns filled the screen. From this vantage point Garcia knew he was looking at a satellite return. The two bogies went into a turn. The bogie on the outside of the turn suddenly split into two pieces of video. The inner bogie inside the turn appeared to elongate as it maintained its position to the outer image.

"Looks like three aircraft," Garcia offered.

Stapler nodded. "It does, but there are four of them. In the turns, it's harder for them to maintain speed and distance. The radar has shown as many as four aircraft in a formation."

"Eighteen formations?"

"Yes, sir. Eight more formations than the original ten, but instead of twenty aircraft out there, we may have as many as seventy-two, sir. . . ."

"Seventy-two," Garcia interrupted. "Why in the hell would the North Koreans want seventy-two fighters buzzing around off their coast? It isn't as if they couldn't launch in time to stop anything coming from the east."

"That's not all, Skipper," Stapler said. "Chief, show the large ones."

"Large ones?"

The displayed image shifted. The image dropped away as the focus zoomed outward. Then the display panned toward the west for a few seconds before starting to zoom inward. When the shift of the satellite radar stopped, Garcia was watching four images of radar video in a flight pattern.

"What am I looking at?"

"Sir, these four bogies are flying lower than the eighteen fighter formations orbiting at eighteen thousand feet. They are flying near the Korean landmass at around ten thousand feet. The land smear complicates the radar return. But they are individual aircraft, larger than the four-aircraft formations, and slower."

On the screen four aircraft trailed one another as they executed an oval racetrack a few miles off the upper North Korean peninsula.

"What are they?"

Stapler shrugged, then said, "I think they're heavy bombers."

The sound-powered phone talker, standing near the Electronic Warfare AN/SLQ-32 suite, pushed his mouthpiece out of the way. "Commander, sonar reports they have a submarine contact."

"Whose?"

"They didn't say, sir. Just said an unidentified submarine bearing 240-degrees true; directly off our starboard beam. Beam?" the young seaman repeated, wondering for a moment where the beam was on something such as Sea Base. On a ship, it would mean directly off the left or right side of the ship; in this case off meant in the right-hand direction to Sea Base.

"Ask them range?"

"They have no estimate at this time, sir."

"Tell them to give me an estimated range!" Stapler shouted. He turned to the Chief. "Chief, I want a sound-powered phone talker right there beside the skipper's chair," Stapler ordered, pointing to an empty space between Garcia's chair and the plotting table. "I don't want to have to shout over the weapons and radar consoles to relay orders via the sound-powered phones."

"Haven't we straightened out the communications problems, yet, Commander? Are sound-power telephones all we have?"

"No, sir. I have regular telephones and some limited intercom, but the most reliable and most widespread comms at this time is the sound-powered telephone system the chief engineers managed to rig."

"The submarine bothers me, Stan. We need more information on it. The aircraft are 400 miles away and we'll know if they decide to get froggy."

Stapler turned to Garcia. "Sir, the submarine is the immediate issue, but whenever the North Koreans are doing something it makes me nervous."

"Makes two of us, Commander."

"You never know what they're going to do."

Garcia nodded. "Whatever it is, it is always something dumb, arrogant, and unexpected. What do we have out there?"

"We have a two F-22A Raptor formation. Distance, Chief?"

"Raptor formation is one hundred forty nautical miles, bearing 340 degrees, sir!" He ran his hand through his rich crop of blond hair. "They've been out there a couple of hours. We'll have to relieve them sooner than I expected. Raptor 10 is already complaining about fuel consumption."

"Do what you have to do, Stan," Garcia said softly. His eyebrows furrowed as he asked, "What's the weapon status of Sea Base?"

"Sir, laser and rail guns are in place, but we've only done limited testing of them since the engineers finished the installations. The fire control radars for them are up and running. I had the fire control spectrum for the railguns switched from gunfire support to anti-air warfare mode."

"So, they're activated-up and running?"

"Not yet, Captain. I have them manned, but I have them powered down. I was concern about keeping them activated for too long."

"But if we wait until we need them to turn them on, Stan, we run the risk of discovering problems we could have corrected. Let's activate them and have the crews do their diagnostics. We want them up and ready for use. Just in case, you know—no other reason, so don't let the crew get nervous about it."

"Sir, you want to go to general quarters?"

Garcia's lower lip pushed up against the upper and eyes narrowed as he thought about the question. The prudent thing would be to call GQ, but if he called it and the North Koreans only continued posturing off their coast, then Sea Base would be locked-down. The work of the platform would come to a halt. Sea Base may have to fight for its survival if the North Koreans do their "Let's show our teeth and be arrogant" thing. Meanwhile, Sea Base still had a lot of work to be done to reach full warfighting capability. When he failed to respond to Stapler's question, the taciturn tactical action officer continued.

"Unless you have other orders, Skipper, I intend to launch our SH-36 LAMPs and lay some sonobuoy patterns around Sea Base. See if we can locate this unidentified submarine."

"The submarine is probably Chinese."

"Yes, sir; probably is. I would prefer it be Chinese and not North Korean."

Garcia's eyebrows furrowed deeper at the thought. He shook his head. "The North Koreans only have a bunch of old 1970s-era Soviet submarines. I'd be surprised if they sent them out of sight of land."

"But they could."

"Any weapons anyone has can be used for things you'd never expect," Garcia countered. "That's what we're doing with Sea Base."

"I hope it's Chinese," Stapler said, gritting his teeth. "Even so, Skipper, we're going to have to do something about it. We can't have it tailing us wherever we go."

Since the encounter a few weeks ago, everyone up and down the chain of command had speculated the Chinese were keeping a submarine nearby observing them. Why after all this time trailing them, would the Chinese let themselves be detected? His eyes widened; unless the submarine isn't Chinese, but is North Korean? Even though he had just argued the North Koreans would never chance sending their submarines far from their coast, maybe they were. Maybe the North Koreans intended to activate their total war plan against the South Koreans and the United States. Worst case for them would be if the North Koreans wanted to make a statement and launch a preemptive attack against Sea Base. America had been attacked unexpectedly in its history and each time the problem was the refusal to accept the expected.

Garcia took a deep breath. "Go ahead and lay the sonobuoy

patterns, Commander Stapler. Have Senior Chief Agazzi send some UUVs out to see what he can find. It'll give them a chance to practice some underwater ballet on those things. As for GQ, hold off on calling general quarters until we really have to do so, Commander." He clasped his hands behind his back and rocked back and forth a couple of times. "Let's keep the Air Force out in front of us until I tell you differently."

"Yes, sir. Raptor formation . . ."

"Raptor formation?" Garcia asked seriously. "You're calling them Raptor formation? That's what the Air Force uses?"

Stapler's eyes shifted back and forth. "Sir, I didn't ask them. Just gave them the formation title recommended by Combat, Captain."

Garcia nodded. "In the future, ask them what they would prefer and as long as it doesn't conflict with doctrine or security, we'll use their preference."

"Yes, sir."

"Meanwhile, keep them between us and the North Korean CAP. Let's see what the North Koreans do."

Stapler smiled. "They don't know the Air Force fighters are out there. According to Naval Intelligence the North Koreans aren't showing signs they have detected the F-22A formation. If the North Koreans do some macho-shit thing, those 22s will wipe the skies with them."

The SIXTH FLEET series
by David E. Meadows

★★★★★
The Sixth Fleet
0–425–18009–3

The Sixth Fleet #2: Seawolf
0–425–17249–X

The Sixth Fleet #3: Tomcat
0–425–18379–3

The Sixth Fleet #4: Cobra
0–425–18518–4

★★★★★

**Available wherever books are sold or at
penguin.com**

b137

From the author of
The Sixth Fleet

David E. Meadows

A "visionary" (Joe Buff) in the world of military fiction, Pentagon staff member and U.S. Navy Captain David E. Meadows presents a bold series that takes America into the next era of modern warfare.

Joint Task Force: Liberia
0-425-19206-7

Joint Task Force: America
0-425-19482-5

Joint Task Force: France
0-425-19799-9

Joint Task Force: Africa
0-425-20147-3

"On par with Tom Clancy."
—Milos Stankovic